CASTLE IN THE SWAMP

Books

BY EDISON MARSHALL

NOVELS

Castle in the Swamp
Yankee Pasha
Benjamin Blake
Great Smith
The Upstart

ADVENTURE STORIES

Shikar and Safari
The Voice of the Pack
The Doctor of Lonesome River
The Deputy of Snow Mountain
The Missionary
The Far Call
Child of the Wild
The Light in the Jungle
Sam Campbell, Gentleman
Dian of the Lost Land
The Stolen God

SHORT STORIES

The Heart of Little Shikara
The Elephant Remembers

Castle in the Swamp

A TALE OF OLD CAROLINA

By Edison Marshall

FARRAR, STRAUS AND COMPANY

PRINTED IN THE UNITED STATES OF AMERICA
AMERICAN BOOK–STRATFORD PRESS, INC., NEW YORK

DESIGNED BY STEFAN SALTER

CHAPTER

1

There are ponds in the woods at Wood Ibis that appear perfect mirrors of a patch of sky fenced in by moss-hung trees, their glass unscratched and unmarred since the world began. Coming upon one of them out of the blind thickets to the scene of a lone white heron perched on a snag repeated with infinite exactitude, the traveler can hardly believe that the blue sheen has ever been ruffled by the wind or lain roughened and gray in the rain.

Once such a traveler with a fowling piece shot a great blue heron winging its way across such a pond. It fell with a splash profane in the silence, and lay in the center of a round wave. The wave rolled in an ever-widening ring. It caused the water lilies to undulate, and the pull upon their roots loosed a little muck that darkened the crystal waters. There was not a reed or grass-blade that did not bend. The ripples ran to every nook and cranny of the pond, one ring after another, appearing to die away only to revive. In the backwash the poor carrion rose and fell with a flopping motion that had an eerie semblance to life. It seemed that the pool would never again regain its virgin stillness; but finally it did, and the only apparent mark on its glassy surface was a blotch of blue feathers that would soon disappear.

But, if it could speak, every reed and grass-blade that had bent and every water lily that had tugged at its roots would tell you it was forever a little changed. What a spreading ring of event may follow a trifling cause! When the cause is great—such as a passion so extreme that it rolls billows of passion to the farthest margins of its scene—the ensuing great event may shape a strange, momentous tale. The one I hereby chronicle is at least strange. Perhaps the little ripples of its telling, spreading wide, may calm some waves still buffeting my heart.

My active part began when I was between seven and eight years old. Before then, the lamps are too dim to read by. The light re-

I

mains uncertain for a good while yet—I gaze back and guess at the detail of the scenes and at words spoken of which a little boy did not know the meaning. I was called Dan by the other orphans and our keepers, and knew I was alive as a dog. I had been taught to read a primer, to eat tidily, to stay out of dirt, and to thank God at appointed times for the Christian Orphanage that had saved me from a life of "beggary, want, and sin." I had heard people say, without knowing the importance or barely the meaning of it, that we stayed in Philadelphia. But where I had come from to this chill house of children's woe, and by what disaster, I did not know.

I had been taught also the duty of obedience to those in charge but was always forgetting the lesson. At a certain hour in the afternoon the breadbox in the kitchen was left unguarded. Too, the slop pail from the Woman's table was set out by the back steps every morning, and rashly left there for the hog-man to empty into his cart. Once I promised God I would steal no more and kept the promise for day upon gray day, only to find my sturdy body growing weak while I did not receive the reward I had starved myself for. It happened that there were two words frequently spoken here associated in my mind with glory. One was written in gilt letters on a picture in the parlor—"Heaven." The other was " 'Dopted." The nurses spoke it aloud, but we little orphans whispered it in awe. I had thought that, beholding my good behavior, God would at least take me to heaven and perhaps would let me be 'dopted. When the hope failed I went back to stealing for strength to fight for myself.

No few of my playmates sickened and disappeared: we were told they had gone to heaven. Many boys younger than I, or older ones less quick at reading and ciphering, were 'dopted. When visitors came to look us over, on one excuse or another I was not put on view; and on two occasions when I had disobeyed orders and rushed wildly into the parlor where my mates were being shown, I was seized and thrust into the outer darkness of the stairs. I did not know that my frantic efforts defeated their purpose: my keepers considered it a sign of ingratitude for the charity given me and I must learn my lesson. When I was whipped for disobedience, my bite-shut lips and dry eyes persuaded them I was incorrigibly bad, unfit for adoption by anyone.

On a hot summer morning, in the year we had been told was 1840, my listless mates and I were playing in the front yard. We were given this privilege every sunny weekday; there was no hope or inkling in my heart that a great event was marching. When the person we called the Lame Man trudged along the sidewalk with his cane and stopped by the fence to watch us, I was a little excited but only showed off for him by playing harder than before. He had often looked in at us and there was a strong light in his eyes that had both frightened and attracted me. Once he had asked which was the best wrestler and, on being told that I was, he had gazed at me long and intently before trudging on. On that day we had been called indoors and put to work for breaking the rule of speaking to passers-by, and I did not want to take the penalty again.

Presently I saw him furtively beckoning to me. I ran about until I was close to the fence and, after a glance at the windows, darted toward it.

Until I came close to him I had not perceived how great his affliction was. He did not stand tall like other men; his long body was so deeply bowed that his back showed as an arch, his head thrust top-foremost only a little above mine. His clothes hung loose on his frail form and his face was very thin. But it was a beautiful face, I thought; and, as he gazed at me from down under his forehead, I did not feel that he was weak *inside*. Truly he seemed stronger than Mr. Lewis, Superintendent of the Orphanage, whom we had thought second in strength and wrath only to God.

"What is your name, little boy?" he asked in a gentle voice.

"Dan, sir." I thought of telling him I must run back before I was seen from a window, but I looked into his face and my heart thudded and I would take a whipping rather than let him know I was afraid.

"What is your last name?"

"The Woman says I haven't any."

"Are you happy here, Dan?"

He might tell them what I said! But I told him the truth.

"No, sir, I'm mighty mis'able."

"You do not love this home?"

"I hate it! I hate it!"

"Do you know what it means to keep a promise?"

"Yes, sir."

"If I take you away from here, will you promise me something and die before you break it?"

"Yes, sir, I will."

"If I promise to adopt you, do you promise, before God, may you die and go to hell if you lie, that you will do everything I bid you, good or bad, safe or dangerous—willingly, with all your might and main—until when you are a grown man I release you from your vow?"

My throat filled but I gasped out, "Yes. Yes, sir—"

"Say nothing about this to anyone. I will come for you soon."

He trudged on. Weak and dizzy I joined my playmates. The rest of that day and throughout the next I waked and slept in a happiness of expectation too deep to express in play or laughter or to share with anyone. Indeed it was so solemn and sacred that I had no trouble hiding it from the Woman, whom I heard remark to one of our keepers that I "looked seedy" and needed a doping or a whipping, she didn't know which. Not once did it cross my mind that the Lame Man would not keep his bargain. It was not to get on God's good side that I refrained from stealing bread and slops. I was trying to show my gratitude for His blessing upon me.

Early in the afternoon of the following day the nurses began dressing four of our best-behaved boys in their Sunday clothes. My watch of the street had been necessarily sporadic: still my first thought was that someone else had come to 'dopt a boy and for once I need not be jealous. My Lame Man had promised to come soon, and I would rather go away with him than with anyone in the world. A quick glance through the window revealed a horse and chaise and colored driver outside the gate. That was a comforting sight—I had pictured him trudging up slowly with his stick. But as I listened to the women's talk I became at first uneasy, then terribly frightened.

"Well, he came in style," one of them said.

"Pew! He hired that rig at a livery stable."

"I don't see how he gets up and down to the seat. Mr. Reed's a good name for such a reed of a man."

I knew then, in icy terror; yet some instinct warned me not to appeal to them openly. I began walking about, trying to catch their eyes and whistling "Jesus is my Shepherd," one of our clergyman's favorite hymns. They continued to dress my playmates without a glance at me.

"Please, ma'am, let me go too," burst out of my twisted throat at last.

"The Matron picked out the ones to be shown," one of the women answered, without glancing up.

"Please let me go! I'll never ask again—"

She turned to me with a puzzled look: there were tears in my eyes, which she had not often seen there.

"You'll be shown to visitors when you've learned to be thankful for your blessings."

I was about to cry out that the Lame Man had come here just for me—he had promised he would! Instead of my voice, I heard his, speaking quietly over the fence—*"Say nothing about this to anyone."* I had promised, stronger than cross my heart, I would do *everything* he said. I did not know then how strange a thing this was—a child not yet eight years old biting back a secret of such terror and woe as mine. Perhaps the Lame Man loomed larger than human in my child's eyes. He had said he would come for me; and he would tear down the Orphanage with his frail hands before he would break troth!

My mates were coached and led downstairs. Desperate now, I crept to the hall door, where I could hear the murmur of voices in the parlor. Plain but distinct came the voice of my Lame Man.

"I am sure there was another boy of this age playing in the yard that day."

"I repeat, Mr. Reed, these are all we may offer you," Mr. Lewis replied.

I flung open the door and burst into the parlor crying:

"I'm the one, Mr. Reed! I was playing in the yard that day—"

"Get that little wretch out of here!" Mr. Lewis shouted. Then to the visitor, "Pardon me, Mr. Reed, but that boy has tried my patience too many times—"

"Dan!" It was the Woman's voice, most feared in this house of fear. "Go to the dormitory this instant, where I'll attend to you shortly. Mr. Lewis, the boy is incorrigible—"

5

She stopped, because Mr. Reed was speaking in a quiet tone.
"He is indeed the one."

"You don't want this boy, Mr. Reed," Mr. Lewis replied. "That's why we didn't show him to you. Most of our little charges are from impoverished but Christian homes and are obedient and a credit to this sanctuary. But this boy—you will pardon me—is a child of sin."

"Still, let him remain with the others if you please. I would like to talk to him." The Lame Man's voice went up and down like music.

"I've already ordered his dismissal—"

"What is your name, little boy?"

He already knew. I had told him by the fence. But that was a secret between us, like stealing a wagonload of bread—an infinitely greater secret than that—part of our promise that I must die rather than break.

"Dan, sir."

"He seems a sturdy little fellow—" This to Mr. Lewis.

"Ah, but you haven't seen his hand. Show him, Dan."

I held out my left hand, the little finger of which lay flat against the palm, immovable and useless.

"How did he come by that mark? Was he born with it, or did he—"

"We could tell you, if anyone knew who his mother was," the Woman answered in her hateful voice. "The child was abandoned at our door, five years and more ago. He was dressed in dirty rags and the message left pinned on them was ill-spelled. It gave the child's name as Dan and asked us to be kind to him—which we have done in vain."

The Lame Man took my hand and squeezed the fingers together. "It would handicap him somewhat in learning my trade, but not much in other pursuits. He is my choice."

He said this last in the same mild tone as the rest, quite without emphasis, causing his grown-up hearers to doubt their ears. I did not doubt mine, knowing in my heart that he would keep faith with me; and now that I had seen him stand against the Woman, my keeping faith with him became at that instant part of me like my blood and breath. But the scene was etched forever in my

6

memory. Usually the blinds were drawn in this chamber of hope and despair, but someone had opened them today and the summer sunlight burst through lacy curtains adorned with silk butterflies of gay hue. My four playmates still stood in a row, each one relieved that he was not chosen, and I gloried that all were afraid of my Lame Man. He had risen from his chair, his head a little higher than usual, his eyes smiling into mine. Mr. Lewis and the Woman sat as straight as though they too were standing.

"Mr. Reed, I'll ask you to consider," the Woman said. "We have our duty not only to the children but to those who wish to adopt them. We must put the *right* child in the *right* home. Both Mr. Lewis and I feel strongly that this boy of bad blood—"

"You will pardon me," Mr. Reed broke in. "I have already established my fitness to adopt a boy. I am of good name in the town and pursuing an honest trade. More than that, I am mentally competent to make my own choice. I see no sign of bad blood— his brow is wide and good, and his eyes clear. There are things worse than bastardy, sir and madam."

As he spoke to them I moved forward and stood at his side.

"It's hardly a fit word, Mr. Reed, for these little ones to hear." Mr. Lewis turned to the Woman. "Send for Dan's clothes. At least it's a good riddance."

I caught the Lame Man's hand. He turned and spoke to Mr. Lewis in a voice that reminded me of organ music.

"You may call it so, sir, if you please. You may say what you like about one of your charges. But be very careful what aspersions you cast upon my son."

He looked at me and I thought my heart would burst.

"Dan, I have never had a wife to my bosom, or child to my loins. But now we are father and son."

Mr. Lewis had what he was no doubt proud to call the last word. As the Lame Man and I walked slowly hand in hand toward the gate, he flung it through the open door behind us.

"You're not father and son until the judge signs those papers."

My companion did not look back and I could see no concern in his face. A great wave of pride in him swept through me; and I stopped tugging forward at his hand, and my throbbing ache to get in the chaise and drive away became less heavy. When he took an endless time trying to gain the seat, I stood the sight better than the tall, black driver.

"Please, suh, I'll pick you up and lif' you in, if you'll let me. De hoss won't move a foots."

My pride in him took no fall as he was being swung up featherlight. Instead it was exciting to see the Negro looking sorry for him. We had another secret, the Lame Man and I—his strength inside. His lameness was something like a cloak to hide it, I thought. It enabled him to do great things no one would guess. Sitting close beside him as the horse jogged off and the houses slowly passed, I did not glance back.

But I remained deeply uneasy about the judge and the papers. "Can I stay with you forever 'n' ever?" I asked.

"As long as I live, I hope."

"Will you know tomorrow if I'm your little boy for sure?"

"I know that already. It will be thirty days before the decree of adoption—that is a paper made out by a judge—becomes final. Your next-of-kin have that long to claim you, if they are alive. But we became father and son when we made our bond by the fence. No paper can interfere with that. If we are parted, it will be only for a little while. I will get you back somehow."

I understood perfectly, despite not knowing some of the words. "I'd run away from 'em and find you."

"That is what I mean by being a real father and son." A little

8

color flowed into his pale face. "From now on, Dan, you will be called Dan Reed, and you shall call me Pa."

I sat a little closer to him, wonderfully happy. Little dust clouds pretty to my sight rose at every cheerful footfall of the ambling horse; he shook his head and whisked his tail, and his harness jingled a little and the creaks and rattles of the old chaise played a tune. I had hated the lone tree standing in the Orphanage yard, grim and growing switches, but along this road the trees were strong giants, making pleasant shade. We passed some big houses, then turned into a narrow street of little houses. At the last of these we stopped.

"This is our home, Dan," Pa told me.

Grass and weeds grew rank by the board walk. The paint was old and flaked, not neat and new as at the Orphanage. I did not know why this pleased and excited me: perhaps it had to do with Pa's and my secret. By the door was a painted sign, the first word of which I could read phonetically but did not understand. The sign spelled out:

Professor Reed
Violinist

Before long, the door closed behind us. We were in a kind of parlor with drawn shades and nice-appearing furniture, including two metal racks for sheet-music. Still it was just a room. It had no interesting smell or feel.

"That room is locked," Pa told me, pointing to a door in the inside wall. "You may play in the others, including our bedroom while I'm resting there."

He left me, and my patient exploration occupied all the remainder of the afternoon. The parlor was for company, I knew: it was the bedroom with one middle-sized bed and one cot, and a kitchen that was also the dining room, where I sensed Pa's life and found his tracks. He had lived all alone in these rooms until now. They had an oily smell and battered-looking books lay everywhere, but there was no dirt to be seen. I spelled out the name printed in big letters on top of a newspaper and it was "The Charleston Post." On a shelf in the room where Pa lay asleep stood two elegant candlesticks, of whiter, brighter metal than the knives and forks on the Woman's table at the Orphanage. In a little hall outside was a fascinating object that I could not identify: later I learned it was the polished shell of a sea turtle.

Finally I returned to the parlor and peeked through the keyhole of the locked room. Quite plainly in its dimness I made out a pale oval like a life-size human face. Someone was in there sitting up high and very still, I thought. Maybe it was a dead person who had never been buried. It might be the body of someone Pa had killed and hidden from the policeman. Pa had very strange bright eyes.

The thought came to me with a cold creeping of my skin that he might intend to kill me. No, or he would not have made me promise to do everything he bade me until I was a grown man. Maybe he had got me to help him kill other people and put them in that room: I wouldn't be surprised. What seemed to me most likely was that the body belonged to the man who had made Pa lame. Pa had laid for him and finally killed him in the dark and no one ever knew what happened to him.

I heard Pa getting up and tiptoed quickly to the kitchen. He told me we could have bread and milk for supper, and then I must go to bed. He would let me sleep with him, he said, except that his mattress was fixed to fit his back. When I had undressed I stood in the dark doorway and saw him bowed over the kitchen table, reading. There was no sound, and no movement save the pages being slowly turned.

I dreamed happily, that night, except for one dream I had had hundreds of times before. In it I was playing in a sunny far-off place when there came a kind of signal, like a gun going off, and I found myself in the Orphanage. It had always wakened me and I had lain in hopeless sorrow to find it true. Tonight it wakened me the same but I lay in warm bliss that I was in this house— Pa's and mine—instead. I—Dan—Dan—*Dan had been 'dopted!*

In the following days Pa talked to me very little, being either busy with the people who came every weekday to take music lessons, or with his books or his thoughts. Sometimes he sat what seemed an hour, his eyes half-closed, making not the slightest movement. But he always smiled or made a clucking sound when he encountered me; his voice and manner were ever kind, and I did not worry about how little attention he paid me, thinking that he had vastly more important matters on his mind. I had to stay near him but that nearness was like an elastic cord, every day stretching farther. Before the week was out I could go into the road and into neighboring yards to play without fear of it breaking.

One morning at breakfast he told me that a month had passed without anyone claiming me, and the judge had sent him some papers declaring me his lawful foster son. I heard the news in silence, in the way of children; then he called me to him and put his thin arms around me and kissed me quickly on the cheek. I had seen such a thing happen to other children but had hardly imagined it ever happening to me. Now I had a sense of lightness as though I could float out of the room. It was a kind of joy that I would like to put in a box and hide away and keep always.

Yet he was gazing at me in deep anxiety.

"Would you like to kiss me, Dan?" he asked, in an odd, strained voice.

"Yes, Pa."

"You need not unless you want to. I am so ugly, marked as I am, and to touch me with her lips—" He stopped, and from his look I thought his back had given him a stab of pain. But he smiled and said quietly, "I mean I wouldn't blame anyone."

"I want to kiss you awful bad."

I did so, on his cheek, and thought a little tremor passed down his body.

"Now I will say a little more about that promise you made me. It was to do everything I bade you, but that's too hard a rule between father and son. Some day you may forget, or want so much to do something else that your promise might seem a burden. Your promise is binding only on some important things to prepare you for a great task when you are a man. Then you will go about it your own way—I will not stand over you—I will give you no commands. For now you must grow up, and grow strong, and play with the other children, and be like any other little boy with his father."

"That will be good," I answered.

There was a question I wanted to ask him and it took all my courage. "Pa, how did your back get hurt so bad?"

He looked at me strangely, yet, I thought, with satisfaction.

"When I was your age, my back was as straight as yours. But I had had fever when a baby, was very frail, and one day my brother Ralph, a year younger than me, but bigger and stronger, played Indian-and-Paleface with me. He played too rough—and after that I grew crooked."

"Is it your brother's body you keep in the locked room? I looked through the keyhole and thought I saw a dead person fastened on the wall."

He smiled faintly. "No, my brother is alive and well. He is the rich master of a great plantation, and married to the most beautiful woman in the world. But he told my parents, Dan, that he had not meant to break my back. He only wanted to tease me and make me cry. He did not succeed—I fainted instead—and I have never cried since. I want you to learn never to cry."

"I'll try hard not to, Pa."

He left me, and late that afternoon I heard his music pouring through the house. It was Sunday and no student had come to take lessons; presently I discovered that the music-streams were flowing through the cracks in the locked door. Was Pa playing to the dead man he kept in there? It might be so, even though the dead cannot see or hear, for the music was not like any I had ever heard. It was *stronger* than the kind he made for the students. I sat very still by the wall, listening.

Sometimes the music grew soft and sometimes it raved like wind. It raged like the wind that one day blew off the sea, wet and almost salt-tasting and so strong that every window in the Orphanage rattled, and the boards groaned, and all the children but me were frightened. The nurses were frightened too; they could not hide it and I felt good, watching them. My eyes felt good to see their white faces and watch them running about. It seemed to me that some big black angel-thing in heaven had become "incorrigible" and was trying to tear down the Orphanage and my heart danced and sang. There was a wonderful, great noise in the chimneys and shingles from the roof went sailing through the air.

The music brought back our marching downstairs, marching upstairs. It brought back the other boys dressing to be shown to company, while I must stay out of sight. It took tunes like we sang at Sunday School and tore them into little pieces and made something else out of them—like a tune yet greatly different—then I laughed aloud at the Woman's ugly face when Pa told her I was his choice. . . . But to Pa it brought other things: I could almost see them in the sound. There were people lying dead, and blood spilled everywhere, and a big bell ringing. . . . There were great seas rolling and crashing and hate as red as the blood and terror as white as the bodies. . . .

The music stopped briefly, then began again, soft and low. He was playing about something or someone wonderfully beautiful, that waked in me a longing for something Pa could not give me. Yet I was excited in a new way, the longing heavy in my heart but tingling throughout my body, and my hand crept inside my clothes and clutched where it tingled most. Then the music changed once more. Pa had told me he had never cried since his back was broken but the music was crying with a broken heart, every note like a tear. It died with a soft sob, and in a moment the door opened narrowly and Pa came through.

He walked more strongly than I had yet seen him. The skin of his face was stretched tight over the bone and was very white, but his eyes were too bright to look at. Through the partially open door I caught a glimpse of seven candle flames in a slanted row, and above them a human face, not the same I had seen through the keyhole. There were no dead bodies in the room, only some lifelike pictures.

"You have been listening to me play?" he asked.

"Yes, sir."

"Did you like my playing?"

I could not tell him how much, only nodded my head hard. "Was it church music?" I asked. "It didn't sound like it."

He smiled so dimly that I could hardly be sure he was smiling. "Of a kind, perhaps. In that room dwells what might be called our household god. But he did not come down from heaven or even from a mountaintop. I think he came hence from some thick woods, very dark with moss and vines, steaming hot in summer, along a tidal creek, where birds of many feathers light in the live-oak trees and among the palms."

He beckoned me to lead the way into the room. The blinds were drawn, but the seven candles set in a frame under the picture revealed it as the center one of three, all with vivid faces and lighted eyes. Except for the two stools in the foreground there was no other furniture.

"The candlestick was no doubt stolen from a Spanish shrine—I found it in a pawnshop—but it affords a good light to see the pictures," Pa told me. "Look at them closely."

The one in the center was of a woman, the most beautiful in the world. Pa had spoken of such a woman and I did not doubt that this was the one. The picture was in color and showed her upper body but not her skirt. She was a young woman with bright-gold hair and very large blue eyes. No such woman had ever come to the Orphanage, one who sat so high, with such wonderfully shaped cheeks and eyebrows and lips. Her shoulders were bare—her red dress barely covering her full bosom—and in the candlelight her skin looked glossy, soft as silk. She wore a heavy gold necklace to which hung a round piece of jewelry, and in each of her earrings glowed a red stone. I could not get enough of looking at her. She looked as though she were about to speak a command that all would rush to obey, and the one who got there first would be so glad and proud. . . .

On the right side of her was the picture of a man, the one I had seen through the keyhole. His lower body was not shown, but I could see that he was a tall, big man, and very strong. He had black hair and bold black eyebrows and a big nose. But unlike the woman there was nothing strange or wonderful about him; had he walked by our house I would have looked at him only once or twice. He wore a black coat with broad lapels and a ruffled white shirt with a black stock. On his chest was a jewel that I later learned was a diamond stud.

On the lady's left was the picture of another man, not nearly as lifelike as the other two. He had black hair and sallow skin, and his small eyes glimmered in his broad face. He too had a big nose but not as shapely as the other man's and his lips looked large and heavy. He was not dressed as finely, I thought, as the other.

"Sit on the tall stool," Pa instructed me, when I had stopped looking at the pictures. It took a long time for him to get fixed on the low stool, his left arm bent and braced against his knee, his right arm supported by his hand on the head of his stick. "I have something of great importance to tell you, Dan. Some of the words you may not know—much of the meaning will not be clear to your child's mind—but listen closely, and follow me the best you can."

"Yes, sir."

"Ask no questions, and make no sound. Later, as you grow older, all that puzzles you now will become clear. Fix your eyes on the picture in the center."

Pa's eyes were fixed on it too, and they shone like a moth's on a curtain. He began speaking in a low voice. It rose and fell a little as he spoke on, his tone deepening at times without becoming louder, the effect like a piece of music played on his violin. It was as though he were reciting a story that he knew by heart.

"That is a portrait of Madeline D'Arcy. At the death of her father, Honoré D'Arcy, she inherited the most beautiful plantation in all the Southland—Wood Ibis, named for a bird that frequents its woods and swamps. Despite her great beauty, great name, and great wealth, wherefore she was wooed by the highest in the land, she fell in love with and married my brother, Bruce Dunbarton, oldest son of a poor brewer in Charleston.

"Fix your eyes on his portrait that hangs at the right-hand of the lady. Mark his manly face and form. By honesty and thrift he had become overseer of Wood Ibis; by his marriage to Madeline he became its owner, and master of Ibis Hall. But in less than three years of bliss in each other's arms he was sent to his grave by secret murder.

"Fix your eyes on the portrait at the lady's left-hand. It is of my brother, Ralph Dunbarton, a year younger than I. Mark the cruelty in his countenance, the lust in his eyes. By Bruce's generosity and goodness he had succeeded him as overseer. At his death he preyed on Madeline's loneliness and grief, seducing her in ways unknown, and six months later married her. So now he is owner of Wood Ibis, master of Ibis Hall.

"Fix your eyes on mine, as I speak my troth. God will take no vengeance on Madeline, whose heart is pure as her face is beautiful, in this world or the next. In the next world He will surely take high vengeance on Ralph; can I not wait His good time? Nay, I cannot suffer him to live out his life, rich, and in honored place, lying nightly in his brother's bed, beside the most beautiful woman in the world. But mark me well. Mark my bowed back and frail limbs. I am a lame man, and my sorrow and thwarted fury have in some measure deranged my mind. I cannot take his trail through the dark swamp, bring to light his deeds of evil, and haul him to the gallows. It is forbidden to me to make atonement—eye for an eye, tooth for a tooth, life for a life. Vengeance is Mine, saith the Lord, God of all might; but patient though I am, how may it yet be mine?

"So I asked of my soul—in vain. Then, in the middle of the night, when I had laid bow to the strings of my Jacob Stainer, there rose deep-toned as the distant roar of the Tyrolean avalanche —heard at its birth in Absam under the master's hand—music that seemed to make words. What banished god had made my violin an oracle I know not, unless it be gray-eyed Pallas speaking with the tongue of Apollo. Close your eyes, Dan, to give the prophecy freer passage to your ears and heart.

"'It shall come to pass through one whose name is lost. One who has naught to gain for himself, save that one he loves may die in peace. One unknown now to the murderer and seducer, but who at last will steal upon him like a thief in the night, bringing fire and sword.'"

The music—it had no longer seemed Pa's voice—stopped. Bracing a wildly shaking hand upon his stick, he rose from the stool. Then he signaled me to follow him as he crept along the wall, blowing out the candles.

3

The seasons chased each other like cloud shadows on the sea, and their brief rings made years. I grew taller and stronger and better versed; my features changed from an urchin's to a stripling's. Pa never elaborated on the story he had told me in the picture-room; when he went there to play on Sunday afternoons he never again recited it in full; but in speaking of Madeline and his brothers he often employed the same phrasing, so that I knew it word for word. Often I asked him to repeat the prophecy that ever thrilled my heart. Sometimes I had feared that he would lose patience waiting for its fulfillment, and employ some other minister. Actually the idea could not cross his mind, so fixed on this design. So I developed and matured far faster than most boys of my years —it seemed in gratitude for his choosing me.

It had long been apparent to me that the master of Wood Ibis did not know that Pa still lived, let alone had adopted a son. Yet he did not rest easy in his bed beside the most beautiful woman in the world! That fact was brought home to me on another summer day, when I was about thirteen. Pa returned from an errand in town walking faster than I had ever seen him. His excited gesture brought me sprinting to the gate to meet him.

"Dan, we are in great danger," he told me. "Ralph Dunbarton is in the city, and someone has told him about a lame violinist named Mr. Reed. He will be here within an hour or two, to see if I am his brother Noel."

"Tell me what to do."

"We must trick him. My dearest friend, Mr. Linsey, will help me. You know he too is lame—he will come here and open the door to my brother and tell him he is Mr. Reed, the violin teacher. You will be playing in the yard—if he asks you if Mr. Reed is at home, tell him yes—if you have need to speak to Mr. Linsey, call him Pa. I will not return until he has left Philadelphia. Play your part well."

He did not ask me if I understood the instructions—he knew

that every word hammered on my heart—and at once hobbled on down the street. Perhaps it was not strange that I waited my first meeting with our great enemy without deep fear and with concealed excitement. Preparation for it had been going on five years. Mr. Linsey, who looked much older than Pa, of much shorter frame and with the affliction called a humpback, came hurrying up the street and entered our house. I waited for the sallow-skinned man in the picture.

In one sense that man never came. The man in black broadcloth driven to our door in a carriage was not the same. There was a general resemblance in features, but his mouth was not as coarse, or his jaw as heavy, or his eyes as fierce as the portrait had revealed them. An even greater shock to me was what seemed his commonplaceness. He seemed too ordinary-looking to bear the name of Ralph Dunbarton, despite his tall, big frame. I could have met him somewhere, talked to him perhaps, and never remembered him. But all that was a kind of mask, I thought, and made him an even more dangerous enemy.

Utterly different than that was a little girl beside him on the seat, perhaps ten years old. I had no time or attention to give her now, but knew that her white face set off by raven-black hair was the prettiest and most memorable I had ever seen.

The visitor read Pa's sign, then called to me in a lordly tone.

"Is Professor Reed at home?"

"Yes, sir." I ran up on the little porch and flung open the front door. "There's a visitor to see you, Pa."

"Wait right here," he ordered his driver. "Cleo, I may be here a good while."

"Can I get out and talk to the boy?" The little girl's voice was soft but clear-carrying as a bird's.

"If you like."

She sprang down, followed the man through the gate, and, coming around the house, advanced slowly toward me. Still I only pretended to look at her, meanwhile watching the front door through which the man had gone and listening in extreme tension. It was through my skin, it seemed, that I got such a vivid, exciting picture of her. Her hair was black but very fine and soft-looking and it grew down to a point on her forehead in what is called a widow's peak, causing her face to appear somewhat heart-shaped. Her eyebrows were black, narrow, clean-cut, long, and grew somewhat higher on her forehead than most. I did not yet know why the whole effect was so strange. . . .

"What's your name?" she asked me, her eyes straight on mine.

"Dan Reed." Then, because she was expecting the question, "What's yours?"

"Cleo Dunbarton. The man I came with is my papa."

"Do you live around here?" There was no sound from within the house.

"Oh, no. I live a long way from here, on a plantation in South Carolina. My papa owns it. But I like this little house."

At that instant I heard the front door open, and her father's voice. "It was a natural mistake, considering you too are a cripple," he was saying. "I'll bid you good day, Professor Reed."

Cleo's father came down from the porch scowling. "Come along, Cleo," he called. "I've been on a fool's errand."

"I wish I could stay here and play awhile."

If I could have done so without danger of arousing our enemy's suspicions, I would have made some excuse to get rid of her, so he would not come near the house again today.

"Well, you may, if you want to," he said, after a sharp glance at me. "I've got a long and tiring ride out to the docks. I'll send the carriage for you in an hour or two."

That made it all right! I breathed in joy instead of air, that this lovely little girl would be with me awhile, without danger to Pa and me. She was Ralph Dunbarton's daughter but I did not hate her for that—every least drop of hate squeezed out of me by some other feeling I had about her, caused by her face and voice. Partly it was wonder at her happiness over being left here a brief while, suggesting that she had very little happiness and maybe a great deal of sadness. It was not her fault that she had such a father, and Madeline Dunbarton was her beautiful mother! Some day I would come upon him with fire and sword, as the prophecy told, but I would not harm a hair of Cleo's head.

Well, I too was as wonderfully happy! Her face was the prettiest I had ever seen, and in a very strange way. It made me feel warm and strange. I saw now that her eyes were the pale brown called hazel with a soft luster. Her long straight lips were such a delicate pink color that they were not easy to see.

"How old are you, Dan?" she asked.

"I'm thirteen."

"I'm going on eleven. My birthday is the sixteenth of October. When is your birthday?"

I started to say Christmas Day, then bit my tongue. Pa's birthday was on Christmas—he had told me that was why he had been named Noel—and I could choose it for my own; but if she told her father about that, it might turn his mind again to Professor Reed. I had learned to be alert and cunning while stealing bread and slops at the Orphanage.

"Mine's next winter," I answered her.

She looked at me with growing curiosity and then asked, "Where is your mama?"

"My mama is dead."

"When did she die?"

"When I was a baby."

"I'm so sorry. But you have a nice papa?"

"Yes."

"So do I, and my mama is the most beautiful in the world."

"I think you're awful pretty too."

Her eyes shone at that. "You wouldn't, if you could see my mama."

I showed her my rabbit-hutch and anything else in the yard to interest her. She wanted to go into the house to see my turtle shell and other treasures, but I could not trust Mr. Linsey as Pa and I trusted each other—he was not bound, as we were, body and soul— and he might say or do something to cause her to suspect he was not my father. It was a nice house, she told me. She wished she lived in it instead of the big house, named Ibis Hall, on her father's plantation. She asked me what its name was and was surprised that it had none. Music Hall would be a nice name for it, she thought.

All the time I was more fascinated by Cleo and excited over her. Her voice reminded me of a bird singing in the woods. Her skin was whiter than ivory and so transparent that tiny blue veins showed around her eyes and on her temples, and when I looked at her wrists I saw them there. I was touched by them and by her slim white throat. They had meaning for me that made me feel sad and happy both at once, but I could not have put it in words—they belonged to Cleo. I could not get enough of looking at her, with growing wonder and joy. She was not so pretty when she laughed—her lips took the shape of a jack-o'-lantern mouth—and her laughter was a little shrill and excited-sounding. Yet I found myself inciting it in every possible way, both delighted and troubled that she could laugh so much with so little cause. Her eyes never laughed with her mouth; only their quiet luster became brighter.

Yet for long, aching periods we stood about in silence, glancing at each other now and then, but avoiding each other's eyes. In one of these it came to me what ache it was that had tied my tongue—to kiss her pale-pink lips. I suddenly craved to do so with that intensity known only to those who have known what it is to starve. It shook and perhaps shamed me, so deeply and strangely it struck, and I walked about whistling.

"What is that tune?" she asked. "I never heard it before."

I was almost frightened as I recognized it. It was a tune that ran through Pa's music when he played to the picture of Madeline, the same that affected me so strongly the first time I had heard it, and always excited me to a half-guilty, half-blissful pain.

"I don't know its name, or where I learned it," I answered.

"It's mighty sweet, but—queer-sounding."

I walked quickly behind the woodshed, hoping she would follow me. She did in a moment or two, a little color in her face, and with big, shy eyes.

"I wondered what you were doing here, so long."

"I was just thinking."

"A penny for your thoughts. That's what my beautiful mama sometimes says to me, but half the time I don't know."

"I never saw a girl like you before."

"I guess I never saw a boy just like you."

"I like you better than any other girl."

"Even those you've known a long time?"

"Yes. A whole lot better."

"Well—I'm glad."

"Do you like me?"

"Yes."

"As well as any other boy—" I was stammering and sweating.

"Yes. You told me so I'll tell you—maybe better than any other."

"Would you be mad if I kissed you?"

"No."

I thought that only I would be made so happy by the kiss, but I was mistaken. Her pretty face turned beautiful in my sight, and we stood with our arms about each other, kissing each other with a joy and longing strange and somehow pitiful in two children of our age. Still I felt and recognized natural forces that were the merest instinct in her. Her summers of growth had not quite overtaken my winters—I was entering a gate she was just approaching —and a complete innocence remained on her lips that I had begun to lose.

"Someone might see us," she said in sudden alarm.

"Come into the woodshed."

Frightened of her own compulsions, still she did not try to resist them. There was something like a desperateness upon her that I did not understand. In the dim room, fragrant with the sawdust of pine, our lips clung longer than was meet for innocence. Together we went into danger that had struck many even younger than we, and together—each of us striving as much for the other's safety as his own—escaped. I think a wise Mother helped us. The precocious fever was broken by her palliative measures. There was only a shadow of shame and guilt on Cleo's face.

Fear was their inevitable follower.

"What if Papa would catch us in here?" she whispered.

"If we hear him, we can hide till we get a chance to slip out."

"Where?"

A tier of stovewood, that had stood against the wall, had been reduced by use before two other tiers were neatly stacked in front of it. There was just room for a child to squirm around the end of these and gain the vacant space. Cleo followed me there, and by sitting close together on the floor, we were well hidden from anyone looking in the door.

"What a wonderful place to hide!" she told me, trembling with excitement.

22

"We can hug and kiss all we like, and nobody could see us." We could barely see each other, so dark the corner was.

"Papa would look and look, and never find me." Her eyes narrowed and shone in the gloom.

My heart began to beat wildly. "Then you could stay and live with Pa and me."

"Oh, I'd love to—for a while. He's got Mama and all that big plantation and—Mama would miss me, but she's so beautiful—and has everything. I love your little house. I'd be so happy with you and your papa—" She caught her breath between every sentence. "Oh, it would be wonderful."

"Do you think if I hid here, you could tell him that I got tired—and started back for the inn—and maybe got lost—or maybe that another man came for me—to steal me? He wouldn't look very long, would he? He'd go back to Wood Ibis in a day or two—he's got so much to look after there. Could you bring me food and water till he's gone? I wouldn't need any bedclothes this warm weather."

Already the bitter truth was breaking on me that the plan was impossible. Ralph Dunbarton would turn Philadelphia upside down looking for her. For that reason alone, Pa would not let her stay—besides she was the daughter of our great foe, by evil marriage to the most beautiful woman in the world. But I could not tell Cleo yet. She would find out for herself so soon. It was a wonder she had not, already. She was blinded by the power of her vision.

Gazing at her, I was beside myself with intense longings and confused thought. I yearned to keep her always, with an equal yearning for her to escape the house I would some day tear down. A need as strange and deep as mine was upon her—it met and joined with mine, without her dreaming how I was involved, only sensing that I understood it somehow—and from that instant we were linked in a bond more adamant than iron. There in that dark hiding place we both felt its grasp. We gazed at each other in a wild wonder of recognition and the air came sharp and strange to my nostrils as though we were out of the world.

We were both trembling and gasping for breath. Then in some instinctive fear of so great a thing—perhaps fear of believing it in vain—she tried to go on speaking of her pitiful plan, trying to defend it, making out she was in her right mind.

"I've heard—of gypsies—stealing girls. . . . Later I could send—for Obo—he's my servant. . . . I guess—it wouldn't work—"

Her lips were twitching, and suddenly my arms flung up around her. She enfolded me with hers and began to cry, asking, "What is it? What is it?" in a bewilderment of grief and joy. We were on the floor of our woodshed behind the stacks, the light dim and tinted grayish-blue, the summer heat confined and bringing sweat on our faces mixed with her tears, the afternoon brilliance through the unlatched door only a narrow shaft in which dust motes floated. Here we hid together from searching fate. I saw its shape but she did not. Yet the wonder and the mystery was no less to me than to her, even though I knew from what deep root it stemmed—she Ralph Dunbarton's daughter, and I Noel Dunbarton's son.

"What is it, Dan?" she asked again, wide-eyed and white, when she quieted a little. "It hurts so awful—"

"I don't know."

"I love you more than anyone except Mama—and she's like a queen."

"I love you more than anyone but Pa—and it's not like this."

"But it couldn't be like grown-up young ladies and their sweethearts love each other. . . . Could it be?"

We were staring, wonder-struck, into each other's eyes. "Maybe this is 'way, 'way more. I reckon so."

"What can we do? Tonight Papa and I are starting back to Wood Ibis. How can we keep from losing each other?" She leaned close and spoke in a frantic whisper. "Would it do any good—would it be wrong—if both of us took off all our clothes—don't think I'm a bad girl—and put our arms around each other—and promised forever and ever? I will if you will. No one can see us—we'll be ashamed to see each other but then it would be a promise —we couldn't—break."

"Yes, but be quick." The rest came in painful bursts out of my choked throat. "Your papa might come and kill us both. Nobody in the world would believe us. I won't do anything wrong—what I know and you don't. Oh, then we'll never break our promise!"

24

Neither of us understood the symbolism: it was too deep and old. We only performed it with bursting hearts. Her hands flew and so did mine and our acute shame became, somehow, our troth. Then, I thought, her body was as white as an angel's.

Afraid to stand, crouched awkwardly in the cramped, dimly lighted space, we put our arms about each other's necks and made our vows.

"I promise forever and ever, Cleo."

"I promise, Dan, forever and ever."

In our desperate fervor and haste we did not declare what we were promising—it did not seem then there was any need, so well we knew. Then we kissed in a like swift urgency and our hands flew again. Time stopped for us after that; we were sitting in the shady yard, our fingers intertwined, unable to say a word, when the carriage came for her. Standing on the sidewalk I watched her grow small, until the white face under its black hair that had turned again and again to me faded in the distance.

for horsemanship. Actually it was no more than good balance, a strong wrist, and no intention of being worsted by a beast. I was born, it seemed, rigidly on guard and that alertness had never left me. Shrewd in most dealings, in an emergency I found a ready cunning that might too have been forced upon my infant mind. I was not tongue-tied or timid, nor was I boastful or overconfident: the business pending was too grave.

Christmas of the year 1853—it was also Pa's fifty-fourth birthday —we shared a bottle of whiskey and at our good dinner talked more freely than usual. He reminded me that we had been together thirteen and a half years. I was at least twenty-one, no doubt nearer twenty-two. I had changed so much, he so little. His fine hair was untouched by gray and his bowed body only slightly less gaunt. Next year a bell would ring for both of us.

"When it's all over, will you resume your own name, so I can take it?" I asked.

"Yes, and I'll tell you now one reason I was forced to take another. Even then I contemplated adopting a son—for no other, no hired hand, could perform the task that my broken back forbade. What did I care for waiting fourteen years? They have sped like the wind across the salt marshes of Wood Ibis. But the existence of such a son had to be concealed. The other reasons you will discover for yourself. It is my best and studied judgment that you start with open mind and eyes lest the little that I know, mixed with so much that I suspect, might mislead you."

I would wait patiently until spring, I thought, and did not dream that event would not wait for me.

Returning from an errand in town a few days after the new year, I passed on our block a figure somewhat strange in the old, quiet streets of Baltimore. He was a Negro of around thirty, wearing rather quaint blue livery, and at first remarkable mainly for his immense size. I had rarely seen its equal in the slave gangs, never in house-service—stature of six and a half feet at least, gigantic breadth and depth. But when he passed me I gazed with greater wonder at his countenance. There was savagery in it, of the kind that slavers see sometimes in the faces of new-caught cannibals, but which planters rarely see because such untamable captives usually die in their chains in the Middle Passage. But also there was a stillness and a dignity to become an African king.

He turned the corner, walking with long, swift strides. Then limping to meet me I saw Pa, anxiety on his face and feverish excitement in his eyes.

"I am tracked down again, Dan, and this time there is no hope of avoiding discovery," he told me. "But you must not be seen. Ralph must not know that I am not alone and helpless."

"How soon is he coming? Can't you get a neighbor to say—"

"It is not Ralph in person. He has sent an emissary. Her servant came to the door and took me by surprise—"

"*Her* servant?" My skin prickled all over my body.

"Yes. A giant Negro, whom you must have met on the street. I could not trick his keen eyes. He will describe me in detail to his mistress. But you must be gone when she comes—"

"Is it Madeline?"

"Oh, no. God, no! It is Cleo, Ralph's daughter, a maiden of eighteen. I never told you that Ralph and she had a daughter—"

I knew it well! I had never told Pa of the girl who had come in the carriage and been here, close with us in the house, ever since.

"Hark, Pa," I broke in. "Instead of going uptown I'll stay in our picture-room with the door cracked. She won't see me. I want to hear what she has to say. It's time to begin. I want to know what she's like before I go to Wood Ibis."

"I see little to be gained—but I have told you you shall operate in your own way. It is possible you will get a hint or two useful to you later." Pa led the way into the house and shut the door.

"But don't admit you're Noel Dunbarton until there's no longer any hope of deceiving her."

"I will not—but I am sure there is none."

I watched out a dim window and presently nodded to Pa. A stylish carriage had stopped outside our door and a fashionably dressed young lady was getting out. Was this Cleo? In my waking life I knew she had grown up, eighteen now; but in my dreams where I knew her best she was still a slim little girl of ten, with an angel-white body and raven-black hair. She was of marriageable age, an heiress with many wooers; perhaps she returned no more to the hiding place behind the woodpile at the little house in Philadelphia. Perhaps when she came to me in dreams she did not know of the visits.

Was the chain we had welded—joining our hearts and souls, I thought, forever—broken? It was still around me fast but had she dropped the coil on the bloody ground of Wood Ibis, where it lay rusting and forgotten? Now she was coming through the gate, her huge Negro servant walking behind her like a trained lion. The bright daylight showed her hair still raven black and her face almost snow white, but not yet could I look and see if they were still mine. I fled into the picture-room, with the portraits of the living and dead, and, leaving the door ajar, waited in an icy cold, extreme suspense.

Pa received her at the door, where her servant remained in attendance while Pa escorted her into the parlor. Although grown tall, she was still slender, and walked with long, light steps I seemed to remember. Indeed the white body I had seen had grown and taken form just as I might have known. But I had not envisioned its spring ripening. Perhaps she had married some planter's son and was in the flush of love with him, and what I had glimpsed in that dim light of long ago was now his sole possession. . . . Perhaps she had told him, with a little shyness, a little laughter . . . The painted faces on the wall behind me had not changed. I had thought she would grow up but not change. To pay them their due I had stayed here instead of going on a journey to validate our due to each other. . . . Dark heart, I could not help myself! Save for them, we twain would have owed no due.

Pa offered her a chair in excellent light, in front of the door behind which I kept hawk-watch. There was no danger of my being seen in these deep shadows, and he wanted to give me a clear view of Bruce Dunbarton's wife and his brother Ralph in their joined flesh. Her mouth was still wide and straight, the delicate pink of her lips unchanged; her eyes, under straight, extremely narrow, black, high-set brows, were of that pale brown called hazel, and their soft luster had neither dimmed nor brightened. She looked so innocent! Perhaps that was only because she was a little abashed in this first meeting with her uncle who had hidden away his very existence, in vain.

"What can I do for you, Miss Dunbarton?" he was asking.

She would reply, I thought, that since she was his niece . . . In listening to her voice I did not at once realize she had said something quite different. It was the same and it flooded my heart. Whether or not she had forgotten, I would always remember.

"I'm afraid, Professor Reed, I've taken your time for nothing."

I held my breath. Pa paused to take great care.

"A mistake in identity?" he asked.

"Yes, sir. While it was only a chance that you were the gentleman I was looking for, I thought I'd make certain. It was a long time ago that I saw him—only a glimpse in a doorway—but I'm sure you're not he."

She was not very steady. I stopped trembling in order to watch and listen without fail.

"Was it at this house?" Pa asked.

"No, it was in Philadelphia. I'll explain the mistake. I had driven with my father who had some business with a Professor Reed who was also a music teacher. When I came to spend the Christmas holidays in Baltimore—I've been going to school in Norfolk and one of my schoolmates invited me here for a visit—I heard of you and thought he might have moved here."

"It was quite a natural mistake, Miss Dunbarton. It happens that I have heard of a Professor Reed who teaches, or used to teach, the violin in Philadelphia. I was told of him because of another coincidence, which you have been too polite to mention. He too is lame."

"Yes, sir, I had that impression. Well, I won't take any more of your time—"

She was giving way, now, to an intense disappointment. I heard it in her voice and saw it in her lovely face. If she only knew that I was giving way to exultation! She had not forgotten, she had not broken her promise! I would not let her go back to Wood Ibis thinking she was alone.

"If you wanted to see him about taking music lessons, I would like to offer my services," Pa said with great cunning. "However, my hours are already taken."

"No, sir. It was a personal matter between me and his son. I wanted to ask the other Professor Reed how to reach him." She was having trouble going on. "Now I will have to make a request of you. It will seem a very foolish one, I'm afraid. Please don't mention to anyone I came to see you, because my mother is well known here—she went to school here—and she and my father might hear I've been in Baltimore. She wouldn't care but he would be very angry. Understand that the only wrong I've done is to disobey him, in not staying in Norfolk over the holidays. I have been visiting Miss Harriet Howard."

"I've heard of Miss Howard. I will certainly keep your innocent little secret."

"That's very kind. And I don't suppose you happen to know—where the other Professor Reed is living now."

"I didn't know he'd left Philadelphia."

"Yes, he has. The letters I've written his son in his care have come back 'address unknown.'"

"I might hear of him later—we have so much in common. Would you like me to give him a message?"

"Oh, yes. Tell his son to write to Dr. Sams, at Little Ibis Plantation, Ibis Island, South Carolina, and give me his address. It's very important I get in touch with him."

"He would be flattered that you remember him so long. Will you be leaving soon for Norfolk?"

"No, I've finished school and am sailing tomorrow for Charleston." She looked away from Pa, but I saw tears in her eyes. "I wish I could stay here longer—Mama's friends would be glad to have me —I would like to take music lessons too—but it's impossible—"

Tears blind some people; to others they are lenses for deeper vision. Through the mist I saw Cleo with new clarity. She was unique-looking in a lovely way and had a unique being. I could not picture her as the daughter of a great plantation house as well as an inmate of thick woods. It was a very strange impression, as though her face was virginal of the sun's torrid kiss and the light that she knew was dappled. A very quiet, hard-to-see dryad might describe her to a man of poetic fancy, or a witch-child whose sweetness had exiled her from her evil sisters. Thinking of birds, I recalled a wood ibis I had seen in Georgia. It was a tall, graceful creature, white, with black head and wings.

32

"Miss Dunbarton, may I serve you some inferior wine, but quite good cake?" Pa was asking.

"Thank you, but I've borrowed Mr. Howard's carriage and must take it back at once." She rose with a wood creature's grace and I watched her, my heart still, cross the room and go out the door. I was by the window before she got in the carriage. The wheels turned, and tomorrow the sails, bearing her back to Carolina, would fill with wind.

"Pa?"

"Aye, my son." His hand was shaking on the handle of his stick.

"It wasn't what we thought, was it?" Yet I had had a premonition of the truth, too strange to believe.

"We have escaped again. She will not even tell her father she has been to Baltimore to meet a Professor Reed with a broken back."

"Who is Dr. Sams, of Little Ibis Plantation?"

"He is my old and loyal friend. He lives on a small plantation once part of Wood Ibis, really a separate island since a tidal creek flows between. My brother Bruce Dunbarton gave it to me when he was master: I leased it to Dr. Sams when Bruce was killed. It affords a modest but comfortable living, and I mean for you to have it when I am gone. Not as a prize for success in your undertaking, mark you, but because you are my son."

"Then Dr. Sams knows you are alive?"

"Aye. I hear from him at long intervals. But he keeps my secret. He pays the small rental to a bank, where it is accumulating for my return. My brother Ralph has not yet petitioned the courts to declare me deceased, whereby to claim the land and the rent. Rather than rake over old coals he chooses to wait until I am lost sight of for twenty-one years; then no petition will be necessary."

"That's a year yet. You'll return before then. Does Dr. Sams know about me?"

"Nay. It is well that no one knows so dangerous a secret."

"He is evidently Cleo's confidant."

"That would be quite natural, I think. But you, too, Dan, have ties with her that I did not dream of. I did not even know she was with my brother, that day in Philadelphia. She is very eager to meet you again. I am deeply troubled."

33

"You needn't be. She doesn't know I'm in any way connected with you. To her I'm a boy named Dan Reed, whom she played with one day. It's true we became very close friends. I guess I felt sorry for her for being Ralph's daughter. You could see today how she might need such a friendship."

He stood very still, staring into an unseen distance, until he felt my questioning gaze, then he nodded slowly.

"Still, it is very strange, after all these years."

"I think she's very lonely and remembers how happy we were together as children. Well, the friendship might be a great advantage to me when I go to Wood Ibis, if I could re-establish it. A close friend, who'd talk to me freely, in the enemy camp."

"Ah, but you cannot! If she knew you as Dan Reed, the boy she played with in Philadelphia, Ralph would remember the call he made on Professor Reed, whom he once thought might be Noel Dunbarton. He would start wondering at the strangeness of his son coming to Wood Ibis, and put two and two together. In no time your true identity would be exposed."

"I agree with you, but—"

"Why, if she remembers you as the boy she met, my long concealment of you will be in vain!"

"I see that, now, and that's why I must make a bold stroke at once. I was only thirteen when we met and my face has changed far more in these eight and a half years than anyone would expect. Far more than usual with boys. My voice has changed too, of course. I grant you that, if I appeared suddenly before her at Wood Ibis, she would at least ask the question in her mind if I could be Dan Reed. But if I met her on neutral ground—apparently by chance— gave another name and showed a different personality—I don't think she'd even associate me with the boy she played with. Any little reminders of him she'd pass over and forget. Doesn't that stand to reason?"

"Aye, it is good, straight thinking."

I was being forced to think straight—and fast. So much was at stake.

"I'd prepare her for my coming to Wood Ibis this spring—on some good excuse. Then when I do come there'll be no question in her mind but that I'm just a shipboard acquaintance—"

"Shipboard?" he broke in, staring.

"She's leaving for Charleston tomorrow. Why shouldn't I be on the ship, going to Charleston on some business? It would be the natural way to meet her."

"That is true." Pa sank into a chair and wiped his face. "And the acquaintance you thus make might be not only a protection from a danger out of the past. It might be of value to the future. It would be well to have a friend, innocent of your design, at Ibis Hall."

I did not reply. His brain was turning over fast. I knew it by his expression.

"It is a bold idea from a bold mind. Even on the journey you might gain information of value to your quest. People's tongues are loosed on shipboard, their shores receded and dim. Aye, the money for the ticket will be well spent!"

"It will be the real beginning."

"But I spy a danger. Not that you, Dan, will speak too freely—but feel too strongly. Even as children you came very close. Unless you are on strict and unremittent guard, you might fall in love with her!"

Sweat came out on Pa's face as he searched mine. "She is Madeline's daughter," he went on, in an intense tone. "Although having only a tittle of Madeline's beauty she has yet enough to stir a young man's heart. She would be very vulnerable to you on shipboard—and perchance you to her. But remember she is also the daughter of my brother Ralph."

He was thinking of more than that. Slowly he rose, moved to his violin case on the stand, opened it, and drew the bow thrice across the strings. The gut could be silk threads as far as my ear could discern. Perhaps they made a sound inside his head. He closed the case and turned to me, gazing from down behind his forehead.

"Dan, tell me, if you will, have you ever lain with a girl?"

"Only in dreams. I've had the desire—at least the symptoms of it—but I was busy with other things, and it passed off." I did not tell that my varied partners in these dreams had always black hair and white skin.

"Dan, would you say this young girl is a virgin?"

"Why, yes."

"I am by no means certain. Mark her mature form for a maiden of eighteen. The sun of Carolina is a beguiling sun. It may be she is lascivious. Still waters run deep, and there are signs of sensuousness in her face and body. You are young, of manly face and form, with impounded natural fountains. You might be greatly tempted by her, and if you yield to that temptation, I dare not contemplate the consequences."

I had never heard him speak so solemnly. His lips trembled and his face was ashen gray.

"I told you I would not direct your operations, but I must give you the most solemn warning. You must not become the slave of passion for her. You would not be free to destroy her father. Guard yourself, Dan, or all will be lost."

"I will," I told him quickly. "Don't be afraid."

"I believe you—yet I must break another rule that I had set, which was to let you find out as much as possible for yourself, without my coloring your viewpoint. Dan, you may sometimes be prey to doubts as to the need, the good, the gain of the task for which I made you my son. I am a marked man, and deranged. Perchance you fear at times that I have made you the victim of a tragic illusion."

"Pa, I never have."

"Yet you realize the strangeness of our lives and consecration. You wonder why I did not employ a hireling long ago. I would have done so, were the task only to avenge my brother's murder. Instead it is to battle monstrous evil spawned in my own clan, darkening my name and my door—unlike any I have ever known or heard of. I know the events but can only guess their meaning. I crave that it be better, more human, less monstrous than my terror hints; but at best the truth will be more awful than you dream. It is your dread fate to unearth it, a fate more strange than your life so far even approached presaging. The shadows you have seen—those across my mind, across your life, even in the face of Cleo—are thin and pale compared to the realities that cast them. In Jehovah's name take warning! Do not let yourself be weakened by one jot or tittle. Let not your steps be led astray."

Again he went to his violin and took it from its case. With his eyes on mine he drew the bow across the strings. This time they did not remain mute, and the music that came trilling forth was not made to Bruce, Ralph, and Madeline Dunbarton. Pa was playing to me.

To one whose name is lost. To one who has naught to gain for himself, save that one he loves may die in peace. . . . *Come like a thief in the night,* the music trumpeted, *bringing fire and sword! Be true, my son, be true!*

But there were two to whom I must be true—no, three. . . . We three.

Before the day was out I had assurance that Cleo had engaged passage on the steam packet for Charleston sailing on the morning tide, and a fair confidence that none of the other passengers or the crew knew me by sight. I bought a ticket under the name of Dave MacDaniel, the first that entered my head, hardly realizing that after meeting Cleo I might have to wear it for years.

In cold blowing mists the auxiliary sails were hoisted, the paddle wheels turned; the passengers who had made short shift of their goodbyes hurried to the fires below. Cleo was among the last to leave the deck.

Aloneness and loneliness seem to me two different things. The second is the sad awareness of the first. No one had seen her off, she stood alone by the rail, she looked and spoke to no one; yet I did not feel that she was lonely. She was too full of deeper emotions to be aware of solitude. She was gazing back toward Baltimore not with grief, it seemed—as though she could not give time and attention to that; it too did not matter—rather with a kind of desperation. Once she glanced down at the waters just under the rail. I could not read her face. Although one would expect it to be telltale, being delicate and childish-looking, actually it was quite an effective mask. Presently she turned and, walking with a long, light step, went below. It was so very light that it gave the impression of her walking on tiptoe. It was a sign of the secretiveness of her soul.

I saw her again in the dining saloon at noon. It seemed to me that she had accepted the fact of a departure and need not yet confront the prospect of an arrival. This was an interim that she was trying to make not the best but the most of; if so, it indicated a strong and realistic mind. She was taking pains with her selection of food and having a delicious and quite hearty meal. She made a swift scrutiny of her table companions as though wondering about every one in view of cultivating acquaintances.

But her first great animation, so intense that it arrested all other expression with a kind of start, came when she caught her first clear sight of me.

She looked away quickly; then, when she thought herself unobserved, her gaze stole back to my face. It was searching and deeply curious yet without any conscious recognition. I thought that her excitement ebbed after later glances. Perhaps, wondering what had caused it, she had wilfully repressed it for a vagary: at most she would like to meet and talk to me. Once I met her eyes and looked at her as might any young man at a pretty girl.

Late in the afternoon the waves lulled, the weather cleared and turned fairly warm, and she was among a scattering of travelers on the passenger deck. She was alone again—remote from the others—and that was the real condition of her being. Her beauty was very marked in the marine light. I wondered why the people did not gaze at it more often. Perhaps it was a kind they did not recognize—not an enhancement of common prettiness but a fresh creation. I thought her beautiful beyond thought.

She turned to me as I approached her, perfectly willing to be addressed, displaying no eagerness but quite possibly concealing some.

"Miss, I saw you riding in a carriage yesterday, and I thought the team of bays was the finest I'd ever seen." I had taken some care with this opening, and thought from her expression that it had told.

"So you've an eye for horses," she replied, honestly delighted with my loutishness.

"Oh, I saw you too. How would you think I remembered you? I thought the whole outfit was mighty fine."

"That's a lot better. Who are you?"

"Dave MacDaniel. I work for a horse-breeder in Anne County and I'm going to Charleston to see the country and look for a job, perhaps."

"I'm Cleo Dunbarton and I'm going home after visiting in Baltimore."

"Have you got kinfolk there? I know a lot of Baltimore people."

"I've friends there, but no kinfolk."

So two shipboard acquaintances made conversation. My voice

sounded fairly steady and my heart was beating in slow, strong bounds. Was she wondering at a dim memory, which had no apparent connection with this scene, of a hiding place behind a woodpile long ago? I was back there, as though in a dream.

It was a long, long dream and at its present point she and I were here. She had grown tall with small, lovely breasts and tapering lines, but fine blue veins were still visible around her eyes and on her wrists and I longed to kiss her lips the same as then. The intensity and timbre of the longing was the same, a thing I had never felt since in waking life—childishly fierce and painful.

"Have you any brothers or sisters?" she asked, when we had talked awhile about the weather, the ship, and the fine sights of Baltimore.

"No, I'm an only child."

"So am I." She started to ask a question—thought better of it— then asked it anyway. "Are both your parents alive?"

"No, they're both dead." I did not know if this was true but it sounded like truth. The very occasional times I had wondered about them—always with a sense of disquiet—I had thought of them as dead. That might arise from their not mattering to me in the least.

"Why did you ask, Cleo?"

"I had a feeling they might be. I'm not a mind reader—I don't know where it came from. Did you lose them recently?"

"No, a long time ago."

"Have you always lived in Baltimore?"

"Yes."

I knew then that she had been thinking of a boy named Dan Reed in Philadelphia—against her better judgment—and perhaps now she would put him by.

"Are both your parents living?" I asked, leading up to something.

"Yes, thank heaven."

"You speak with such feeling. You must love them very dearly." That was it. I had to know—especially if she loved Ralph Dunbarton. It would make no difference in what I had to do, but might make a bleak world of difference in what happened between her and me. I had been asking the question, under cover of my desire, for eight years. She might say she did, but her eyes might belie her words. My common sense had told me that she could not, and her despair at returning home was strong evidence that she did not.

"Of course I do. My mother is very beautiful—"

She paused and, pressing her, I said, "Why don't you go on?"

"I've heard that ships were wonderful ice-breakers and now I know its true."

"I'd love to talk to you if you've nothing better to do."

"I'd like to talk to you. I like your name—David MacDaniel. It sounds honest and—plain. I like plain things. I've nothing else to do at all."

"Well, there's a cushioned seat in the saloon, and it's warm in there."

She sat beside me, her arm touching mine; and the lamps were not yet lit and no one was in hearing.

"You spoke of how much you loved your mother," I said.

"I adore her. I always have, as long as I can remember. As a little girl I thought of her as a queen, with a golden crown and jeweled eyes."

"Do you love her more than your father?"

"I feel about him in a different way. I don't adore him as I do Mama—you see, he's not of high birth like her. But I love him just as much."

Her eyes and lips were saying the same thing.

"He's strict with me," she went on, "but more demonstrative than Ma—always kissing and hugging and praising me—especially when he's had a drop too much. He worries about me a great deal."

"I don't see why he should worry about you. You're slender but you look healthy. I wouldn't think a plantation would be a danger-ous place."

A short, faint vertical line appeared between her long, narrow, black, high-set brows.

"I've never been sick a day in my life. But I ride a lot—he's afraid I'll have an accident, I guess—and love to go into the woods and swamps with Obo." She began to talk with eagerness and joy. "He's my servant, quartered below with the others. You might wonder I'd have him with me at school, but I wanted him and he was sick to go and Mama arranged for the school to let him help with the gardening. You ought to see him, he's such a giant. Papa gave him to me when he was first brought from Africa, thirteen years ago. He was only about seventeen then, very tall and big-boned but so thin that everyone thought he would die. He had eaten almost nothing on the slaver and was brokenhearted, and Papa bought him for a hundred dollars. He would have died if Papa hadn't given him to me. I named him Obo because his voice sounds like one—Papa has one that he can play a little."

I had thought that Pa was the only musician in the Dunbarton family.

"I was lonely and set out to try to make him play with me," Cleo went on. "Even a little girl of five is full of guile. Before the day was over, he had learned to swing me in a rope swing, and I had coaxed him into eating some of my picnic lunch. In a week he had learned to smile. After that he wanted to be near me every minute; he slept on the floor outside my nursery door. Still Papa can't believe I'm perfectly safe with him, even miles away from anyone. He wouldn't want people to know how we make the most wonderful excursions together, because they'd condemn him—and that worries him too."

"I see. Where is your plantation?"

"About thirty miles from Charleston, on what's called a sea-island —the last one of several islands separated by salt creeks."

"Is it very beautiful?"

"I think it's the most beautiful in all Dixie."

"There's about ten thousand acres in cultivation and pasture," she went on, after a brief silence. "All the rest is wild woods and swamps."

"You must be mighty glad to be going home."

"Well, I'd never been to Baltimore before and would have liked to see more of it. But Papa would have raised sand if he had known I was there—he thought I was still at school in Norfolk. Besides he's kept writing me to leave school and come home—I guess he can hardly stand to have me away."

"If he loves you that much, it's a wonder he let you go away to school."

"He said I couldn't, but Mama made him. I wanted to go to

Philadelphia—there's a fine girls' school there—but they settled on Norfolk. Of course I'm mighty glad to be going home." She gave me a quick glance as she said this last.

I had business to attend to. "Have you any other close kinfolk? It's so nice to have uncles and aunts—"

"My mother's brothers and sisters died in the plague, when she was a little girl. Papa had two brothers but one died two years before I was born, and the other—he was lame—went away about the same time and never came back. Papa doesn't know if he's still alive."

"I had a cousin who was born lame." My mind was becoming very alert and the invention came easily.

"I don't think Uncle Noel was. I can't remember clearly, but I think someone told me he was injured when a boy. I never heard how."

"I had a little injury three years ago." I opened my left hand that I had kept closed until now and showed her my little finger.

Her eyes rounded and she gave me a wild glance. Only by the utmost effort of will could I keep my countenance.

"What's the matter, Miss Cleo?"

"Oh, nothing." Her hand gripped the edge of the bench, the knuckles hard against the skin. "A boy I knew had hurt his hand the same. It surprised me so. But it's a small world—"

"I hurt it in the woods and it was a good while before I got to the doctor. That's why he couldn't straighten it. The little finger has such small bones, it often happens like that."

"I see. . . . There's the supper bell."

"I wish we could eat together. I'm a farm boy without extra-good table manners."

"Papa was a farm boy too. He was overseer of Mama's plantation when they got married. Anyway you seem mighty good-mannered to me."

Some of the people stared at such a plainly dressed young man eating with a young lady rich and highborn, but Cleo seemed unaware of it and in high spirits. I began to sense a new hope in her heart concerning her return to Wood Ibis—perhaps wild and reckless but warming her like wine. I could not imagine what it might be. I kept thinking it was empty, and could hardly stand her eager laughter. It was the same as on that day—excited and a little shrill —and as easily invoked—as though the same hope had placed it ready in her throat. Still her eyes did not laugh but remained soft with subdued luster—maybe they had seen too much to take stock in that hope.

After supper we walked the deck awhile, she with a light and lovely carriage. I was trying to get my own feet solidly on the ground. I did not succeed at first—the strangeness of our walking together had an uncanny quality. Although convinced we were new acquaintances, still she was recapturing some of that old joy. The mysterious, almost metaphysical bond we had made eight years ago was working on her beyond her knowledge—exciting and touching her deeply.

There was an aching blind urge upon me to tell her that I was her partner in that bond. I could not have resisted it, if I could have stopped at that—and not exposed, sooner or later, my identity as the adopted son of "Professor Reed." Only a little putting of two and two together in her father's mind or even in hers would certainly disclose that one of the two lame music teachers was Noel Dunbarton. I could not swear her to secrecy, on any excuse, while I went about hounding her father to the gallows. I could not ask any loyalty from her during the performance of that task—it would be unspeakable.

So the bond we had made must remain a thing of the past, making no demands on my immediate future. Even our promises to each other had ended in the air, unburdened with eventuality, and must remain so a long time yet. That meant we must not fall in love. Only when my work was done, when she would know what wounds I had dealt her, would we both be free.

It was a good resolution. I had made it just before we stood at the companionway to say good night. But she would expect some courting from a swain of new shipboard acquaintance—and the darkness here invited a common address between such fellow-travelers as Cleo and Dave MacDaniel. The words were loutish enough, but something went wrong with my voice.

"Are you used to being kissed good night?" I asked.

I could barely see the lift at the ends of her long lips.

44

"Since you ask, why, yes. Both my parents kiss me, if they're around."

"I'd like to make you feel at home, while on the sea."

"Why, you needn't, if that's your only reason."

It sounded not at all coy, only a little jocund, and hiding behind her humor was some other mood. Perhaps intense curiosity. Perhaps intensity itself.

Hiding behind my trickery of her and of myself was a giant in leash. He was breaking free. A warm wave of desire swept through my blood and bone to my finger tips.

"It's because you're so beautiful and lovely."

She spoke quaintly then, a curious consequence of her attempt to hide her excitement. "In that case, you may have a good-night kiss."

It had been eight years since her lips had pressed to mine, yet it seemed I would have known them in blind dark. They came upon mine and withdrew; and it was like waking from sleep. It was true in a sense—I had dreamed this a thousand times, but sleep had softened its realization; in my dreams it had ushered in a bliss that was still out of the world, yet which had satisfied a sleeper. It could never again. Those forces were all the greater for being so long leashed. They would never rest again.

Buffetted by my own gales, dizzy, and bewildered, I could not at once observe Cleo. My first thought in regard to her was to hide what had happened to me. . . . I must deal with it in secret. . . . It was at once a great joy and a great danger. . . .

"I'm going down, now," she was saying, in a queer, thin voice. "I'll see you tomorrow—"

"It was such a nice—"

She had turned a little toward the companionway; suddenly she faced me.

"I've got to ask you something, Dave." Her voice enriched with courage. "Maybe you'll think I'm out of my mind, but—have we ever met before?"

"Not that I can recall."

"Well, you keep reminding me of a boy named Dan Reed I met in Philadelphia and played with. I keep looking for his face in yours and sometimes I think I see it. He was the boy I spoke about having a broken finger. Well, on thinking it over I'm not sure of that. I can't remember noticing it but when I saw yours it seemed so familiar—as though I had seen it on that boy and had half-forgotten it. You've got a 'Dan' in your last name. Just yesterday he was very much on my mind—I had an idea we were going to meet again. Will you tell me how old you are?"

"Certainly. Twenty-four." I looked to be that age, and it would help get me started at Wood Ibis.

"Well, Dan wouldn't be over twenty-two. You say you've never lived in Philadelphia. Yet when we kissed just now—I had the strangest feeling that somehow you *were* Dan—come back. To be satisfied I've got to ask one more question."

"Why, ask me as many as you like—"

"There couldn't be any reason, could there—that you'd lie about it—"

"Yes, if I'd done something—got in trouble—and had to change my name."

"In that case, you wouldn't have come near me. Well, it was just a mean trick of my mind—"

"I reckon you're mighty disappointed—"

"Not in you, Dave. I didn't intend to compare you unfavorably with him. I like you a lot or I wouldn't— If you had turned out to be him I'd 've been so glad. But you didn't—"

She was speaking now in a low monotone that had more desolation in it than have most tears. There could be no longer any doubt that the chain we had put upon each other in our childhood was as strong and binding upon her as upon me. There was a joy in my heart like music at the thought that it was unbreakable, despite her being Ralph's daughter and I Noel's son. Maybe it was of such mystery and wonder that no barrier could prevail. . . .

I tried to steady myself. It was a great barrier—no exultation could eclipse that stark fact. Besides there was a dark inkling in my mind of which I did not yet clearly see the shape: it seemed to be of some even greater barrier. I did not admit it, only asked some curious questions.

"If I had turned out to be Dan, what would you have done?"

"That has no connection with this."

46

"It's none of my business, I know. Yet—"

She stood so still it gave the effect of a start. A desperateness was fighting against pride, I thought, and suddenly it won.

"He and I made a promise to each other. I don't think we said what it was—but we both knew. If I could find him, I was going to ask him to make it good." She spoke in as calm a way as possible, but her voice shook more and more until it broke.

"Will you tell me what the promise was?"

"Yes. That we'd go away together and live in the woods."

"Why in the woods? Why not stay together at Wood Ibis, your beautiful plantation?"

"I don't want to live there any more. He promised to take me away. That's what I've lived for, ever since—and the time's up."

I had known in every dream of her that had been the promise I had made.

If I could talk to her only a minute or two more I might learn exactly what it was she was trying so desperately to escape. In gaining that knowledge I could be true to Pa and to Cleo too. The time might not be quite so long until, if Pa died, he could die in peace, and until I could take Cleo away from Wood Ibis. But she was fighting with tears, and reviving pride made her bid me a hasty good night—she'd talk to me again in the morning—and hurry down the companionway.

After a night of many, long wakenings and dreary dreams I waited in turmoil for her to appear on the deck. When she came it was with every appearance of composure. She was able to talk cheerfully of casual things a moment or two before mentioning the events of last night—as though they were not of any great importance after all.

"I'm afraid I made a mighty big fool of myself last night, Dave," she said. "I'm of a romantic disposition, I reckon, and sometimes I get too sentmiental over that childish affair with Dan Reed. You reminded me so much of him, that last night I let myself go—and you know there's something about an ocean voyage that encourages romance. We haven't got our feet on the ground." She had taken great care with this.

"Well, all it did was make me jealous of him," I said.

"It's not that serious. And what I said about not wanting to live at Wood Ibis—well, that might have given you the wrong idea. I should have explained that while it's a beautiful plantation, it's awfully lonely. It's had a sad history too, which I suppose affects me. Anyway I believe that when a girl marries she and her husband ought to have a home of their own. In spite of loving Papa so much—and adoring Mama—I'd like to spend a few years in a different country altogether. Just for a change."

"That's natural enough. But you said—you and the boy wanted to live in the woods."

"I didn't mean that—exactly. That was our childish notion—and I said it without thinking. I love the woods but I can't imagine us trappers and hunters. Still, we might be—if we went West. What made it so silly was, we haven't seen each other since that day. What chance is there that we ever will see each other? If we did, why, we'd be so changed—"

"Yes, you'd better remember it as a sweet experience and let it go at that."

"Of course."

"You don't think you dreamed the whole thing, do you? Maybe when you had a fever——"

"I never thought of that. But I've done a lot of dreaming."

"You spoke about your plantation having a sad history. That sounds interesting." I was trying, the best I could, to retrieve my lost opportunity. It was not possible entirely, in broad daylight.

"Papa's brother Bruce died in an accident, and another brother—I guess I told you—was terribly injured." Ghosts rose before her eyes—I could almost see them. "But I've talked so much about my family and you've hardly mentioned yours."

"I reckon mine is so outclassed."

"That isn't true." There was a childlike earnestness in her tone and there were motives in her mind that were very secretive and strong. "My name isn't D'Arcy, like Mama's was—it's Dunbarton. The Dunbartons were never aristocrats—not even gentry. My uncle Bruce—the one who died not long before I was born—could hardly read and write."

Pa had never told me that. Since he was such a great reader, remarkably learned, I was astounded and incredulous. The marriage to her overseer by a Carolina beauty of great name had been an accepted fact in my mind—I had pictured a man far above his station not only in native gifts but in education and culture. Perhaps it came about by an illicit intimacy.

"Was Bruce the one who was lame?" I asked.

"No. The lame one, Uncle Noel, disappeared but may still be alive. Uncle Bruce was very strong—almost as strong as Pa, the old colored people say—and quite handsome. We had a portrait of him but it was stolen long ago."

"Why should anyone want to steal a family picture?"

"Oh, some are quite valuable, if painted by well-known artists. Maybe the thief thought these were, but they were only Sullys."

I had the impression that the theft had not crossed her mind for many years and she was startled a little by the remembrance now.

"Was more than one picture stolen?" I asked.

"I remember hearing there were two. Both my Uncle Bruce's and Mama's. They were cut out of the frames, which the sheriff said showed a practiced thief. We think he took the pictures first, as well as a pair of silver candlesticks that someone—Uncle Bruce, I guess—had given Mama; but he was frightened away before he could break in the silver chest or find Mama's jewels. I reckon that's the way it happened. An old colored woman insisted that the shell of a sea turtle was missing from the woodshed, but that was silly."

Not as silly as might be, I thought. Not as unlikely as that a practiced thief would stop with two unsalable portraits and a pair of candlesticks. I wondered whom Pa had hired for the raid. The turtle shell was no doubt a trophy of childhood. Maybe Pa had found it on the beach and polished it prettily; perhaps he had caught a splendid live turtle before his back was broken, a great feat he had never forgotten, for later the slowest crawler could outdistance him.

That thought had a curious effect on my thoughts about Cleo. Stuffing back some of them—tender and glowing thoughts that I could not afford—I gave free rein to others that were their natural accompaniment but which, stark and unblessed, were exciting in a way that had a quality of cruelty. . . . Pa had wondered if Cleo had been deflowered. Still water ran deep and the Carolina sun made love to thin, white skins. It might be this girl was lascivious, he had said. She had kissed me with such soft and mobile lips. . . .

"A penny for your thoughts," she said, not wanting to be anxious, not knowing why she was.

"I was thinking how I'd like a picture of you."

"Was that it?" Her face appeared to brighten, probably an effect of her quick and eager smile, although I might have fancied a diffused light glimmering outward through her skin. "There was a very queer expression on your face—much stronger than ought to reflect a little whim like that. But maybe you have very strong feelings. I mean—whatever you want at all, you want mighty bad. Some people are like that."

I would have to guard my countenance more carefully in the future. Actually it was no ready traitor; instead far from expressive, something like an Indian's in that respect. It had started to grow that way on stolen bread and slops. It had helped me cover many lies and preserve much bitter pride. Looking at it last year, a medicine-show doctor had told me I was of phlegmatic disposition—wasn't I born under the sign of so-and-so?—and I would make a good watchmaker.

"I reckon that's right."

"I guessed right at first that you're more intense and high strung than you seem. Anyone can see you're strong, but might think you're stolid too. Your big body is quite graceful and your movements very quick. You have big features but they're quite nicely carved. Your eyes are gray with a blue rim and you look at things quick and hard."

"You're very observant, Cleo."

"I reckon you've had to fight pretty hard too, your parents dead and all."

"Tolerably hard."

"You've got a Scotch name and your skin has a ruddy cast but your hair is almost as black as mine."

"I've seen a lot of black-haired Scots. But we've wandered off the subject. You were saying that your father's people weren't like your mother's—"

"Judging by Papa—I never knew my uncles—they were as different as black from white. But I'm glad of it. I met some of the D'Arcys—Mama's uncle before he died and two old-maid cousins —and they need some good common blood to mix with theirs. They're all beautiful and charming but they look like full-blown flowers about to go to seed. I think Mama felt that too—she has many feelings no one knows—and that's why she married as plain a man as Papa. So when you say your family can't hold a candle to mine, you're mistaken. I'm just as proud of the Dunbarton name as I am of D'Arcy. Papa's family has come up instead of gone down. You can come up too, Dave. I know you can."

Of her father's family, one brother was down in his grave and the other had taken his broken back into exile. That too gave right-of-way to those exciting, cruelty-colored thoughts. They obscured a little in my sight the unworldly loveliness of her face. But when she spoke I saw it clearly again.

"Obo says I have wonderfully sharp eyes," Cleo was confiding. "In the dim live-oak woods I often see birds and animals before he does. But my eyes *feel* different then, very wide awake. At home—in the house—they feel half-closed—or as though I'm looking through a dirty window pane."

Was she mortally afraid of them being opened? Was that one of the fears from which she was trying to flee? I could not run away with her to the deep, still woods she loved, and I could not play with passion's fire without danger of falling in love. I resolved on continence. It was my only safeguard. During the daylight hours, a good number of them spent with her, the resolve seemed not too difficult to keep, despite the forces freed against it. Not until the darkness fell, lust's element, did I know that the very strength I counted on, always standing by me until now, young, thrilling—the very intensity of my nature that she had seen—turned against my will-power. My attempt to curb the more gross desire brought into relief a beauty she was giving me, out of her great store.

Even so, I might have avoided the perilous path if she too had tried. Instead she was eager to get out of sight of the other passengers and welcomed every dim retreat. I sensed a kind of recklessness upon her, wildly exciting to me; before we knew it we were sitting atop a cubby of linen in a warm companionway. Here her lips were soft and yielding to mine, and she was allowing herself to become aroused. I did not get the impression that she was very happy. At times her face had a forlorn cast and her eyes looked very dark.

"Do I still remind you of the boy you knew?" I asked on impulse.

"No, it was all in my imagination."

"Maybe you'll hear from him, wherever he is."

"No. He isn't anywhere."

"What do you mean, Cleo?"

"I told you this morning that my affair with him—if you can speak that way of a childish love—was not very important. I was lying, because I was ashamed of confessing so much the night be-

52

fore. It was terribly important. You find that hard to believe—but it's true. But it's over now. It has to be over because—he's—dead."

"What do you mean, Cleo?"

"He died. I know he did. I've often thought so, when he didn't receive my letters, and now I know it."

"How could you know it?"

"You won't believe me, but I'll tell you anyway. Last night I went looking for him in my dreams—I searched the little house— and the woodshed—and behind the wood. He wasn't there. At other times that I lost him, I called and he'd come. But I called last night—and he didn't come."

We were silent a long time. Maybe she was regretting speaking so.

"Do you think he's been dead a long time?" I asked.

"Long enough that he can't come back—when I call."

"Will you look for him again tonight?"

"No. It's no use."

"Well, in one way I wish—"

"I didn't mean to sadden you, Dave. I'm so glad you're with me. Giving him up for good was something I had to do sooner or later—and you've helped me." Without my asking, she put her arms around my neck and kissed me.

"That was good night," she said.

Our parting for the night only arrested, briefly, a journey we were making together. I meant it to end in a cul-de-sac at the ship voyage's end—that was the compromise I had made with my desire; she had other intentions not yet disclosed. From that cul-de-sac I would go alone, in due time, to Wood Ibis. She might be there or perhaps she would have escaped from there by then: in either case we would be separated at least until my task was done. What the future held for us thereafter was so far removed that I did try not to link it with the happiness this present held.

Still I did not fall in love with Cleo—at least with complete surrender. I was helped by various devices, one of them oddly enough by thinking of us two as Cleo and Dave, not Cleo and Dan— shutting in a locked room of the past not only the promise I could not keep but the whole event of our childhood love. Her not knowing that I was Dan helped me turn the key. So did its perfect beauty that I did not want to expose to the hard light of future realities. This would be a shipboard love affair only. As such, it too was perfect.

The weather served it well—unusually warm for January, with gentle winds—and the long nights afforded it a grateful share of darkness before bedtime, which grew later as the voyage progressed, since Cleo was like me in getting along well with relatively short sleep. We clung and kissed more and more, like any young shipboard sweethearts, and did not confess to each other that we were both experimenting with ecstasy. Often I saw guilt in her glimmering eyes, not of what we were doing but of what she craved to do and did not dare. Her soft kisses grew fierce sometimes, until she drew back ashamed—and such ferocity was so unexpected in this strange, pale child! Its effect upon me was all the more powerful because of her virginal loveliness—her inmost beauty.

On our last night at sea, she and I had the dimly lighted saloon to ourselves. I had persuaded her to lie across my lap on the wall seat, her breast close to mine, her upturned face reachable at my merest bow. She was happier there than I had yet discovered her, I think because she sensed my physical strength, the long rolling muscles of my arms and my chest's big bellows. It was the happiness of present safety, warmth, and of new hope, I thought, in the future. She did not know that my strength could not serve her for a long time yet, if ever, or dream how, during that parting it would be used.

Since I seemed her protector, she was not afraid of my embrace and passionate kisses. Never was such a sweet return as her little arms stealing up sometimes and her lips still hungry when I had feared them surfeited. We were giving each other a magic feast that never blunted, ever whetted, the appetite for more; and it was a wonderful and new thing to me, to be able to receive such joy, at once that I gave it. I ached to give it in this same measure, which was immeasurable. Other swains of my years were wisened to this wonder: it did not break upon them like a new creation. Other swains did not have Cleo.

"Have you a sweetheart in Baltimore?" she asked.

"No."

That satisfied her for a moment, in the way of words; they were incidental anyway to this communion. Then when she was again flushed and palpitant: "Have you one anywhere?"

"No."

"Dave, have you—ever?" She lay very still.

"What do you think?"

"It stands to reason that you have. And yet—"

"I never had one."

"Do you know? I felt that. You see, I've never had one either —except Dan."

I could not tell her of my solemn, thrilling wonder: I could only act surprised.

"I can't believe it. You—the heiress of a great plantation—beautiful—a highborn lady—"

"All the girls of my age at school had at least one. I pretended that Dan was mine—and made up stories about us—once or twice I forged letters to show them. I've had beaus at the few balls and parties Pa let me go to, but—they didn't come to see me at Ibis Hall. A distant cousin came—I liked him pretty well—and soon went away. We're in the same boat, Dave."

"Will you be my sweetheart, until we part?"

"Yes, and you'll be mine. It's as though we'd both lost our partners—at the biggest masquerade ball ever given—and found each other."

Just then she had to sit up primly beside me, for two men were coming into the saloon. They sat down under the dim lamp—only one was lighted—and began to play cards. In that little wait, in which neither of us could think of anything to say, I remembered that this was our last night at sea.

Tomorrow Cleo and I would part, this little parting now its dreary forecast. I was greatly wrought up—facts and images, desires and fears, in a whirling flux in my brain—yet I tried to get my bearings. I had not been false to Pa by this love-making; instead I had come nearer to betraying Cleo and myself, by refusing to link the present with the past. I had not fallen in love with her in the way I longed to, for no reason that I knew save that I could not keep my promise to her, the due of that love. It was a strange but seemingly a certain fact. There was a holding back in my heart as though by an outside force. How then could I ask her to give her love to me?

Yet I had asked her to, in every act and word. Even now my thoughts were clamoring to her, as Pa's thoughts clamored soundlessly sometimes, when he drew the silent bow across the silent strings. They were confused, uncontrollable thoughts. . . . Fall in love with me, Cleo. Love me with great passion, need me, give me your beauty, and don't blame me because I am forbidden to love you. . . . I would if I could. . . . I would inundate you with my love. . . . *But if I do I will keep my promise to you!*

I was asking for her love as a free gift. I wanted her to come with me to some secluded place and give it to me. Would she come? Where could we go?

Then the thoughts made sound, a low whisper in her ear.

"Where can we go?"

"I don't know," she whispered. "There are men working on deck." We had become like guilty conspirators.

"There's no one in my cabin. My roommate got off at Wilmington."

"If anybody saw me go in there, they'd think—"

"No one will see you. The companionway is almost pitch dark. It's the last door on the left. I'll go first, and then you come."

"Someone might know—"

"No one will know. The walls are solid. It's next to the funnel and is warm as toast."

"All right. Pretend to say good night." She rose, and her voice rose. "Good night, Dave, and thank you for a pleasant evening."

"The pleasure is all mine, Miss Cleo."

Presently I was in my room, the door ajar. The wait became long —perhaps she had decided not to come, seeing the danger of it, and worse than that, the futility. Dizzy with desire, I envisioned another door—leading into our picture-room where Pa played to the portraits. It was for that, that I could not have Cleo. . . . I had seen Ralph Dunbarton in life, and his face was not like the face in the picture. . . . It was for that, that Cleo had called and I had not come. She had looked behind the woodpile, and I was not there. . . . Now I was calling her, in vain. I had lost her for the sake of a Lame Man's music that tonight I did not believe.

There was a murmur on my lips that terrified me. . . . "If she'll come, I'll keep my promise to her!"

Exactly then the door opened and my Cleo, my wood ibis in black and white, came in to my arms.

The long dream went on and, at this point in it, I was sitting on my bed, she lying again across my lap, her breast against mine. Again we toyed with ecstasy but more rashly now. We were taking a path that led to a great deep forest . . . not the green woods where we had promised each other we would go and dwell but a wilderness dark with moss and vines . . . steaming hot in summer . . . where birds of many feathers light in live-oak trees and among the palms. . . . Someone had described it to me once: I could not think who, or when, or where. . . . Once she had unbuttoned a little dress. That was in a strange rite of innocence and beauty that began a dream. But at this point in the dream the jeweled pin at the collar of her gown had become unloosened. . . .

"Cleo! . . . Cleo!"

But she sprang from my arms and stood trembling, her hand on the door.

"I don't blame you," she said when she caught her breath. "I shouldn't have come here—unless—" She paused, watching me.

"Unless we love each other enough to "

"To be engaged—and marry? I wasn't going to say that."

"What were you going to say?"

"Something that may shock you, but I don't care. No, we don't love each other that much—yet—we're just shipboard sweethearts. There's something holding us back—I don't know what. I felt that tonight. But maybe we could learn to love each other if we were together a long time. Anyway you could have me—" She paused again.

"Please, Cleo, tell me everything."

"You can have me tonight," she said in a low, clear tone, her eyes fixed on mine, "if tomorrow you'll take me away."

"You mean without being married?"

"I'll marry you, or live with you without being married. I'll do anything you want, right or wrong, for as long as you want. But you've got to take me so far from Wood Ibis that no one can find me."

She did not know that the very reason she would pay this price was now my reason, its great validity proven beyond question, for paying Pa's price. The thing she was trying at such cost to escape was the thing to which I was bound.

I had asked her to meet me on the deck, where the sea-winds would cool our fevers, and the quiet stars return our sanities. There we could take our bearings. But as I waited for her the air was sharp and strange in my nostrils the same as on the day we had found each other, as though I had passed, for the moment, out of the world. I had felt then what now I knew—how inextricably our fates were joined, and how strongly, by the same token, opposed. It had been true from the moment Pa and I had made a promise across a fence—although then I did not dream of her existence, a little girl of five, daughter of Ralph Dunbarton by his wife Madeline. Now that I knew the reality of the evil at Wood Ibis, all that had happened to me fitted in a fateful pattern, the part already woven perfectly clear, but its final shape undreamed. As Pa's avenger I became, inevitably, her deliverer. That weaving was plain.

When I saw Cleo emerge from the companionway, I had already seen my road. I would deliver her, as I was bound, but not by the means she proposed—indeed if flight could be called deliverance, instead of its empty shell. I did not know yet how to tell her that the time was yet far off, or how even to hold out hopes.

She was very pale in the moonlight but she did not hang her head. I could find no shame in her face for her desperate offer.

"Will you tell me, Cleo, why you would pay such a price to go away from home?"

"No, Dave. You'll have to take it for granted."

"Are you sure you even know?"

"I know enough. There's a great deal I don't know. If you're not going to do it, there's only one thing more I ask—that you won't tell anyone in the world about it. Not a word that I've said. I'm not ashamed—I felt I had to say what I did."

"You needn't have the least fear. You'll have to take for granted that I can't take you away now—it's impossible for reasons I can't give. Some day I can. I'll be free then, and I believe we can fall in love and marry. In the meantime can't you go somewhere and be happy? Haven't you friends or distant kin—"

"I wouldn't have made that offer, if I had. It's impossible to go anywhere—and stay. I've thought of everything—and nothing will work. Just believe me."

"Then there's nothing but for you to go back to Wood Ibis?"

"Yes. Maybe it won't be long before I can marry someone. I don't believe it—but it might happen."

"Cleo, would you like to have me come to Wood Ibis?"

She stared at me in wild disbelief. "What do you mean?"

"To get a job there, and live there?"

"When? It doesn't seem possible, but—"

"I'll come now, on some excuse. I could get acquainted with the overseer—or perhaps there's some close neighbor who'd need a man. I'm an experienced plantation foreman. I'd have to go to Baltimore to settle up my affairs—but would come back as soon as possible and then we'd be near each other."

"My father has a hired overseer but all his foremen are intelligent Negro slaves. But I've a friend who lives on Little Ibis—his name's Dr. Sams—it's a small plantation that was once part of ours—he might give you a job. Didn't you say you worked at a stock farm?"

"Yes."

"Well, he breeds horses and mules to sell. It's just a side line with him but since you've had experience—"

"I know more about that than any other work." And it did not just happen so. Pa had encouraged me to pursue it. I wondered if the idea that Cleo had hit upon had occurred to Pa long ago, as a possible means of establishing me at Wood Ibis.

"How long after you get home can I come?" I asked.

"You'd better wait a week. Then it won't look like a put-up job. First thing tomorrow I'll go to Cousin Mattie's—she's a D'Arcy connection by marriage—and she'll send word to Papa to send our carriage for me. He won't likely send our sailboat this time of year. You can go on Captain Weaver's boat that leaves Charleston every Monday to carry mail and small freight to Bull and other islands."

"Fix everything as well as you can."

"I will. I'm going down now. If you change your mind in the night—"

She wanted to say a great deal more but found herself unable to do so. Her roving eyes suggested to me that she was already frightened of the consequences of our plan, and the fear was mixed with guilt. I was intensely alert, every perception quick and clear, my brain working fast; the guilt might be a dim sense of betrayal of her father by our conspiracy, which I must ponder later; or it might be from letting passion sway her judgment. But my coming to Wood Ibis, if only as a stopgap to her terror and woe, would give her new hope.

"I'll see you when we dock tomorrow morning," she said.

"We'd better not seem too well acquainted. I'll shake hands with you and thank you. Patronize me just enough."

"All right."

"You know the kind of goodbye I want to take with you now."

"That's the kind of goodbye I want, too."

She came into my arms with a quick movement, as though fleeing from something. There were more happiness and hope in her kiss than in any she had given me since long ago, and these quickened rather than dimmed her shy, lovely passion. It was telling me not to fail our rendezvous. There was such bliss to find. . . .

I was afraid that some kind of a spell would be broken on the busy docks in Charleston. These were no more the wandering waters and the living island. It could not break, because, save for each other, saying formal goodbyes, we were still alone. She was as friendless here as I. Only the poor gazed at her with admiration or kindness; the purse-proud upstarts looked as though they knew a malicious joke about her; the aristocrats were occupied as she came by and not one spoke a welcoming word to her. Impotent fury surged through me. She was still the daughter of Madeline D'Arcy, the most beautiful woman in the world; by her highbred grace and delicate, dreamy beauty she put their blatant belles to shame. I saw her engage and then get into a hackney. It was as though a bird of the heron tribe, white with black-tipped wings, had soared in from seaward, lighted a moment on the pier, and again taken off.

For the next week I lived in an inexpensive inn and saw the sights of Charleston. On Monday morning I set sail on Captain Weaver's lugger, by Capers and Bull Island across Bull Bay. Hitherto I had seen only long, brown beaches with grass-crowned dunes and scattered clumps of palms, but now we touched at little landings among live-oak trees, and skirted shores thick with virgin forest, and gazed into inlets where the water looked almost inky black, and what looked like huge white flowers on the tree-boughs took wing in effortless flight. To planters who passed the time of day with me, I spoke of a stud farm in Maryland looking for wider markets for its thoroughbred horses.

On the following morning we rounded another wave-washed beach and sailed up a tidal creek to the dock of Little Ibis. It was like the others I had seen, rudely built of cypress, salty and fishy-smelling, with sheds that served for warehouses, rickety ladders, and barnacle-incrusted piers. Our approach had been seen, and a rather plainly dressed man of middle height and age and a pleasantly homely square face came down from his cottage among the live-oak trees to greet me. I did not doubt that this was Dr. Sams, whom both Pa and Cleo claimed as friend.

He gave me a keen glance, more critical than a traveling horse-trader deserved. Plainly Cleo had not been able to conceal her involvement with me and perhaps had not even tried. I was not as disturbed by that as by the scene—Little Ibis that belonged to Pa, given him by his brother Bruce for a happy home, from which he had been turned out by events not yet known. It was once part of Wood Ibis . . . named for the bird that frequented its woods and swamps . . . the ancestral home of the D'Arcys. Once I had been behind the fence at the Orphanage and now I was here.

"Is this Dave MacDaniel?" the gentleman inquired.

"Yes, sir. Have I the pleasure of meeting Dr. Sams?"

"Thank you, I'm he. Miss Cleo told me you might be out this way, and I'm glad to see you. Join me in a toddy."

While a slave carried my bags, Dr. Sams led me up a cobbled path to the house. It was larger than it had looked from the dock —nearly twice as large as Pa's present cottage—and comfortably furnished. Since I was on business, he took me into what he called his office—really a library where he kept accounts—but he did not stint his hospitality. Over our toddies we were soon talking horses and horse-breeding at a lively rate. Actually I was better versed in the subject than he. It was a side line with him and no part of my schooling had ever been a side line with me.

He struck me as a rather garrulous man who was also lonesome. Before we had emptied our glasses twice he proposed that I let the boat sail without me when she put in here tomorrow: he would see that I had transport to Charleston later. He would be pleased to have me look over his stallions and brood mares and make recommendations. Was I fond of hunting? He had a bay he would like to have me try.

"Perhaps you'd like to renew your acquaintance with Miss Dunbarton," he suggested in a rather nervous tone.

"It would be most agreeable to me but I'm not sure it would the same to her," I replied. "Young ladies are expected to be democratic on shipboard, but among their own kind—"

"Her father is quite strict with her, I must say. However, he has no reason to be toplofty with a young man who has his way to make. He certainly made his own way."

"I hope that will make a difference."

"I admire him for it, you understand." This was a gentleman speaking. "But it's quite a step from overseer to master of Wood Ibis. I'll take you over there tomorrow and I'm sure that both he and Mistress Dunbarton will make you welcome."

When we had inspected his stables, my chance came to congratulate him on owning such a fine plantation, which might lead to his talking about Pa.

"Actually, I don't own this land," he told me. "It belongs to an uncle of Cleo's, Noel Dunbarton, an old patient of mine when I was in practice. I rent it from him."

We were standing on that land, at the gate of the paddock, the immediate scene seeming commonplace. But my sight had quickened as he spoke and the subdued colors of the winter landscape stood out. I noticed things not seen before—a flock of ducks diving and sporting beyond the dock, their visible numbers never the same; a broken, dim white line of cranes on some certain solemn errand across the sky and sometimes catching the sun on their seraphim wings; a gang of Negroes bending and straightening in unison in a distant field. Dr. Sams had seemed a loquacious man but under his easy flow was a deep pool of silence. He was a bystander in the world. An able physician if his thoughtful eyes and clever hands gave the clue, yet he had forsaken his practice for a lonely life on a seagirt plantation—perhaps because it had involved him too deeply in people's lives.

I feigned a faintly puzzled look. "Excuse me," I said, when he glanced at me sharply, "I thought Miss Cleo told me she had no uncles or aunts. I misunderstood her—"

"No, you didn't. As far as she knows, she hasn't. You see, my old friend left here under unfortunate circumstances nearly twenty years ago and no one has heard from him since. I pay my rent—it's very small—to a bank in Charleston. It's piling up there for his return or for his heirs when he's declared legally dead."

"I thought in just seven years—"

"Yes, his brother Ralph—master of Wood Ibis—could have obtained provisional title years ago. He chose to wait until the courts award him the land and rent as a matter of course. Perhaps he can't bring himself to confess his brother deceased—also, he's reluctant to have some unpleasant stories start again." Dr. Sams looked troubled: he did not want to talk about these matters, but civility had made him reply to my questions and a stubborn honesty, rather characteristic of gentlemen, demanded a reasonably full answer lest I be misled. "You're likely to hear a garbled version even now. I'd rather give you the main facts."

"I'd thank you kindly."

"Bruce Dunbarton, the first of that name to own Wood Ibis, was killed in a peculiar accident while making for Bull Island in his sailboat. He had set out on a dark, cold night, and in some fashion a small cask of gunpowder, brought from Charleston only the day before, exploded and blew up the boat. Presumably it had been set off by a charcoal burner in the hatch, but rumors flew about that it had been rigged."

63

"I see." My face felt cold and wet and I feared for its color.

"The bodies of Mr. Dunbarton and his black boatman were found, badly mangled, in the rigging. But there was also found what seemed to be a piece of fuzee that presently disappeared. The last to have it in his hands, as far as anyone could remember, was Noel Dunbarton. He was accused of dropping it overboard."

"He had come out in a boat to investigate the accident?"

"Yes, and his behavior attracted a good deal of unfavorable attention. It was frantic in the extreme. And you see—he was a marked man."

"I'm not sure I know what you mean."

"His back had been broken when he was a child and he could not stand erect. The ignorant people regarded him with superstitious awe. 'Beware a marked man'—you've heard the saying. That day he fairly ran to get in the boat. Some people said afterward that he didn't touch his stick to the ground and stood perfectly straight. He had been seen loitering about Bruce Dunbarton's boat earlier in the day and was known to be very clever with his hands. You see, I'm repeating to you the hazy, childish reports that were the basis for the silly story that he had murdered his own brother."

"They condemned him on no more evidence than that?"

"The poor fellow made it worse by disappearing the rest of the night and all the next day. He was found all but unconscious and covered with muck at the swamp: of course people said he'd been driven to flight by his guilt. His frantic attempts to explain his absence were wild and contradictory."

"The storytellers must have fabricated some sort of a motive." I had regained control of my voice and kept my countenance better, I believe, to appear a rather stolid young man listening to an interesting piece of history.

"Unwittingly—and to his later regret—his brother Ralph suggested one. He had remarked how kind Bruce had been to both himself and to Noel—making him overseer of Wood Ibis with a share of the crop, and giving Noel Little Ibis for his own. Ralph went on to say how much Noel loved having a home of his own and how he had come to Ralph only a few days before, shaken with terror lest Bruce take back the gift. He had heard there was a flaw in the deed—a report without foundation—and that Bruce had repented his generosity."

Dim and dainty-sounding on the wind came the notes of a bell.

"There must be a church near by," I said.

"That's the big bell at Wood Ibis. It came from a churchspire in France. It's ringing for the hands to come in from the fields. God, how it rang the night after Bruce was buried—tolled, I mean, all night—by some crazed slave, I guess. But nobody ever found out who it was. Ralph went out several times to try to stop it—it was driving the blacks into a frenzy—but the ringer hid from him, only to come back when he was gone and start tolling it again."

"Was the lame brother—Noel, you said—ever charged with the crime?"

"Of course not. Everybody who knew him at all well had only contempt for the story. Noel loved Bruce more than anyone in the world—" Dr. Sams stopped, a sharp remission of expression in his face. "He loved him as Jonathan loved David," he went on presently, in a quieter tone. "Bruce's every triumph became his own."

"If he wasn't charged, why should he disappear?"

"There was no good reason. I reckon the rumors worried him and he couldn't stand the Low Country without Bruce. But pardon me—you used the word 'crime' a moment ago. You must understand that the coroner did not find a crime. The verdict was, 'death by accident'—the only possible verdict under the circumstances. Intelligent people hereabouts have let it go at that."

8

I had bought riding clothes in Charleston, of the plain, ready-made sort suitable to my station, and the legs in the breeches knew how to fork a nag. When Dr. Sams had me mount his mettlesome mare Lizzie, he knew that my knowledge of horse-breeding was not all from books. Indeed I enjoyed a marked rise in his estimation.

"She's a fine piece of horseflesh, to have such a plain name," I proposed, as we ambled off.

"I named her for a neighbor of mine, who's a fine piece of woman-flesh. I'm not speaking ribaldly, mark you—although I don't doubt that too would be true. Not fine-haired, not even pretty, but mettlesome. By Jove, I'll introduce you to her!"

"I didn't know you had any neighbors, except the people at Wood Ibis."

"She's the daughter of a Danish sailor who settled at Turtle Inlet forty years ago. He had been a ship chandler from Copenhagen, and set up a store here to supply pirates and smugglers and prawn-fishermen. Little Ibis wasn't in cultivation then and he obtained squatter's rights to a quarter-section of sandy, valueless land. She and her husband, Sam Childer, are the only permanent residents, but fishermen and fowlers put in there and keep them company. She knows more about the history of this section than anyone I know."

"I'll look forward to meeting her."

"I'm out of 'Ginie for my pipe—don't care for our native leaf so we'll go by there now. It's hardly two miles out of our way. You'll find her an interesting woman. If she were a lady—and unmarried—I'd go after her. But I reckon being a lady would have spoiled half her charm."

Skirting the sea we came to her abode, a two-storied frame shack scantily shaded by half a dozen wind-stooped palms beside an inlet coldly green as beryl. A ramshackle dock had been built out over

66

the oyster shoals; a rack for drying fish nets, a shed for driftwood, an anchor half buried in sand, and a crazy-leaning privy were the only other signs of habitation. We found Lizzie Childer behind her counter and looking fully as mettlesome as Dr. Sams described her. Her gay striped skirt and red shirt looked gypsy—more likely they had come up tax-free from Cuba—and this torrid attire gave the observer a pleasant jar, in contrast with her heavy flaxen hair and sea-blue eyes. She was over forty, of middle height with a not heavy but powerful peasant build, her face not pretty but engaging. Her sinewy feet were bare.

"Where's Sam?"

"Out fishing," she replied in a full-throated alto voice.

"No customers?"

"Not even the smell of a shrimper."

"Why, it's the opportunity I've been waiting for—if I hadn't brought company."

"I notice, Dr. Sams, there's always something wrong with your opportunities."

"This is Dave MacDaniel. He's representing a Maryland stock farm."

"MacDaniel, did you say?"

"Yes, ma'am."

"Scotch, I reckon, and no hope of a nickel's profit."

"I've told him about our little kingdom, Lizzie, and he's interested in meeting all the subjects," Dr. Sams went on.

"I'm not one. I hold by old Gustaf Neilson, descended from vikings who used to run kings off their thrones and ravish their queens." She turned lively eyes on mine. "Dave, have you met the crowned heads of Wood Ibis?"

"No, but I had the honor of meeting the princess, on the ship down."

Lizzie's expression changed but I had no inkling why.

"She's not as beautiful as her mother was, Doctor will tell you. Madeline D'Arcy was toasted as the most beautiful woman in the world—not the county or the state, mind you, but everywhere this side of heaven. Still—Cleo's no mud fence."

"Why do you say Madeline 'was,' not 'is'?" the doctor asked.

"What a slip! Son, she ages like a wonderful ivory statue, or a piece of Paul Revere silver, or something elegant. Her wrinkles are the sweet writings of Father Time!"

"Dave," Dr. Sams told me grinning, "you'd almost think that Lizzie dislikes the mistress of Wood Ibis."

Oddly enough, I did not think that. I had a feeling that her brazen, coarse sarcasm to a complete stranger concealed some other attitude. Her eyes had changed color subtly but there was nothing in them that I could read.

"At least I don't kiss her feet as so many free-and-equal Americans do. But, young man, why don't you aspire to that pale-pink mouth of her entrancing daughter? Get a job as overseer of Wood Ibis—that's the way the present owner got his start, and his brother before him—the ladies of Ibis Hall having a weakness for overseers if they're big, hearty fellows like you. Maybe you've already laid the ground, aboard the ship."

"I didn't get the idea that she would be that democratic," I answered, not in the least wishing to defend Cleo, only deeply curious and excited.

"Her mother was, believe me! Haven't you ever heard the saying that it takes a great aristocrat to be a great democrat?"

"You're in a vile mood this morning, Lizzie, and I'll take a pound of your best Virginia and we'll go."

"Are you calling on the Dunbartons? If so, tell the mistress that Lizzie Neilson sends love and kisses."

Suddenly she broke into a notably musical laugh, fine and hearty, and cheerfully transacted the business. Inviting me to call again, she took us to the door and waved us goodbye.

"Lizzie doesn't give a damn what she says," Dr. Sams observed, when we were out of hearing of the store.

"So I noticed."

"But her spite against Mrs. Dunbarton is half put on, I think. At least it's become a mere habit. However, she did have a grievance at one time."

"It must have been a pretty big one—"

"Some people might consider it mighty big. She was 'keeping company,' as she would say, with Bruce Dunbarton when he was first made overseer of Wood Ibis. She was somewhat below his station yet people assumed they would be married. When he saw his chance to marry his employer, Madeline D'Arcy, he jilted her. But what in the devil could Lizzie expect?"

"Anyway you'd think she'd be too proud—"

"That's what puzzles me. She knows human nature remarkably well—has few illusions. At the time she took the hard blow like a sportswoman—in fact she told a skipper friend of mine that it was Bruce's great chance and she wouldn't dream of standing in the way. She even went to the church with some of her friends and to an oyster-roast that all classes attended. The shrewishness began to come on her some years afterward."

"How does Mrs. Dunbarton feel about it? Excuse me—but you've made my visit here so interesting."

"Thanks. I'm enjoying it immensely. Madeline is gracious to her, as she is to everyone. She's not one to wear her heart on her sleeve."

I wondered if Lizzie was!

We left the beach and soon came into a dim road winding through Fern Creek swamp. The mild frost and rough sea winds had unclothed the deciduous trees—gum and cottonwood and white oak—letting a little light into its fastnesses, and the water reeds were brown; yet the effect was still of voracious green dozing while it waited for the sun. We came in sight of a long pond amid a water-oak grove, perfectly mirroring every branch and twig of moss-shrouded cypress, up to their gnarled knees in unrippled water. A solitary wood ibis in stark black and white perched with ineffable grace on the tallest tree.

"That's a pretty scene," I remarked. At least it was like an Eden older than Eve's.

"There are too many snakes to suit me. Cottonmouths thick as your arm and six-foot rattlers. We can't hunt here with dogs on sunny days—we lost so many—and old René D'Arcy lost plenty of hands, getting out the cypress for Ibis Hall. By the way, we're on Wood Ibis now. The border's that creek—Little Run we call it— that we just crossed."

I was on "the most beautiful plantation in all the Southland."

"This swamp connects with Gator Creek swamp, which runs clear to Sweetwater Pond, just below the mansion. Two or three thousand acres where no earth was ever turned or seed planted."

As we gazed the angels came—spiraling down from the sky, lightly lighting on the brink and standing primly. They dropped out of the sunlight on silver wings but turned into alabaster in the forest dusk. They were egrets, Dr. Sams told me.

We crossed boggy ground on a corduroy road, wound through a sandy stretch of palmetto and dwarf oak, and then came out on a good cart road, flanking cultivated fields and pasture as far as we could see. These were on our left hand; on our right and within a stone's throw, rose the abrupt rim of the swamp into which we could not see at all. There was sound on our left— the squeak of corn leaves and the rattle of stalks or a very subdued murmur of cotton plants in the breeze—and silence on our right. Where the wind blew free, the smells were innocent and good; but in the eddies lingered the faintly sulphuric, dank, moldy breath of things that swiftly grew and swiftly died.

We passed the overseer's cottage and a fair-sized village of cabins, big barns, and shops. Soon we turned into a driveway of ancient live-oak trees, huge of bole, with enormous lateral boughs draped with greenish-brown moss. I began to catch glimpses of a roof and chimneys, then of windows and glimmerings of white, finally of tall pillars fit for a Greek temple. Then suddenly Ibis Hall moved grandly into view.

Grandeur was the word. It had been deliberately sought and obtained. The mansion lacked the long, breezy veranda of so many Southern plantation houses; instead it boasted a noble portico, two stories high with five enormous columns, reached by a flight of marble steps thirty feet wide between stone abutments and the height of the ground floor. The main structure was of wood, three and a half stories in all, and crowned with a rotunda.

The style could be called classical, I supposed, and presumably an anomaly on the South Carolina sea-island, neighbor to a primeval swamp. But it was not my uncultivated taste that found it in strange but touching harmony with the scene. Truly it was like a temple in the ancient grove, and of stately beauty.

"Madeline's grandfather built it, replacing an older manor house, hardly sixty years ago," Dr. Sams told me in a sober tone, "but we think of it as having been there forever."

It was curiously castle-like, I thought. No wonder that Madeline, born and raised within its austere walls, became a queen in Cleo's childlike fancy and Lizzy's tart jest. Bruce Dunbarton, a plain man who could barely read and write, had become at least its regent, plainly a position of great peril. But his brother Ralph had reigned a long time and no doubt felt himself safe. I might stand face to face with him in a minute or two more without his having the least inkling of danger. I might then be able to measure better my own danger. My childhood memory of him had become dim and untrustworthy.

"I reckon Cleo will be outdoors this time of day, so sunny and all," Dr. Sams was saying. "She's the proper person to present you to her parents. Let's go round to the stables."

These would be the family stables, housing carriage and riding horses. We rode under a porte-cochere at one side of the mansion, and at once discovered Cleo leaning against the paddock gate, in easy conversation with a tall young man of singularly powerful frame. Both wore riding habits and made a peculiarly vivid picture in the clear, winter sunlight. Rather they were the central figures of what would be to me an unforgettable scene. A fine bay horse nuzzled at Cleo's hand, thrust through the bars. His coat gleamed like burnished copper. In the middle distance appeared the family's private landing on Gator Creek, the waters a pale-blue sheen below a neat, well-painted dock with a railed ladder for guests arriving by boat. Still beyond, dark blue water glimmered amid cypress trees, its farther expanses lost to sight behind somber woods.

"Why, it's Dr. Sams with the young man I met on shipboard," Cleo told her companion, her voice carrying as clear as a thrush's. She hurried to meet us, trying to conceal a happiness and an anxiety both of great depth. Perhaps she succeeded with the on-lookers. They did not know her face, as I did, for I had looked at it with wider-open eyes. It had spoken to me in lovelier language than any I ever learned. It had been with me, waking and sleeping, every moment of the past week, no matter how busy I had been with other matters, other dreams.

"So you did show up, after all," she addressed me, telling Dr. Sams as well as the young man at the paddock gate that I had expressed very little likelihood of coming.

"Well, I found some time on my hands—" I had dismounted, and a stable boy took the mare.

"Dr. Sams, when Mr. MacDaniel introduced himself and asked about your stock-breeding, I thought you'd be interested in talking to him."

"We've had very interesting talks, Cleo," Dr. Sams remarked. "Thank you, dear, for putting him my way."

"Saul, I want to present my shipmate, Dave MacDaniel."

Thinking at first the young man might be a visitor, later I had been struck by his air of belonging to Wood Ibis. He had loomed ever larger on the scene, and suddenly it seemed that Wood Ibis belonged to him. No new acquaintance had ever impressed me so powerfully before. I could have described him minutely after one intense gaze—his curly, dense black hair, his large gray eyes looking very light-colored in contrast with the pale olive of his big, broad face, his strong features boldly and handsomely carved, his lusty bull-neck, and his expression of good-natured arrogance. He stood lightly on his feet, despite his heavy frame—did everything lightly and easily by some gift akin to grace—and appeared as much less than his real weight as younger than his real years.

"Mr. MacDaniel, this is my brother, Saul Dunbarton," Cleo said.

The ground rocked under my feet. Cleo had told me that she was an only child! Anyway this man was too old to be Ralph's and Madeline's son. Great God, if Cleo too had been 'dopted—!

Then Saul Dunbarton laughed pleasantly at her.

"Your half-brother, my sweet. You're always forgetting. Mr. Mac-Daniel, I'm the son of Ralph Dunbarton by his first wife, Miss Cleo by his second. He came up in the world at his second try; and so, while Cleo is half aristocrat, I'm all chawbacon. You'd better get our complicated relationships straight at the outset to avoid embarrassments. Welcome to Wood Ibis."

It was a strange experience to discover suddenly a full-blown, unknown foe.

There came strongly upon me an eerie inkling that he was my mortal foe. At present all that I knew positively against Ralph Dunbarton was Pa's positive statement that he had broken his back in cruel play: the rest was a legend of hate devised by a deranged mind. I had considered this often these late years, always with a sense of shame. But I knew by the testimony of my own eyes and ears that Saul Dunbarton was hated and starkly feared by Cleo, and had no doubt that he was the main cause for her tragic proposal to me. This he took as lightly as the ground in stride. That was why he had laughed.

Cleo's not mentioning him on shipboard was staggering evidence of the same thing. Pa had not told me about him so I could discover him for myself, but why had not Dr. Sams? Saul was not too unimportant in this ménage, I could be sure of that. Perhaps it would have brought up an unpleasant subject that the doctor did not want to discuss. To tell me of Ralph's son the doctor would have had to tell me of Ralph's first wife, whose death had cleared the way for him to pay court to his brother's widow. When did she die? Was it many years before Bruce died or in the same insalubrious season? What was the manner of it?

"Your trust in him, in letting him ride Lizzie, was well placed, Dr. Sams," Saul Dunbarton remarked.

"I thought you'd see that."

"You have a good seat, Mr. MacDaniel."

"I thank you, sir."

"Miss Cleo tells me you're a breeder, as well."

"I'm in the employ of a breeder, sir, and some day hope to have a farm of my own."

"A laudable ambition, which some members of my own family have achieved. Can you read and write?"

"Why, yes."

"It's not necessary, but an advantage. So can I, for a wonder. Miss Cleo is well educated, as you no doubt perceived aboard the ship. You must have had some elegant conversations."

"She certainly didn't go out of her way to make me feel uncomfortable."

"Well said. I was just teasing her, not you. She's been very eager for you to come and didn't conceal the fact very skilfully. Charleston beaus are scarce around here. They are dunces, of course, not to recognize the charms of Ibis Hall. But horse-traders are famed for their acumen."

"I find your humor rather coarse, Saul," Dr. Sams said blandly.

"Oh, I'm used to it," Cleo told him, her eyes sunken-looking and unusually bright, "and I'm sure Dave won't mind."

"I'll call you Dave too, if I may," Saul went on. "And I assure you, you're an unusual horse-trader and I quite understand Cleo's interest in you. It's a pity you don't live in this section."

"I think I would, if Dr. Sams would give me a job as foreman of his stud farm." The iron could hardly be hotter than just now, when he was championing Cleo and me against Saul.

"By Jove, I'll think that over," he broke out. "It's not much of a farm now, but I've often considered enlarging it— You might be just the fellow to take charge."

Despite this urgency, I had been conscious for the last few seconds of a man moving toward us from the house. At a distance I could tell that he was elegantly dressed in black broadcloth, was a big man over fifty, with black hair and heavy black eyebrows and a sallow complexion. I could not doubt that this was Ralph Dunbarton. As he came nearer, my boyhood memory of his appearance, which had seemed faded and pale, proved vivid as ever. I matched it against his present aspect and the resemblance was far closer than with the portrait in our picture-room. And suddenly a fact that I had once perceived and later disavowed was again revealed— despite his big bulk he looked commonplace. My clearest memory of him was of his seeming anonymity. His countenance was neither good nor bad—merely nondescript.

"I haven't met this young man," he remarked, rather querulously.

"He's a dealer in horses whom Cleo met on the boat and persuaded to come here," Saul replied, hardly giving him a glance and reveling in the game he was playing with his half-sister.

"He asked her about my little breeding ventures," Dr. Sams broke in, "and since he came out to talk business with me, I brought him over to call."

"What is your name, young man?"

"Dave MacDaniel, sir."

"I'm glad to have you. I'm Ralph Dunbarton, master here."

This was the protagonist of evil in Pa's and my faith, to whose destruction my life had been dedicated. But his eyes, set wide apart and of an indifferent blue-gray, were dim and jaundiced, his sallow skin bilious, and his belly had a distinct paunch. Even his strut appeared assumed. It was as hard to believe that he was the arrogant Saul's father as beautiful Cleo's; and both made sense compared to his being the murderous usurper-king of Wood Ibis. Far away a man with a broken back played his frantic fiddle, but the music made no sense.

"Saul, why don't you ask Dr. Sams and this young man in for a toddy?" Ralph Dunbarton asked. "The weather's a mite chilly."

"A hot day would do just as well, wouldn't it, Papa? But it's a notion."

With what seemed to me faint mockery, Saul gestured for his father to lead the way. We did not mount the magnificent steps below the splendid portico but entered an ordinary-looking door from the porte-cochere. The interior of the house was only the exterior turned wrong side out. It had the same grave beauty, now obtained by high ceilings with noble moldings, huge chandeliers each with a hundred crystals, deep carpets, heavy drapes, marble fireplaces with dark-red fires that cast highlights on the silken polish of wine-red furniture. Pompously the master led us to a small parlor with a score of lighted candles, sat us down, and pulled a bell cord.

"I'll see if Mistress Dunbarton can receive visitors today," he announced. "She's suffered from headache lately, Dr. Sams, and I wish you'd prescribe for her."

"Ralph, I've forgotten all the medicine I ever knew."

A venerable Negro came and went. We waited in silence, with

grave expressions, although there was a twinkle in Saul's bold eyes. "Just like church before the first prayer," I heard him whisper to Cleo. Then Ralph Dunbarton, whose eyes were fixed on the door, rose solemnly. The rest of us, including Cleo, made haste to our feet.

"She cometh," Saul muttered, deep in his throat, his eyes cast down, his hands folded.

But truly the woman's entrance was breath-taking. When the servant drew aside the curtain, she walked in like a queen; and Pa's far-off music making hopeless love to her did not shame him and me. His estimate of her beauty had been exaggerated but not fantastic; in the day of its full flower its equal would have been hard to find in all the Low Country. Comparing it to the beauty in the portrait I could see that it had faded a little—dimmed might be a better word, as might a portrait in too strong light—but as though with deep regret and great gentleness. I could imagine her entrance at the Saint Cecilia Ball still electrifying the aristocratic throng; and when a young woman she descended broad stairs, the chivalry of Charleston must have worshiped her.

She was one of the tallest women I had ever seen—close to six feet. Her carriage was at once stately and gracious, her full-bosomed form both voluptuous and majestic. Her hair, worn high with jeweled combs, remained a magnificent gold; every feature was exquisitely carved; her flesh tints were warm and lovely. She bowed with touching grace and what seemed a little shyness.

"Dr. Sams, what a pleasure to see you," she said in a rich voice. "You don't come half often enough."

"That's the way of advancing years. We don't do half the things—"

"Mine don't advance. At least with any ceremony. They charge down on me like Cossacks." She fixed her splendid blue eyes on mine. "And who is this gentleman you've brought to see me?"

"He brought him to see Cleo, Mum," Saul broke in. "But he'll take a look at our main attraction while about it."

A curiously intense expression flicked across Ralph Dunbarton's face—I thought it was stifled anger—but no one else in the company appeared to notice the insolence. Dr. Sams introduced me with great punctilio.

76

"So you've met my daughter?" she asked, after the amenities.

Flustered by her gaze—by being in her presence, by all these forces in assemblage—I spoke too hastily and not well.

"Yes, I had the pleasure of sailing with her from Baltimore."

Saul slapped his thigh. "Now you've put your foot in it," he cried with great glee. "Cleo led us to believe she got on at Norfolk, where she primly attends the seminary."

"What were you doing in Baltimore, Cleo?" her father demanded in an outraged voice.

"She was up to no good, you can be sure of that."

"Fiddlesticks," Madeline Dunbarton broke in. "Cleo, don't condescend to answer Saul's loutish comedy. Ralph, Cleo wrote me she might visit one of her school friends for a few days. I told you so."

"I'm sure you never did, Madeline."

"Mr. MacDaniel, pardon this silly scene. We've lived out here so long that we've forgotten how to act like civilized people."

"I never knew how, Madeline, and it's too late for me to learn." So spoke the master of Wood Ibis, and an intense prickling sensation moved from ear to ear across the back of my neck. "You've told me a thousand times that no gentleman reprimands his wife or his child or even his servant in front of strangers; but in the face of disobedience if not worse, I can't heed your instruction."

"Ralph, be good enough to wait—"

"Mark you, Madeline, I'm not a gentleman, as you and all the rest here know full well. I'll pretend to be, in front of strangers, although they laugh behind my back. I'll not pretend to these."

"Remember, Papa, yon horse-dealer is still a stranger hereabouts, no matter how well he may know Cleo," Saul said, his cold eyes dancing. "But he too will regret this blight on our humble but honest name. Pray tell us more."

Saul's testimony was not valid; he mocked everyone. Cleo loved her father and was looking at him in dismay. It appeared that Dr. Sams watched with only intense curiosity. But there was one here who could not help herself from knowing whether a wickedly great actor was performing for us. She had been his wife at least in name for nineteen years. With a frozen heart I searched her beautiful face.

The jewel-like brilliance of her eyes became less marked and they were fixed on him not in hatred or accusation or even suspicion but in sorrowful compassion. Her beauty waxed, not waned, as a forlorn expression eclipsed all signs of humiliation and alarm. She had forgotten all of us but him.

That was her whole reply. It shook the main pillar of the temple Pa and I had built, which I had felt tremble at today's first sight of my foe. What a wonderful thing if it would fall! High-minded Dr. Sams had told that the jury's verdict of Bruce's meeting his death by accident was accepted by all sensible people. Perhaps with more evidence to support it, and the lack of any evidence of murder, Pa too would accept it and at last die happier and more sane than if gorged with vengeance. In that case, Cleo and I could build a temple that Saul could not knock down.

The thought had the beauty and some of the tenuousness of a dream. I was looking at Cleo now and she always invoked dreams. Still my attention never wavered from the continuing movement of event within this room.

"Saul, the young man is concerned in this matter," Ralph was replying, by his obliviousness to his son's cheap sarcasm rebuking him more tellingly than with a blow. "My daughter told a lie, perhaps because of what's between them. He won't be shocked at my speaking in front of him—he understands how we plain people do—he is one of us, unless I miss my guess. But I will be polite in front of my lady wife and Dr. Sams. I will question Cleo alone and, if she's guilty, I will punish her in plain folks' ways."

"It looks like you're in for it, pussycat," Saul remarked cheerfully. He leaned forward eagerly, his big hands on his powerful knees. "But if she's guilty, Papa—and personally I don't doubt it— what are you going to do with her gallant?"

"I'll only ask him to leave Wood Ibis. If he molested her on the ship, there were plenty of officers in call."

"There's another thing, old man. You can properly punish your daughter according to us common people's customs, but maybe not Mum's daughter. Mum isn't one of us, you know."

"Every young girl flirts a little, Ralph," Madeline said quietly.

"I've heard enough of this elegant talk," he replied. "Cleo, I'll ask you to come with me to your old schoolroom."

"Well, by God, I'm going along," rose the voice of one I had thought a bystander—Dr. Sams. "Mr. MacDaniel came out to see me on legitimate business—I can vouch for him—and as your one-time family doctor I've got a little vouching to do for Cleo. Ralph, you're making a mistake."

I expected Ralph Dunbarton to refuse him, but he did not. "If you can help me prevent making one, I'll thank you kindly."

Cleo had already risen and, with a strange glance at me, she led the two men out of the room.

"Note that she didn't walk humbly behind her sire, like a plain farmer's daughter ought when going off for a tanning," Saul remarked, his eyes shining.

"He won't tan her," Madeline answered. "Your hopes, my charming stepson, are in vain. Even if Doctor hadn't intervened, he would not."

"I guess you're right. Not that fine, round bottom, reminiscent of the D'Arcys'."

"Mr. MacDaniel, if you are in the least worried, pray compose your mind. I won't bother to apologize for my stepson's vulgarity."

"I like that," Saul cried, greatly entertained. "It may have been ribaldry, Mum, but not vulgarity. The vulgar—I remember my Latin, Dave—are the most prim people on earth. At that moment I was aping the free speech of the aristocrats."

"You don't know how to do it, Saul. Mr. MacDaniel, I must ask you to excuse me. I've enjoyed your visit, and hope we may see more of you under more pleasant conditions."

She returned my bow and with great beauty of movement went out the same door. Saul and I resumed our seats. He sat snapping his fingers: I had never seen a more vital being, beast or human. He kept reminding me of a wild stallion shaking his mane, scornful of any fence. What made so, this baseborn heir of Wood Ibis? On what food had he fed?

"You're not lively company, my lad, and I'll find more excitement in the schoolroom," he suddenly burst out.

"You needn't stay on my account."

"Besides, Papa is badly outnumbered by the nobility and gentry, and I'd better lend him a hand. Not, of course, in the way of tanning hides, if it comes to that."

"I wouldn't think so either."

A man of abrupt, swift movements, he was out of his chair and half across the room before he heard that. He stopped in his stride, balancing on the soles of his feet, then lightly turned and faced me, deeply interested.

"Are you suggesting you might interfere?" he asked thoughtfully.

"I'd dislike seeing my pretty little shipmate strapped, even by her brother."

"Her half-brother, I informed you. It wouldn't be any fun if I were her whole brother."

"I see."

"How do you expect to sell stud horses around here, if you get in trouble with me?"

That was the second mistake I had made today—perhaps the far greater of the two. I was in no position at present to antagonize Saul.

"It would be bad business, I grant you."

"Are you in love with pussycat?"

"No."

"It would be fun if you were—fun for me." He held up his big hands, admired them, and strode off.

The door had hardly closed when one behind me opened. It opened softly to let someone slip through: an obsequious slave, I thought, on some household errand. But the silence held so long that I turned to look.

A white woman stood behind my chair. She looked to be very old—eighty, perhaps—and senile. At least her rather full face was a maze of fine wrinkles and her eyes had a vacant stare, although her somewhat fat body appeared strong. She wore a faded wrapper and her scanty white hair hung in dejected wisps.

"Are you a real person?" she asked in a husky whisper.

"Quite real."

"I thought at first you might be a spirit—another one. I peaked at you, as you came in, and thought you were one of the dead, come back. There are so many."

"No," I said to her as to a child, "I'm just a visitor."

"Don't tell them I came in and talked to you. It's my right to meet company, but they think I'm not in my right mind."

"Who are you?"

"Don't you know? I'm Sadie's own mother."

"I don't know who Sadie is."

"Oh, you must have heard of her," the old creature told me in a desperate whisper. "She's Ralph's wife. His first wife, before he married the rich woman. Why, Saul is my grandson. I have a right to come and meet the company. But you won't tell them—"

"No, not a word. Is Sadie in the house too?"

"She stays at the little house but she comes here sometimes, crying, and holding her side. It still hurts awful, she says."

"She's a spirit?"

"Oh, yes. I thought you knew. I feel so sorry for her. I'd do anything I could to make her rest."

"Maybe I could do something for her, if you tell me what's the matter with her. How did she come to die? Did some one kill her?"

The woman shrank back. "I never said that. I never, I never!"

"Hush! They'll hear you. Her husband killed her—Ralph killed her—so he could marry the rich lady. Isn't that so?"

"She says so, over and over, crying and crying, but I never. Even when he married the rich lady—before the grass got high on Sadie's grave—I never said it. It grows right smart high on graves, you know, but it was still short on Sadie's when he married the mistress of Ibis Hall and crawled into bed with her."

It was something in her voice as she said this last that invoked an image of horror.

"How did Sadie die?" I asked.

"It crawled into her bed, and then she got in, and then Ralph crawled into the rich lady's bed. Do you see the connection?" She rolled her eyes at me and looked wise.

"No. Tell me everything, quick."

"There's too much getting into beds, on this island. Wrong beds. Oh, terrible wrong."

"What did you mean, *it* crawled into Sadie's bed?"

"The cottonmouth. It was wintertime and it went there for

warmth, Ralph said. Its head was as big as your fist. Ralph killed it, and I saw it. But before he killed it"—her whisper became muted and madly furtive—"Sadie got into bed and it bit her on the side and she *died!*"

"Did he put it there?"

"I never said so. She says he bought it from the man who made whiskey in the swamp, but I haven't breathed a word."

"Don't tell anyone you talked to me."

"I won't. I never tell the living what the dead say, but I keep thinking you're a spirit—"

"No, I'm a man who can kill people. If you tell anyone I asked you about Sadie, I'll kill you."

The door opened again, very softly. The old woman whirled to face it, her expression half-cunning, half-defiant. A strong-looking, pleasant-faced colored woman of about forty hurried into the room, terror on her face.

" 'Scuse me, suh," she gasped. Then in a low breathless tone, "You gotta come now, Miss Granny. You know what dey do to bof of us when you slip off—"

"I got the right to meet the company. I'm Mr. Saul's grandmama. I didn't tell him about the spirits—"

The Negress had seized her wrist and was tugging her toward the door. "Suh, please don't tell de white folks she come in, please suh. Massa, he take me to de woods and beat Debbil out o' me."

"I'll not tell them."

"I won't say a word," Granny told her in a deeply sad whisper as the door was closing softly. "Not a word. Not a word—"

Not a word could I say to Cleo, of soon hope and promise. The little temple she and I were building must wait how long?

Dr. Sams returned, followed by Ralph Dunbarton. They were talking quietly of crops and weather. Both men looked greatly relieved.

"I trust you'll excuse this troublesome incident," the master of Wood Ibis told me. "I'm naturally very concerned for my daughter's welfare and a girl of her age is liable to mistakes. I'm completely satisfied about her journey to Baltimore, and her deceit was a childish one. She has assured me you behaved very properly toward her aboard the ship and Dr. Sams, quite an expert at reading character, speaks highly of you."

"I thank you both."

"By the way, you made a very favorable impression on my son Saul. A young man himself, he understands this generation better than I. I'm a bit old-fashioned, I'm afraid."

"He's a son to be proud of."

"Thank you. If Dr. Sams decides to enlarge his stables and finds a position for you, we'd be glad to have you for a neighbor. Now we will have our toddies. My butler will bring them in a moment. The ladies ask to be excused—they have household duties—and Saul is occupied elsewhere."

"I'm quite serious about that horse business, Dave," Dr. Sams said. "We'll discuss it later."

The butler entered with punctilio, bringing six drinks in silver mugs. "You dunce," Ralph Dunbarton burst out, "I told you there'd be only three of us!"

" 'Scuse me, massa," the servant answered, not in the least embarrassed. "It done slip my mind."

"Well, now you've brought them, you might as well leave them."

After praising the drink, I complimented Mr. Dunbarton on his beautiful home.

"My wife takes it for granted—she was born here—but not I," he replied, his face lighting. "I was born in a three-room shack in

Charleston. Especially I prize its strong construction. The walls are so solid that when the windows are closed, we can't hear the wind outside. It may be blowing almost a full gale, but we would never know it save for threshing boughs."

Nor could an outsider hear the winds that blew within.

"It should stand centuries, unless destroyed by fire," he went on. "Wouldn't you say so, Dr. Sams?"

"Certainly."

"A great monument to the D'Arcys, a family that built strongly, both their houses and their stock."

Ralph Dunbarton gave me his hand when Dr. Sams and I rose to go. It was warm and its grasp firm, not in the least surprising me, so completely human he appeared: only afterward did I fancy that it should have been cold and a little slippery from holding unclean ministers of death. The stable boy who had taken charge of our horses waited under the porte-cochere, and gigantic Obo, Cleo's servant and bodyguard, was tamely helping a gardener clip a boxwood a short distance off.

But his gaze flicked swiftly and covertly to meet and signal mine.

"You're a big fellow," I told him, when I had mounted and the stable boy stood back. "How much do you weigh?"

"I don't know, suh, but more'n half a bale o' cotton. A big bale, not a short bale." His high-tenor voice had indeed the timbre and melody of an oboe.

"Can you lift one?"

"Yes *suh!*"

"There goes my whip. Hand it to me, please." If cunning was not native to me, it was long ago acquired and practiced.

The stable boy sprang forward but Obo was too fast for him. I imagined that a big lion could spring like that. As he handed me the quirt his immense pink palm brushed mine. I was expecting that and no one noticed the passage; what surprised me was the expression that swiftly crossed his broad, black face. It was as though he had suddenly seized an illusive memory, and not merely of seeing me on the Charleston dock. Most Negroes have wonderfully acute senses and Obo was Africa-born. Could he be remembering now where he had seen me first, on the very block in Baltimore where his mistress went to call on a lame man?

"I hope that unpleasantness this afternoon didn't embarrass you too much," Dr. Sams was saying, when we were riding away from the great, glimmering mansion.

"No, sir, I wasn't very embarrassed."

"Good. I'm getting the idea there's a lot to you, Dave. For a complete stranger who never heard of Wood Ibis until a few days ago—suddenly confronted with that situation—well, you kept your head mighty well."

Not too well, I thought, remembering Saul as he held up his big hands. Was I in love with pussycat? Perhaps Cleo had not kept her head in sending me the note cupped warmly in my palm.

"By the way—he wouldn't have laid hand on her," Dr. Sams went on. "She knew it as well as I did. He whipped her only once —when she was about ten—and something happened to put a damper on him ever after. No doubt Madeline threatened to leave him if he ever did it again, but this occurrence was more dramatic. According to the colored people's story, a few days after the whipping he met with an accident."

"He'd been conjured?"

"Nothing so unsubstantial. It appears he'd made a habit of walking down from the stables into the swamps about Sweetwater Pond to look at a nest of sandhill cranes. He went every day or two before breakfast, interested in the hatching and growth of the little birds. That morning as he was creeping up to the nest he stepped into a pit cunningly screened with leaves and grass. In the bottom was a sharp stake. His first impulse was to start a manhunt for a would-be murderer—it would have been a very short hunt, or I miss my guess. But he changed his mind when someone—I think Madeline—showed him that the stake was set in such a way that he couldn't have impaled himself on it. The device was meant as a warning."

"A kind of grim one, I should say."

"The pit was the sort used in West Africa to take buffalo. Yet I believe that Obo was not even whipped, no doubt because Ralph prizes the man's devotion to his daughter. You see, he does love her very much. He regards her as a vindication before the world of his marriage with Madeline—blue blood mixed with some red.

Of course he's bent and determined that she'll make a top-sawyer marriage herself."

I looked at the swamp on the left of the road, where serpents lay in cold sleep and bright birds flew, and then to the broad and fertile fields on the right.

"I think there'd be plenty of young men to choose from, especially if she's coming in to this."

"She'll get some of the D'Arcy jewels but I reckon Saul will inherit all the land. It doesn't seem right when she's half-D'Arcy and he's none. Except when it's entailed, a woman's property becomes her husband's at marriage. Through Bruce Dunbarton's will, Madeline became owner again, but now Ralph's the owner. He and Saul have a good many disputes but Saul usually gets his way. They're a lot closer than they seem."

He wanted to say something more—perhaps of encouragement to me—and native restraint interfered. He said it finally.

"For Cleo to make what is called a brilliant marriage won't be as easy as he thinks. Ralph Dunbarton is *persona non grata* in Low Country society—Madeline has been virtually ostracized because of her two marriages into that family—and very few young men have ever paid court to Cleo. Saul's sense of humor hasn't helped any either."

As Dr. Sams led the way through the swamp I read the note Obo had handed me. "If you can, meet me at Sweetwater Pond at twelve tonight." It was signed "Cleo" and was in precise, girlish handwriting.

Half-expecting something of the kind, I did not expect such a dizzy rush of joy. To meet Cleo again, alone—to have her in my arms in the dark of night—the very danger sweetening the fruit. . . . It was forbidden fruit. That had been established when an old loon shut away in Ibis Hall, told me about her ghosts. But I would find some way to get around that. The joy became mixed with a stealthy excitement as I rode deeper into the dark and tortuous swamp. She must wait a year or more before I would be free to keep my promise to her—hate, not love, had the right-of-way—but in the meantime there could be stolen nights in woods like these. Nights of such love as would not interfere with my great affairs, of the kind the swamp-folk knew. . . .

86

"Damn these devil-dens," Dr. Sams suddenly burst out.

"I don't know what you mean, sir."

"These swamps. They bring out all the bad a man's got in him. I never ride through them without feeling it surging up from the pit that opens in us all. In summer it's worse—everything hatching and growing, hungry for life, pitiless, dog-eat-dog. Look at that water hemlock. Poison as hell—but typical of the cursed place. Eat one of those red-capped mushrooms and you're dead as a dog."

Instead I looked at the entwining forms of branches, stout trunks and vines in wild embrace, and the voracious greenery that winter could not kill. A humid warmth exuded from the muck. White birds with black heads and black-tipped wings stood primly, with no hint of their ruthless hungers. Doves that looked too delicate to breathe, but monsters of lechery in spring, made sad, hypocritical sounds. The green-stained light receded as the swamp became more rank, then slowly cleared as we gained higher ground, with the effect of a solar eclipse. But hours must pass, I remembered, before real night would fall.

They went by wasted. I did not lead on Dr. Sams to talk of long years past, for my mind could dwell only on a near, future hour. In his warm house he wanted to sit up late with me—eager to talk and listen—but I told him the fire made me drowsy—feigned many a stifled yawn—yes, the day's ride had fixed me for a long night's sleep—I must go to bed at nine.

He sat alone by the hearth a full hour, then I heard him come upstairs—and a servant extinguishing the lights, banking the fires, locking the doors and windows. Was there danger of thieves in this lonely outland? Perhaps a renegade whiskey-maker still dwelt in the fastnesses of the swamps, turning his hand to what profited him, even a cottonmouth moccasin, old and fat, turning, twisting in his hand. I could not put my mind on that. I was waiting, my skin prickling, for the house to grow silent.

I crept down the stairs, unlocked the back door and pocketed the key, and, avoiding the glimmer of the winter moon, made my way to the stables. Lizzie kept the bargain she had made at her colt-hood's end—submission to a fate that came and went on two legs —and not the dimmest wonder crossed her mind as to what business I might be on. I walked her on soft ground until out of hearing from the house, then gave her the spur.

The track through the swamp was a black tunnel with moonlit chinks in its roof. When Lizzie tried to turn back—scenting peril that she could not see—I forced her on. I had prepared a pine knot to light the ground for her, but did not stop to kindle it: I loved the wild-scented darkness for the sense of power it gave me. Wide-winged cranes and herons, making free of the skies only a few hours ago, perched in impotence as I pressed on. The ducks were water-bound; the wild turkeys flushed from their roosts but swiftly lighted again, afraid of the dark passage; even the owl flitted uneasily through the very tree-tops, where the blackness thinned to blue. I shared the night with the hungry fox, the stalking wildcat, perhaps the great panther on silent feet. I was as wildly alive as they.

Saul Dunbarton kept a pack of bear and bobcat hounds in a kennel close to the barns. They caught my scent and clamored, a great and noble outcry in the silence, as though entreating me to take them hunting, for often they were freed on such a night. The sound carried clearly to the big house. Cleo, waiting at the door, perhaps already at the meeting place, knew I traveled fast. But soon I checked the mare, put her across soft ground, then dismounted, and tied her to a live-oak limb. Skirting the mansion that loomed in the moonlight like a huge forsaken temple to an Attic god, and fetching a circle about the stables, I gained the bank of Gator Creek where my feet found a little-worn path.

There was an old clearing, now overgrown with underbrush at the inlet of the pond, and the moonlight picked out a rustic seat where Madeline might have daydreamed as a young girl. Its rail was broken but its cypress wood unrotted; it was the exact point Cleo had chosen for our assignation. Later it could serve its turn. Now I stood poised for sudden movement, searching the shadows.

In hardly a moment one shadow moved silently out of a swarm, spread swiftly and greatly across little pools of moonlight, and stopped almost at my feet. Its shape was of a monstrous man, but I could not yet see what cast it. A voice like a muted oboe came down to me.

"Miss Cleo come in jist a minute."

"Thanks."

The shadow vanished as though lifted instead of drawn away, and I could not hear the slightest sound. Then the grass rustled and dead leaves crackled and Cleo stood beside me.

"Oh, Dan," she whispered.

"What did you call me, Cleo?" My voice shook.

"Forgive me! It was just a slip of the tongue. Dave, I'm so glad you came."

"How dangerous is it? You better tell me."

"There's practically no danger, or I wouldn't have asked you. There's none whatever of anybody taking us by surprise. Obo's standing guard and he'd warn us before Papa—or Saul—could get past the stables. You could sneak off and hide. I'd just pretend to be taking a late walk, for I've taken lots of them—at all hours of the night—when I felt like it. Papa would have no choice but to believe me."

"He wouldn't whip you?"

"No, that's all bluff."

"Saul wouldn't believe you'd just been out walking!"

"No." She wanted to say something more about Saul but put it off for the present. "Let's sit down. I wish we had a fire to go to, but the weather's mild and both of us are warmly dressed."

"How much time have we?"

"'Till two o'clock."

"Surely no one stirs around that early—"

"Well, the tide turns at two tonight and then the marshhens holler. They almost always do at the turn of the tide. Papa sleeps with his window open on mild nights. He's a very light sleeper and often they wake him up. They make a big racket, you know. If he does wake up, he usually roams around the house testing the doors and windows. I reckon he helps himself out of the decanter while about it. I don't want him to find a certain window open."

She sat with her hand under her chin, gazing out over the pond. I took the place beside her and her other hand. I was much more calm than when riding through the swamp and somehow happier. The moonlight was a good medium for her delicate, dreamy beauty.

"I've got something important to tell you. It's terribly disappointing too. This is the last time we can see each other for a long time. If Dr. Sams offers you a job—and I think he may—tell him you can't take it until spring."

"Will you tell me why?"

"I don't want Papa to suspect that we know each other any better than it seemed today. If you leave and nothing's heard from you he won't think I had anything to do with your coming here, and then if you come back you won't start out with him set against you."

"What harm would it do if I stayed on with Dr. Sams? If I had nothing to do with you for three months, it would allay his suspicions as much or even more than if I stayed that long away from the Low Country."

"No, because you would be having something to do with me. Your job would bring you over here constantly. Besides—we might both get lonely and meet—like tonight."

"You said it was safe tonight. Why not other nights?"

"Papa knows you haven't had a chance yet to write or talk to me alone and he wouldn't think I'd be so brazen as to write to you. But later on—if you stay at Little Ibis—he'll set a watch over me. He has plenty of slaves. He can have them take turns, like soldiers."

She was speaking rapidly, in a nervous tone. The reason she had given for my leaving Wood Ibis so soon and for so long did not seem good enough, considering her joy at the prospect of my coming. Still I did not look for any other, partly from looking at her face and form in the moonlight, partly from searching my own heart. We were alone once more, perhaps for the last time in long months. The scene, the silence, our close warmth, and the shadow of Ibis Hall upon us both made potent magic to re-weld a weakened chain. She had called me Dan and an almost irresistible urge was upon me to answer to the name.

"You see the danger," she was saying out of a tight throat. "I hate—to have you—go—"

I was seeing a greater danger. No, there must be no other nights. I had been brought too near a child's hiding place of eight years ago—too far from the picture-room and Pa's music. I was too happy beside Cleo—too deeply moved by her.

Her hand was warm and confiding in mine. Her lips would be

soft and yielding. Even now I was fighting against loving her with all my heart, but there was another kind of love than that, running riot in the night, and this was our last night for how long? It was as though in closing one door to happiness, another opened. We were sitting by the edge of the swamp where the old gods of Nature reigned supreme. The moon, her ancient agent, gave misty light that softened every austere shape and rigid line, obscured the distance, and cast us away on a little silver island in a sea of darkness. The deep waters of the tarn were full of shadows.

Why not have her this hour, and keep my promise to her in my own good time? She had met me by stealth, still in hope that I would take her away: that very hope would breach her walls, perhaps lay her in my hand. The tide was rising fast and the dark waters whispered in their grasses to the tide of desire mounting fast in Cleo. *"Lie down, maiden, and yield."* She was gazing at the moon, and perhaps it promised what her overwrought imagination craved. *"I will shine on your face, maiden, and he will gaze down upon the beauty he has waked in you, and you will see his face darkly in shadow, and half-vision, half-dream his joy."*

If she were fighting with guilt, the old moss-hung cypress trees, gray and wise, standing still and watching for so long, might reassure her. *"We know not evil here, because we know not good. This is not Eden, where God sits on guard, but an older realm."* If she were ashamed of her passion, a wood ibis somehow kin to her, perhaps her totem in an ancient nature cult, moonlit on a naked snag, might speak to her what she craved to hear. *"Lie down, innocent and lovely one, and yield your whiteness. We make our loves in the day, for we know naught of shame, but you and he can hide from all the world in this soft darkness, yet not conceal one ecstasy from each other."*

We would know each other then—but that was our right. We would love each other too—I was not deceived—but that was our long-fixed fate. I was bending toward her when a harsh sound rose from the reeds. It was only a wakeful marshhen—the tide had not yet turned. Yet the moon rocked in the sky and my heart reeled and, with a great surge of my will, I spoke.

"The reason you gave, Cleo, isn't the real reason you want me to go."

She rose out of a trance and her round eyes meeting mine, slowly shook her head.

"What is the real reason?"

"Maybe you think I'm hoping you'll take me away with you. But I'm not, now. I know you told me the truth when you said—"

"I don't think that."

"I have to tell you the truth—no matter if you never come back. My voice won't work—it's so awful. The real reason is—you're in terrible danger."

The chill that ran over me was more than skin-deep. The scene at the edge of the swamp had been sensuous only a moment before; suddenly it was ominous. The pond looked sinister, the shadows like something in ambush, the moon only a weak lamp against what walked the night.

"You must tell me everything, Cleo."

"That's the trouble. I know so little and what I do know—I've got to tell you, to make you believe me—makes me so ashamed."

"Don't be ashamed. I knew there was something awfully wrong here, to make you so desperate to run away."

"It's Saul. He gets sudden hatreds sometimes—no, that's not the right word—a kind of malice more evil than anything you can imagine. I was frightened when he praised you to Dr. Sams—urged him to give you a job. That was so unlike him, when he suspected I wanted you to stay here—ordinarily he would have been content to humiliate you terribly so you'd leave and never come back. Wanting you to stay showed he'd picked you out for—special —treatment."

"What do you mean by that?"

"Wait. Right then I wrote you the note and gave it to Obo to slip to you. All the rest of the day he asked cunning questions about the voyage, his eyes shining as I've never seen them shine before, except—but maybe I can get out of telling you that. Dave, you wouldn't believe that any man living could be so completely bad as Saul—it doesn't stand to human nature—there's a reason for it, I feel sure, but I can't imagine what. Right now he's tired of hunting bears and wildcats with his dogs. He hasn't got a new young Negress to amuse him. That might make him want a new butt for his jokes—the cruelest he can think of—but this goes deeper than that. He has senses as sharp as a wild animal's. He is a wild animal with unbelievable human wickedness. He knows we're sweethearts and thinks we're in danger of becoming more than that. I'm trying to tell you everything—as you asked—and it's so

93

hard. Maybe he's convinced himself there's more between us than there is."

"Something that we ourselves don't know?"

She gave me a great wondering glance, then fear and despair filled her eyes again. "I meant he imagines something that isn't true. . . . What did you mean?"

"Only that you might feel about me—a little anyway—as you felt about Dan."

"He knows about Dan. At first only that there was such a boy that I loved and dreamed about. You can imagine what he did—no, you can't. The only wonder is, I could keep on dreaming about him—waiting for the day he'd come to take me away from here—loving him if a little girl ever loved anyone. You'd think Saul would have made me too ashamed to let myself think of him again. Letters from Dan that he forged—so cleverly that I was fooled by a lot of them—saying he was coming—and I'd go off to the meeting place—and wait for him hours and hours. He took my diary in which I'd written my heart out and once when a kind woman from Bull Island brought her children and neighbor children for a picnic here with me, he read it aloud to all of them. Only last year he got a young Negro to come here—everything fixed so cunningly that I never suspected—to tell me that Dan was in Charleston and would meet me at midnight in a restaurant. I got a girl I know in Charleston to invite me there, and Mama made Papa let me go—and I went to the restaurant—dressed like a girl who could go there alone at night—and pretty soon three of Saul's friends came in and began to make fun of me. I knew then, of course—that night I tried to get on a fisherman's boat to run away —but Saul came with the truant officer—and I had to go home."

"Good God, Cleo!"

"I didn't mean to tell you all of that. It doesn't—really—concern—"

"Did Saul ever find out the boy's name was Dan?"

"Yes, from the diary. Then when Papa told him that he'd left me to play with a boy whose last name was Reed, in Philadelphia, he put two and two together."

"Did Saul think I might be Dan Reed?"

"At first he did, when I mentioned meeting you on the ship, and saying you might come out to see Dr. Sams. I told him you weren't, and since I'm not a good liar—he's always able to trick me and find out the truth—he knows now you're not. He knows I've given Dan up for dead. But he suspects you might come to take his place —I had hoped you would, I guess—and he knows I care about you far more than anyone I've met since. That's all Saul needed to set him off. Besides—did anything happen between you and him after I left the room?"

I told her of the mistake I had made.

"I should have warned you on the ship, but I was so ashamed— hated so to speak of him—and I never really believed you were coming to Wood Ibis. I guess it's hard for me to believe any promise, after the one Dan and I made each other. Maybe I was afraid that if I told you—about Saul—there'd be no hope of you coming."

"Well, I did come, and though I've got to go back to Baltimore for a while, I'm going to come again."

"Don't think of such a thing. I won't let you. There was only one hope for us—and it failed. You know what it was—my pride's all gone—that you'd fall in love with me and I could run away and we'd live in some far-off place. We'd have to be married—I was wrong about that before—or you couldn't hope to keep me away from Saul. He'd track us down and somehow make me come back. Even if we were married, the things he'd do—" Her voice filled with sorrow and failed.

"If I were free—"

She broke in quickly, for the sake of my pride. "There's another reason I know he's planning some awful injury to you. You won't believe this part—but I do. Granny says he is—that you are in real, great danger here. She's Saul's grandmother—the old woman who came in and talked to you today. She's in her second childhood and out of her mind most of the time but she's got second sight."

"How did you know she'd talked to me? Did the old Negress—"

"Aunt Lucy wouldn't tell a soul that Granny slipped off from her. She hasn't done it for years. She saw you come in and some- thing made her go to you—she didn't know until after you'd gone, when she went into the closet with her 'spirits.' Then she asked Lucy to bring her into my room to visit me—she has a lot of cunning—and I could see she had something to tell me so I sent Lucy on an errand. She was half-frantic but almost rational."

"Did she think Saul would harm me on account of you?"

"Partly. She gave another reason too—but her mind was wandering then. She said you'd come here for some purpose besides getting a job and being near me—and if Saul found it out, he'd kill you. She said you were a born enemy of both Saul and Papa. But often when she's talked to her 'spirits'—in her own imagination of course —there's a lot of craziness mixed with the truth. That's common with people with second sight."

I did not think Granny's mind had been wandering too far in this instance. My questions about her daughter were good evidence of a secret mission here.

"Cleo, is there any special reason—besides pure malignance—why Saul won't let anyone court you? You'd better tell me."

"It's not what—yes, I'd better tell you—what you think. At least —believe me, Dave—if I weren't kin to him but living in the same house, he'd still make life unbearable for me—perhaps because I'm half-D'Arcy and he's not. But because he's my half-brother, because it would be so awful—every law and decency and Nature itself bars him from me—he pretends to want to keep me for himself, never let me love or marry anyone. All he does really is say awful things and be dog-in-the-manger."

She sat quietly a moment, trying to find words to tell enough but not too much. I had to know all.

"I'm not afraid of humiliation, Cleo," I said. "Unless he goes farther than that—"

"He went a little farther even with Mama's nephew by marriage who visited us last winter. Lucas was about eighteen and he and I made a little puppy-love. Saul didn't respect him as he does you —he was a sort of mama's boy—but he was good and sweet and I was so happy to have him here. Well, Saul played jokes on him. When Lucas went shooting his boat drifted off and he had to walk two miles through knee-deep, half-frozen muck. He was in the last stage of exhaustion when he got in and has never completely recovered his strength. Are you satisfied with that?"

"No. I want to know—"

"When I was a little girl we owned a strong, intelligent mulatto named Bert. I don't know what Saul had against him, but he was whipped time after time for nothing until he ran away. Saul had a wonderful time hunting him with his dogs. He never caught him though—and the pack never got to worry his body. Bert swam out to sea until he drowned."

I could not run away from Wood Ibis! A murdered slave named Bert had become another reason for staying here. What had he seen that had made him dangerous to Ralph's life and his son's great expectations?

"There was another Negro—a simple soul called Slewfoot—who tried to run away just last summer. At least he'd gone into the swamp without Papa's orders. He had to run, even if he had never intended to, when Saul rushed in and rang the alarm and turned loose his pack. The pack treed him and he got shot out stone-dead —no one seems to know just how. We don't talk about those things in Ibis Hall."

Cleo's father had no doubt told her that he had not given Slewfoot orders to enter the swamp, and the simple soul could not return to dispute him. Had he talked too freely before then, or merely looked too wise?

"Did your mother know about this?" I asked.

"No. She knows of nothing she doesn't want to know. She's like a real queen on a throne. I'm not supposed to know about it either —but I hear whispers."

"To talk plain—do you think Saul might kill me?"

"Granny says he will, if you stay here. If you were enough in his way and he couldn't get rid of you, you'd either be killed or you'd die."

"What do you mean?"

She was whispering in a way that reminded me of Granny, a terribly sorrowful, hopeless sound.

"I don't know. I know only that he always wins. He isn't human. I mean he didn't grow into a human being but something different. It's not conjure—I don't believe in that—it's real. What can anyone do against him? He lets Obo live but when the time comes—"

Cleo had assured me, without knowing she had done so, that Saul was running her through the swamp for the monstrous sport of it, letting her escape to run again. The fact remained that there were sloughs and quagmires there that might swallow her, save for Obo's love and strength. If he were queerly killed or more queerly died, I would take her away from Wood Ibis, no matter how long my other tasks were postponed. As it was, she would be safer staying here, I thought, while I took ax to the root.

"I'm going in now," Cleo told me.

"I may not see you for some months."

"You'd be better off if you never saw me again. All the young men in the Low Country know that, without knowing half what you know. I tell you, you'd better not take a job here. We're too drawn to each other—"

"That's one reason I'm going to take a job here, as soon as I can get one. I told you—and it's the solemn truth—I'm not free to take you away—not free even to love you. God knows I want to—I'd fall in love with you this minute if I were free."

"That's such a strange thing to say. Nobody can make themselves love anyone, or make themselves keep from it."

"You're wrong, Cleo. I know. I've seen it proven our last night on shipboard—and again tonight. People have more control over their hearts than you think—when there's enough at stake. Love waits until the people find out how desperately they need each other—usually through passion. If I'd taken you in my arms tonight it would have come to me. That's why—for a while anyway —in spite of wanting to so terribly—"

"Don't talk about it, Dave."

"I'll go to Baltimore and come back as soon as I can. I'm going to leave an address with Dr. Sams where you can write me and, if you say to come at once, I will. When I do come, I won't make love to you. Saul will soon be convinced that there's nothing between us but a shipboard acquaintance."

"You'd better wait three or four months, I tell you. Even then unless it comes about naturally—"

"We'll have to quit being shipboard sweethearts. It may be a long time—a year perhaps—before I'm free. But when I am—"

"Don't say it, Dave. Just let it go."

"I'm not free because I've made a contract with someone else. But it will be all over—"

"Don't make any promises. We're not sweethearts any more and if you come back, come only to be Dr. Sams's foreman. I know you care about me and want to help me—but I don't think you will come back—and if you do—nothing good will ever come of it for you and me—and maybe more bad than you can imagine. There's only one thing that can save me—and that won't happen."

"What do you mean, Cleo?"

"For Ibis Hall to burn down and every acre of Wood Ibis to sink into the sea."

There was only moonlight where Cleo had stood. In the morning I stood with Dr. Sams outside his paddock, looking at his stallions and brood mares. It was a bright, warm day, a fine day to follow hounds after a fox or to hunt partridges or to fish for winter trout; not a day for following on with last night's business. People's optimism would be out in front. They would want to dwell on the future instead of the past. I wanted to ask the doctor about two Negroes, Bert and Slewfoot, and a whiskey-maker who once lived in the swamps, but it was not the right time. He started to talk about horses.

"Is Saul Dunbarton a good horseman?" I asked, to break this thin but hard, bright ice.

"Top-sawyer. You'd expect him to be able to master them but they seem to like him. He can call them to him after very short acquaintance. Dogs are crazy about him—jump all over him whining for his pattings."

"Well, there must be a lot of good in him if dogs are drawn to him."

"Well, I've heard that."

"If the Negroes like him too—is he a hard master with them?"

"Not particularly. Rather indulgent, in fact. You can't tell how they feel about him. White people have their own world, there's another that they share with the colored, and the colored have their own world, hard for us to enter."

"I'd like to know how big Obo feels about him," I said in a tone of idle curiosity. "He must resent the way Saul talks and acts toward Cleo—"

"If Obo hates him, he never gives a sign. Still—I wouldn't like to be Saul at his mercy down in the swamp." Dr. Sams had the sense of talking too much and too fast—I saw it in his face—but the Dunbarton family was more interesting to him than the ancient four-legged family of Eclipse. "He's a very primitive African, you know," he went on hastily. "As you say, he might resent Saul's badgering his Cleo. On the other hand, Saul's never made any trouble for Obo."

"Cleo told me that he was named after the oboe that Mr. Dunbarton plays. Does Saul take after his father and the lame brother by being musical?"

That question was intended to disarm Dr. Sams—show him I took a broad and friendly interest in the family.

"He sings extremely well." Dr. Sams spoke rather absently, I thought: I followed his gaze to a nursing colt in the lot. "By the way, Dave: come into the house a minute. I have an idea I want to discuss with you."

I followed him into the library and somewhat to my surprise he closed the door. Then he turned to me with his dark eyes full of thoughts.

"How did you know that Noel Dunbarton was musical?" he asked.

"Why, you mentioned it." I was able to keep alarm out of my voice. "Don't you remember? You said he played the violin."

"I thought perhaps it might have been Cleo."

"Well, perhaps she did say so, on the ship."

"No, she didn't. He'd never had a violin in his hands when he disappeared. If she's heard that he's alive and since become a violinist, I have every reason to believe that she wouldn't mention the fact to anyone. I know it, but I wouldn't have mentioned it. It would have indicated contact with him since his disappearance. I ask you again, Dave—how did you know that Noel is a violinist?"

I looked Dr. Sams in the face. "It's quite a mystery. Someone certainly told me—"

"It's not as great a mystery to me as it might be. Last night after you'd gone to bed I got out my gazetteer of stud farms, and there's no Fairbrook listed. You're well informed on horse-breeding and are a wonderful rider, but you're far more interested in the Dunbarton family. That started me thinking, and I would have figured it out even if you hadn't made that break about Noel. In fact, I've got the main facts already."

"Well, we'd better sit down."

"I think so too."

"If I tell you everything, would you promise—"

"I promise nothing, yet, and it's for me to ask questions and for you to answer them. Cleo told me about a boy she met in Philadelphia years ago. Ralph had gone to see his father, a lame musician— thinking he might be Noel—but the man he met in the house wasn't Noel. Since her return this time she told me about calling on a lame musician in Baltimore. From her description of him I had every reason to believe he was Noel. I asked her if he had a son and she said she didn't know—she didn't see anyone else. But you got on the boat that night. You came to Wood Ibis. I think that Noel sent you and I think it likely you were the boy she met in Philadelphia. In other words I think that Noel got some other lame man to put Ralph off the track. Is that right so far?"

"Yes, sir."

"You're Noel's adopted son. What is your real name?"

"I don't know. Pa took me out of an orphanage when I was about eight. I'd been abandoned there as an infant—no doubt by an unmarried mother."

"Do you think Noel would like to come back here? I wish he would. If he would want me to live here with him and operate the farm, I'd do it gladly."

"He won't come until the mystery of his brother's death is cleared up."

"And if it proves to be murder—if Bruce was done to death— doesn't he want the murderer brought to the rope?"

The sunlight flooded through the windows and I saw the faint lines and tiny blemishes on his fine, tight skin. He had very clear, deep, dark eyes.

"Pa could hardly expect me to do anything about that in a brief visit, Dr. Sams."

"I think this is a preliminary visit. I've always felt that sooner or later Noel might 'revisit these glimpses of the moon'—not in person, I thought, but vicariously—as it seemed to me he used to live in his brother Bruce. I have been hearing from him at rare intervals for about seventeen years. Reading between the lines I surmised this intention. Lately I've perceived in his letters an increased hope of clearing up the affair—as though, after all these years, he was about ready to act. But it would seem a mad act to anyone—we've got to deal plainly—to anyone but a madman."

"It would seem so to you, I know."

"In his long absence has Noel uncovered any fact that would hold out the least hope of success?"

"No, sir."

"He would send you—or some other—to start at the beginning?"

"I reckon so."

He turned to the window, white of face. "It's raving madness," he murmured.

"It's a cold trail, I know."

"Yet there's a certain method in it, if he's enlisted you. I don't know who would have a better chance to accomplish the all-but-impossible feat than a young man of his hands, intelligent, unknown, of humble station seeking a job on the plantation. But where would you find the resolution, the patience, I'll say the zeal, necessary for such a task? You're an adopted son. You never knew Noel's brother Bruce. Noel must have promised you a great reward."

"I'm supposed to have Little Ibis, at his death."

"Don't think I blame Noel. Even I, a bystander, have lain awake nights wishing that this shadow could be lifted."

"Do you mean, sir, even if it means a noose around a neighbor's neck?"

"Dave, I practiced medicine for about fifteen years," he told me, speaking slowly in low tones. "I fought to save life. If for greed or lust or hate someone did my friend Bruce out of his life, I want to see him on the gallows. It's not possible for me to take an active part in sending him there. I withdrew from life, in a sense, when I stopped practicing medicine; but I'll tell you everything I know—the little that I know—and give you a base of operations by offering you a job here. If a bloody-handed murderer is now enjoying the fruits of his crime, I yearn for his destruction."

He went to a cabinet, filled a glass from a decanter, and emptied it in one deep swallow. "Please pardon me," he said. "I can't meet any crisis without this help. Luckily I hurt only myself with it, these days."

"I thought to go back to Baltimore, talk to Pa, and smooth

the way for my return. I mean, lead up to it in such a way that no one would suspect my real business here."

"That can be done, but not hastily. You and I can exchange letters about enlarging my stud farm. Weeks and months must pass before we come to an agreement—that will give Ralph's and Saul's suspicions time to die out." The drink had changed Dr. Sams: he seemed more alert and somehow more capable and shrewd. "Have you anything to tell Noel—an impression or a fact picked up on this trip—to encourage him?"

"I can tell him about you! That's a mighty lot. And I have a feeling that I could make friends with Lizzie, at Turtle Inlet. She's spiteful against Madeline but that's put on, I think. She strikes me as an honest, highly intelligent woman who would make a strong ally."

"In time, perhaps. My feeling is that you'd better not trust her with your secret—just visit there and let her talk. Well, I'm going to show you something—a somewhat grisly souvenir of my practice. Of course Noel told you there was another sudden death only a few weeks before Bruce was killed."

"Yes, Sadie's, Ralph's first wife." I was not yet ready to tell Dr. Sams about my conversation with Granny.

"I did what I could for her, including cauterizing the wound. It was too late, of course; I believe no treatment could have saved her, no matter how soon it was given. You'll see why in a moment."

He left the room to return shortly with something wrapped in paper. It proved to be the head and neck of a water moccasin that had been preserved in alcohol—a prodigious specimen to judge from the breadth and depth of this part. When Granny had said that the creature's head had been as big as my fist, she had not missed it far.

"What is the first thing that strikes you about it?" Dr. Sams asked, a little like a master in a school.

"The unique size."

"In fact, that was my excuse for cutting off and keeping this memento of a truly horrid tragedy—and even so it seemed a shocking breach of taste on my part. However, I don't think that occurred to the widower," the doctor went on with a faint, mirthless smile. "Among Ralph's many admirable qualities—as you will find on better acquaintance with him—so-called good taste is not conspicuous. It's not his fault. Those fine shades of feeling are hardly natural to man—more the consequence of artificial environment and little contact with the tough realities of life. They're a hothouse growth on which I once set store, but I've come to realize they're not very important."

"Yes, sir," I said, not even wanting to hurry him, intensely interested in him as well as in his story.

"The crushed and broken body of the snake was lying in Ralph's chicken pen where Saul, I believe, had carried it. Ralph had killed it with a poker some two hours before, when poor Sadie had leaped out of bed screaming that she had been struck—she was prostrated in twenty minutes and lived only a little over an hour. Dave, you'll see a few moccasin skins stretched to six feet or over, but this brute was six feet before he was skinned—an imposing length even for a diamond-back rattler. I measured him to see. I didn't weigh him, to my regret, but the thick of his body was a good three and a half inches. Well, I was at once struck not only with this oddity—the extraordinary size of the creature—but also with another. I refer to its odd behavior in entering a house and crawling into a bed. Taken alone, either one or the other could be remarked and dismissed. Corn snakes, for instance, frequently enter houses to hunt mice. Taken together, they terrified me."

His tone was too calm to go well with this inherently exciting story, and with the fever in his eyes.

"I think I see what you mean," I answered when he paused. "If someone had plotted to murder Sadie in this way, he'd want to use a big snake with plenty of venom. A bite on the hand or foot would have to do the business relatively quick. But the murderer carried a good thing too far."

"That's about right. I could hardly face the possibility of such a crime—both Ralph and Sadie were patients of mine; I liked them both—but I'd studied under Charles Bell in London, and one thing we students dared not do before that fierce old man was to overlook symptoms. I protested to myself that such a murder would have been too risky to undertake. This snake would likely crawl out of the bed or betray its presence. Then I thought if a determined killer knew as much about snakes as I did—"

"Yes, sir?" I prompted him when he paused.

"I was raised on a rice plantation near Beaufort, where they were thick. That night the weather was quite cold—the snake would naturally have been very sluggish. Brought into the warm house and put under the heap of quilts it would have grown gradually more alert and dangerous, but not likely stirred for a good while, especially as it had not quite completed digesting a frog, its last meal. One side of the bed was against the wall, the quilts tucked in tightly. When Sadie got in the other side and rolled to her usual place the brute struck her, probably, before she became aware of its presence."

I had an inclination to rub my eyes, so clearly the scene was being re-enacted in the front of them. It was bedtime for Sadie, hard-worked wife of the overseer of Wood Ibis. The night was quite cold and she was grateful for the warm room and the bed with its many quilts: Ralph would soon join her there. I could see her face, almost: a man of ambition such as Ralph—although its seed was barely planted when he had met and married Sadie, then he did not dream its future monstrous growth—would have chosen a wife for a solid farmer to be proud of, a good cook and housekeeper, of pleasant face and disposition, tidy and thrifty, strong like her mother before her. She had washed and braided her hair and put on a clean nightgown and got into what she thought was a clean bed. Suddenly the humble little warm world she had made turned into a pit of horror beyond imagination's pale. And now her very strength served her murderer's bent. Wildly her staunch heart pounded, fiercely driving its head of venom-laden blood to every cell of her body.

"I knew about the frog," Dr. Sams was saying, "because I examined its stomach. But that wasn't the only dissecting I did. Now I'm going to tell you something that I've told only one other person, and that as a grim matter of duty. The person was the sheriff; and when he asked me if I would testify before a coroner's jury that the evidence I had discovered strongly indicated murder, I of course answered that I could not.

"When Ralph killed the snake, his blows missed its head and neck," the doctor went on. "At each side and on top of the neck

106

I found unmistakable trauma—bruised flesh—such as could readily be caused by the pinning down of the head with a forked stick, the countryman's device for catching snakes alive. The bruises were only two or three days old."

"I think you should have given that evidence to a jury."

"What would it have amounted to? Not a presumption—only a suggestion—that a horrible murder had been committed. The snake might have caught its head in a hole in a sunken log. Some slave might have tried to capture it and let it get away. However, you may be right. The real reason I did not testify could be that I'm a moral coward. I've been demonstrating that, for him who has eyes to see, all my life. Why fight what you can't beat? That's my motto."

He spoke this last with a faint, evil smile and in a horrid mockery of self-praise. Then he went again to his cabinet but his hand shook as he filled the glass, and some of the liquor spilled on the floor.

"If the charge of murder had been made," I said, "even though it could not be proved, perhaps the murderer wouldn't have dared try again."

"Do I need you to remind me of it, God damn your soul!"

"It started a fashion of pretty murders, didn't it? A boat that blew up—a runaway slave driven by a pack of dogs to drown himself in the sea—another accused of running away but maybe sent into the swamp by ol' massa, escaping the dogs by climbing a tree and then shot out of it."

"I didn't know that Noel had heard of those incidents. I never wrote him about them."

"Cleo told me, in warning me to stay clear of Saul."

"You've been in communication with her since coming here?"

"Yes."

"Of course she knows you're the boy she knew as Dan Reed."

"No. I reminded her of him, but lied out of it. I was afraid she'd mention me to her father, and when I came here he'd figure me out as you have done—that I'm Noel's adopted son. I know now she wouldn't have mentioned it for anything, still I don't want her to know it."

"Because she would then suspect your real business here?"

"After while, yes. I wouldn't want her to know that the boy she's remembered so long came here to hunt down her father."

"I won't tell her. She loves her father. And she gave you good advice about Saul. I'd better take you into Charleston tomorrow. It will look as though our business has been completed and that there was nothing between you and Cleo. He'll dismiss you from his mind and look for other excitement."

"Dr. Sams, is he as bad—?"

The doctor sat still, as though he were looking at something that he could not believe. "I'll go into that later," he said. "I'll tell you now that his hands are bloody with the blood of those two Negroes. I have no doubt he fired the shot that dropped Slewfoot out of the tree. No one else around here was marksman enough. It came from across a pond three hundred yards wide. He certainly had nothing to do with his mother's death. He loved her deeply— the only person he ever did love, I think—and he was only ten years old."

"Good God, I never imagined he did have anything to do with it! I want to ask you a question. Was Ralph ever known to handle snakes? He had an interest in natural history. You told me about him watching the crane nest—"

"I think he's always had a morbid fear of them. He acts like it, in snake country."

"It would be hard to find a Negro who'd have anything to do with a snake. Was there any white man available to supply him? If so, is he still alive?"

"There was a renegade living in the Santee swamp, making whiskey that he traded to the Negroes for stolen goods—a real swamp rat. His name was Cliff Todd, and last winter—I haven't heard of him since—he was trapping otters on the salt marshes. Listen, Dave. I've talked all I can about this now. Anyway I've told you practically all I know—later, when you come back, I'll try to have recalled details that may or may not be useful to you. I'll lay the ground for you taking a job here in a way that won't look suspicious. Provided—you're determined to go ahead with it."

"I am."

"You're doing it for love of him—not for any reward. Only love —or hate—can engineer such an enterprise as this."

"I reckon you're right."

"Well, I've got to say one more thing before you start. We've talked plain today and this will be mighty plain. You've heard the story of Bluebeard's key. You're going to try to open a locked door to the past. You think you know what you'll find there—but do you?"

"What do you mean, Dr. Sams?"

"I put this forward as the merest possibility, but one you must face. It was the custom of Ralph to get in bed before his wife did. She usually blew out the lamp and locked the door. That night he sat up reading. He was not much of a reader—but Bruce lent him a book."

"That was just an excuse—"

"Assume, for the moment, that the death waiting in that bed was meant for him. He had one implacable enemy—a man whom he'd crippled for life in a cruel game played when both were boys."

I felt nothing but aching cold. "Go on, please, sir."

"He was far more intelligent than his brothers Ralph and Bruce. After his injury, he devoted himself to reading and became highly educated. It caused him to look down on their mentalities—sometimes he made remarks indicating that he held them both in contempt, even while he envied desperately their strong bodies. What counts the most, he asked—physical or intellectual strength? Who had the greater right to the prizes of life? I told how he seemed to live in Bruce. But I'll tell you now I've never known a more ruthless man than Noel Dunbarton, or a more cunning one."

"I wish you'd hurry this up. Granted he might want to kill Ralph. But Ralph lived—and Bruce died."

"I'll give you the rest—the horrid, remote possibility that I warned you you must consider. Suppose Ralph had died in agony, instead of Sadie. No one would blame a helpless cripple—so the scheme went—no one knew his resources by which, for instance, he was able later to steal two portraits and a pair of candlesticks from Ibis Hall. True, I don't know that he turned the deal, and no one else but Lizzie Neilson ever dreamed it might be he, but I had no real doubt. But if that horrid deathtrap was Noel's work, which

God forbid, it killed the wrong person. Noel would not dare strike again for some months—and this time not directly at Ralph. Could it be that he struck at Bruce, figuring that his covetous brother Ralph would be hanged for the crime? If so, that crime too went wrong. Noel was seen dropping something into the sea—one man said he *thought* he saw him do it—I who said nothing *did* see him do it, drunk as I was that day. People found in him a more likely suspect than they found in Ralph. He was a marked man—and not always in his right mind."

"I can see the next step in your reasoning," I said, my voice husky with cold. "He still thinks that a murder he committed himself can send Ralph to the gallows. That's the job he's given me."

"There—or to his grave by a shorter route. Hasn't he ever suggested more direct punishment for a fratricide? You're a desperate man, Dave—and a dangerous one."

"But you haven't supplied the motive for murdering the brother who always befriended him—who gave him a plantation—"

"If you're looking for a motive, he had the strongest in the world. Bruce, who could hardly read and write, had married the woman whom Noel loved with the most desperate, mad, tragic love I've ever seen."

Dr. Sams dropped into a chair, his hands limp on his lap. "Well, I've said it," he went on. "I want you to know I don't believe it. It's only the worst possibility imaginable."

I already knew he did not believe it. What I did not know was why he had gone to such pains, employed such ingenuity, to show that Ralph was not the only suspect.

"But the truth, whatever it is, will be bad enough," he went on, his eyes haunted with visions. "If it's brought to light, all of us may wish we'd never been born."

"Those are strong words, Dr. Sams."

"Dave! Dave! Forgive me all I've said—forgive my frantic fears. But if these were murders and not strange accidents, the truth will be an awful thing. I tell you it will be abominable beyond abomination. The evil done here will be beyond the name of evil."

Pa saw me enter our gate and rushed with such slow rushing to the porch to greet me. I knew then that we loved each other and he had not sent me on an evil errand. If he had committed what in man's sight was high crime—and I did not believe a word of it—it had been an act of madness. I would protect him, as far as possible, from the consequences. Through that madness I had become his son.

The brisk wind off the Bay blew his thin, pale-colored hair. He gazed up at me, from down under his forehead, his back in pitiful arch. After its first flush of joy at my return, his face wore an expression of harrowing anxiety. So the door had hardly closed ere I must speak.

"It's all right, Pa."

"What, what? I do not know what you mean."

"Dr. Sams is going to give me a job on Little Ibis. It will be ready for me when spring comes, and will be a fine base of operations."

"That is good news. You have done well, Dan, I know. Have you had supper?"

"I'm not hungry—"

"Eat a bowl of bread and milk, the same as you did on your first night in my house. Then you may give me the news of Wood Ibis."

We spoke little during the simple meal and, I thought, had never felt closer to each other. The brief daylight was failing as we finished, and Pa started to light the whale-oil lamp.

"Why not sit by candlelight, from candlesticks out of Ibis Hall?"

"I never told you they came from there."

"Cleo Dunbarton mentioned their being stolen, about the time she was born."

"They were not D'Arcy candlesticks—perhaps she told you that. They were a gift from my brother Bruce to his bride, bought with his humble earnings. I could not suffer my brother Ralph to sit by them."

"Let them be a token of full trust between you and me."

"I see you have come into your full manhood." He lighted the candles, their flames reflected in flickering bright points in his eyes. "If you ask what I may answer in full knowledge, that I will do."

"You've never said, in so many words, that Ralph killed his brother Bruce. Can you now?"

"Nay, I cannot. I did not see him do it."

"It would strengthen my hand a great deal if you could establish the innocence of all others on and about the plantation. Not that I have any real doubt."

Pa sat still so long that I thought he might not have heard me. "Why, then, do you ask?" he replied at last.

"I'm bound to do so."

"I cannot establish their innocence, including my own."

"I ask you to be patient with me. Others deeply involved in Bruce's life were his former sweetheart Lizzie Neilson, and his wife Madeline. Saul Dunbarton was only ten years old. There are no more unless I count Dr. Sams."

"You speak, Dan, as might an officer, investigating an unknown crime. But speak on."

"Was Dr. Sams living thereabouts at the time?"

"Aye, Honoré D'Arcy, Madeline's father, had employed him as his personal physician—he was then in failing health—and to see to all others on the plantation, including the two hundred or more Negroes. He was quartered at his present abode, then called the Summer House, and part of Wood Ibis. He continued to live there after Little Ibis was detached from the main plantation and deeded to me."

"Was he in love with Madeline?"

"He always was, and always will be," Pa told me with gleaming eyes. "He was neither blind nor dull."

"Would he have had an opportunity to rig the explosion that killed Bruce?"

"I do not think so. The powder arrived only the day before. On the preceding day Dr. Sams had begun a drinking bout of his tragic solitary kind. He was deep in its effects throughout the period and, I believe, helpless."

"Will you tell me where you were living then? I'd like to know the lay of the land."

"My brother Bruce had given me quarters, with separate board, on the ground floor of Ibis Hall. He was going to build a carriage road across the swamp to Little Ibis, whereupon I would live there with Dr. Sams."

"If the coroner had found that Bruce was murdered, the sheriff would have questioned Madeline."

"You, Dan, may question me."

"I don't like to do it."

"Madeline loved my brother Bruce enough to reject all her high-born suitors and to make him, hitherto her overseer, her lord and the lord of Wood Ibis. It so happened that she had gone to Combahee to visit a sick uncle when these events occurred. I was present when the summons arrived and saw her reluctance to leave him even for a few days." The sweat came out on Pa's face and he drew a slow, deep breath and spoke on. "She was a girl of deep and lovely passion, and could not get enough of lying in his arms."

"I have heard that Lizzie Neilson loved him too. At least the report was, she expected to marry him."

"Poor Lizzie was not to blame for loving my brother. But even when merely overseer, he was far too great a prize for such as she. I think she took his loss in good part. She spoke spitefully of Madeline, but bore neither her nor Bruce any great ill will."

"Well, then, I'm satisfied, except on one point. It would occur to anyone trying Ralph for his brother's murder. How could he know he would profit by it, unless Madeline had already promised that he would? I do not accuse her. I only want to know the answer."

"The answer is, his vaulting ambition and malign heart. The position of overseer was the first round of his audacious ladder. But when he reached it, he was not content—he had seen his own brother leap from there to that dizzy height. Was he not the better man of the two? Had not Madeline given him secret signs of favor? Oh, that he could be at once so cunning and so blind! Oh, that to the wicked all things are wicked, and God would

113

suffer the innocent, by their very innocence, to provoke evil! Madeline was too trustful to be wise. When Bruce invited his brother to sit at his table, Madeline received him with a sisterly kiss and plenteous welcome, oblivious to his faults, thinking that because he was Bruce's brother, he too must be of noble mind and heart. When she lay blissful with her beloved, rejoicing in his manly strength that went with his manly soul, could she picture his brother lying awake, taut with evil passions, hating the poor woman who lay beside him—one of two obstacles between him and his goal—busy with his plots to wipe both from his path? He had reduced to tottering impotency one brother of whom he had been jealous—if he had accomplished so much as a boy, how much more could he do as a man? Oh, he had learned his lesson young! He had maimed one without punishment being visited upon him. Need he hold his hand from the other?"

I had fallen under the spell of Pa's voice and was startled when it ceased. Comprehending fully every word, yet I had only the vaguest sense of the passage of time. I looked at him, his head bowed over the table, his face white but almost expressionless.

"Madeline married him six months after Bruce's murder, for which the blind world blamed her," Pa went on, as though he had lifted his bow again. "She did not wait even the customary year. But I tell you, it was because she mourned her husband more, not less. Had she waited a little longer, she would have found out who this was, who paid her such bashful court. So she was seduced and betrayed, and who can wonder, when he was able to deceive even you!"

Tears came into my eyes not of shame as much as of redemption. They were the kind that penitents and converts shed, when they know that their breach with the father-power is healing and they will be taken back within the law and the love.

"You are not to blame," Pa told me in a gentle voice. "Sometimes I too have doubted Satan in this world, thinking that what seemed evil was only the lack of enough good. It is the way of weak-spirited man. If there are two possible motives for one's wrong-doing, one good and one evil, we will believe the good one. If, of the two, one is more evil than the other, we will believe the lesser. Not so, the staunch tall men of olden time! They did not flinch, weak-kneed, faint-hearted, from the reality of the Devil, miraculously born in God's world. They sought him out in every den and corner where he laid his ambush, and did battle with him. They smote his children hip and thigh. Those who loved him they punished with fire and sword, and left them for a feast for ravens.

"Hark to me well! When I first told you of my mark, I said that Ralph had not meant to break my back, only to make me cry in cruel sport. I looked into your face, that of a little child, and, lying to myself, I lied to you. Could I not be so generous to my mother's son out of my father's loins? It was not generosity, but cowardice. I hated him, but not enough to stand beside Jehovah against Baal! Ralph had discovered that my mind was far better than his. My body was weaker, from infant fever, but it was mending and would soon be as strong or stronger. He wanted me broken at his feet, so I could never race with him to any goal."

Pa began rising from his chair, his wildly shaking hand on the knob of his cane, speaking on meanwhile, his voice strengthening as his head rose higher. "If you still doubt, if your heart is still hardened against me and softened unto my enemy by its love for his daughter, then behold him dealing with his horse or dog that has lost him a race for a prize. If you are still weakened for the battle toward, even as was Samson in Delilah's arms, watch him punish a slave who by mistake or misdemeanor brooked a jot of his greed. Behold me, now—mark me well—as I stand as tall as I ever can again. My bowed back will break again ere it lifts another inch—my heart presses upward against the rigid arch of twisted bone until it fain would break—what do I care for pain if it will raise my head a jot? But no pain will avail."

I cried to him to stop his torment and mine—frantic words as one gasps out in a nightmare and as instantly forgotten—and he stood still as I wiped the sweat from his face. But he was not done with me yet. I must be chastised with rods and scorpions for my whoring after false gods.

"My brother left me broken at his feet, lest I race with him," Pa went on. "Did he do his work well? Watch closely, Dan—at this pace could I win the goal? Yet it is my fastest." Pa had brushed away my hands and was scurrying up and down the room. I dared not seize and hold him and could only reel along beside him, to catch him if he fell. "See, I strive with all my might and main," he gasped. "But I cannot hasten more by one jot or tittle. If tongues of flame were licking at my feet—if sheets of fire leaped in pursuit—still I could go no faster. If Madeline stood with outstretched hand, promising her hand to him who won the race, *smiling in radiant beauty—still I could not—*"

But that vision drove him to a final, convulsive effort. His frantic scurry became a hideous run; then he toppled into my arms. I carried him to his bed, where he lay panting, his face as white as the sheet. It seemed to me that he slept a moment or two, then, discovering me in a chair beside him, he gave me a weary smile.

"You made one mistake, Pa," I told him, after I had served him a drink of whiskey.

"I know of one. A very great mistake. But perhaps you have discovered another."

"If Madeline had waited a year before marrying Ralph, she still wouldn't have found him out. She hasn't found him out yet. You should know that, by her continuing to live with him."

"Does she—live—with him?"

"As far as I know. If she ever loved him, I think that love is dead, but she seems to be fond of him."

"It is a wonderful mask he wears."

"Nor has his daughter Cleo found him out. She loves him very much. However she may have weakened my will, for a little while, it was not by intention. She's completely innocent and guiltless."

"That brings to mind the other mistake—of letting you sail with her on the same ship, the shores of restraint lost behind you. Tell me, Dan. Speak plainly. Have you lain with her in the embrace of love?"

"No."

He had spoken in low, quiet tones but I had sensed an extreme urgency all but concealed behind them and in his white still face. It seemed to me that my answer had relieved it.

"Then never do. Let it not come to pass, no matter the temptation, the wildest hunger, the safest retreat, even in the transport of honored love. But resist loving her, even if you see her as Madeline incarnate. Close your heart to her. Avoid any pass whereby you might fall under her spell. Every jot and tittle of love you bear the daughter will reduce by that much the hate you bear the sire."

"I will do the best I can."

"That's all I ask." A beautiful expression stole into his haggard face. "Now is there something that you desire of me?"

"I want to hear you play in our picture-room. But I think it had better wait until I've done a hard chore in preparation for my return to Wood Ibis."

"Very well."

"It will take at least three months and keep me away from Baltimore almost the whole time. I'll come back only to get Dr. Sams's letters and to answer them. I'll be up and down the Bay, and perhaps as far south as Currituck Sound in unseasonably warm weather. It's something we both overlooked in our preparations and very necessary."

Not wanting to tell him what the task was, lest it worry him, I weakened and did so. It was simply to gain enough skill with rifle and shotgun that in some all-too-imaginable instant of trial I could be a better match for Saul. That task I performed, working at it early and late, and in all weathers. To put hand to it I had only to get a job as a market-hunter on one of the boats supplying the poultryers with wild ducks, geese, and swans. A rifle was not a good arm for these slaughterings. I had to buy one, and powder and balls, out of my pay; and I practiced with it on distant targets in otherwise idle hours. There was usually time at midday to fire fifty or a hundred rounds, and although I would be hard put to it to shoot a Negro out of a tree at three hundred yards, by mid-March I could make a fair score at swimming ducks at a third that distance. I left swivel gun shooting to others, as far as I could, but never missed a chance to shoot from a blind, taking the birds as they bunched or passed one another in the darting, dipping, towering flocks. Almost always one plummeted down ere the smoke cloud whisked away, and sometimes two or three. The nip and tuck of timing quickened my eye and hand. Through practice with a fowling-piece, my rifle began to level more quickly and surely. I learned many a stratagem of hiding from the sharp-eyed fowl, not the least being to stay perfectly still until they were in range, and many a trick of stalking them through reeds and squashy muck. Even the spyglass eyes of the Canada goose were no match for my wiles. Once I staggered to the boat with fifteen of the big birds after an hour's shooting.

In mid-March the flocks thinned, and in early April only a few stragglers remained. I collected my small wages and counted my great gains: even the time spent in the task did double-duty, for Dr. Sams had prepared for my return with patient cunning and care. Several letters had passed between us, which the Dunbartons had either seen or discussed. His decision to enlarge his stables had been reached, it seemed, after due forethought; he had had advice from experts and a beautifully forged letter recommending me as his foreman. Now I received his final letter offering me the job, and bidding me assume its duties on the first day of May.

"Dan, do you think I'm a good violinist?" Pa asked, on the night of our leave-taking.

"I've never heard your equal."

"I learned all I know of the violin after I left Little Ibis. I had some bent for music—at least I loved it—but no money to take lessons. It is said that a violinist must begin young. Yet violin playing was one of the few pursuits by which I could earn bread and a certain solace for my loss, and in two years I was the best in Philadelphia. Remember that, when a task seems too hard."

He played first to Bruce—an elegy to a fallen captain, splendid heroic passages interwoven with dirge-like strains—and if Pa did not love him his fiddle lied in its throat. The tribute ended in the resounding oaths of soldiers amid clashing steel. His custom was to address Madeline next, but instead he fixed his eyes on the portrait of Ralph, and it seemed to me the soaring strains cast a shadow like Furies in flight almost to his feet.

Every time Pa had played our Oratorio the strains had varied somewhat; and today he told Madeline something I had never heard him tell her before. It seemed a new sub-theme introduced into the fugue, and I had an impression of deep remorse for some wrong he had done her. I knew Pa's playing well. I had long ago learned to know his moods, almost to read his mind, by its strains. Though it did not make sense, I felt downcast and afraid.

Most of the music was a sensuous tribute paid to her beauty; but the portrait with its golden crown and jeweled eyes dimmed in my sight, and a face of sharper contrasts and more strange fashioning rose between. The hazel eyes had a quiet, lovely glimmer. I had kissed the long, grave lips and they pressed again to mine, making for both of us an undiscovered bliss. Still it was no more than an old haunting, the echo of a lost, forbidden passion.

The violin sang no more, and there came to me another echo out of the past.

"I wish the house would burn down and every acre sink into the sea."

CHAPTER

14

The beaches of the outer islands seemed little changed since I had seen them last—long and low and brown, with palm scrub beyond—and the riverbanks had the same aspect save for a richer green. Only when Captain Weaver put into Little Ibis did I surmise what spring had wrought in the Low Country. It was no mere change of color and temperature but one of mood, almost a transfiguration as occurs to things in dreams, as though a farmer's slattern daughter, drowsy in the daytime, a little strange-looking and -acting but not alien to the house, became at night a vampire. You had the feeling not that the sun had moved north, rather that the land had shifted, bag and baggage, a long way south. Wood Ibis had come into its own as a tropic kingdom.

A little browner of skin and a few pounds off in weight, Dr. Sams greeted me with a business-like air. Had I a good trip down? I had brought real summer with me: few could remember a milder, pleasanter April than had just passed. Presently a houseboy "took care" of my belongings and the doctor and I were seated in his office behind a closed door. Startling to me was how close I felt to him, the due of his feeling of closeness to me, wrought in my absence by his lonely heart. To him I was not only Noel's son and ambassador, not only Noel himself—a kind of reincarnation with an unbroken back—but in some measure he himself, a deputy Dr. Sams, sans his moral cowardice and weight of years.

"I kept thinking that at the last minute you wouldn't come," he told me.

"I don't see how you got that impression."

"It wasn't an impression. It just seemed to make good sense. The rest doesn't, you know—as I told you before, it's madness—or else an awful kind of sanity that lies on the other side. I confess a faint hope you wouldn't come—a hope I'm ashamed of but it never weakened the strong need and desire that you would. You can understand that, and forgive it."

"Yes, sir. But there never was the slightest doubt."

"I knew that, too, despite the vagaries. How did you leave Noel?"

"Just the same. He's deeply grateful to you for arranging everything for me."

"I've arranged only a place for you to live and work from. That I've done successfully, for no one at Ibis Hall has the least suspicion of your real business here. Well, I'll except Granny. Who can guess what goes on in her senile mind? I have a sneaking belief in second sight, and she's always had a little of it—perhaps more than a little. But she hates Ralph and is in mortal fear of her grandson Saul and, whatever she divines about you, she won't tell anyone. Both men are mildly interested in your apparent business and in no way adverse to it. Cleo has convinced them that the flirtation never did amount to much and is water over the dam. She herself has evinced no curiosity about you. That may not be very flattering but it's certainly for the best."

"I agree with you heartily as to that."

"Just take pains that she doesn't become interested in you again. Ralph has only to lift his hand to take over Little Ibis and put us both off—unless, of course, Noel comes back to life. For the time being Saul is amusing himself with his hounds and a young witch of a quadroon he bought at Port Royal and installed in one of the cabins. But if you give him the least reason to think you're worth hunting, God help you."

"I'll have nothing to do with Cleo at all."

"I wish that could be true, but it won't be. You're bound to run into her every few days and a great deal will depend on your manner toward her. However, you'll have very little occasion to enter Ibis Hall. It would be improper for you to call there, now you've taken a foreman's job. Of course if Ralph or Saul invite you, you'll have to go."

"I'd like to renew my acquaintance with Lizzie."

"Well, we'll ride over there today. Her husband, Sam Childer, has arranged for me a shipment of marl at a low price—I'm going to sweeten some sour land close to Little Run. I think it will pay you to spend a good many evenings with her and Sam."

We ate a farmer's midday meal and went out to the paddock. Dr. Sams had bought a fair English hunter stallion; with his stylish

Hackney and big Jack we had the makings of a small, general stud farm by which we could improve the breeds of saddle and carriage horses and work-mules throughout the region. He had some part-thoroughbred brood mares and intended to buy more; Little Ibis afforded plenty of grain and year-round pasture for the colts. The job of supervision would keep me fairly busy and necessitate frequent visits to surrounding plantations; but two black henchmen, Joshua and Ben, who could "speak horse" if any linguist ever could, would relieve me of many a night watch and allow plenty of leisure for other pursuits.

"So you're back," Lizzie greeted me bluffly, when the doctor and I dropped in at Turtle Inlet. She was wearing a loose cotton dress with scanty, if any, petticoats, its whiteness accenting the pleasant sun tan and wind brown of her plain attractive face; also her sturdy, woman figure was well presented. "I knew we hadn't seen the last of you."

"Are you a Circe among other things, Lizzie?" Dr. Sams asked.

"It didn't take a Circe to know that much. Doc, are you a little Cupid among other things?"

"A Cupid only to amorous mares and lusty stallions."

"Dave, shake hands with my man, Sam Childer."

I did so, finding him self-respecting, plain, hardy, and salty. He let Lizzie do the talking for both of them but plainly she esteemed him highly.

"Cupid has achieved some wonderful feats down here," Lizzie went on, her eyes shining into mine. "It must be the climate. I expect great things of you, Dave."

Dr. Sams and Sam Childer went out to look at some stores. Lizzie served me a drink of fine Cuban rum from a flask kept behind the counter.

"I'm afraid the opportunities here aren't what they once were," I told her, to get on with our game.

"Why not?"

"Assuming the princess would follow the example set by the queen, how would I get rid of Mr. Saul?"

Her face, for a brief second, became very still. When she spoke it was in the same jovial tone but with a different expression of eyes.

"Do you refer to his little game of dog-in-the-manger?"

"Well, I've heard a lot of gossip about the royal family since I was here last. A cat can look at a king, you know—and hear the rumors."

"That game doesn't take much of his time. Mighty few young men come to Ibis Hall." Lizzie laughed harshly.

"I hear she has no dower to interest young planters hereabouts. Is Saul heir presumptive?"

"Heir apparent." She put back the jug and I thought she was taking the opportunity to get her voice and countenance under strict control. "It's pretty late for the queen to present Ralph with a crown prince. Even if she did, this late in the day—I doubt if he could nose out Saul. Quite a fellow, Saul."

"He impresses me a good deal."

"Not a good fellow to fall foul of, as the saying goes."

"I reckon he won't be interested in a neighbor foreman."

"You'd be surprised the people that Saul gets interested in. Almost anyone who allows himself to get interested in the Dunbarton family. But you'll be pretty busy with Doc's mares and studs. Maybe that's a good thing."

"Well—thanks."

"You're a newcomer here and Sam and I are right neighborly people. You seem very likable, in spite of a lot going on behind that stolid-looking jib that nobody knows about. To stop joking—it would be a good thing if you don't look above your station."

"Would you like to speak a little plainer? I'd be much obliged."

"Yes, I will. I'm a fool. Cleo would be very lucky to get you, I think. I know you'd be damned unlucky to get her. Let it go at that."

"Well, I'd like to drop in here often, to pass the time pleasantly."

She changed the subject to fishing—her husband would give me some fine sport with red drum—and presently Dr. Sams was ready to leave. We visited the pastures, made plans for the farm, and ate supper. After the meal we sat on his small veranda, amid failing light and deepening stillness. We heard a great horned owl trumpeting his feasts of blood, and a 'gator bellowing his lordship of the waters, and a sweet-voiced mockingbird humble and happy in her bowers, but were out of hearing of everyone but each other, so I told him my day's gains.

"So I want to ask your advice again about taking Lizzie into my confidence," I told him.

"I'm more than ever convinced you should keep your secret," he answered. "You, too, suspected her spite against Madeline was put on—it's a little too shrill. What if her real feeling was idolatry? Plain girls such as she was, often idolize such great beauties as Madeline—live in them—real heroine-worship. If so, she'd be ashamed of it—hearty, earthy, realistic woman that she is—and make fun of it. It was rather borne out by what happened some months after the marriage. Madeline visited French kinfolk in New Orleans—the old city went wild about her, by the way—and Bruce, very lonesome, began dropping over to Turtle Inlet. What did Lizzie do but take off herself? I think she was running away from temptation and, if so, it wasn't from moral scruples—although she has her own code. I think it was for Madeline's sake. The Bull Islanders thought that the marriage was breaking up, and Lizzie wasn't going to help the smash along."

The skin tightened over the bones of Dr. Sams's face giving it a masklike aspect. "Madeline came back," he went on. "I *knew* she would."

"And I shouldn't confide in Lizzie, because she doesn't want Madeline's house pulled down?"

"That's about right."

If so, Lizzie and Madeline were strange bedfellows. There was too much crawling into wrong beds around here, Granny had told me.

"I want to ask you something, Dr. Sams. If Ralph killed Bruce, does Saul know it?"

Dr. Sams reached for his decanter, drank, and set the glass down with a trembling hand. "Dave, I believe that for the last few years he's been as sure of it as—you are."

"As you are?"

"I didn't say that."

"Do you realize that then he'd be reasonably sure that it wasn't Ralph's first murder?"

The doctor's face was turning gray in my sight. "Saul's a bad man. He could easily stand the thought of his father committing fratricide that so benefited himself. But the other—his own mother —Dave, it's unthinkable."

"If he does suspect it, he and Ralph are strange bedfellows."

"I won't admit the possibility."

"So are Ralph and Madeline, when you come down to it."

"Dave, if you as much as hint that Madeline suspects by now that Ralph killed Bruce, I'll have to ask you to leave. I know that the thought must have crossed her mind in some dreadful moment of despondency, but she wouldn't treat with it. Every word and action show that. I'm sorry to take that stand toward you, but I must."

"I shouldn't have said that. I beg your pardon." I was begging Pa's too—more than that, his forgiveness. "It's no wonder she couldn't imagine Ralph committing such a crime. He doesn't look or act or talk like a man who could commit even a common murder, let alone those two. He doesn't give me the impression of being that crafty and resolute. It troubled me a lot—"

I was holding Dr. Sams's brief, I thought—explaining well Madeline's blindness—but to my amazement he interrupted me in a voice harsh with inward torment.

"My God, didn't he break Noel's back?"

I made haste to vary the subject. "Will you tell me, Dr. Sams, why you think Saul suspects the second murder?"

"Yes, although the evidence is like the rest—rather vague. You mentioned Bert—an intelligent mulatto who tried to run and swam out to sea and drowned to escape Saul's hounds. He'd been whipped within an inch of his life on at least three occasions and couldn't face it again. In each case the charge was trumped up, my man told me—the real reason was he knew something he wouldn't tell. It was something that went back to that bad winter when Sadie and Bruce were killed. Saul took charge of that torture and Ralph consented to it—according to my informant."

"Bert knew something he'd die rather than tell?"

"That's the impresssion I got."

"Who was he protecting? Would he be capable of protecting anyone that far?"

"If you don't know it already—some of the most noble hearts and minds in this world belong to 'niggers.'"

"Who do you think might have won such loyalty from him?"

Dr. Sams helped himself to another drink. "I was afraid you'd ask that and I tried to ward it off. I dread answering you—but I will. Bert had belonged to Honoré D'Arcy. He was Bruce's account-keeper, being much better at figures and a better reader and writer than the master—and attached to him, I believe. But he was much closer to Noel, who'd furnished him with books and talked with him about them. Not to mince words, he loved Noel. Do you know how deeply one man can love another in nobility and honor? It's a rare thing but it passeth understanding. Bert was the kind to go to hell without an instant's hesitation if it would help Noel."

"Well," I said with deliberation and a great surge of my heart, "I'm glad of that."

Dr. Sams's eyes became luminous, then deep and still.

"What could Bert have known about Pa that he would die by torture rather than tell?" I went on. "Please talk plain."

"I tell you, I don't know. It wasn't just that Noel's alive. Noel authorized me to reveal it in an emergency and would have done the same to Bert."

"It must have been evidence so black against Pa that Bert thought it would send him to the gallows."

"Good God, Dave!"

"It would make no difference to me. But it might have been an even more terrible secret. Anyway—Bert has begun to loom mighty large in this affair."

"One of four who are dead. Bruce, Sadie, Bert, Slewfoot."

"Slewfoot went into the swamp for unknown reasons, was accused of running away, the dogs were set on him, and Saul shot him out of a tree. Did this occur after or before Bert's murder?"

"Afterward. Bert was killed five years ago. Slewfoot only last year."

"It took me too long to grow up and get here, didn't it? At least there was a chance—if Pa could have moved sooner—sent someone to wage relentless war against Ralph and Saul—those two murders would have been prevented."

"You talk plain, Dave, but I'll not gainsay you. I'll not curse again for speaking the truth. Let the chips fall where they may! In this case, at my feet. I was here—I was free to act—in my heart

I knew that each of those four deaths was by horridly wicked, cold-blooded murder. I've never said that before to any man. I never said it in plain words to myself, but I knew, God help me— I could not save myself from knowing. But I thought every one was the last. I went to my bottle, stroked and comforted myself with its oblivion and its lies, retreated a little more. Have we seen the last even now? I wish I could believe it."

"You weren't free to act, Dr. Sams. I can feel that. I'm free to act and must stay that way. Have you any idea how Slewfoot's murder was related to the others. What was his relationship with Ralph and Saul?"

"I never knew him well. He seemed rather stupid or at least childish—a somewhat low-type Negro. Ralph used to have him for an errand-runner and handy-man helper and later Saul used him as a boatman. There was no apparent reason for him to try to run away. My Negroes whispered that Saul sent him into the swamps on some trumped-up errand and then rang the bell and set the pack on his trail. But what he knew of danger to them I can't imagine."

A rather stupid, at least childish, somewhat low-type Negro. He rose too plain before my eyes, black, kinky-headed, broad-nosed, heavy-jawed. He laughed extravagantly at Saul's jokes; he boasted among his fellows of the confidence "young massa" put in him; when the two were out in the same boat, they were more like friends than master and slave. One day last year Saul had put enough confidence in him to send him on a secret mission into the swamp. Thin and pretty from the distance came the brassy ringing of the bell. . . .

"Wonder why dey ringin' 'at bell! Aint time for de han' to come in from de field. Dey ringing it mighty fast, wonder if one of de buildin' done caught fiah." . . . Faint on the breeze, a little riffle on the tarn of silence, there stole to him another sound; he had to stop and listen, his head lifted, to make sure. ". . . Sound like dem hound o' Massa Saul's. Dey raising sand, sound like he gone huntin' wif 'em. . . . Dey sho raisin' sand, like dey hot on de scent. . . . Wonder whedder dey chasin' a bear or a bobcat? Critter mus' be runnin' dis way, sound gittin' louder. . . . Sound gittin' louder and closer sho nuff, look like de bear or de bobcat

127

might run right pas' me. . . . Don't reckon one of 'em new niggers run away. He don't know what good for him, if he try. Maybe dat why dey ring de bell, given de 'larm. Hope he don't come runnin' by me, for dem dogs mighty mean. . . . Dey gittin' mighty close, but no call for me to start runnin'. . . . De bayin' gittin' mighty loud, but no bear or bobcat run by me yit, or runaway nigger. Massa Saul done tol' me to go into swamp, runnin' he errand. He know I aint runnin' away, and Ol' Massa know it too. . . . But it look like . . . it sho look like dem dogs got off de scent and got on my scent by mistake. . . . *Dey comin'! Dey comin' sho! Hee dey come right whar I done cross de branch on de log. . . . Jesus mercy hee dey come . . . .*"

"I once thought there couldn't be a worse crime than fratricide," I remarked to Dr. Sams.

"Well—there is." He was looking at a ghost hidden from me, in the darkness by the river.

"It's beginning to look as if blowing up Bruce in a boat was a fairly decent job, by comparison."

"I warned you, Dave."

"What is the source of all this evil? Does it steam out of hell through a hole in the floor of Ibis Hall?"

"There's kind of a hole here that seems symbolic of evil. The Swamp. The hot sun above and the primordial muck below. There's a lust for growth and fructification—rapacious, ruthless, heartless—dedicated to Ashtoreth instead of to God. Even speaking as a onetime physician, I think it affects us all. And granted a cancer of ambition and greed devouring Ralph—"

"You once said that only love or hate could engineer my undertaking here—to let light into these malignant swamps so that murder will out and be avenged. I would think that only love or hate could have engineered the whole event."

"Overweening ambition and greed are symptoms of self-love that has become poisonous. And mark you, Dave—when we jest about the king and queen and crown prince there's many a true word spoken. Wood Ibis was founded by the truly regal D'Arcys, French aristocrats of the haughtiest sort, with a name as old as Bourbon or Valois. René D'Arcy had a divine-right doctrine—and utter contempt for American civilization and law. We are only a day's ride from Charleston but he didn't give a damn. As you know, Wood Ibis produces everything consumed here except luxuries, and those are got by direct trading with Europe. Wood Ibis pays no excise, even the slaves are imported direct from Africa. René set up what amounted to a small absolute monarchy, with a bailiff and his family subject to his law, two hundred or more serfs over whom he had not nominally but actually the power of life and death, and built a castle from which to reign over it. He used intelligent slaves as foremen instead of illiterate whites—Ralph still does. Madeline rebelled so strongly against the monstrous folly that she committed at least the well-meant, high-minded folly of marrying a commoner. But don't you see how a false sense of values could come into force here—'I am the State'—'The king can do no wrong'—? Amoral—godless? Ralph saw his brother made king —why not he? Not just a plantation owner but husband to Madeline and monarch of all he surveyed?

"I hinted there might be other killings," he went on after a moment's brooding. "Why not, if Ralph is another Roman king of the wood, winning his kingdom by murder, knowing if he loses it through the truth coming out, he will also lose his life? Saul is the heir apparent. And you, Dave, are no adversary to be defeated by half-measures. You're a young man as age is reckoned, yet you've spent fifteen years preparing for this task. Isn't that true?"

"Yes."

"It doesn't astonish me, knowing Noel. A ruthless, implacable avenger. Still, if he'd picked the wrong boy out of the Orphanage —but I reckon he took great pains with the choice."

"He looked us all over many times. But I think my hand had something to do with it. It was a little mark, he said, to go with his great mark."

"I noticed the slight deformity the first night you were here. Were you born with it, or is it the result of injury?"

"I have no way of knowing."

"May I see it, please?"

"Certainly."

He put on eyeglasses and looked closely at the little finger immovable against my palm, and then felt the bone.

"I would say it's an injury occurring in rather late infancy." But he could not explain the diagnosis. It was by perceptions so faint that they could not be attributed to any one sense and seemed to him like intuition. Doctors learned by long experience to receive and integrate such dim impressions.

"There is a great deal of something like intuition in successful medical practice," he went on, taking what he called his nightcap. "I could not tell you why I think so, but it comes to me that this little infirmity might have affected you more than you know. Abandonment at the Orphanage and the kind of life children live in such places affected you far more, of course—it could be called a wound to the soul. Well, that fits in with a theory of mine. If it's true it would explain why you're here, fit for the job before you."

"What is the theory?"

"I'll give it in five words—but not elaborate on it. Just think it over. *Only the lame can love.*"

CHAPTER

15

If it were true, only the lame can hate. That was the other's inexorable corollary. I knew that my love for Pa cast a long, black shadow.

Full into that shadow—rode Saul. He came my third day at Little Ibis, mainly on business with Dr. Sams, partly for a look at me compared to his memories of me. I hoped these last were not too vivid. Spring had come since we met; now full summer was at hand; time, like tide, had swept slowly but evenly across this island kingdom since then, scouring no new deeps, forming no bars, leaving little flotsam on the shores. He had fished and hunted, helped Ralph direct the planting, let Cleo alone while he played more gratifying games with his new, pretty quadroon, and apparently had taken only a neighborly interest in Dr. Sams's enlargement of his stock farm. He sprang down with horsemanly grace, immensely vital, his pale-colored eyes brilliant in contrast with his olive-colored skin, handsome, and superbly free.

"Hello, Dan," he burst out, enveloping my big hand with his.

Thank God, I had learned to control my countenance when a bread and slop thief in the Orphanage. Dr. Sams looked hard at the horses.

"I see you've forgotten my first name," I told him, grinning.

"I beg your pardon! It was Dave, wasn't it? How did I get the idea it was Dan!" Then and there he put a boy whom Cleo had loved, Dan Reed by name, out of his mind. "I'm glad the doc persuaded you to come."

"I didn't need much persuading. It's the opportunity I've been looking for, and I'm out to make good."

"Well, it's a worthy enterprise. The horseflesh in these parts can certainly stand a little improvement. So can the nigger-flesh," he went on, looking at weazened little Joshua who was grooming Lizzie. "How about it, boy?"

"Yes *suh* boss!" Joshua cried, showing all his teeth in a grin.

"Why don't you and the doc import three or four two-legged

stallions straight from Africa?" Saul asked, turning again to me. "The size of Obo, say, but with more vim? Up country, where slaves are few, they are at least getting more brains bred into them, along with more white in their skins. Down here they stay black and dumb, African savagery dying out and nothing taking its place, and getting lazier and more thieving every day."

I did not think he had any ulterior motive in saying this. He was entertained by the notion and its impact on Dr. Sams and me.

"I hear that Sally, Cato's young and pretty wench, had a mighty bright baby a few weeks ago," Dr. Sams remarked. "Maybe that will help a little."

"Yes, but I can't begin to make the rounds on such a big plantation, and you won't lend a hand. You and the rest of the Low Country gentry are too damned toney and our most valuable livestock is being neglected. How about you, Dave? Wouldn't you like to be remembered as a father of your country?"

"I've got other ambitions, Mr. Saul."

"Well, that's commendable. There are a lot of pretty young girls at Georgetown and about, some of them with broad acres." If that was a warning to stay away from Cleo, he had put it neatly and diplomatically, and I could see nothing but buoyant spirits in his big, broad face.

"Speaking of thieving," he went on, addressing Dr. Sams in a more business-like tone low enough to be inaudible to Joshua, "it's started up again at Wood Ibis. We've lost a couple of wagon loads of rye and some other stuff. We haven't got our man yet—but we think we know who it is—and are hoping to set a trap for him. I rode over to ask you if you have any reason to think it's going out through Turtle Inlet."

"Good God, no," Dr. Sams answered indignantly.

"Why so emphatic? Lizzie and Sam are friends of yours, I know, but that needn't stop them from turning a little trade with a thieving nigger. Have you forgotten that old Gustaf Neilson got his land by outright theft from Mum's *papa*?"

"If you demand proof of their innocence—wagons would have to come along this road, and I'd hear them. They couldn't get down to the beach across the dunes. My fences haven't been broken.

Dave and I rode them just yesterday. There are no wagon tracks off the road."

"To me, every man's guilty until he's proven innocent." Saul gave me a good-natured grin. "I judge others by myself—completely untrustworthy. Well, I'll be on my way."

"I'm glad you stopped by, Saul."

"Thanks. Dave, who sent you her greetings but the chatelaine, her majesty Madeline."

"Please thank her kindly."

"She says for you to drop in and give her the news of Baltimore, when you have a chance. She went to school there! She was a great belle there! You're a bit young for her, but she likes big fellows with a faint flavor of manure, and since Pa is getting stale—"

"My soul, Saul, but you're a rotten cad." So spoke Dr. Sams without anger or even disgust, only stating a disagreeable fact.

Saul laughed boyishly and sprang on his great gray stallion. "I thought that would nettle him, Dave, his skin is so thin. If he hadn't been so refined, he might have got her himself. Well, both of you drop over, when you've no horse-marriages to solemnize. Things get pretty dull at Ibis Hall."

He was far out of hearing before Dr. Sams spoke. "You'd think a man who so parades his badness must be better than he seems, instead of worse."

"Yes, you might think it was a cloak for a tender heart," I answered, the mockery born of fear.

"Once I had two shepherd puppies. One of them kept running off and finally became a renegade, living in the swamps. Various people caught glimpses of him at rare times. He'd grown nearly twice as big as his brother and was a wanton killer of deer and everything he could catch. I borrowed a pack of hounds and went after him but he killed more than half of 'em before I could put a bullet in him."

"I see."

"But you can be grateful for Saul's visit. Without meaning to, he gave you a valuable tip."

"I'd remembered that you said the swamp rat, Cliff Todd, a whiskey-maker and maybe a snake-catcher, used to buy stolen produce from the slaves. Do you think he's up to his old tricks?"

"Yes, and not far away."

"Why didn't Saul suspect him at once, instead of Lizzie and Sam?"

"He didn't know of the other deals. Cliff is a remarkably furtive animal. The swamps helped make him so, I reckon. He's not a po' white but a low white, a species spawned in this deep, hot South, with great capacity for survival. I believe he provided that huge water moccasin. He was the most likely purveyor, and had had other dealings with Ralph. Assuming he was the one, do you find yourself marveling over something?"

"Yes. . . . That he's still alive."

"How do you suppose he managed it? Ralph might leave loose ends—both his cunning and farsightedness are subject to odd lapses —but Saul would be inclined to tie them neatly."

"He must be a real fox."

"He fawns on both of them—I've seen him—rather characteristic behavior of low whites to those who can do them favors, as opposed to the independent manner of po' whites. That flatters them. Both are so newly rich and powerful, so little civilized really, they might mistake bootlicking for real loyalty."

Was a swamp rat named Cliff Todd Ralph's and Saul's Achilles heel? I would base my first strategy on that assumption.

My first meeting with Saul was behind me, well managed, well gone, but to meet Cleo again was still up a dreamy road. It too would be well managed, over and done, I thought, but my heart did not subscribe to that calm assurance. It sank or soared or thumped at every thought of her, the prisoner of Ibis Hall. I visited her in every dream at night—at least I never wakened from one without a sense of her presence or could recall any ungraced by her beauty. In return her wraith appeared to me countless times, often unsummoned, and stood a little distance off, smiling with long pale lips, a subdued luster in its eyes. Its skin was whiter than ivory and its little throat had been soft and sweet to my lips.

As though materialized out of solid longing, late one afternoon she herself came riding out of the swamp. I was putting marl on some new corn-land close to Little Run; she had come down the corduroy road and, seen from a distance, appeared to burst through a solid, green wall. A servant was in her attendance but he needed no horse. Trotting along behind her, effortlessly keeping pace, appeared Obo. When I waved to her she cantered toward me. The giant Negro lengthened rather than quickened his stride and the distance between them hardly increased. When she stopped at the rail fence he dropped to the ground as instinctively, it seemed, as her horse lowered his head to nibble grass.

There was nothing we could do but greet each other, exchange a few commonplace words, and part. But my heart rebelled again: it was hammering, "Cleo! Cleo! Cleo!" with stupid violence. I saw again the strangeness of her beauty, so deeply touching, reminding me of a white heron's, untainted by the dark swamp waters that imaged it. Only a rail fence rose between us, and, if my hands were free, I could tear it down with one.

"Hello, Dave." She controlled her voice well.

"Hello, Cleo. But what a strange thing to say to each other!"

"There doesn't seem much else we can say—except I'm so glad you came."

"Thanks, but it was a sure thing."

"How are you getting along?"

"Very well. How is everything with you?"

"A lot better than when you left. I've visited Charleston twice since I saw you. I may spend next winter there."

"I hope you can."

"I've been wondering about something, Dave. It's not important —I'm just curious. When you first spoke to me on the ship, you said you saw me riding in Mr. Howard's carriage. What part of Baltimore was that?"

"Why, it was in Jonestown, where I boarded at the time."

"Well, I was in Jonestown that day—on some business—and we came near to meeting face to face. Obo passed you on one of the little streets. He remembered when he saw you later—he's a wonderfully close observer—and mentioned it to me."

"Unless fate intended us to meet—and missed the first try—it was just a remarkable coincidence."

She was still a little troubled by the coincidence—I could see it in her telltale dark eyes. She decided to make a clean breast of it.

"It's more remarkable than you know. I was down there, in the hope of finding Dan. His father was a lame musician named Reed, then living in Philadelphia. I heard of another lame musician named Reed living in Jonestown, and I went to see if he was the one." She waited for me to speak.

"I reckon he wasn't. At least if the Professor Reed who lived in our neighborhood had a son—I saw him a few times and have passed his house often—I never heard of it."

"I had caught only a glimpse of Dan's father and I wasn't sure from just looking at the lame man in Baltimore. But he told me he was not the one."

"Cleo, why did you say this wasn't important? Obo seeing me close to the house started you thinking that I might be Dan, after all."

"I suppose I could hardly bear to abandon the idea. Well, you see where my mind might go from there."

"No. Will you tell me, Cleo?"

"That wonderful thing happened a long time ago—we were mere children. It's just common sense that it might not mean to him what it meant to me. A great many things could happen in the years to make him break his promise. Maybe I haven't got any common sense. I was living at Ibis Hall with Granny and Saul and a wonderfully beautiful queen, who never goes farther than the garden any more, and the only happiness I had was dreams. But he was out in the world where dreams die. Maybe just another girl could put an end between him and me. In that case, if I met Dan by chance he might lie to me about being Dan. If he was out of the house when I visited his father he might still care enough about me to take the boat to see how I still felt—and in case I still loved him, to tell me it was no use any more. He might go under a different name until he found out—and then when he did find out—and found himself still caring for me a good deal but not enough—with the other girl still between us—he might feel so sorry for me—perhaps a little shamed he hadn't ever come back to me—that he couldn't bring himself to tell me the truth."

She sat very still on her bay horse and perhaps that was the reason he stood so still. But it suggested a steed of war standing at attention in tribute to some great bravery. Cleo's bravery seemed so strange in one with such a white face and gauze-thin skin.

136

"You might carry it a little farther," I told her, so shaken by her beauty and bravery, going hand in hand, that I could not steady my voice. "If Dan cared for you a good deal, but not enough, he might still want to help you. Needing a job anyway, he might take one near you. Yes, and if he were in love with another girl he might temporize, to see if in the end you and he might fall in love. Haven't you considered that?"

"Of course. Well, is it true? If it is, I want you to tell me so. I'll relieve you of your promise."

"It's true I took a job where I could be near you. Cleo, if I was Dan Reed, why should my father deny it?"

"I don't know, but I thought of a possible reason. You see, I thought of everything. Obo went looking for the house and told Professor Reed I was coming. There was plenty of time for you to ask him to say he was not Dan's father."

"As it happens, I've talked to Professor Reed since you have." My brain was rising to the emergency and working at great intensity.

She was not able to speak and the respite permitted me to shape the lie plausibly.

"Soon after my return to Baltimore I met him on the street and remarked I had been down here. He asked me what ship I had taken and, when I told him, he was curious as to whether I had got acquainted with you. That was natural enough, since you had called on him. Then he told me that you had confused him with another Professor Reed, with the deformity known as a humpback."

"A—humpback," Cleo murmured, her eyes rounding.

I knew then that my long shot had gone home. To my best memory Pa had not mentioned to her the nature of the lameness afflicting Mr. Linsey, who had impersonated him in Philadelphia.

"That's what he said."

"Well, that settles it. You're not Dan, and I was out of my mind to think you were. I had only a glimpse of the Professor Reed in Philadelphia but I remember now—perfectly clearly—his—back. It was not at all like the other. I remember now thinking so when I first came in the door. Well, I'm sorry I've made so many mistakes. I'm sorry I kept accusing you of lying to me—you must have got mighty tired of it and you've been very patient with me. I'm not ashamed, though—you see—I had to find out for certain. Not one doubt remaining."

"If I were Dan, I'd be so proud of that." I was ineffably proud—and at once so saddened that I could not tell her why.

"I'm disappointed, of course. That's a weak way to put it, and you know it. In spite of everything I kept on dreaming. But in one way—one great way—I'm glad."

Her voice seemed to come from far away, so lost I was in thrilling thought. If I told her I was Dan, long lost and found again, she would not tell Saul. I could devise a plausible reason why she must conceal it from her father. . . .

"Dave, I don't want to come between you and the other girl," she was saying.

"I didn't say there was another girl."

The words said themselves, it seemed, without causing the slightest whirlpool in the rushing stream of my thought. . . . I need not tell her I was Noel's son or of my deadly business here—I could hide both things from her for a long time yet, perhaps until I had proven her father a murderer. She might never forgive me for it—but she would know the justice of it, know I had been true to us three—and in time. . . .

"You should've said so—at the first. I know now you love someone else. If you had intended to marry her soon, I want you—"

Her voice faded out. She was gazing at me with startled eyes. Mine wandered to the fence between us—only rails I could leap over to take her in my arms. I could tell her and see her face before we were both blinded with tears. The time had come, without a warning bell, taking us by surprise. . . .

But in the time just passed, in a moment just gone, she had said something important in this affair. I could not at once remember what it was; it only cast a shadow across my course. It was very dim—perhaps imaginary—yet with a wrench of my will I returned to that moment and listened to her again. Then against my will, it seemed, and by what guidance or command I did not know, I waited there, long enough to ask one question. Time stood still.

"You said in one way you're glad I'm not Dan. Will you tell me what you meant?"

"Of course. It's nothing to hide, when you know all the rest. Dan is either dead or lost. Maybe too much came between us. But I can still believe that if he and I had met again—and I'd told him what I told you by the pond—he would have kept his promise that very night."

She raised her head high and looked me proudly in the eyes. "I can still believe that—in spite of what I told you today—and I still do," she went on, her voice low but ringing. "Not anyone or anything could have stopped him. That's the kind of boy he was— the kind of man he'd have grown to be. He and I would be gone from here forever. I'd be safe in his arms."

She wheeled her horse and, sitting high in the saddle, sped away.

CHAPTER

16

It was my fate and my fierce joy to go on with the hunt. But I could not make the haste I craved. I must stalk the quarry, not bay upon his trail.

Dr. Sams had warned me not to make one move that would attract Saul's searching attention, so I must wait in patience for a seemingly casual encounter with Cliff Todd. Meanwhile an event was moving beyond my knowledge, with deep importance to my enterprise. My first inkling of it came three days after I had talked to Cleo, at almost the same spot. I had been at work in the field when Dr. Sams rode up, dressed in his best riding coat, twill breeches, and well-polished boots, followed by Joshua carrying a leather bag. "I've been fishing and caught some nice bream," he called, beckoning me furtively to the fence. "I'm taking a mess over to Mr. Martin and thought I'd drop in at Ibis Hall."

Mr. Martin was overseer of Wood Ibis.

When we met at the fence he began to speak hurriedly, in low tones. "Ralph's caught his thief. One of my boys told me. The whipping's coming off at half-past eight tonight. I'm going to appear by chance, for what good I can do. There certainly ought to be a doctor present if it's as I expect. I'm not one any more, but Ralph doesn't know that."

"I'd like to come too."

"My God, why? If I could get out of it—"

"I want to be better acquainted with Ralph." Maybe I wanted to see him with his guard down and discover his weaknesses, but maybe I still needed the testimony of my own eyes, not circumstantial evidence, that Cleo's father was capable of murder.

"It's awkward. Well, Ralph won't care. He calls in all the hands for these affairs—believes in making examples of the poor wretches for discipline's sake—the same argument I've heard put forward by ship captains for public whippings at sea. You can say you heard the bell at an odd hour and wondered what was up. I wish you could go in my place."

140

He rode on, sitting heavy in the saddle, and vanished behind the swamp timber. The bell at Wood Ibis began to ring for the hands to come in from the fields, as always at this hour, and I sent our men and wagons to the barns. It had a pleasant sound, I thought, for man and beast. But alone at the border, ready to ride, I dreaded the next summons from its brassy throat. Throughout the island the people waited, not listening for it, listening instead to the silence as long as it would last. The innocent stock was being fed, cows milked by lean, black, pink-palmed hands, the white jets played a bell-like tune in the pails, supper was being cooked that would be eaten late and cold, if at all, smoke rose with pleasant shapes and scents from cabin chimneys; but all this was just a prelude to the bell and there was no reality but its soon clang. The pickaninnies did not play this evening. They stood looking at the parents with big, anxious eyes. "Get on wif yo suppah, chillen." But it took hard breath and a wringing of the heart to say even that little. I had never heard so deep and wide a silence.

The late summer sun had dipped behind the swamp and made a faint red-gold haze in the less dense tree-tops and sometimes winked fierily between the boles. The water birds flew sedately to their roosts—long flocks of white cranes that had made room for an occasional black one, streamers of delicate egrets, shy bands of wood ibis in elegant black and white, marauder crews of pelicans with rapier bills and greedy pouches, sweeping to their coves, their powerful pinions beating, resting, beating again. The summer ducks were the latest of the water clans to be up and out. God made them wondrous gay of feather, and as long as the least light displayed their multicolors they flew in fancy circles, darting handsomely, whistling to attract attention from plainer folk; but their vanity became pitiful as the dusk deepened, and soon they were mere black shapes against the still-glimmering sky. Ignominiously they perched in the cypress trees, for while fashioning them so prettily God had seen fit, in jest or justice, to alienate them from their webfoot order, and they could not settle among the murmuring crowds in the reedy pools. Of all the flyers only the owls on velvet wings, the night hawks that the Negroes called bullbats, and their grisly companions, common bats, the element of all of whom was darkness, remained aloft when, at last, a little tremor in the air swelled to the deep clang of the bell.

It had a cruel sound. Perhaps the hand at the rope was hurried, parched for blood, or perhaps the notes had been conjured while traversing the swamp. But I was not conjured by the humid, heavy-scented thing as I rode to meet the crowding clangings, swiftly loudening to my haste. I hated it tonight with a righteous hate. I was not seduced by its lascivious whispering—perhaps the rustle of greenery in rank growth, the hot pantings of vines intertangling and entwining in insatiable copulation. The swamp was alive and breathing with infernal life, all the innocence of the nesting squirrels and little birds in abeyance while they slept, and the invisible poison serpent wriggled through the muck on his lethal errands; but I did not dream of Cleo's white body torn down for my prey. Steadfast, I did not turn aside to yearn even for the beauty of her love. Tonight I rode for Pa, swiftly and relentlessly, and for our union.

When I emerged into the cleared land, the bell had stilled, and distant lanterns bobbed and converged, and pine torches flared. But I was not the only late-comer: on the cart road I overtook a Negro, running lest his laggardness be found out, and stumbling from near-exhaustion.

"What was the bell ringing for?" I asked, slowing my mare to his gait.

"Dey gwine whip Big Mose for stealin'," the man gasped, "And us 'bliged to watch."

"Catch my stirrup strap and you'll make better time."

"Bless God!" Then when he had caught his breath, "My cart wheel done broke and I'd been late sho."

As it happened, we were in plenty of time. The affair was far more ceremonious than I had expected. The colored people still hung in wretched clumps and clusters. Big Mose stood with his hands bound but had not yet been tied to the whipping-post behind the mule barn. Ralph was talking to Mr. Martin; Dr. Sams and Saul waited a short distance off. Not discovered yet by any of them, I took careful note of the lord of Wood Ibis.

He was dressed finely in black broadcloth coat and trousers and

142

brocaded waistcoat and had a judicial air that seemed completely sincere. It was somewhat pompous and yet in no way ludicrous: it would become a simple, plain man made judge of a high court. Presently he strode forward and appeared to be looking the prisoner up and down as though judging the condition of a horse for heavy labor. Mose stood before him with bowed head.

Saul seemed as much amused by the doctor's sick expression as by his father's solemnity. Presently he caught sight of me and called in mock-solemn tones brimming with high spirits.

"Ho, friend Dave! What brings you here, at this pregnant hour?"

"I heard the bell and thought maybe you had a fire—"

"Make way for him there, you black baboons," he commanded. And when I had come onto the torchlit ground, "You're just in time to see the law of Moses executed on his thieving namesake."

"I'll thank you, Saul, for a little less levity," Ralph told him in grave rebuke.

I would do the same. Perhaps Mose was too dulled by terror to know what Saul was saying, but the other Negroes perceived how lightly he took their tragedy and, despairing that they were men, wondered if they were counted even beasts. Indeed I caught myself championing Ralph, seeing him as the lesser of my two antagonists, and was suddenly cold and sick with shame.

"Pardon me, Judge," Saul had replied. "We are all sensible to the gravity of the occasion. The long arm of Wood Ibis law has reached out and now will smite an evildoer—*by—Gum!*"

"Dr. Sams and Mr. MacDaniel, I welcome your presence here tonight for this lamentable but necessary event," Ralph told us. "You will see how justice is administered at Wood Ibis, without fear or favor—punishment to a confessed thief, but inflicted in the open as an example to others tempted to wrongdoing. That punishment will be stern but justly measured. I trust that every stripe laid on will prevent a dozen in the future."

It came to me eerily that Saul might have made precisely the same speech, save in mocking instead of solemn tones, and it would have been equally characteristic of him. Saul clasped his hands and bowed gravely.

"I appreciate that," Dr. Sams answered. "I suggest, though, that the punishment fit the man as well as the crime. Mose is big and young, but he looks apoplectic to me. I'll gladly keep track of his pulse—"

"His punishment will not be abated one jot by the state of his pulse. That would not be justice but weakness. A whipping is moderate punishment for his crime—often it is imprisonment for life—and is the noose to be loosened a little because the criminal is in delicate health? If Mose should die beneath the lash it will be not on my conscience but the result of his own wrongdoing. Let others fear and tremble!"

My eerie feelings of a moment ago were like the presentiment of a nightmare. I fought a little battle with the Powers of Darkness ere the mists dissolved and I could again set my teeth in reality. There watched Dr. Sams with a white face. There waited a black foreman with a bull whip. There stood Saul, his eyes shining, turning the tragic scene into an obscene jest by his sanctimonious posturing. Mr. Martin's lantern glinted on a naked, sweat-wet back. Its muscles flexed here and there as its nerves jumped and twitched. The throng of Negroes looked bowed down under a weight of doom beyond their ken, with unspeakable shame and sorrow in their eyes.

But in that grasp of reality, I could no longer explain Ralph as a colossal, deliberate hypocrite, mouthing cant while he did to death those who brooked his greed. He was not feigning his judgelike manner but glorying in it, I thought. He was living the role of Ralph, *Rex* of Wood Ibis, and I could not believe that in this moment he remembered how he had gained his crown.

"You colored people shall watch every lash," he told the hushed throng. "Be glad it is Mose's back and not your own. You will remember the fair treatment and the good care you get, if you do your duty, and know what will happen to you if you transgress. The way of the transgressor is hard—remember that."

"God ha' mercy on us," an old woman whispered.

"Mark you, Mose was caught stealing and has confessed other thefts. He swore on his knees that he was alone in it, tempted to do it by an unknown Negro—he was to put his stolen goods in a certain place on Little Run, and return and find money hidden there. It may be the story is true. We will soon know."

"If it aint true, massa, let bless Jesus send me to hell," Mose cried. "Not one o' dem was in it wif me and I never seen de nigger 'fo or since."

"We will see. Mr. Martin, we're ready to begin. Have Mose tied securely to the post."

The man was led forward, his feet shuffling, by two black foremen. They took a long time with the ropes, and Mr. Martin tested the knots.

"Yes, sir," he reported in a dry tone.

"All you colored people form a circle, with the short ones in front. I want every one of you to be able to see well."

Many bare feet shuffled, and the circle was formed. I saw no liveried servants from Ibis Hall, but did not doubt that every slave in the Quarter big enough for field work was part of that black umbrage of the lurid ring—big-muscled bucks in their prime, lean wiry wenches, boys and girls and white-powed elders who lagged behind the crews. All struck the same posture—leaning forward slightly from their hips, their arms a little bowed—and the porcelain-white of their eyes lit up and went out here and there in the interplay of torch and lantern light with the effect of a huge, elaborate kaleidoscope of insane invention. Their gaze was not fixed on their doomed fellow—they could hardly afford pity on him, lest the Wrath fall on them. Instead they watched with desperate vigilance Ol' Massa's every move.

"Mr. Martin, have Zeke lay on twenty-five lashes, hard as he can for a starter."

The overseer made no reply save for a straight, somewhat prolonged glance into Ralph's face, and a low-voiced command to Zeke.

"We'd better stand back," Saul murmured to Dr. Sams. "If he's as apoplectic as you say, we might get sprayed."

"I'll stay where I am, thank you," the doctor replied. "I can see better here."

Zeke was a powerful Negro. The bull-whip coiled, stretched out, hissed, and its cruel lash made a sharp cracking sound against Mose's naked back. It left a gray mark, perfectly visible in the torch light, and before the whip could coil, whirl, and strike again it was a dull-red color. The deeply red welt was not manifest until two lashes later; the others appeared after about the same interval. Mose grunted at each of the first half-dozen strokes, although ever more deeply, and after that the sound changed and loudened until it was a horror in the night. But Saul's fears proved in vain. Only where the stripes crossed one another did the strong skin break clean, then there was only a trickling flow, garish in the yellow gleam of the doctor's lantern. The watching Negroes did not want to make a sound—every lonely desolate soul wanted to hide its very being—and truly not one raised an outcry; yet the stifled gasp of each as the hissing snake of leather darted toward its prey combined to make a dull, heavy noise like a shovelful of sand thrown on hard ground.

The youngest and dullest stripling did not miscount the strokes. Long before the last, their sound was no longer a sharp crack but a soggy thud. At their end Mose had sagged in his bonds, his big body grotesquely jackknifed. Dr. Sams was palsied and very pale, the Negro watchers' faces had a uniform gray cast. Ralph stood tall with folded arms, aloof from everyone, it seemed, his expression stern but rather regal, the whole effect that of a monstrous boast before us, entirely justified in his mind by what he deemed his well-won place and power. I had a sense of the uncanny, but not of insanity in him: this was not an illusion of grandeur, rather a horrid form of the thing itself.

Saul alone had been unaffected by the event. He stood lightly, animated and graceful, not in the least interested in Mose but highly entertained by his father's majesties. At that moment what I took for a small bat that had slept all day head-down, like an inverted cross, in the recesses of the swamp, was attracted by the light and flitted over Saul's head. But at its second dart I saw that it was only a very large moth.

"Mose?" Ralph called imperiously.

The sagging head moved a little but there was no other reply.

"Give me the whip, Mr. Martin," Ralph ordered. "I'll see if he can still speak."

"I can talk, massa. Please massa don' hit me agin."

"Was it true, you were spoken to by an unknown Negro?"

"Yes, massa."

"You don't know who he worked for?"

"No massa, 'fo God."

"No other of my slaves helped steal the things?"

"No massa, 'fo bless Jesus."

"I'm persuaded you are telling the truth and that mitigates the offense. I think twenty-five additional lashes will be sufficient to teach you your lesson, a good one to all the others."

Dr. Sams's flaccid countenance became more lifelike. "Ralph, I wouldn't call that any considerable mitigation of punishment," he said in a low but firm voice.

Ralph turned to him rather stiffly but with less antagonism than I expected. "Fifty stripes for confessed thieving? I count that a very proper number. If he had lied as well as stolen I'd have ordered a hundred."

"You forget that most whippings are administered by men of ordinary strength. Zeke is not only unusually strong but very expert. Muscular collapse rarely occurs before fifty lashes; in this case twenty-five has brought about the condition. Mark you, too, that the blows will be largely wasted as far as rubbing in the lesson goes; his outcries have been spasmodic for the last several strokes and although they may continue he will be too shocked to be aware of pain. Considering that further blows will only delay his recovery I feel that he has had enough."

"I am sensible to your argument and respect your medical knowledge. I will remit more than half of the remaining punishment, but you will oblige me by not petitioning any further remission. Mr. Martin, have Zeke lay on a round dozen more, full strength."

Zeke coiled his whip. Dr. Sams reeled off and I heard him retching in the darkness. I was not troubled in that way—indeed had never before felt so strong.

When the sentence had been executed, Mr. Martin had two of the field hands free Mose's inert body from the ropes and carry it, with such life as it still contained, to his cabin. His wife and young son and daughter followed, dry-eyed as far as I could see, although the boy was whimpering in terror. The other Negroes scattered quickly and silently. Somewhat to my distress—although, oddly enough, not to my great surprise—when Dr. Sams returned, he did not offer to treat Mose's wounds. His explanation for what seemed cruel neglect of duty he made with an interesting indirectness while addressing Mr. Martin.

"If Mose were my patient, I'd venture he wouldn't be fit for heavy work for a good fortnight. He's fairly young and the wounds will heal rapidly under Aunt Kate's good care. You know she's a wonder at herb doctoring. Some doctors laugh at Negro medicine, but I've never known better palliatives than some of their poultices and herb teas."

"He's a badly punished nigger," Mr. Martin commented, not caring who heard him, a grim expression on his homely, honest face.

"Well," Saul broke in, "now the Roman holiday is over—excuse me, Papa, I meant that Justice has triumphed—why not make a night of it?"

Instead of rebuffing his son, Ralph spoke quickly to the doctor. "At least come to the house for a glass. I confess I need one. The business of keeping two hundred Africans in something like orderly control is no sinecure. I think you too can do with a stimulant."

"Thank you, I can."

"Will you join us, Mr. MacDaniel? The ladies have no doubt retired, and we can be free and easy over a bottle of good brandy." His eyes glistened.

"I thank you kindly."

"In brief, we will now doff the cares of state, and be fiddlers' bitches," Saul remarked.

Ralph turned to him gravely. "We are neither of us gentlemen, Saul, but I can drink like one, and expect others to."

It seemed a commonplace thing that we four were presently riding toward the mansion, Ralph in the van, the doctor close behind him, Saul and I abreast and discussing horse-breeding. I had in some fashion obtained a new calmness toward my undertaking, a quietude almost; my patience would not be tried by necessary delay; if any profit could be turned by a drinking bout with my two adversaries and my well-wisher, well and good; anyway I would lose nothing by it. There was no danger tonight of my betraying feelings to endanger my cause.

Stable boys took our horses and Ralph led us through the side

148

door under the porte-cochere to his handsome, well-furnished office. His butler cleared a table, and provided a decanter, glasses, a water pitcher, and four chairs. Despite our polite behavior—the Dunbartons talking of politics and farming, I listening or briefly answering questions—no one could mistake the purpose and nature of the gathering. In a sense there was no gathering: I was an outsider and each of the other three was alone with his desire. This might not have been as true of Saul as of Ralph and Dr. Sams: he was at least amused by his cupmates' zeal. However, he too had set out to get drunk.

Within the hour the condition was developing well and in two hours obtained. Saul, who had drunk twice as much as either of the others, was the least befuddled. His enormous vitality was not noticeably reduced; constantly he shifted his big body, moved his hands in buoyant gestures, and frolicked about the table. Ralph's gestures were lordly, his tones loud and boastful. He smirked now over not being a gentleman: he had pulled himself up by the bootstraps! Truly he became a clumsy personification of a peasant-born king, winning his throne through iron will, and there was no doubt that he believed in it. Dr. Sams swayed a little in his chair, saying almost nothing, and I was troubled by the deep red of his skin.

"Dave, you're too damned sober," Saul told me. "You're a dull dog on a booze and, unless you liven up, we won't invite you again."

"I'm having a mighty fine time but a little overawed by the company I'm in."

"You don't have to sit back 'cause o' that," Ralph replied. "When I drink with a man, I count him a man, and on top o' that you're my guest. We aint drawing any lines tonight."

"The king chooses to be gracious," Saul mocked.

"Dave's a good fellow," Ralph told him blearily. "He's just as good as you and me, 'cept he aint got so far. Dave, I'm glad Doc gave you a job. I'd give you one myself, if you needed it. I'm glad to have you on my plantation."

"Uncle Noel's plantation, remember," Saul corrected him. "He hasn't officially kicked the bucket yet."

"Little Ibis is mine any time I want to have the court declare him deceased. It will happen anyhow next year. It's hard for me to reconcile myself to him being dead, but I don't doubt it no more. When the title passes to me, I want Doc to stay right on."

"At the same rent?" Saul asked wickedly.

"Doc and I won't have no trouble about the rent, will we, Doc?"

Dr. Sams heard his name called and looked dazedly into Ralph's face. "You bet we won't," he muttered.

"I'll want Dave to stay on too. He's a good fellow, and knows horses."

"Thank you kindly, Mr. Dunbarton," I said.

"He knew a pretty little filly on a boat, but don't any more," Saul remarked, rolling up his eyes.

"You got no business mentioning it, Saul. If Dave was a little too forward on the boat, it was before he was employed down here. He knows better now."

"Yes, sir, I do," I assured him.

Saul's eyes glistened with mirth. "It's an awful thing, Dave, for a man employed on a plantation to be forward with a lady of the big house. Papa would be so shocked at the idea, and so would our dear Uncle Bruce, if he sat here with us. He's here in spirit, I know."

"Saul, I get damned tired of your damned constant making fun of serious things." Ralph was momentarily a little less drunk.

"Doc too knows it's improper for a mere vassal to court the queen," Saul persisted, "even though a gentleman and never doing any dirty work."

"The practice of medicine has its unpleasant aspects," Dr. Sams emerged from his stupor to say distinctly.

I feared mightily that Saul would persist with the subject, but the doctor's florid face put him on a new tack.

"Doc, you said Mose was apoplectic. Looks to me like you should prescribe for yourself."

"You notice I didn't pay no attention to that, Doctor," Ralph boasted. "Niggers don't belong to have a disease with such a long and fancy name. If Mose had it, I still wouldn't paid no attention, but gone ahead and done my duty. He's worth twelve hundred dollars alive and not a pigskin dead, but I'd done it just the same. But when you talked sense, like about Zeke being stronger than most whippers, why, I listened to you."

"Thank you. Thank you, sir. Thank you."

"I'm still not sure that another twenty-five wouldn't have got out of him who bought the stuff," Saul remarked. "Laid on slowly and judiciously, that is."

"I know niggers, and know when they're telling the truth."

"I wouldn't wonder but Cliff Todd was behind it, after all."

"Cliff wouldn't have paid him in cash. He's never had that much, and never will. He'd of made whiskey out of the rye and sent him some. Anyway Cliff wouldn't dare do it. He's under my thumb."

Ralph's thinking that, true or untrue, was the reason Cliff Todd was still alive.

"Let's talk about nigger wenches. It's a more interesting subject. Dave, I'll pick one out for you who'd melt an iceberg. The whole Low Country knows I'm an expert."

Ralph was nothing loath and his boast of being able to drink like a gentleman went by the boards. Dr. Sams was not too drunk to look a little sick: I feigned a zest for the subject, hoping that it would keep Saul off the subject of Cleo. But it soon palled on him.

"Hell, this is dull," he broke out. "Let's wake up Granny and get some brandy down her and have her call up some ghosts."

"Hold your drunken tongue!" Ralph cried, unmistakably alarmed.

"Maybe she's still roaming through the house, chasing spooks. She'd be a barrel of fun." Saul rushed to the door and flung it open, roaring at the top of his great voice. "Granny! Where are you, old witch? Come and wet your whistle!"

Ralph tried to spring up only to topple back in his chair. His old black butler, standing outside the door, turned to Saul in desperate entreaty.

"For Jesus' sake, Massa Saul—"

"Stop it, God damn you," Ralph shouted. Then, as though alarmed by our sight of his great alarm, "you'll wake up the ladies!"

Saul was arrested on the balls of his feet the same as on my first call at Ibis Hall when I had hinted interference between him and Cleo. Then he shut the door softly and with his eyes gleaming walked in long light strides to Ralph's chair.

"I might wake up the ladies?" he asked in low tones, smiling.

"Sit down, son, and have another drink!"

"Mustn't wake up Madeline and Cleo, with my drunken noise," he went on. "Are they the owners of Wood Ibis, or are we?"

"We are, of course, but—"

Saul's empty chair stood between them; he seized and flung it against the wall with one incredibly swift and powerful movement, and it crashed to the floor in three pieces.

"Then why aren't they entertaining your guests in the parlor? Why haven't you got Madeline down here helping you, sitting with us, throwing her smiles around, being Lady Beautiful, making high-class talk? Why haven't we got Cleo waiting on us? That's the way plain men do with their women—are you trying to be gentry after all? She married you, didn't she? Or isn't Cleo your daughter?"

"I wish you wouldn't talk that way—"

"In front of Doc? I know you don't care about Dave, but Doc's a gentleman. For a Sams of Beaufort to become a doctor instead of a planter was a little comedown, but look what drink did for him, eh, Doc? You got drunk once too often and now you're in a more respectable business." Saul laughed uproariously. "The same we're in, Papa! Low Country planters—by—God! Well, if you're scared of the women, I'm not. Come with me, Dave, and I'll show you something pretty."

"What are you going to do?" Ralph gasped.

"What I said. I'd show you all, if you weren't so hog-drunk you can't walk. Come on, Dave."

I got up, looking toward Ralph.

"Go with him," Ralph cried in a desperate, almost hysterical voice. "What does it matter? Let him have his way!"

"Follow me, Dave, and make it lively."

Saul appeared to bound up two flights of steps, sped along a dimly lighted hall, snatched a lamp from a table, and then began to pound on one of the many doors.

"Who's there?" It was Cleo's voice.

"Your half-brother Saul and your old friend Dave MacDaniel. Open up."

"Saul, I've gone to bed—"

"*Open up!*"

"I beg you, Saul—"

"I want to show Dave what a pretty little thing you are in your nightgown. Open that door."

"I won't! I won't—"

"All right. Here goes. One—two—three!" At that he lunged powerfully, and the impact of his shoulder against the door shook it on its hinges. Another such lunge would break it down.

"I'll open it," she cried. "Wait just a minute, *please*."

This last, not the words but their sound, was an entreaty for his pity. Saul did not know what a fateful thing that was.

"That's the way to handle 'em," he told me, greatly amused. "Take a tip from me."

"I'm embarrassed, Mr. Saul—"

"Over seeing a lady in her nightgown? Cleo, don't take time to cover up those charms, or down goes this door."

The door opened and the lamplight flung through in a broad shaft, making a yellow frame for the pale figure standing there. Perhaps it was then or perhaps in remembrance of then that I had a vision of a young woman, a saint or a witch, being burned at the stake in some long-ago infamy. There was no shame in her posture. Her black hair flowed and her feet were bare. If she had looked for a dressing-gown she had not had time to find it. The cambric, low-cut, sleeveless nightgown clung to her damp skin and barely covered her bosom.

"*Aint* that pretty, Dave?" Saul burst out.

"Ma'am, I beg you to excuse me. Mr. Ralph Dunbarton told me to come with him—"

"You're not to blame, Dave," she replied.

"How pretty," Saul remarked. "But not as pretty as the picture. Dave, if you don't show more enthusiasm I'll think you've seen it before."

"May I go now?" Cleo asked.

Saul hardly heard her. His quick ears had caught the sound of a door opening farther down the hall. He turned with gleeful anticipation.

"If I live, here comes the queen!"

Madeline came out of her room wearing a lustrous blue robe and with a lighted candle in her hand. Even at this distance the small blue-yellow flame limned the gold of her hair. As she came nearer, her beauty and stateliness became a great, real wonder.

"What's the matter, Cleo?" she asked quietly.

"Saul made me get up. Dave's not to blame."

"I know it. You can go back now, Cleo, and close the door."

"We must all obey her majesty," Saul said to me, when Cleo had gone.

Madeline stood quietly, looking him in the face.

"Cleo was really enjoying it, you know—being a martyr and the same time showing off her pretty figure—but nobody appreciates the favors I do them," Saul went on in a mock lament. "Well, let's go back and drown our grief."

"I'll bid you good night, Mr. MacDaniel," Madeline told me. "Perhaps I should apologize for another scene, but I don't think it's worth while."

The next afternoon Dr. Sams and I rode down to the beach and sat and talked in the sunlight. The amber-colored sand, all bright save for our own clean-cut shadows, the summery sea, and the sleepy surf and the leisurely flight of gulls were antidotes for the poison of last night; and our cleared heads worked well.

In discussing Saul's mention of the swamp rat, Cliff Todd, I told Dr. Sams of my conversation with Granny on my first visit to Ibis Hall.

"That is remarkable, Dave," he said, his tone and expression revealing greater amazement than he perhaps intended to reveal. "In the first place, she hasn't slipped away from Lucy for some years. Not that the watch is so strict, rather she's so terrified of the consequences. You see, every time it's happened Ralph ties her in a chair all day as punishment. It's really very severe punishment, because she has terrors at times and her only relief from them is to go into a closet where she says the good spirits stay. He also takes Lucy to the woods and gives her a terrific beating with a strap."

I had a horridly clear vision of the old woman screaming and sobbing to be set free. But I made no comment on Ralph, being past all that.

"Why do Madeline and Cleo stand for it?"

"Madeline goes in and stays with her and comforts her all she can. In this particular thing she's not able to restrain Ralph—he knows how dangerous Granny is to him and that he has to take strong measures."

"Then why doesn't he take the usual measures and get it over with?"

"That's even more dangerous, I reckon. Perhaps Madeline too is deathly afraid of her talking to visitors—sure that what she says is raving insanity but horrified at anyone hearing it. Cleo is sent off for the day with Obo. I don't think she knows how bad it is—she shuts up her imagination for one thing, in matters she can't help, and there is a conspiracy among the servants to protect her as far as possible. They know she needs a lot of protection. I'm in that conspiracy. If it wasn't for her—for lovely little Cleo—I would have fled this accursed spot years ago."

I nodded to him. "Yet she loves her father."

"Very deeply. It goes hand in hand with her worship of Madeline. She blinds herself, I guess. I long for the day she marries and shakes this muck from her feet. Maybe Saul has given her some graphic descriptions of Granny tied up—it's his idea of sport—but perhaps that particular torture doesn't entertain him. Well, what I started to say was, Granny took a terrible risk in slipping off to talk to you. She must have wanted to terribly. Why?"

"I don't know. A mad vagary, I suppose."

"Besides that, it's very odd for her to mistake you for a spirit. She's usually very definite about her spirits."

"It doesn't seem to me important."

"I guess not."

"The important thing is how to get hold of Cliff Todd. I mean, to get a hold on him."

"You'll have to work that out. Even to find him is not easy—he's like a swamp fox, always on the go. He throws together a little shelter of palm leaves and bark—rather his woman does, a free quadroon named Clara—and in a little while moves on. There's only one white person who's likely to know where he's operating right now—colored people will swear they don't know. That's Cleo. At least she can find out from Obo."

"You don't know anyone else?"

Dr. Sams thought hard. "No. Cleo wouldn't know either, save that she's almost a swamp fox herself. The woods and waters are her salvation."

"What excuse could I use for wanting to talk to him?"

But as I asked the question, I found the answer.

This little tributary to the main stream of event flowed fast. I watched for an opportunity to meet Cleo as though by accident, and it was not long in coming, since she had been watching for the same. Of late I was bossing the job of running a fence to inclose one end of the island: I thought she knew that, when in early morning she and Obo came to fish in a pond in distant but clear view. I at once appointed tasks to keep the hands busy, then rode over to join her.

"Any luck?" I called—the same call that passers-by made to anglers in Pharaoh's Nile.

"A little," she told me with a childish smile, "now you've come."

"Were you expecting me?" I was cutting a fish pole.

"I wanted to talk to you." Her smile flickered, a little like a small flame, and went out.

She gave me a spare piece of line, a buckshot sinker, and a hook; a small twig did for the cork. I baited and threw in beside her; we both sat down and Obo moved out of hearing. "Look like a good hole down dis way," he announced in his soft, high tenor. By his saying that, I thought he had been especially instructed. Almost at once I got a bite and landed a pound stump-knocker. Cleo squealed, and then was better able to talk to me.

"I love Papa," she began, "but he's too severe with everybody except Mama and Saul. With Saul—well, he's clay in his hands."

"I know that."

I did not look straight at her but watched her still, perfect reflection in the deep waters of the pond. Perfect meant not distorted; actually the face I saw there appeared different in a very subtle way from the one I knew by direct gaze. The beauty of it seemed more mysterious; it proposed, I imagined, traits I had not yet discovered. Both were marvelously beautiful to me today. Something had happened to my eyes now that I hated Ralph so deeply that no other emotion could interfere with the coming battle. I could look straight at everything.

"You know now what I told you about Saul—before you left here—is true. He's not like other men—not even a little like them. He never did before what he did the other night—he never does the same thing twice—but it was entirely characteristic. But I wasn't humiliated after I saw your face. I'll always be grateful not just for what you said but for how you looked. I was glad we'd been sweethearts, although it's over with now."

"I'm glad too. I wish it didn't have to be over."

"You're safe from Saul only for that reason. If it wasn't over, he'd put a horrid end to it. You know that. You couldn't live here after that."

"My wish stands."

"I wish he'd die." It seemed to me that it was the girl in the water who said that. "I'd kill him in a minute if I could do it without getting caught."

I would attend to his death when the time came.

"What I really wanted to talk to you about, was Papa," she went on. "Liking you so much, I hate to have you think about him as you are—after drinking with him and seeing that horrible whipping. He believes so much in stern justice that he can shut his eyes and heart and mind to suffering. He really thought that whipping would prevent a great many more. He sees himself as a kind of Old Testament judge and thinks mercy is a weakness. He's always afraid of being weak. And he thinks too that he was fated from the first to be master of Wood Ibis—maybe that God appointed him because he was so fit to rule it."

"Why should he think that?" I asked, my skin prickling.

"Well, I reckon you've heard by now that his brother Bruce was Mama's first husband. But Bruce was too good-natured and kind to be a good ruler, he thought. As you probably know, Bruce was killed by accident. Only a few weeks before that, Papa's first wife, Saul's mother, was killed by snakebite. He thinks Fate can be that cruel, to bring about what's best. He thinks that he too must be cruel to bring about what's best—for the whole plantation."

"He's a terribly cruel man, to talk plain—I wish you weren't his daughter."

"I take pains never to see his cruelties. I couldn't stand them—and then—maybe—I couldn't love him any more. I need to love him so much. That sounds weak—but I can't explain it or help it."

"What are you going to do—about Saul?"

"Stand him off until I can get married."

"When will that be, you think?"

"When the first man—except you, if you ever should—asks me to marry him."

"Why do you exclude me?"

"Pride, for one thing. But there are some other reasons."

"Have you anything more to tell me?" I asked.

"No."

"Well, I have something to tell you. Mose was whipped for

stealing. There's been stealing around Little Ibis too. If there wasn't an incentive to steal—someone who'd buy the things—it might save some whippings in the future."

"That's perfectly true."

"I think I know who's behind it, and I want to scare him so bad he won't tempt any more Negroes to steal. Your father knows the man but wouldn't believe he's guilty. That's one reason I ask you to say nothing about this to anyone. The other reason is I'd like to handle it myself—get the credit for it with Dr. Sams. His name is Cliff Todd."

"I know him," she said in a strained voice. "Obo and I have met him several times in the swamps."

"Well, I don't know how to find him, and thought Obo might know."

"He very likely does. I think it's a wonderful idea and want you to succeed." She raised her voice very little and called. "Obo!"

I was surprised that he heard, but he did, and came running.

"Yassum."

"Do you know where Cliff Todd is hanging out?"

"Yassum."

"Tell Mr. MacDaniel how to find him."

"I kaint, Miss Cleo, but I could show him where he stay right now. Maybe he be out when massa git there, but maybe not. Mas' Todd live in de swamp. He layin' snares for egrets, to sell de plumes to de French ships. I couldn't tell no one how to git to him, dey no path, and de hummock look all alike, and half de time you kaint see de sun. Mas' 'Daniel couldn't find his way haf in, let alone haf out."

"Well, you'll have to take him in there."

"I not gwine leave you for de time it take, not now," the huge Negro replied with a sullen look.

"You see, Dave? I'll have to go too."

"Well, I'm glad of that."

"Obo, will Cliff still be there Saturday?"

"I reckon he won't move on for a while yit. But he hard to catch at home."

"Saturday's a good day. Saul's going to Capers Island to look at some slaves put on sale. Obo and I can start out like just for another day in the woods. Obo, where can we meet Mr. MacDaniel?"

"I reckon where Little Run come into Whale Branch. Mas' 'Daniel, you gwine get mighty muddy and wet, but to go around de island and come in de easy way take t'ree hours' sail in good wedder and a hour pole in a bateau."

"I'll wear old clothes, Obo."

"De fewer, de better. We bes' meet noontime, so we'll have half-ebb to cross, and dead low to come back," he went on after a brief calculation. "De tide back up de swamp water right smart. You bes' go barefoot too, but I'll look out for snakes."

"It will be nice to have an outing with you," Cleo remarked, "considering it's business."

I had no idea where we were going from Little Run: Dr. Sams had told me that Deep Swamp, just beyond, was impassable, no boat able to get over the hummocks and through the snags, and the sloughs much too deep to cross on foot. On Saturday I found Cleo wearing an old dress tucked into knee-breeches, her shoes and stockings and some petticoats literally hung on a hickory-like limb, and with happy anticipation in her face. Obo wore cotton trousers slashed off at the knee, his immense naked torso a lustrous ebony in the sun. I had never seen such powerful neck and shoulders and arms on a human being. But he wore a curious homemade harness of which I could not guess the use. It consisted of a strap over his shoulder fastened front and back to his belt, with strong leather loops at the bottom and the top. Also in his belt was a short-handled ax. In one hand he had a smoothly-worked oaken pole, about two inches in diameter and six feet long, and in the other a coil of rope.

"We needn't hurry," Cleo told me happily. "Obo, lead the way."

I thought he would cross Whale Branch into the water-oak swamps; instead he followed down it straight toward Deep Swamp. Almost at once we were on boggy ground. The vegetation thickened and became more rankly green. Obo kept us clear of heavy muck—apparently he could identify it at a glance—but we waded through many a shallow pool and crossed runs on fallen logs. He wove through thick growth like a catamount. I saw his head turning constantly in a narrow arc, and the focus of his gaze seemed about ten feet in front. Presently he turned to Cleo with a grin and made a little movement with his thumb. She grinned back. He veered a little in his course, and peering closely, I saw what had amused them. It was a full-grown cottonmouth moccasin asleep on a log.

The sight of him did not amuse me: it recalled too clearly the grisly memento Dr. Sams had shown me. However, I escaped any sense of horror. After all the creature was merely a swamp denizen, innocent of his own deadliness, an eater of frogs, a biter of human beings only in sudden fear. A stranger thing was my different feeling about this swamp than about the others I had seen. I could not identify it yet, or trace its source. Perhaps it was more beautiful; if so, I did not know why. We were full in it now, the light dim and mysterious, the trees festooned with vines, the sulphuric smell strong, the pools seemingly unrippled since the world was made, the solitude unutterably deep.

A flock of wild turkeys, swift and vigilant, crossed a hummock ahead of us. Every vista revealed water birds—assemblies of cranes, lone blue herons, small bands of wood ibises, egrets so delicate and lovely that their vanity over their plumes became a little touching. A timber rattlesnake crawled away—Obo had seen to it that we did not take him by surprise—and a few minutes later Cleo whispered,

"There's a bear."

Obo discovered him in one glance. "Bless God, you seen him fust, Miss Cleo." She had to point her finger before I made out a black shape in the dark shadows on our flank. He had heard us no doubt, but had not seen or smelled us: presently he was reassured and went on with his affairs. He rambled about, sometimes tipping over logs and lapping up some sort of tidbits he found beneath. My companions watched him in childish delight, turning bright faces to mine with the most wonderful sociability. I was more absorbed in my feelings about Cleo.

Her face and form were never more lovely in my sight and I longed for her more powerfully than ever before. Yet that longing was different than when we had met by the tarn—sweeter and less predatory, wrapped in tenderness. The scene, deep in this profound, primeval swamp, was impassioning. The deep shade wet yet warm, not as though from the sun but from the blood of the swamp itself, from the bodies of its growing things and the life-force in its ooze. The air that stirred so little seemed to have been here always, native to the Swamp, part of it like its ponds and runs, a permanent warm lake engulfing it, in which trees grew and vines hung and white birds swam by wingbeats and on whose bottom serpents crawled and bears fed drolly. The light was very soft, but perfectly lucid now that my eyes were accustomed to it, and obscuring no shape of beauty, indeed enhancing every one by stimulating my imagination. Everywhere was the triumph and the ecstasy of procreation.

We pushed on into this archaic world, seeing shy deer, ten-foot alligators sleeping on the mud flats of the runs, hearing little sound but the occasional croak of a swamp bird and once the clamor of a flock of small green parrots, the first I had ever seen wild in nature. Cleo and I were already wet to the hips from wading, and now Obo paused at the brink of a swale.

"Mighty mucky, dis place, and a far piece around. Maybe you better—"

"We'll both just hold on to the rope."

"Yassum."

He passed the end of it to us. I took hold of it behind Cleo, not knowing what the procedure was, only to discover that he was going to tow us through the muck. I was at first a little ashamed to need the help, and then accepted it in great joy. The black mire was nearly waist-deep. I would have worn myself out fighting it in brief time. Obo's slow, thrilling conquest over it was not alone a matter of gigantic strength. That alone was exalting to me—the wonderful sinuous movements of his muscles under his black skin. Also it was a triumph of intelligence and skill. Each forward step was superbly controlled, the extended knee used as a plowshare, the other muck-clutched leg drawn at the exact angle of least resistance.

We gained relatively firm ground, laughing at our mud-plastered bodies. "Dey's a clear branch wif good bottom a short piece ahead," Obo told me kindly, coiling up his rope, "where you can wash off." Apparently it was not necessary to instruct Cleo.

All three of us rinsed fairly clean, crossed a long hummock, and then came out on what seemed a scene from Dante's abyss of lost souls. It could be called a cypress pond—actually the slough was two hundred yards wide and ran out of sight to the right and left. The cypress trees, some of them the largest I had ever seen, hundreds of years old, their tops higher than the flight of swallows in the afternoon, were all dead. This was a drowned forest. The inundation, probably of seawater in a hurricane, that had killed the giants must have occurred a century or more before. A great many were sturdy skeletons, appearing to be waiting for a spring that never came to breathe them back to life. Many had toppled as the dirt had washed from around their roots and lay in fantastic ruin. The tops of others were broken and some of the limbs fallen so that they took weird shapes. The boles were clothed and the limbs draped in melancholy moss.

"Dis here's why dey say nobody kin cross Deep Swamp. Dey's quagmire at each end, and nobody kin git a boat in here. But de swamp rats know how to swim it, pushing along a limb to hold dey guns, and de strong ones can wade it at low tide. But us can cross it at 'mos' any tide."

He waded in, again having Cleo and me cling to the rope. But the water deepened rapidly, and when it reached Cleo's waist, he put the pole he was carrying through the loop at his shoulder and fastened it to the other loop at his belt, so that it stood rigid against his chest and about three feet over his head. Then he turned to Cleo and put his open hand deep in the water. I saw her place her left foot in his palm; lightly he lifted her until she could stand on his shoulders. Taking hold of the pole her strange perch was instantly secure.

She gave me a droll smile as Obo waded on. My heart swelled with joy, and tears that I could not understand stung my eyelids.

I too waded on, putting no load on Obo yet, although I knew he could bear it staunchly. He had a great surplus of strength made free to others. But soon it was apparent why only a swamp rat, who knew every channel in the big slough, could cross it by swimming. Great quantities of silt had washed in, forming a dirt-and-water mixture often within a few inches of the surface. These places were hard but not hopeless to wade, and by trusting him, I was able to follow him and his passenger through deep water and shallow to the bank.

Obo crouched and let Cleo down. At that instant he saw something in the reeds that caused a startling change in his happy-child expression. I thought at first it must be another poison snake only to remember that he had shown not the slightest animosity toward the others. Ferocity came into his face but could not remain there long: he had been too gentled since he waged war for his tribe in Africa and had been sold into slavery. Sadness took its place.

All I could see was a loop of iron chain fastened to a root, and a dead fish. Seeing my mystification, Obo grinned, and, kneeling down, very carefully brushed away dead leaves and dirt from the barbed, spread jaws of an iron trap. It was the largest I had ever seen.

"I can spring it, Miss Cleo, and Mas' Todd won't know dat de bear didn't come by and brush it wifout gitting caught," Obo proposed.

"All right."

A wave of heat seemed to move across my brain. "He'd just set it again," I said in a queerly strained voice.

"Yes—"

"Obo, can't you make it look as though the bear had been caught and broke loose with the trap on his foot?"

"I sho kin. Bears bus' loose a heap o' times. 'At root aint so strong a real big bear couldn't yank it out."

"Then he'll never catch another bear with that trap," Cleo exulted.

"It de onliest bear trap Mas' Todd got, too," Obo rejoiced. "Dey cost a heap o' money, and de grease aint worf it to him to buy anodder."

Obo began digging the dirt from around the root. Nearly a foot below the surface he found a rotted place and hammered it with his ax until he could break it with his hands. With good forethought he packed the dirt around the broken piece again, then drew it out. For several feet around the trap he cut and harrowed the ground and made long, perpendicular scratches in the bark of the tree. The watery place could not be expected to hold perfect footprints and his hand thrust in the muck did the trick well enough.

"We needn't play-like leavin' a trail," Obo remarked. " 'At bear come from de water and took to it agin, like dey do sometime. Now I'll hide de trap and on de way home drown it in deep water."

But I had another plan for its disposal.

We rinsed ourselves in the first clear branch we came to, and sat on its open bank to dry in the sunlight. Then, by Obo's directions, I followed up the branch to a white-oak hummock and came on a shack made of bark and logs, roofed with palm leaves, not more than ten feet square and hardly distinguishable from the wild landscape. A Negro woman of perhaps forty, tall and lean and savage-looking in a buckskin garment, was broiling venison over a low fire. She withdrew within the shack as I approached and I thought it likely that a firearm was close at hand.

"Are you Cliff Todd's woman?" I called, not approaching the doorway.

"Yassuh."

"I want to see him on some business. I'm Dave MacDaniel, the new foreman at Dr. Sams' stock farm."

"I reckoned 'at was you, but Cliff aint here."

"I've come a hard way to find him. I got Miss Cleo and Obo to take me across the swamp, pretending I wanted the outing, but they don't know my business. When do you expect him back?"

"Boss man, I don't know when to speck him. He lef' at fust light and was figurin' on findin' a egret roost. He might get in tomorrow but maybe not till the next day."

I was not greatly disappointed. There was some advantage in not taking Cliff Todd too much by surprise.

"Well, then, will you tell him to meet me at the junction of Little Run with Whale Branch a week from tomorrow? I won't say anything about the business I want to do with him, except I'm not getting paid very much money and I think if Cliff and I got together we could make some. Tell him I'd meet him here but I can't cross the swamp without Obo."

"I knowed you crossed wif 'em, as soon as I laid eyes on you. Nobody else can git across but 'em and my man Cliff." Her face had lighted. "If you tell 'em you jus' happen by and talk to me, would it be all right to send 'em some of dis venison roas' ovah de coals? It'll go mighty fine befo' you all start back."

I thanked her for the well-cooked meat and returned to my friends. They were almost as excited by the gift as over a "surprise" they had for me, hardly a half-mile's walk over fairly firm ground. When we had eaten, Obo led the way to a clean grassy bank, half-screened by vines from an arm of the slough. The scene was peculiarly poetic from causes I could not trace. Perhaps it was some grouping of the trees, permitting moss-hung corridors of gray-green light—standing so a little above the deluge that had drowned their great companions—and looking down on them as in grave thought, not rejoicing in their own escape, only dreaming of the mystery of life and death. I was told to watch or wait without sound or movement.

Before long there was a dramatic swirl of water. Some powerfully swimming creature left a splendid wake. Another swirl broke close to shore and a doglike head appeared and disappeared. Already I knew the "surprise"—only a family of otters dwelling near by and making this pool their playground. Presently we were treated to a fine exhibition of fancy swimming, one moment the water as still as at creation's dawn and the next in sudden tempest from the explosive feats of four performers. Cleo pointed her little finger up the shore. I caught the signal because I was observing her as closely as the show. The bank was elevated there perhaps by an old Indian kitchen-midden long covered by decayed vegetation, and what looked like a narrow trail led from the crest to the water. There the moss and grass had been worn off and shiny wet mud exposed.

Suddenly an otter appeared from nowhere on top of the mound, leaped off, and slid fast as a toboggan to hurl into the water with a glorious splash. In a moment all four of our entertainers were taking turns on the slide, often colliding with one another in their wild play, like urchins on a frozen hillside. But they did not know we were watching them in stealth, our eyes filled with delight, and Cleo did not know I was watching her.

I saw not the beauty of her face or body but the beautiful person that these signified. I had often thought what a wonderful thing it was that Cleo, the child of that haunted castle, born there by the event of murder, daughter of a fratricide, companion of Granny's ghosts of grief and horror, prisoner to a monster, could possess either outward or inward beauty. Now I knew that those very specters had in some mysterious way shaped her to this rare, unique, and lovely being. They had caused a certain lameness, in the sense Dr. Sams had used the word—a wound of the soul, it might be called, that caused it to grow different from other souls and banished it to solitude save with other wounded ones—but that lameness was manifest in beauty.

Only the lame can love, he had told me. That might be because only by loving or being loved can they escape from exile. Love is their only medicine. Suddenly it came to me who had given it to her in this measure. One of its givers was I, Dan, long ago. The gift was real and imperishable, the undiluted juice of a boy's heart. The other, who gave it at the beginning and would at the end and with every breath he drew, was Obo.

Wondering at this, I felt the first thrill of a great discovery. It was bursting upon me in flashes of insight—as, at night, lightning-flashes might illumine reach after reach of a dark road. My spine was tingling strangely. I had never felt such freshness and sharpness in the air.

I had wondered why this swamp had seemed different from the others—it would not have done so had I come here alone, or with only Cleo. This was Deep Swamp, the darkest and most primeval. Here poison serpents crept; breath was bought with blood; here almost every life grew out of death and the battle never ceased; here the cruel-fanged lynx stalked his innocent prey and killed it screaming and the red-eyed weasel slew the song birds. Yet I did not dwell on vengeance, or gaze with lust upon my sweet companion. The reason was, there was no evil here.

That too was Obo's work the greatest wonder I had ever known and yet undeniable. His only holy water was his own innocence and love.

Cleo, you too are innocent but, unlike him, you are afraid. You are very brave in the face of that fear, yet it curtails your powers. I am neither innocent nor fearless, thus I can never conquer the dark powers around me and within me; the most I can hope for is not to be conquered by them. But today they are exorcised. I am suddenly clear-eyed and very strong. Cleo, you told me that in Ibis Hall your eyes felt half-closed, as though you were gazing through a dirty windowpane, but in the woods with Obo they were opened. I understand that, now. Then look upon me with those open eyes and behold at last, at long last after a long blindness, the gift I have for you.

It comes, I think, of knowledge of you, second only to your great protector's. Next to him I know the fullness of your beauty in and out, and you will never find another in this world who sees it as clearly as I, and for whom it has such meaning. That meaning is transmuted to my gift to you, again second only to the one he has given you, although of a different kind. The kind he gave you is beyond the power of men like me. It is not the kind of which Dr. Sams spoke: his saying does not apply to giants. Obo is not lame.

Perhaps he was so, and you made him whole with a child's love. He has been through the valley and come out on the high hills. The love you gave me when you were yet a child and that I returned was the aura, the intimation of mature passionate love— the whole love of the lame.

Even then I knew you. If I had not met you then I would have dreamed you, small and childish-looking as you are—I do not know the need of that—and with eyes of quiet luster and your long lips curled in such a pleased and childish smile. I wanted your skin to be gauze-thin as some kind of symbol, and your little throat so slim and white as another symbol. I implored your love at the first sight of you, such hidden need I had of you. Since then I closed my eyes, but again they are open wide.

That need too is revealed. I have agreed to its pain and have conquered any fear. Sitting beside you here, while your wild companions play about you and the dappled light reveals you, I know its name.

Cleo must have felt my gaze because she turned to me. She was still smiling over the otters but instantly grew grave and her eyes rounded a little.

"You look startled," I told her, smiling.

"You were looking at me so strangely—"

"I know. With wonder and happiness and tremendous excitement, as though I had just found you. Well, that's true in a way." It did not matter if Oho heard me.

"I don't think you ought to say that, considering—"

"It would be all right to say it, even if I were in love with some other girl. But I'm not. I never have been."

She was still a moment and then asked, "Why did you let me think so?"

"I was afraid to love you. You were out of my reach."

"Why have you taken it back?"

"You're not out of my reach now. At least I can give you a gift I have for you."

She drew a deep, troubled breath. "What is it?" she asked in a low, clear tone.

"My love."

I had called the gift by a word of many other meanings, yet a single and definite meaning to both of us now, perfectly simple, entirely clear. The sense of mystery that came upon me was of the thing itself, such a strange visitor to our lowly earth, partaking of that earth yet with wide pinions—a slim white heron might be its symbol, delicate-appearing, beautiful, yet calling from the high skies, sunlight on its wings, lighting to feed earthily and soaring again, free from horizons. The thought came to me with great joy that the gift was not restricted to the great, that kings and clowns were alike eligible, and that the rash and foolish young were more equal to it than the old and wise.

Cleo had been looking off as I mused, in wonder but not surprise, an indescribable beauty on her face, but now her eyes made a swift search of mine and again turned away.

"You don't know what you're saying."

I laughed happily at that. "Both of us know perfectly well."

"What changed you?"

"I haven't changed. I loved you in all my dreams and had you in many of them. I just now found out about it."

"Maybe it's just passion. You felt it so strongly, when we were at the edge of the swamp that night."

My mind took hold of the problem, and moving with unwonted power, instantly solved it.

"There's plenty of that but it comes from loving you and knowing it. It isn't a substitute for love I didn't dare give you, as it was then. I think that's the difference."

"When did you become sure?"

"Just a few minutes ago."

A lone white heron, with sunlight on its wings, soared down from its unhorizoned sky to the reedy shore. Others had been coming and going, but I picked out this one as a sending to us alone, emblematic of what was sent from more profound skies. Its lighting down, I fancied, had symbolic meaning. Only a few minutes later Cleo and I had to get down to earth and see to its affairs.

"Dave, if it's true—and your face and voice tell me so—I'm afraid to have you love me."

"Don't ever be afraid of that."

"You know what I mean. Besides, there's something—I can feel it—I keep thinking of Papa. I keep thinking of Dan, too. I want you to love me, Dave—you don't know how much—I've dreamed of you too—but—what are you going to do?"

I did not reply at once, for the scene had a sudden uncanny aspect and the flakes of sunlight through the moss appeared to float in the air like the notes of a violin, and Pa was speaking to me.

Have you lain with her in the embrace of love? Then never do. Let it not come to pass. Resist loving her, even if you see her as Madeline incarnate. Close your heart to her. Every jot and tittle of love you bear the daughter will reduce by that much the hate you bear the sire.

This last was not true. It made all the rest invalid and set me free, whatever chains Cleo might wear. . . . Dr. Sams was speaking, the night of my return to Little Ibis. *Just take pains that she doesn't become interested in you again. Ralph has only to lift his hand. . . . If Saul thinks you're worth hunting, God help you.*

Part or all might be true, but my hand too would be lifted. So swift is thought that a shred of palm frond fluttering down against the rising earth-heat had hardly touched, so light a touch, the water, when I spoke on.

"Ask you to marry me."

"I'm glad you stopped a minute before you said that," she murmured after a little while. "It showed that you wanted to be sure." There was fear in her face, but I thought a great joy, too.

"Will you, Cleo?"

She smiled. "Remember I said I'd marry any man who'll take me away from Wood Ibis—except you."

"That doesn't hold now."

"In part, it doesn't. I was ashamed of trying to change you into Dan. Would your being so like him—I mean, reminding me of him—make us happier together—or—" She paused.

"It would make us happier, I know."

"Could you take me away at once?"

"I can protect you. I'll promise that."

"I'm awfully confused—wonderfully happy that you love me but afraid too—we'll have to let it go for now. Just hold me, like you did that last night on shipboard."

I went to her and sitting down, drew her across my breast. Obo sat a little distance off in plain sight of us, but if she wanted him to leave she would tell or signal him to do so. It did not seem strange to me that I would like to have him near us. His power was so great, his protection of her so true, and my own strength was new-found and untested. I had a feeling about him that he alone could raise the curse that lay on Wood Ibis, its shadow falling so darkly on Cleo and me. The only movement he made was to edge a little forward, so that we were barely behind his field of vision, and I thought he did that on my account rather than on Cleo's—lest I not understand the closeness of their bond.

We talked of gone-by things and stopped to kiss and I knew immeasurable joy. I had fought through a deep and perilous swamp to come out on this green bank.

Our passion for each other welled, but it was no cruel, predatory thing, and it did not prevail over our care of each other or increase our danger. At last Obo spoke softly, as though waking some loved one from sleep.

"We gotta be startin' back pitty soon now. De tide about to flow."

So would time flow, from this moment onward, deep and strong, and perchance drown us both as once a tide had drowned the cypress forest, for we grew in perilous ground. Suddenly Cleo's eyes were wide with terror.

"What shall we do, Dave?"

"Do you love me, Cleo?"

"I think so, but I'm afraid."

"Will you meet me again soon?"

"As soon as I dare. But it's so dangerous—"

"When and where?"

"Is there a hand on the farm you can trust? Obo could get him a message."

"Yes—Joshua."

"If it's a long time, don't think it's because I don't want to. I wish we could always stay in the woods. Then I'd love you and we could be happy."

"Wonderful," I whispered.

"We are so lonely, both of us. Your parents dead—and mine cut off from me—in some way I don't understand. I think we need each other as much as any two people ever in the world."

I whispered to her and kissed her eyes that had filled with tears.

"A thought came to me just now—I was afraid it might sound silly to you—but it won't," she went on. "Do you know we're like the babes in the woods? We're happy here, because we're together —and the birds sing to us so sweetly—but we're lost—and don't know where to go."

She kissed me with tear-wet lips, sweeter to me than any other sweetness life could hold, and got slowly to her feet. Obo led the way back to the crossing. But before he entered the slough he retrieved Cliff Todd's bear-trap that he had hidden.

"I'll drop it in deep water," he told Cleo.

Then, so swift upon the wonder and the beauty that had just now come to pass, its echo and its hope still illumining Cleo's face, I heard the voice of Dan speaking calmly and persuasively out of the lips she had just kissed.

"No, don't throw it away. I want to look it over. Bears have to be trapped sometimes and I might invent a trap that would be more merciful.

"Yassuh."

But there were other animals to be trapped whom I would not spare the great barbed jaws.

Sunday was windless and sultry. At noon a few buzzards kept a lazy watch aloft, but the perching herons stood as still as in the Chinese picture Dr. Sams had bought from an Indiaman, the dragonflies looked like tassels on the reeds, the busy marsh wrens loafed in the grass, and the low tide of Little Run trickled slowly. I had expected Cliff Todd to be late for the rendezvous, but he was not: he merely delayed awhile informing me of his presence. Indeed he thought he had kept it a secret. As he watched me from one thicket and then another, sizing me up with his swamp-rat eyes, figuring whether I was for or against his survival, he did not know that I too had been a rat, stealing bread and slops in the Orphanage kitchen, whatever bird or beast I might be now. I could not swear that I had heard or seen him: it was as though I smelled him.

He withdrew and presently advanced boldly in the open. He was a small, spare man with little hands and feet, delicate-looking almost, yellow-brown in color save for his icy blue eyes and scant black hair, so tight-skinned and wiry that no one could guess his age. He was dressed in cotton trousers and shirt and carried a rifle and powder horn. He had small, sharp white teeth like a squirrel.

"I reckon you're Mr. MacDaniel," he said.

"Yes, sir. I take it you're Cliff Todd."

"That's me." He sat down on a log and waited.

"Do you want me to get to business, or shall I beat around the bush?"

"I reckon you wouldn't of sent for me, just to pass the time o' day."

"I got your name from a nigger on Little Ibis. I'm not saying which one."

"Niggers know a lot sometimes, and sometimes they think they know a lot what they don't."

"I'm not sure this one knew what he was talking about, but he said, you could make as good moonshine whiskey as any man ever put in his mouth."

"He could be right about that."

"You know I came here from Baltimore. A man I know up there's got a lugger that he runs all the way to Florida. He told me he'd pay cash for all the good rye whiskey I could furnish him."

"I could make him some whiskey but I aint got no grain and sugar."

"I could furnish you with both, for half what the whiskey brings."

He took his hunting knife and began to whittle a stick. I took the opportunity to pick up what looked like a rotten stick an inch or so in diameter and dug in the ground with it.

"I don't love to get in no trouble," he remarked.

"You wouldn't get in any."

"Then you better talk plainer than that, mister."

"Dr. Sams don't keep track of his cribs and stores like the Dunbartons do. I reckon you know he keeps pretty busy counting his bottles."

Cliff Todd laughed softly. "I reckon them horses use a lot o' grain."

"They could use twice as much, and he'd never know it. The main thing is, there mustn't be any wagon tracks leading off, but I've figured out how there wouldn't be any. A bateau doesn't leave any tracks."

"It sure don't, mister."

"It could go in a wagon to where the road crosses Little Run and be delivered right here—or better yet, a little farther down Whale Branch on the opposite shore."

Cliff sat like a thinker, his chin cupped in his palm. However, he was not thinking as much as communing with his instincts. I feared those somewhat. He was a long-time dweller of the swamps. However, I had taken great pains to be convincing—preparing and rehearsing my speeches—and was a long-time practicer of cunning.

"I reckon that might work out all right," he remarked at last.

"Do you know a good landing over there?" The extreme tension in my chest did not tighten up my voice.

"I sure do. I'll show it to you."

He got up and led the way across Whale Branch on a fallen water-oak. I was carrying the stick I had picked up, for it had not just happened to be there on the ground. It was what actors call a "property" needed for this scene. Nor was it as rotten as it appeared: beneath the mossy shredded bark it had an inch core of solid black oak. The first time Cliff stopped to draw aside some branches I brought it down across the top of his head with about half the strength of my right arm.

My first sensation was of surprise at how easy the act was. Actually I had tried to persuade myself of this beforehand but had never believed it. The very importance of this first stroke had hampered and frightened me. Now I knew what Dr. Sams had meant when he called me a man of my hands. Even the weight of the blow had been well measured. But my next sensation was more strange and momentous—a high wave of exultation washing every cell of my body. Cliff had wilted and dropped at my feet, his animal strength ebbed, his swamp-taught cunning in abeyance, his avid life in my hands.

The wave receded but left me changed. There was a pleasant hardness in my heart, excluding both fear and mercy; my eyes felt bright and sharp, I had a sense of deadly capability. I rejoiced in the completeness of my plans and was eager to get on with their execution.

Cliff made a light load to the place I had picked out—a small slough running into Whale Branch. A little water was trickling seaward from puddle to puddle in its black mud bottom when I arrived, and the fiddler crabs scuttled in all directions. Before I had completed my preparations, the creatures were again venturing out of their holes. The mud made a smacking sound and the little wet remaining in the sinks had stood perfectly still and then began to trickle in the opposite direction.

The chain of Cliff's big bear-trap had already been fastened to a cypress root deep in the mud, unreleasable by a one-handed man. I had already prepared two small blocks of wood which, placed against the sides of Cliff's left wrist would act as buffers against the barbed iron jaws and prevent them compressing the big veins and arteries and cutting off circulation. His right was free, but when the time came for him to try, he could not open the trap with it—indeed he would not be able to loosen its clutch by a fraction of an inch. Only by his full weight efficiently applied could the powerful spring be compressed. It was a horrid-looking append-age to his left arm but that was why I had employed it, instead of a rope that would have done the actual business just as well. Now he was lying face upwards, low in the mud as in a feather bed, his head in a slowly spreading puddle of water. I might have to move him a little, if he took too long to regain consciousness, but I thought the lapping against his throat and into his ears would soon bring him to.

I withdrew behind some thickets, out of sight of Cliff when he would wake, but able to watch him through the vines as might a catamount in ambush. Such a beast would be likewise alert to his every move, his blood tingling, waiting his moment of supreme pride and power. . . . Suddenly I remembered that our panthers almost never attacked human beings. I pictured the beast watching instead a deer caught in the quagmire—and how different the whole scene became!

It would be innocent of evil, as were similar scenes on the day I crossed this swamp with Obo and Cleo. The air would be humid and warm as now, the vines would enmesh and perhaps strangle the young trees, and plants would eat the carcasses of their fellows, but the snags would not take diabolic shapes, no steam would rise from hell, the shadows would not be haunted with the monstrous creations of human imagination. The only evil here was what Cliff and I had brought.

My captive began to stir. He raised his right hand, let it fall, raised it again and touched the top of his head. It dropped into the puddle and he was puzzling, in his half-sleep, at the warm wetness. He shifted his left arm a little but there was a weight upon it he did not understand; perhaps he heard too above the smack of the mud a clattering sound. His ears and the back of his neck felt warm and wet. Presently he turned his head on one side—perhaps trying to ease the pain at the top—and suddenly his mouth and nose were filled with muddy water.

With a spasm of coughing and violent movement he sat up. Vision was returning to his eyes, a sense of time and place to his brain, and instantly he remembered the war he was waging for survival. He saw the muck around him and the tidal water trickling in. Only as he was lunging to his knees did the tension on his left arm draw his eyes to the bear-trap fixed to his wrist.

For an instant he was arrested by horror. The evil brooding over the swamp thickened like mist as he began to struggle. Again he started to spring up, lifting the trap from the muck with a sucking sound, but the chain was shorter than he thought, and he could not raise it more than a few inches above the water. Then in a frantic effort to apply more strength, he surged to his feet.

His back was more bowed and his head lower than Pa's! I thought of that with a stab of joy sharp and hard as steel. His body twisted as he clutched the chain with his right hand and heaved with all his might against the horrid yoke.

Then he remembered he must keep his head. . . . He had been in tight places before and escaped by cool cunning and ability. I did not believe he had yet considered how he came to be in this fix—he had seen the buffers of wood protecting his wrists from the iron teeth but they had no more meaning for him than the rest of the horror. Now, very bravely, he began to function like a man instead of a beast. He took time for one desperate glance about him, perhaps in terror of the enemy who had brought this about, possibly in irrational hope of appealing to his mercy. Then he sat down in the muck and reached for the knife he had worn at his belt.

His hand groped in vain for the hilt. In one horrified glance he saw that it was gone. His next attack was against the mire itself. He began scrabbling at it with his free hand, trying to dig down to the fastening of the chain. The mud and water flew, but the hole filled almost as fast as he could dig it, and when he stopped to grope for the shackle, his labor showed cruelly in vain. Then he caught sight of a big stone—I had provided it for a later phase of the affair—and threshing through the mire he picked it up in desperate hope. But there was nothing firm against which he could place the chain to pound it. Again he dug frantically hoping to pound loose the shackle from its anchor. With the strength of desperation he managed to force the stone through the resisting muck and water to deal a few feeble blows against the root; I heard their muffled knock. But to reach so far below the surface brought his face very close to its image in the black water. The space narrowed slowly but steadily.

It was then, I thought, that he remembered that the tide running up from the creek was the New Moon tide. He knew that tide of old, filling every swale and gutter in the swamp and forcing the marsh hens out of their hiding places to swim on its brimming flood. He looked at the banks of the slough, where the reeds were still muddy-wet from the early morning tide, and to find the high mark he had to twist his head and raise his eyes. It was then that his mouth opened and gave vent to a wild ringing cry.

"Help! Help!"

I stepped smiling out of the thickets. Maybe the smile was feigned, but not hard to force.

"What's the matter, Cliff?"

"You devil!" he howled. "Why have you done this to me!"

"Why, you've caught your hand in your own trap. It's happened before to bear-trappers. The trigger's too easy."

"Take it off me, for God's sake. Hurry, before the tide—"

"Oh, the tide will run a long time yet. By standing up and holding it as high as you can, you can keep your nose out of water for an hour or more—"

"Take it off! Please, mister—"

"All right—for a price."

This too was madness if he stopped to think—what possessions did he have to pay me for the trouble I had gone to—but he spoke wildly on.

"I'll give you anything I've got—my gun—my woman. I've got more than a hundred egret plumes—"

"I don't want any of that. The price is just that you tell me about something that happened about twenty years ago. After you've told me, you'll write the gist of it on a piece of paper, and sign your name."

There fell a silence complete save for the trickle and lap of water, the smacking of the lips of the mud, and the distant cawing of a crow. Again Cliff was forcing his head to work—trying to appraise accurately the situation, employing his eyes and ears with utmost sharpness, calling on every resource of cunning and strength. Perhaps he did not yet know what I referred to. Perhaps there had been several stories that a stranger, with unknown purposes, might want to hear. The strengthened hope of life gave birth to a hope that he might avoid all further penalty, if he were bold enough . . . cunning enough.

"Who are you, and what's your game?" he asked.

"That's of no matter to you."

"What do you want to know?"

"How you supplied Ralph Dunbarton with the cottonmouth moccasin that he used to kill his wife."

"Are you some kind of policeman?"

"No."

"Well, I didn't. If anybody else caught that snake and sold it to him, I don't know who it was, unless it was one of his niggers. I didn't have nothing to do with it. As far as I know the snake got in the house and crawled into the bed for warmth. I've known other snakes—"

"Why are you protecting him?"

"I'm not. I'm telling you the truth, so help me God."

"Well, that's too bad. If you're protecting him, you won't any more. If it's the truth, you're going to be drowned for sticking to it."

"You don't dare let me drown! People would know you'd murdered me—"

"Talk sense, Cliff. I'm coming back at low tide, take the trap off your wrist, and unwind the chain from the root to its usual length. You won't know when I take it off, or put it back on—you'll be dead as a dead fish. I'm going to lay a dead fish or some other kind of bait handy. You were setting the trap to catch a bear—"

"I wouldn't set it in a tidal slough—"

"You might, if you know a bear came in here at low water to catch fish or crabs. There'll be plenty of crabs here, you know, after the first one finds you. Nobody else will find you for a long time. Poor devil—he got caught while baiting his own trap. If you should happen to be found in time for some one to see that bump on your head, you must have knocked it against that rock. You'll flop around quite a lot, you know, when the tide gets high but not quite high enough."

180

Cliff had got to his feet in frenzy, then he sat down in the water with an air of resignation at once courageous and grotesque.

"Then I reckon I'm in for a drowning," he remarked, when I remained silent.

"Yes—unless you tell the truth."

"Well, I'd rather drown than tell a lot of dirty lies about some feller. I never have done that, and never will."

I did not answer, only found a comfortable seat on a log and lighted a pipe. I had a sense of histrionics, but felt they were effective; and in a moment the actual drama eclipsed them and took me out of myself. The water soon girdled Cliff's waist, completely submerging the trap. It gurgled no more, only welled upward. The light dimmed a little as the sun in the hazy sky went behind a cloud; I strained in vain for the slightest sound. A member of the heron tribe, dark, so thin it looked emaciated, started to light at the brink of the slough, saw its strange inmate, squawked, and flapped away. Cliff's right hand crept to his left and was desperately strained—I saw the tension move into his shoulder—then it relaxed.

"Why do you want to know about that snake?" he asked.

"That's my affair."

"I don't say I didn't give a moccasin to Mr. Dunbarton one time. He said he was going to keep it alive until he found somebody who could make him a belt out of the skin—I gave it to him in a potato bag. It wasn't a very big snake and I don't think it could of growed enough between when I gave it to him and the time his wife was bit to be the same snake."

"How long a time was that?"

"I reckon six months or a year. It was so long ago—"

"That couldn't have been the same snake."

"I don't say it wasn't, or it was. I caught it in a fish net and gave it to him in a potato sack. But that was the only snake I ever supplied him with, so help me God."

"Cliff, they say if a man dies with a lie on his lips he'll go to hell sure."

"It aint a lie."

"You caught another snake two or three days before his wife's death, and you didn't catch it in a fish net, but with a forked stick."

"Where did you hear that, I'd like to know?" he asked.

"You were seen doing it."

"Who seen me."

"Granny, Sadie's mother, in a vision."

Until now it had not occurred to me to make use of the senile old woman of supposed second sight but the invention of the moment had a more powerful effect on Cliff than the speeches I had so carefully prepared. He had fought with terror and forced it down with quite notable courage; now that inward citadel began to crumble. I saw a change in his face and posture.

"That old witch," he gasped.

"Why are you shielding the killer? You can say you didn't know why he wanted the snake, and after the woman's death you were afraid to say anything."

"Would I have to stand trial?"

"No. The statement in your handwriting is all I want. Then you can disappear in the swamps and nobody will bother you."

"Will you let me go as soon as I tell you?"

"As soon as you've answered any questions I might ask."

"He came to me and said he wanted a big moccasin. He said what he wanted it for was his business, and I wasn't to say a word to anyone. There was a mighty big one that used around a pond near the river, and I caught it with a forked stick as the old woman said. That night I took it to him. He met me where the road crosses Little Run, and he gave me five dollars. Three nights later Sadie died of snakebite."

"All right, I'm wading out with a notebook and pencil. Write just 'I furnished Ralph Dunbarton with a big cottonmouth moccasin three nights before his wife died,' and sign your name."

When I was in reach of his free hand I braced the notebook against my thigh: although he had been trembling violently he steadied and wrote rapidly and far more legibly than I expected.

"Now take off the cursed thing," he gasped, "and let me go."

"There are just a few questions more, and we've plenty of time. Did Ralph ever give you any more money, to bribe you not to tell anyone about the snake?"

182

"I never asked him for none."

But I saw in his eyes that he regretted this answer, and was again terrified.

"Why did he trust you?"

" 'Cause I'm a man o' my word. You may not believe that—"

"Ralph Dunbarton trusted to that? You'd been dead long ago, if that was all. You heard about Bert and Slewfoot. He had something on you, didn't he? That's why he came to you—because you didn't *dare* tell."

"He didn't have nothin' on me. I was just afraid to tell, mindin' my own business. You said you'd let me go."

"The water's coming up fast. You'd better talk fast."

"I don't know nothin' more about it. He didn't have nothin' on me. For God's sake—"

"You killed somebody and he knew it. He had the evidence against you. But he won't be in any fix to use it, when I'm through with him. If I see it's going to come out I'll give you plenty of warning so you can get out of the country. Who'd you kill?"

The water was up to his armpits now and he scrambled to his feet, and the trap pulled the length of the chain was still under the surface. His left arm shook violently and he was gesturing wildly with his right hand.

"Oh, God, let me go! It was only a nigger belonging to Mr. D'Arcy. He'd been fooling around a yeller girl I had—"

"It was you who rigged the explosion that killed Bruce Dunbarton. Ralph made you do that too."

"Take it off! Take it off! I'll be drowned before—"

"Not if you talk fast. What did you have to do with that?"

"He rigged it himself. Hurry, for God's sake. Look at that water! You promised you wouldn't drown me if I told."

"You haven't told all—"

"He got the fuzee from a slaver that lay off Turtle Inlet. She was the *Clarabelle*—she's still afloat—a sugar boat that comes into Charleston in late summer—I swear that's all I know. Believe me, mister. But it's too late—you've drowned me, God damn you to hell!"

It would have been too late to dig out and unfasten the chain —indeed the task would be all but impossible in this deep tide—

and the strength of my two hands and his free right hand could have hardly compressed the spring and loosened the jaws. When I turned from him and sprang toward the great knees of a cypress tree on the bank of the slough he thought I was leaving him to drown, and his howls of fury and terror smothered the violent splashing caused by both our frenzies. I rolled aside a big stone. It had wedged securely the root I had previously cut from the tree and to which I had fastened the trap. By lifting it I could give enough play to the chain so that Cliff could straighten his bowed back and raise his face well above the tide.

It was a much heavier lift than I had expected. I employed the full strength of my back in a frantic heave—Cliff meanwhile tugging with all his might on the chain—before the packed silt parted and let the black root rise 'gator-like to the surface. Then hauling on it, I dragged its captive to shore.

Then I stood gasping and faint as the silt spread and blackened the water at my feet, the knowledge of evil dark and deep within my brain. I had found out how easily murder could come about, on Wood Ibis.

Cliff Todd and I sat on the bank of the slough await-
ing the aftermath. He looked smaller than ever with
his knees close to his chin; he appeared more pensive
than outraged or chagrined; he was "favoring," as
the people say, his left arm, occasionally shaking his
numbed hand and tenderly feeling his wrist as well
as the top of his head. Otherwise he seemed unscathed by the or-
deal. I was far more shaken than he and had a hard time repressing hysterical laughter at our appearance: mud-plastered from head
to foot. We were both swamp rats in a way of speaking, I thought.
But he was more rat, less man than I and hence was far more innocent of the knowledge of evil. He killed by instinct.

"Well, mister," he remarked at last, "I smelled something wrong
about that trap being gone, but it looked all right, and I didn't believe my own nose."

"Miss Cleo had Obo break it out, so it wouldn't catch a bear.
I'm going to drown it in deep water."

"Well, I wouldn't love to catch a bear with it nohow, now. I
reckon I know how he'd feel."

"Yes, sir, I reckon you do."

After brief, efficient meditation he spoke again. "I reckon you
know that there paper I gave you is no good in court unless you've
got a sample of my handwriting to compare it with."

"Dr. Sams has got a sample of it. You wrote him for some medicine when you had chills and fever. That's the way I knew you
could read and write."

"I forgot about that."

"If you wanted to, you could appear in court and say I forced
you to write that statement. I'd have enough evidence by then to
show the statement is true, and then your killing the Negro would
come out. Ralph may bring it out but it would be more against
him than for him. It explains so well why he'd go to you for the
snake and why you didn't dare testify against him."

"I aint going to go to court if I can help it. If you let me know in plenty of time, like you said, I'll hit for the Okefenokee. I know a feller down there. He said he could hide me till hell froze over."

"I'll let you know in plenty of time."

"I'll say this too. I aint got any hard feelings about this. I never did you no harm, but as I see it, what you did to make me talk, wasn't agin me but agin a man who has harmed you, how I don't know. You took strong measures but they was the only ones that would work."

"I thank you very much, Cliff, for your broad-mindedness."

"I hate Ralph Dunbarton. I hate him to hell, and there's only one man on earth I hate wuss, and that's his son Saul. I've killed and I've robbed, but I'm a clean man compared to them."

"That's true. By the way, Cliff, while you stay here don't buy any more stolen stuff from the Negroes. A big Negro was almost whipped to death for it."

"I did it to get back on them Dunbartons, kind of, and didn't think about the risk to the niggers. I won't do it no more."

"That's fine."

"Well, leave my rifle and knife where we was sittin'. You can unload the rifle if you want to. That will keep you from worrying about me follerin' you and shootin' you in the back."

"I'm not afraid of that. I'll tell you what I intended to do—and I'll do it, though I don't think it's necessary. I'm going to give this paper to a man I can trust, to be opened in case I'm killed."

"That's fair enough. Now I'm goin' to tell you somethin' you didn't ask me. I do it not for a favor to you but 'cause I hate Saul. He found out you was with Obo and the girl last Saturday. I reckon he suspected somethin' and went to look for your tracks. He asked me if I seen you. He thought I might have done a little spyin', which I would of, if I'd been home that day: I reckon he wanted to know if you and the girl was sparkin'. I told him I wasn't around that day and since I didn't know what your business was, I didn't tell him you'd left word for me."

"Thanks for telling me. It's a very great favor."

"A word to the wise, as the feller said. I know that Saul. The next time you walk out with the girl he'll play a dirty trick on you both. He's figuring it out right now."

I had not thought of Cleo for some hours. Her lovely face had not risen between me and my dreadful goals. Thinking of her now, prey to Saul, once entreating his mercy in my hearing, often doing so perhaps in scenes I did not want to imagine, I began to tremble and my love for her became caught up in my hate for him and the two opposing forces, like two gales that meet at sea, formed a tornado of emotion in my heart. The organ is only a blood-pump, Dr. Sams had remarked, and passion has its seat in the lower brain. Be it so, my head was only reeling and dizzy, but my heart felt as though its strong walls would burst.

I could not have Cleo to keep, as long as Saul lived. Cliff sitting there did not reduce the stunning effect of that thought and became involved in it. If Saul had fallen in the slough caught in a bear-trap I could have waited while the waters rose, then while they threshed and swirled as though a wounded 'gator were dying in the mire—sometimes giving glimpses of his throes—and finally flowed quietly again to their appointed mark. Cliff might help me. The Swamp whispered to me of hidden murder. The dark tide rose, the light sifted weirdly through the moss, and the air reeked with evil. . . .

"I hate him wuss than any man alive," Cliff told me in a low, dreamy voice, "but not as much as you do."

"What do you mean?"

"I couldn't of done what you did today even to the man I hated, let alone to a feller I'd never seen, to git at another."

Cliff would not serve. He had become a fellow of the animals he hunted, bears and panthers who killed only that they might live. His knowledge of evil was not of sufficient depth.

We parted presently, and when I had returned to Little Ibis the bloody design descended into a cellar of my brain, out of the way of its other designs, but perhaps gaining strength and taking form down there in the dark. Dr. Sams put Cliff's statement in his lockbox. He did not ask me how I had got it, and I did not tell him. He gave me the welcome information that the *Clarabelle* was a "friendship" ship—meaning that the same men signed on year after year—and on her touching Charleston in late summer, it was quite possible that we could find an old salt who recalled the purchase of some fuzee by the overseer of Wood Ibis nearly twenty years before. Still I could not quite believe that Fortune would so smile.

187

My immediate business would be with Cleo. It was to win her love, if it were not already won, to marry her, and to safeguard her. Cleo too knew its urgency, and at the end of a long-drawn, acheful week, Joshua gave me a note that Obo had handed him. It instructed me to ride about sundown that afternoon to the causeway over Fern Creek; she would meet me there and had something to tell me. I did not doubt that she had already heard from Saul.

I saw her coming and in great joy I raced toward her, freeing my reins or my heart. I flushed the herons from their feeding and they circled wildly, impatient for me to be gone, appearing and disappearing among the tree-tops; and all the swamp-devils ran. My white bird with a black crest! She leaned out of the saddle to receive and return my kiss, and the mettlesome horses stayed still long enough, as though this were a serious matter.

"I've only got a minute," she told me. "I'd have sent you word before but there wasn't any chance till now for us to see each other."

"It's been very long," I told her.

"For me, too, Dave. The day in the woods was the happiest—in many years. I've longed for another day with you—to talk things over—to find out a little more how I feel—maybe just to be with you—and now we can have one."

"Wonderful."

"Saul told Pa at dinner last night that tomorrow he's riding over to Murray and will start early and be gone all day."

I started to speak but thought better of it. The thought seemed a sudden one: actually it was only the out-throw of a long churning in my mind.

"I thought since it's Sunday you could ride with me 'way down the beach toward Bull Island," she went on.

"Why we can, and have a wonderful day. But don't start until Saul's gone."

We arranged a meeting place, but the long night intervened, and in sudden passion we sprang down into each other's arms. In the morning I was up and gone before Dr. Sams wakened, and he would be puzzled by the note I left for him. The dew still glimmered in the fresh-up sun when Cleo and I kept our rendezvous. She was riding her roan gelding, Tuck, the brother of her bay, Nip.

I was on Paddy, the horse I rode in the fields. Obo rode shank's mare as he wanted it: he could never find enough play for his big and restless muscles.

The sea was a charming azure with a low, clean surf. Mainly we kept to the beach, loving its solitude, companions only with the little sandpipers whose bands were always and at once lighting and flying and with great pelicans passing on their marauder journeys and with ubiquitous sea gulls who looked good-sized and fine and bold, but were really handfuls of feathers. Occasionally we had to draw back among the dunes, sometime skirting the palm woods, and fording or swimming salt creeks. There was not a mark of man on these long beaches, for the great manors lay far inland, where fresh-water rivers rose and fell with the tides. The ocean was ours today, and the air, and it seemed even the sun. We were childishly and wonderfully happy. The dark spot of hate and fury in my heart I had somehow walled off for these hours, and it cast no shadow on all this brightness.

We had brought hand-lines and mullet-bait and about twelve miles from Ibis Hall we came on the inlet where often Cleo had had good sport fishing for red drum. While Obo was fixing the lines I rode one horse and led the other to a wide natural meadow behind the dunes, watered the beasts and picketed them under palm trees. Actually this place had been described to me by Joshua the night before. Particularly he had assured me that a horseman could not approach our beasts across the meadow without danger of being observed from the beach, but a man on foot could easily do so. I noticed too where a pointed stone had been placed on another close by the clump of palms.

Content with that, unspeakably happy with Cleo, I threw out my hook beside hers for common fishing. The big drum with spotted tails would not bite: we caught only cat- and toad-fish. When we had shared with Obo the lunch she had brought, she let me lay my head on her lap and often bent down to kiss me. She said very little though—I thought perhaps because she had a great deal to tell me and did not know how to begin. Actually she had already told me by the sweetness of her lips on mine and by the tremulous touch of her hands.

"You've been thinking it over?" I asked her at last.

"Yes, all the time."

"What did you decide?"

"I thought how happy we were together—and how sad I was when you were gone—and I couldn't stand the thought of parting with you again."

"Do you love me, Cleo?"

"Yes, Dave."

"Forever 'n ever? That's what I asked Pa—one day."

"Forever and forever." She put her lips on mine and cried.

"I love you forever and forever, Cleo."

"I know. That's the way you are."

"I've been loving you as long as I can remember anything. I didn't know your name or where you were, but I think I saw you in dreams. In the first dreams you were a little girl taller than I was, and older I guess, and you'd put your arms around me, and I felt so happy and safe. My love for you was mainly a prayer to be loved by you."

"How did I look in those dreams?"

"I don't know." But until I had found her that day in Philadelphia I had thought she had golden instead of black hair.

"Do you remember how your mother looked?"

"No, I'd lost her before I remember anything. I looked for her in my dreams but couldn't find her—she'd been gone a long time, it seemed, before I somehow got lost. It wasn't a real memory—it was only a sense of an interval between losing her and something happening—in my dreams there was a kind of signal, like a gun being fired—that caused me to be left at an orphanage. It was only in dreams that I knew about it. I think that she'd had to leave me in someone's care and after awhile that person couldn't care for me any more. But I started to talk about you—"

"Tell me the other too."

"I don't believe my mother deserted me wilfully, because I had a sense of having been loved. I didn't know the word—it was just something wonderful and happy that I'd lost. Maybe I invented you to give it back to me some day."

"You never told me before that you were in an orphanage."

"No, only that my parents were dead. I was adopted by a kind man who wanted a son. He loved me deeply and I loved him more than I can tell you. I wanted to do everything in the world for him. I kept on having the dream of the signal—and finding myself back at the Orphanage—but sometimes as it was just about to sound— and I had the awfullest sense of doom—you came. You were standing there. If you came in time the gun didn't go off—and I could stay with Pa." But that had happened only after Cleo and I had met.

"How did you know it was I?"

"You were dark-haired and very beautiful. Your face wasn't always distinct but I never had any doubt. Sometimes at first you would just stand there with a little smile, or we would kiss each other, but after fourteen we had each other completely. All young men have such dreams but mine were always about you."

There was a good deal of tension in my chest but her arms about my neck and tears on my face and perhaps a sea gull circling overhead on which I could rest my eyes gave easy passage to the words. I heard the surf—the low-pitched crashings of the waves on the beach and the long hiss of their retreat—and the sound reminded me of rain on Pa's roof when I was warm and safe in bed, with him sleeping in the same room and I could go to sleep without fear of evil dreams. Cleo and I seemed one person saved from the sea, brought up out of the dark into the sunlight. I was conscious of Obo down the beach and of a vision of Saul around the corner of my gaze, but I would kill Saul when the time came. I would see him dead at my feet. The safety and happiness of that fulfillment was upon me now in a kind of presage of what was to be.

"So I waited for you," I told her. "I've never gone to any other girl in search of love."

"That's so strange, Dave. You see—I imagined Dan waiting for me—and it turned out to be you. I went to him in dreams—who I thought was he—and I stood and watched him just as you said, and sometimes we kissed—that was while I was still a little girl— but later on the rest happened too—at least a wonderfully blissful thing not very clear in the dream. There was always the scent of pine. The light was dim and the space cramped. Often when I was awake and would smell piney woods I'd go into a blissful kind of trance. Maybe Dan died—long ago—and by some magic you took his place. There's a lot of magic in the world."

"Will you marry me, Cleo?"

"Yes."

"Right away?"

"As soon as you can take me away. Will that be soon?"

"I'll take you at once away from Saul—to Dr. Sams's house. After you're my wife you'll be safe—"

"Oh—you don't know!" But hope fought with her terror and won, at least for this moment. "Anyway, Dave, I'll need a little time to get my parents' consent. I'll marry you anyway—but I don't want to oppose them if I can help it. Mama's word has been law for me all my life—"

"That frightens me."

"It needn't. She's so beautiful—and wonderful. She'll know it's my only hope of happiness. And if I can persuade her, she'll win Papa over and make him promise not to tell Saul."

"I'm going to fight Saul in the open. That's the decision I came to last night. He's never had anyone fight him before. He's going to be surprised."

"Oh, I love to have you say that. Right now I hope—I believe— that you can defeat him. But you saw how he would have broken down my door—"

"I'm going to be in front of it, before long."

That stirred her deeply, I did not know why. Her eyes turned very dark and she sprang up and walked rapidly up the beach where driftwood had lodged and the heaped-up sand had formed a little cove hidden from Obo's view. I marked that it was also hidden from the palm scrub behind. There she waited for me, as I had once waited for her behind a woodshed.

I wondered if that instant she thought of Dan. If so, it did not cool my welcome when I had overtaken her at the hiding place.

Pa had said that Madeline, when Bruce's wife, had been a girl of deep and lovely passion. Seeing her so regal, not easily imagining her as a vital young princess instead of a stately queen, I had found the idea slightly shocking, unreasonably enough. But if Cleo could not hold a candle to her as to native beauty, which everyone took for granted, my girl was at least her peer in the other gift of life. When in such haste and hunger she flung into my arms I knew that the goal I sought was more strange and wonderful than I yet comprehended.

Her face was a little drawn, and to me the most beautiful in the world! Madeline's beauty was for all the world to worship, but Cleo's was largely hidden away, an enchanted prize for me alone. She was giving it to me now, in as full a measure as time and event permitted. Our small enchanted world, with its cool shade and golden sands and low, white surf was yet liege to the great world. But an old Mother who long had cherished Cleo was kind to both of us; wisely she ministered to us so that, after many exquisite addresses to each other, we could breathe and speak again.

Then the great world encompassed us again. We crept out of the hiding place, glowing from triumph and revelation, and took in our lines and started up in the dunes. I had been afraid for Cleo and a little for myself of the events about to ensue, so grim upon the ecstasy just won and its flush still on our faces. What a fall we might take! Instead, in my case, another joy was superimposed upon the first, of an utterly different realm but in some measure subject to it, and sweeping fiercely through me as Obo gave me a little nod. Even when Cleo, atop the dune, turned to me wide eyes filled with terror and torment, I was still exultant. We could not have each other without great cost, certainly without great hazards. I believed that victory was a little nearer.

"Saul!" she gasped.

She had seen that our horses were gone from their pickets under the palms.

"Don't worry. I was expecting that."

I don't think she heard me in her extreme shame and sadness. But if I had told her of my plans, she would have been terrified, and perhaps opposed them.

"Oh, Obo, why didn't you keep better watch?"

"I seen Mas' Saul when he turned 'em loose. I was lying on de dune, watching for him. But Mas' 'Daniel say to let him, for he was ready for him. He say time for somebody to fight back at Mas' Saul and I believe him. Anyway de hosses will come home and I could kay you every foot to Ibis Hall if Mas' 'Daniel plan slip up."

Hope fought the despair in her face. "Dave, what does he mean—?"

"You'll see. Maybe the plans did slip up, but I don't think so. I had two good helpers—Obo and another. Head for that salt creek where it meets the inlet."

Under the bank, close to the water, was a thick growth of scrub palms. Hidden within it we found two horses from Dr. Sams's stables, neither of them fancy stock, but sound riding beasts and feeling their oats.

"I had Joshua bring them here as spares," I told Cleo. "When you told me Saul had so fortuitously decided to go to Murray Island today I was sure he was going to play one of his little jokes, and what would amuse him as much as turning loose our horses so we'd have a twelve-mile walk home? But I won't know whether we turned the tables on him for a while yet."

I did not expect to know until I could hear from Joshua, whom I had ordered home by a safe route as soon as he had hit or missed, lest he fall foul of my infuriated enemy. Chance, by no great strain, provided that we three companions should discover the outcome before we gained Wood Ibis. Actually the ruse had turned out an outstanding success. It was the second time I had scored heavily against the Dunbartons in the past fortnight—the first occasion being my affair with Cliff Todd—and that luck was almost too good.

Declining to part with Cleo at our meeting place near Turtle Inlet, insisting on escorting her to the border of Wood Ibis and greatly tempted, despite its folly, to take her to the very door of Ibis Hall, I was riding ahead of her when we approached Little Run and caught the first glimpse of someone ahead of us, at the moment all but hidden in the tree-growth of a swale. A few seconds later he emerged in plain sight, casting a long shadow in the lucid, late-afternoon sunlight. It was Saul, and he was walking with long, strong strides. He had only now come into the road, or we would have seen his footprints.

I glanced at my companions. Cleo had turned white. Obo's bull-neck appeared to swell a little and I could see no fear in his liquid-black eyes. I had no intention of trying to avoid the encounter; if we were tempted to retreat it was too late. Saul's quick eyes or ears had discovered our approach and he stopped to wait for us.

He was besmeared with mud nearly to his waist and daubed with it from head to foot. His riding clothes were torn and his face and hands bore livid scratches from his furious assaults of the briar patches and palmetto thickets. But he did not appear tired, and his eyes, as they took in us and our accouterments, were alive and shining. These he fixed on my face.

"You turned that trick prettily, Dave," he remarked.

"So I see."

"You realized my bent for practical jokes and outguessed me. But you must have had some help."

"Not any co-operation, if that's what you mean. I instructed one of our boys to have spare riding horses concealed up there, in case the ones we came on got away. The boy didn't know what I expected to happen and simply obeyed orders. I was watching you when you turned loose Tuck and Paddy, and it was no chore to cut in ahead of you and turn loose your stallion. But I must say I hardly hoped you would have to walk home. I heard you were able to call him to you."

"Well, I am—in the horselot. I'd taught him that—with a whip. When there wasn't any fence, nothing but the great outdoors, he forgot I was his master. I chased the devil for hours. He's got more spirit than I ever gave him credit for."

"Well, I suppose you can whip it out of him."

"I'm not going to—as it happens. I admire his spunk, and want some colts by him. And you, Dave, showed more spirit than I gave you credit for."

"You're not my master, you know. I'm working for Dr. Sams."

"Cleo, did you know about this?"

"She didn't," I said quickly.

"Let her speak for herself."

"I didn't know about it; but if I had, I would have been in it with Dave. I'm so glad he did it."

Profound astonishment, almost a bewildered expression, passed quickly across Saul's broad face.

"You're not afraid of me any more?" he asked in low, even tones, his head cocked oddly as though listening to some far-off sound.

"I'm afraid of the things you do. I'm not afraid of you yourself, as I was before. You may not see any difference—but there is a great difference."

"I think I know what you mean. Obo, were you in it?"

"Yassuh."

"You weren't afraid of me?"

"I nevah was afraid of you, suh. I belong to Miss Cleo."

"I beg your pardon, Prince Obo."

"Cleo, I think you and Obo had better ride on to Ibis Hall and send one of the grooms with a horse for Saul," I proposed.

"Oh, don't bother, Cleo. It's only a short distance, and I can reflect better on foot. In fact, I'll take the full penalty for my joke that boomeranged."

"I want to stay here as long as you do," Cleo told me.

"Good God!" Saul burst out. "A general insurrection against the crown prince! Obviously, you and Dave have fallen in love."

"Yes, we have," I answered. "But Cleo—you and Obo needn't fear leaving Saul and me together."

"None in the least," Saul told her. "He's mounted, and I'm not. Anyway, my next move is going to take a lot of thought."

"Cleo, I want you to ride on and tell Mrs. Dunbarton what happened."

A shadow came and went on her face as though from a bird in flight. "All right," she answered, when her eyes had met mine.

When she was out of sight Saul wheeled his eyes to mine. "Who in the hell are you, that you'd dare strike back at me?" he asked.

"I'm Dr. Sams's foreman and Cleo's lover."

"God in heaven, is the history of Wood Ibis to have a new chapter, repeating the old? Uncle Bruce—and then my father—and now you—the old journey from workman on the plantation to lord of Ibis Hall? I've got an eerie feeling."

"All I want out of Ibis Hall is Cleo," I said.

"Of course, you know you can't have her, unless you're able to beat both Pa and me. That doesn't seem possible, does it? I'd have laughed myself to death over it no later than this morning. I have a notion Madeline will oppose you too, in this respect. Well, I won't laugh at it any more, I assure you. At last I've got a real adversary. Still it's preposterous that you could win. I must advise you not to try."

"Thanks—but this is a settled thing."

"You thanked me," he went on in a deeply startled tone. "You ought to have, by all reason—it's such a kind act on my part. But why did I do it? Kind acts are not in my line. Yesterday I wouldn't have advised you not to try—I would have welcomed the sport on this dull plantation. I'm ashamed of myself—it slipped out. It must have been my real desire. If so, Dave—you've impressed me more than I admitted to you. I've got the uncanny feeling again."

I made no reply. I too had an uncanny feeling that made no sense.

"Dave, I'm going to show you great respect. You needn't be on the watch for any more practical jokes—I'm not in a joking humor toward you. By the same token I shall treat Cleo very respectfully. If you give her up, we'll call this square. You can go on being Dr. Sams's horse-dealer. I'll keep my hands off you as I do off Obo. I confess it would save me a lot of trouble. But to go ahead with the warning, now I've stooped to it—if you keep on I'm going to unlimber my big guns. Do you understand that?"

"Perfectly."

"What big guns have you? None. It's preposterous, I tell you." Again I did not reply.

"Do you realize, Dave, you may be killed?"

"Is that a threat of murder?"

"Not murder. War."

"I've considered the possibility. So might you, for that matter." My tongue felt good, saying it, my eyes delighted in the pause it gave him; my heart leaped.

"I'm considering that too," he told me, with a strange smile. "In a broader way than you know. Before now I played dog-in-the-manger with Cleo for the sport of it. Actually I don't give a damn for any white girl. Not one stirs me in the least—I want the heat and strength and primitiveness of Africa. The only esthetic joy I know is to see my whiteness upon a wench's darkness. If I could be excited by a white girl, it would be Cleo—perhaps because of her black hair and white face, perhaps just because she's forbidden to me by every law of God and man—but I can't. So don't get it in your head it's for that, that I'll fight you to the last ditch. Nor is it because I share Papa's little dream that she marry one of the aristocrats so he can hold up his head a little better in their company. If you were a weak man, Dave, I'd toss her over gladly—provided too I had had a rude awakening like today's. The next weak man that wants her can have her, with no jokes played. But you're too damned strong."

"I don't know what you mean."

"I don't want you in the family. For once I'm willing to forego a lot of sport just to play safe. I'm not the lord of creation. I'm not unconquerable. I just thought I was."

What had made him think so? It was not a natural or a common illusion. What had made Dr. Sams's runaway shepherd dog, becoming a renegade in the swamps, grow nearly twice as large as his brother and so strong and agile that he killed half the pack that had hunted him down? On what food had he been fed?

"Well, I'm going to finish my penance," Saul told me. "Dave, I'll see you later."

"I presume so."

He waved and walked on. Watching his long, strong strides, I knew that my victory over him was dearly bought. For the time being Cleo would escape persecution, but at the cost of Saul fighting instead of playing with me, much sooner perhaps than had been necessary. He was more dangerous to both of us than ever before.

CHAPTER

21

That night I told Dr. Sams all that had happened. Since the weather was breezy and cool, we were sitting in his office. He reflected a long time, meanwhile sipping a glass of brandy, before he replied.

"I must say I'm not greatly surprised—about you and Cleo. How you are going to hunt down the father of the girl you love is more than I know."

"I'm going to keep on hunting him. Sooner or later she'll have to know it. I hope she'll be my wife by then. That would make it harder for her to break with me for his sake."

"That's pretty ruthless, Dave. If she did break with you in spite of the hardness of it, she would be hurt a great deal more than if she broke with you now."

"It's a chance I have to take. You know as well as I do that she's got to find out sometime what kind of man he is. If I'm her husband then, loving her and protecting her, I think she'll get through it better."

"Well, maybe you're right. You can cross that bridge when you come to it. I was starting to say that if you were what you seem—not Noel's avenger—just a strong, decent, ambitious wholehearted man of humble beginnings but good education—I would be overjoyed to have you marry Cleo. Otherwise she'll have a hard time making a good marriage. No real aristocrat would want any connection with Ralph and Saul Dunbarton. She has no money to even that up—I'm speaking now of an alliance such as Ralph craves for her—and she's too strange a girl to appeal to ordinary fellows, even if she were thrown with any. But you are consecrated to her father's destruction. That's an awful thing to contemplate."

"I believe she can never be happy or free until both he and Saul are dead."

"It's a weird, cruel trick of fate, just the same."

"I don't think it's strange, and I wonder if it's cruel. Instead of Ralph coming between us, he brought us together. It's all one war —for her and for Pa and for me. No other man could love her as much as I do, involved as I was with her from early childhood. At thirteen I began to know her awful situation and now see her brave and beautiful in spite of it. No other man would be so compelled to fight for her."

"Dave, that's very fine. I think its true, too. Yes, it was in the cards for you two to fall in love. But while you've got more to fight for than ever before, you can no longer pick the time and the ground. You won't have the months of free operation you hoped for. Ralph will very likely forbid you to come to Wood Ibis, and that may be just the start. Your chances of pinning murder on either him or Saul in any near future are greatly reduced, and you might as well face the fact."

I did face it. My hate of Saul, flaming up in my love of Cleo, had driven me to make a tactical mistake. It was no worse thing—I could not help it—perhaps I gained strength from it to more than atone for the loss of ground. I had not broken faith with Pa. The memory of his music was sweet and imperious in my heart. Its beat failed but grew strong again as I saw, dim and distant but inexorable, the vision of victory demanded by my will.

Dr. Sams seemed to feel my rebounding hope. "You've got strong weapons, Dave," he went on. "Getting Cliff's declaration was a great stroke. There's a possibility of obtaining equally damning evidence from the men of the *Clarabelle*. You also have Noel's weapons, mighty ones, at your side—his patience and cunning and zeal."

"They don't know he's alive and we do," I exulted. "And he, not Ralph, is the owner of Little Ibis."

I think we were both expecting a call the next day from Ralph, addressed to Dr. Sams with proper ceremony, to discuss the folly or the effrontery of his foreman. He did not appear and there was no word from Ibis Hall all day. On the following evening there came a uniformed footman with a letter bearing the D'Arcy crest. It was a request that I present myself at Ibis Hall at four o'clock the following afternoon, to discuss a matter of prime importance, and it was signed by Madeline D'Arcy Dunbarton.

I dressed in my best apparel for the interview, and for the first time in my life, rode forth accompanied by a groom. As I approached the mansion in its grove of live-oak trees, its long shadow crept to me and presently its chimneys hid the sun. But I was not as frightened as on my first visit here, despite the clearer shapes of peril. Before I had only Pa to walk beside me. Now I was new-armed and armored by love of Cleo.

For the first time I mounted the great marble steps under the portico and was ceremoniously received by the Dunbarton butler at the front door. He led me to the main parlor with its great chandeliers and somber grandeur, bade me be seated, and went out. There followed a long wait in heavy silence. Then he entered again, drew aside a curtain, and Madeline made her entrance, followed by Cleo. Both were formally dressed and some of the D'Arcy jewels gleamed on Madeline's breast and in her golden hair. She had a shy look wonderfully telling as a kind of paradox to the native majesty of her bearing and her overpowering beauty.

"I thank you, Mr. MacDaniel, for accepting my invitation," she told me in her rich voice, when I had bowed to both of them. She took a thronelike chair that the butler held for her; Cleo sat on a divan; I resumed my former seat.

"What is your pleasure with me, ma'am?" I asked.

"It arises out of something Cleo told me the night before last. She said that you had proposed marriage to her, and that she accepted."

"Yes, ma'am."

"She said you two love each other despite your short acquaintance, and I see how that could very well be. You are a very winning person, Mr. MacDaniel, and my daughter is beautiful enough to attract anyone. However, it is at most a new-found love, perhaps subject to growth—or to death."

"I deny, ma'am, it could ever die."

"You think so. Young lovers always do. You are mistaken though. And it is impossible, I regret to say, for you and Cleo to marry."

"I don't know why."

"I wish that I need not explain why. If my grandfather, René D'Arcy, were here he would forbid me doing so. He would consider making any explanation a shame upon our house, and the one I am about to make must disclose sentiments and attitudes of mind that he regarded as highly private—not even comprehensible save to his peers and of no concern to anyone but himself and his line. But he did not live in the United States in the year 1854. Actually he did not live in the time in which he was born—rather in the days before the Revolution in France could even be imagined—in a more remote period than that, perhaps, when a nobleman was answerable only to God and the king."

"I'll do my best to understand, ma'am."

"Thank you. My grandfather came naturally by his regal pride. You must understand that even in Europe the houses that could trace without break their male lines to such ancient founders as Acquille D'Arcy, a knight under Charles Martel, can be counted on the fingers of your two hands. He regarded the Low Country aristocrats and the Virginia and New England gentry, who could do well to have been franklins or vintners two hundred years ago, as little more than peasants. But while I had been schooled in his code of life, I perceived it was an anachronism. At least, compromise had to be made with a changed world. So when I came to marriageable age, an only child and a considerable heiress, I was faced with a great decision."

Her voice was putting a spell on me. I was able to shake it off only when I had looked at Cleo, who was gazing at her mother with big, worshiping eyes.

"I wanted to be true to my grandfather's teaching," Madeline went on. "Indeed, I could not help it if I chose, so deeply had I been indoctrinated in it. I believed and still believe that after these storms have passed—these revolutions against kings, the appointed of God—that it will again prevail not only in France but here. An absolute monarch will again sit on the throne at Versailles. The United States will have a king or again be subject to an English king, and not an upstart Hanover. Louis Napoleon is a shopkeeper at heart, but France still has princes of Valois, Bourbon, and Orléans—even though her D'Arcys are all gone." Madeline said this last in a somewhat sad tone, but in no way reflecting the incomprehensible sorrow in her face.

"I'm sorry to hear that, ma'am," I said instinctively, as might any young man of my times and manners, although aware of its inadequacy to the occasion.

"Save for my great-grandfather and his brother, then in Quebec, every male of our house died on the guillotine or in prison." She raised her head a little and spoke majestically. "All that pisseth against the wall."

She ought to be on a throne, I thought, wearing a gold crown and ermine. I felt pity for her, having to explain all this to me. Then a light broke, the light of Cleo's and my love for each other, and what were bones dry seventy years compared to that?

"When I was pondering whom to marry, my father's cousin, Henri D'Arcy of Combahee, was alive, and had a son who would carry down our name. I was to lose that name, no matter whom I married, but at least I wanted our family traditions and beliefs to be perpetuated. I wanted to build for a glorious future in which I believed. If I married one of the little Low Country aristocrats, Wood Ibis would belong to his family instead of to mine. His family traditions and beliefs, at most a century old, infused with vulgarity, would prevail here. So I made a decision for which the *petite noblesse* condemned me—shut their doors to me—but little they knew I was being true to my heritage in a way they could not dream. I decided to marry a man of the people. I was in love with such a man—Bruce Dunbarton, my overseer—as manly and as winning as you are. He and I could found a new house here. His strength and good red blood would be its foundation; the tradition, the culture, the family customs would be all mine. My children would still be better born than the Low Country planters, just as the bastard son of a king by his low-born mistress is better born than most of the nobles of his kingdom."

She was speaking in a low, utterly simple, and unpretentious tone. I saw her stately beauty, but it did not blind me to another —a face more luminous and lovely in my sight, and a form more moving. On that face was growing despair.

"Since then, Henri D'Arcy and his son have died," Madeline went on. "Cleo is the only living descendant of René D'Arcy, and her position is utterly different from mine. My husband was killed, leaving no heir, and I married his brother Ralph who represented him in my mind and heart. In my grief and loneliness I did not consider that he had a son, to whom he would leave the estate obtained by marriage to me. That means that Cleo has no fortune by which she and her husband could found a house. She cannot marry whom she pleases, as I could. She cannot hope to hand down the D'Arcy traditions and culture intact; and unless she marries wealth, all of that will be lost. The original D'Arcy name will completely disappear: it can not be sustained in poverty.

"So I have appointed Cleo a solemn task. She may marry a man of name, or without one, but he must be a man of wealth. He must have or build a seat equal to this one and be willing to name it Arcy, the name of our oldest domain in France. Thus her sons' and grandsons' names will be associated with it, as my father was everywhere known as Honoré D'Arcy of Wood Ibis. In that way my house will be reborn. It will not pass from the earth."

That was the meat of the coconut! The mundane idiom helped me to set my teeth in it—the only substance in the spell she was weaving. Calmly she expected me to surrender Cleo for its sake. Dr. Sams had told me that Madeline had rebelled against her grandfather's divine-right concept of his place and power; actually she was a priestess in the cult. Ibis Hall, castle of Wood Ibis, where she reigned in name but not in deed—a queen of many sorrows, haunted by ghosts she dared not face—had no doubt intensified the "monstrous folly" as he called it; yet I knew, from reading, that family pride and glory amounting to worship of one's own name were not infrequently found in the great houses of Europe. Men died for these things, let alone separated their daughters from lowborn lovers.

"If Henri's son had lived, marriage between you, David, and Cleo, would not have been unthinkable. If she were heiress of Wood Ibis, or if you had great wealth, I would gladly give my consent. I esteem you highly. Your behavior on both occasions you were here was admirable. I am sorry for the pain of parting you will both feel—but it will pass off—and Cleo knows, I am sure— and I hope you too will understand—why it is so necessary."

Madeline paused for me to reply: I did not know what she thought my silence meant. But it held too long, a troubled line appeared between her beautifully shaped brows, and her voice flowed out to me again.

"David, I asked Cleo to give me her word of honor that she would withdraw her promise to you and not see you again, save in such casual meetings as are necessary and pleasant between

204

neighbors. She told me that she could not do so, unless you also gave your word of honor to the same pledge. Will you give it to me now?"

"No, ma'am." The words came easily after all.

Cleo drew a sharp breath. Madeline sat in stunned silence.

"After what I've said—you must have understood me perfectly well—you can't refuse," she said at last incredulously.

"Yes, ma'am, I do. Cleo and I love each other and are going to marry."

"I told you it was impossible. Cleo! Tell him it is. Tell him you understand now, and can't see him again."

"No, Mama. If he can resist you, I can too. Dave! I'm so glad and proud you did." She rose and walked gravely to me to receive and return my kiss.

"Mama, I adore you," she said, turning to the pale, regal woman rigid in her chair. "I always have and I always will. It's very hard for me to deny you anything. But you are wrong about this. What you've been saying hasn't any real sense—I see that now. Marrying someone with great wealth has sense to it if that's my best chance of happiness, but it isn't. The only real chance I've ever had is in Dave's love. I could be happy with him if we lived in the woods."

Madeline sat as still as in the portrait in our picture-room. I could not see her breathe and what light was left in her queenly eyes did not move or change. At last her lips moved.

"I see, now, you are deeply in love," she said sorrowfully. "But will you at least agree to wait before taking some irretrievable step, to discover for yourselves if you are fitted to be man and wife?"

"Oh, of course we will, Mama," Cleo burst out.

"Then I will ask you to excuse me. I am an aging woman of another school, and am very sad. Cleo, will you join me presently? Good evening, David."

She rose and walked with her head high to the end of the long room; there a curtain was drawn aside by an unseen hand and dropped behind her. Cleo's eyes filled with tears.

"I wish you hadn't given your mother that promise," I told her. "You can't tell what's going to happen here. We might have to run away tomorrow!"

"It was so little for her to ask—and once all she had to do was command," Cleo replied. "We didn't agree to any definite time. And Dave—you must understand I've never before refused her anything. I wanted to sometimes—but simply couldn't—I've worshiped her for so long. When I was a little girl I used to think how wonderful it would be if I could die for her. That was before I met Dan—the only happiness I knew was when she was sweet and loving with me, or when I was in the woods and swamps with Obo. I wanted to die, you know. Every night when I went to sleep I prayed I'd never wake up. Now I've found you and want to live I think I'd still do it—without question."

"I wish you wouldn't think of such things."

"You've got to know. There's a curse on this house, Dave—it has darkened every soul in it—twisted every life—and one of its signs is the hold she has on me. I tell you, I don't think I could have refused her today except that her dream could never come true. I wanted to tell her so—so she wouldn't think I too was a traitor—"

"A traitor? What do you mean, Cleo—by using a word like that?"

"I meant to say, rebelled against her. That would have sounded more sensible. Or just disobeyed her. But you see—I did say 'traitor.' It showed what was deep in my mind. That's the name used for people who rebel against a king or queen. Even disobedience is called treason."

"Good God!"

"You see now how I could run away much more easily than I could disobey her. She's my mother, but more than that—I say more than that, an idea so fixed in her mind that it's become imbedded in mine—she's my queen. She doesn't know that except for Dr. Sams and a few old Negroes I'm her last loyal subject. At least she doesn't realize that nobody else thinks of her in that way any more. She thinks one reason no young men come to court me is that they regard Madeline D'Arcy's daughter as out of their reach. For a year now she's been planning a royal gesture of welcome. She was going to show them how gracious she could be to her inferiors—and the young men needn't be bashful. She

206

and Papa were to give me a big ball—inviting all the young people of the Low Country aristocracy. I've kept putting it off on one excuse or another, and got Papa to help me. I know what would happen—and although he doesn't admit it, Papa does too. *No one would come.*"

"Cleo—is she mad?"

"No. Just wilfully blind. She persuades herself that although the planters ostracized her for marrying her overseer, they are eagerly waiting a chance to flock around her again. If Charleston is too stupid to worship at her feet, there's Baltimore—New Orleans —even Paris. That's why I couldn't tell her that her dream of my marrying a rich man is only a dream. She's happier thinking I'm so in love with you that for a little while I can hold out against her. Thank God, I had both reasons. Otherwise—I'm ashamed to say it—"

"I'd have thought one would have been enough."

"It should have been enough. You've got every right to believe I'm not capable of loving you enough." Her eyes had been avoiding mine but now she looked me in the face, and they were dry and aching. "Dave, do you want to let me go?"

I could only shake my head.

"Let me go, before you love me any more—or before you hate me. I tell you again, there's a curse on this house. If I go with you I will carry some of it with me, and it will fall on you. I don't know what it is—but it's more terrible than either of us can imagine."

I walked toward her and took her cold, trembling hands. "Do you love me, Cleo?"

"Yes."

"Then I will never let you go. Don't ask me to, no matter what happens. Don't let anything come between us. I love you—do you understand?"

She gazed at me in a wild hope. I was shaken like a beach palm in a gale and could barely speak on above the storm.

"If we love each other enough, nothing can part us—"

"Don't say that!" It was like a cry of terror.

"Cleo!"

"They'll hear you. Not the people, but the ghosts. They're not ghosts, but demons. If they hear you, they *will* part us. Something will happen—some awful thing—and then—"

Her impounded tears broke their barrier, and I had never seen anyone weep at once so deeply and so silently. I did not know what I said to her; my words were as instantly forgotten as those I had spoken to Pa that dreadful day when he had shown me how fast he could run to Madeline. I knew that my arms were about her and that I loved her beyond knowing; then after a while I found myself on horseback, riding down the aisle of live-oak trees, away from Ibis Hall.

What had wakened me from my trance this soon was the slow-dawning intimation of great fear.

Three afternoons later came Ralph in his part of a plain, just man, whom Providence had made monarch of Wood Ibis.

22

"I came to speak to Dave," he said, when Dr. Sams had seated him with a glass on our little veranda, "and I'll make it short and to the point. But, neighbor, I want you to hear what I've got to say, and I'll be surprised if you don't agree with me."

"I'd like to hear it," his host replied.

"You notice, Dave, that I came over here to see you, instead of sending for you. That alone shows it is man to man, with no lines drawn."

"I thank you, sir."

"I like you, and admire you. You're a fine, ambitious young man. In that respect Mrs. Dunbarton—I'll call her Madeline, Doctor, as you've always known her—sees eye to eye with me. But Dave, if I may be excused for saying so, those reasons she gave you for you and Cleo breaking off are just a lot of drivel. She believes it, mind you. Old René D'Arcy taught it to her when she wore pigtails. She had sense enough to rebel against it but she believes it just the same. Ancestor worship is what I call it. She's thinking of the glory of the D'Arcy name—of course believing that will bring happiness to Cleo. I'm thinking of Cleo's happiness and nothing else."

The pomposity was not as marked, I noticed, as the night he had whipped Mose almost to death; but it was the same man talking. He held his glass out for Dr. Sams to fill.

"She told you one other true thing," Ralph went on. "My son Saul will inherit Wood Ibis. Only a man can conduct a plantation properly—you ought to have seen how Wood Ibis was going down until my brother Bruce became owner, and Doc will tell you how much more it's improved since I became owner. As much as I cared for Bruce, he was too easygoing to be a good planter. Isn't that so, Dr. Sams?"

"He had it such a short time, Ralph—less than three years—I don't think it would be fair to say that."

"Well, maybe not. Anyway Saul is my son and heir. That means that Cleo's only legacy will be some of her mother's jewels. She won't want to sell those, as I would—she's got too much D'Arcy in her. Then how's Cleo going to live in the style she's accustomed to? People can go up in the world and be happy about it, but it's real hell to come down. She was born with a gold spoon in her mouth and had every luxury she could ask for. She thinks she could be happy in a cottage, but does any sensible person believe it? There's only once chance for her to be happy, and that's to marry money."

He emptied his glass and set it down with a thump. "Dave, do I make myself clear?"

"Very clear. You and Mrs. Dunbarton arrived at the same conclusion."

"You're a fine young fellow. I want you for a neighbor. But I won't have you for a son-in-law, because of your position in life. You refused to promise my wife you would break off with Cleo. I told her you'd promise me, once the plain sense of the thing was set before you. I want you to make my word good."

"I can't make you any such promise, Mr. Dunbarton."

"Think before you speak. That's my advice. Dr. Sams, haven't I talked sense? Why don't you tell this young man he's hurting himself and Cleo too, by this foolish affair?"

"I can't do it, Ralph."

"Why not? You're a good friend of both of 'em."

"You haven't given the slightest valid reason for them to give each other up."

"Well, by God, I've given a practical reason, and that's good enough for me. Dave, you've forced me to say what I didn't want to. I won't forbid you coming on Wood Ibis in the way of your work, but the next time you try to sneak off with Cleo, I will forbid you. That will be a real inconvenience in your work here. I wouldn't hardly see how you could operate the stock farm. It would mean you'd have to go around by boat to hit the road to Charleston. That's awkward, especially when you're moving horses. Doctor, I don't see how he could be very useful to you, if he can't go back and forth through Wood Ibis."

"It would be very awkward for him, indeed."

"I reckon you'd have to let him go."

"I'm not going to let him go, Ralph, for anything rising out of his and Cleo's right to fall in love and marry."

"Dr. Sams, it looks like you're against me, in this, instead of for me. I don't like the look of it, when you've been living off Little Ibis, at a fraction of a reasonable rental, all these years."

"I rented from Noel, Ralph." Dr. Sams's face was turning fiery red.

"My brother Noel is dead. I have only to go to court—"

"You don't know that he's dead. He may reappear—"

It had already come to me that the doctor and I were taking a too adamant stand. It was a mistake comparable to the one I had made with Saul. Perhaps it was a great deal worse—a shapeless shadow flicked across my brain and was gone. I spoke quickly.

"Dr. Sams, I wouldn't want to be the cause of any trouble between you and Mr. Dunbarton."

Both men looked at me with grave respect that would have made Saul howl with laughter.

"Now you're talking sense, young fellow," Ralph said.

"I ask you, Mr. Dunbarton, to give me a little time. I'm very much in love with your daughter and I can't bring myself to agree suddenly to give her up. I want to keep my job here—and have Dr. Sams satisfied with my work. I'd like to think it over and then have a good talk with Cleo—"

"Well, you may, if you don't meet her in secret."

"I agree to that, and thank you kindly."

"And, Doc, you and me aren't going to have any trouble. We've been neighbors and friends too long."

After Ralph had gone, Dr. Sams swore savagely and long. "For you to have to knuckle to that murderous—"

"I don't care about that, if we can play safe."

"I was too hotheaded, I admit. Bide your time if you can—but I'm not sure that's possible. Saul and Ralph together can play downright hell with her, and with you too as long as she's at their mercy. Don't do anything for a few days and let them get their guards down. Then when you have that talk with her in the open—"

He paused, and the gleam in his eyes made my pulse leap.

"Yes, sir?"

"You say it. You're thinking of the same thing."

"Have two horses handy—or a sailboat—and hit for the nearest preacher. Then I'll have legal right to keep her and protect her. But we couldn't come back here unless—"

"You thought of that, too. Yes, I'd take you both in here and tell the Dunbartons to go to hell. They wouldn't go so far as to throw us out by force. They'd start legal action and if necessary Noel can come back to life."

Again a shadow flicked swiftly as a buzzard's over my train of thought; but, dazzled by the shining hope he had offered me— struck by a strange notion that he had not intended to give me —I could not then discover its meaning and soon let it pass out of my mind.

The notion was, that Dr. Sams's strong defense of my love affair was not wholly his deep concern for Cleo's happiness and his friendship for me. Indeed, it was almost out of character for him to move actively in anyone's life. I thought it was offering him a most welcome diversion from more grim business. Dr. Sams dreaded opening Bluebeard's door only a little less than he hated the triumph of murder.

If I craved such a diversion, I could not have it.

"I think it's best for all three of us—and for Pa—that Cleo and I put off the runaway until our position is stronger," I told him.

"Any delay will be mighty tough on her—"

"I don't think she'll find it too bad. I believe Saul meant what he said about leaving her alone, if I'd leave her alone. If nothing's heard from me, Ralph will think he has frightened me into trying to give her up. Meanwhile I'll be trying to get that evidence from the *Clarabelle*. If she puts into Savannah on her way to Charleston, it may be in four or five weeks. I'd like to find out more about her run—she may touch Saint Augustine very shortly. If Ralph suspects we have positive proof that he bought fuzee from her as well as the moccasin from Cliff Todd, there'd no longer be the slightest danger from either him or Saul. They wouldn't dare make a move against you or Cleo or me. We'd hold the whip hand then, by God! I could marry her in welcome—and we could play them along until every terrified Negro tells us what he knows and we're ready to put the ropes around their necks."

Cleo too had found compelling reasons for delaying our marriage. She sent me no more messages through our trusty couriers, and week after week went by without her maneuvering to meet me. When chance afforded us a brief encounter on the road, we were in plain sight of Mr. Martin, the overseer. Nevertheless she checked her horse and spoke in one breathless burst.

"I'm still trying to get Mama's consent. Sometimes I think she's going to give it, and then she turns to ice. At least I've got to give her time enough to be reconciled as much as possible. And with Saul leaving me alone—treating me with great respect—it's not too hard to wait."

"I love you, Cleo." That's all I had time to tell her, as she started to ride on.

"Dave, I love you," she called back softly over her shoulder.

Saul's good treatment of her had held, evidently, up to the time of his departure for Charleston. His absence had continued day after day, affording Cleo and me a wonderful opportunity to elope, and every night I had bleakly regretted our not seizing it. Every turn was so critical now; a little losing of our way could cost us our goal; a mistake easy to make could so easily prove fatal at Wood Ibis. Saul would return soon and all that I knew was, he would not be idle. Even Madeline on her throne had decreed that Cleo and I should part—and she need not know the measures employed by her husband and stepson.

On the morrow Saul was still away. Chancing to learn too that Obo had bought some mullet-bait from a fishing smack at Turtle Inlet, I stopped tacking and set a thrilling course. No doubt Obo and Cleo were going to fish the afternoon tide for red drum, in which case their homeward ride would take them by Turtle Inlet at twilight or a little later. I proposed to be making one of my frequent visits of late to Lizzie and Sam, and intercept her on the beach. If she would agree, my small poke of gold might persuade one of the trawler captains to take us to Georgetown. If our marriage were an accomplished fact—so I refuted my own argument for delay—I did not believe Ralph and Saul could put any serious, additional obstacles in my future course.

I was aglow with the prospect as the day waned. Ralph and Madeline would never expect Cleo to elope in old clothes aboard a high-smelling shrimper, and we would be certain of a long head-start. When I dropped into the store to wait for her, Lizzie gazed at me sharply. She and I had become extremely good friends in the past month. Many a nip of Cuban rum we had tossed down together; we had talked pleasantly of everything but not very confidentially of anything: indeed the relationship had been more a relaxation from, instead of a help to, my business. I still got no glimpse of her real feelings toward Madeline. She spoke mockingly and sometimes spitefully of both her and Cleo, but I could never believe she meant it.

"You look like a cat full of warm milk," she told me as I loafed near the door.

The impulse came to me to take Lizzie into my planning. If she gave it her wholehearted approval, the physical difficulties would melt away. The captain of a shrimp boat waiting the tide might not risk antagonizing Ralph Dunbarton by ferrying, for love or money, his daughter and her lover to Georgetown, but if Lizzie told him to, he would. Old Gustaf Neilson's daughter had that kind of a way with the sailors who cast their anchors here. But I did not ask her help, remembering her remark soon after my return to Wood Ibis. *Cleo would be very lucky to get you, but you'd be damned unlucky to get her.*

Now her blue eyes were markedly sharp and clear. "I see now what's in the wind," she said after a quick glance through the window. "Romance comes again to Ibis Island."

I glanced out. Little more than specks on the brown beach in the fading light appeared Cleo on horseback, Obo trotting behind her.

"What a surprise to see them!" I said, grinning at Lizzie.

She replied with what was almost a sneer. "I was going to say, another case of rags to riches—but that don't apply," she went on, pouring herself an unusually big dram. "The riches go to Saul."

"Cleo will get some mighty pretty jewelry."

"All the eligible bachelors from Charleston to Georgetown will weep into their planter's punches when they hear that the belle of the Low Country—Madeline D'Arcy's daughter—has given her hand."

214

"That's pretty raw, Lizzie. Not up to your usual wit."

"Yes, that stung you. You don't often show any resentment at my slanders but it's plain as day you'd like to wring my neck. You must have got pretty thick with her lately."

"Thicker than I'd like to have Saul know."

"Well, he will know it. But it's not my funeral."

She turned her back to me and began to rearrange the stock on her shelves. Not until I started out to intercept Cleo did she whirl, and almost spring to the door. "Invite her in, Dave," she said in an oddly tense tone. "The men won't be back for half an hour— and I've got a present for her." Then she stood in the doorway and called. "Cleo, come in a minute. Someone here wants to see you."

Cleo stopped, then slowly rode toward us.

"For heaven's sakes, Lizzie, be nice to her," I said in an undertone. "Her skin's pretty thin."

"A lovely skin," Lizzie answered gravely. "In that she's the equal of Madeline."

Cleo handed her rein to Obo and gave me an intense questioning glance. Lizzie went about lighting two lamps.

"I've got an extra-fine bottle of French wine for you, Cleo," she said in her heartiest tone. "Don't let your Pa get his nose in it, but save it for one of your and Dave's picnics."

"That's awfully nice of you, Lizzie."

The woman leaned lithely against the counter but I felt that she was sharply alert and perhaps under great strain.

"Isn't it nice to have a young man on the plantation as attractive as Dave? You did us all a favor when you charmed him aboard the ship."

"Thanks, Lizzie," I said, while Cleo stood straight and still.

"What a lucky meeting that was! Dave, you didn't by any chance know in advance that such a lovely passenger would be aboard? Of course not. Saul's grandmother is the only mind reader in these parts. But, Dave, there's more to you than meets the eye. Maybe you came here only to get a job near Cleo—maybe you're just the honest young horse-breeder that you seem—but sometimes I wonder."

"You're being very mysterious, Lizzie."

"To tell the truth, I'm a little bit mystified by you, Dave—and maybe I'd better warn our island princess to take care. Have you had any dealings with Cliff Todd? He was slated to live and die in these swamps where he was born—as much of an institution as Ibis Hall; but he's suddenly hit south, bag and baggage including Clara—and the place knows him no more."

"I'd say it was a good riddance."

"But you don't say anything more. Cliff must have got the scare of his life—from someone. But Dave—it makes us old settlers proud to have a newcomer take such interest in Ibis Island history. You don't go back to the Indians—but the marriages—and the deaths—especially in the reigning house—why, you can't hear enough about them."

"How do you explain that, Lizzie?" Cleo asked, with a quiet voice and manner.

"I don't try to, Cleo. Of course if your old maid cousin, Terese D'Arcy in Wilmington, was writing a family history—and finally got enough money to hire—"

Watching Cleo in cold dread, I did not instantly perceive that this pause in Lizzie's game was different from the others. She had not just left a question hanging in the air in the way of hinters. On her final word something had happened to her voice. When I turned to look, something remarkable had happened to her face. The warm colors had rushed from it, leaving it a cold white; her eyes that had been narrowed a moment ago were widely staring at some calamitous blunder she had made. If any woman ever wanted to bite her tongue off, it was Lizzie Childer.

"Why don't you go on?" Cleo asked.

Lizzie made a powerful and partly successful effort to recover herself and regain her usual manner. "Oh, I've badgered you both enough," she replied. "I'm a mean, spiteful woman, soured on the world. I was making up those insinuations as I went along."

"To make trouble between Dave and me?"

"I reckon so—but trouble you two can patch up as soon as you get out in the moonlight together. You know how I resent your mother's high-and-mighty manner toward me. I couldn't resist a little sport at your expense."

"Well, I'll be going now. Dave, will you ride a way with me?"

"That's what I came here for. Good night, Lizzie."

If Lizzie's eyes did not ask forgiveness of me as Cleo and I went out the door, I did not know what they were saying. Cleo did not look at me and her face was unreadable in the deepening dusk. She took the lead until the beach path intersected the road; then she sprang down. I too dismounted and Obo took both our reins. Some little signal must have passed between him and his mistress—perhaps only a mental telegram—for he strode out of hearing down the beach, leading the horses.

The surf that had been brilliant white half an hour ago was now wan gray. We could not see the waves come in; each arrived unexpected out of the deep, broke, and died. The tide was very high, and about to turn back. What had it brought me, and what would it take away?

"I don't know as I ever mentioned Mama's cousin, Terese D'Arcy of Wilmington," Cleo began in a low voice. "She would have nothing to do with Mama after her marriage to Uncle Bruce Dunbarton. Once we thought she had forgiven Mama—she invited me to visit her—and Mama let me go. But it turned out, all she wanted of me was to ask a lot of what she thought were very cunning questions."

Cleo expected no reply, and I made none.

"It was perfectly plain to me—a girl of fourteen—what she was up to. You know when one man becomes rich by another's death—especially if that death is a peculiar accident—stories start. You couldn't come down here without hearing them."

"Yes, I heard them."

"Terese made up her own. Without the least evidence, she decided that my father had murdered his wife and his own brother in order to marry Mama and get Wood Ibis. She didn't care about that—all she cared about was for Papa to be convicted so Wood Ibis would revert to Mama's ownership by Uncle Bruce's will. A man can't own lands gained directly or indirectly by murder. If it did become Mama's again, Mama was duty-bound and perhaps legally bound to give her a fourth of the island. René D'Arcy made the arrangement in his will, to occur on Mama's forty-fifth birthday, in case no male heir was then alive. Mama will be forty-five next year."

"Well, I guess I know what Lizzie meant. That your cousin, Terese D'Arcy, had hired me to try to send your father to the gallows. Lizzie doesn't want you to marry me—for some unknown reason—and she thought that if you found out my game of course you wouldn't."

"That's about right except—to speak more precisely—she doesn't want *you* to marry me. She doesn't want anyone she's fond of to have anything to do with me."

"Why?"

"I don't know. Uncle Bruce was going with her when he fell in love with Mama—but while that might make her hate Mama —and somehow Lizzie seems to me too big for that—it certainly hadn't ought to make her hate me. I'm not even Bruce's daughter, but Ralph's. I've thought sometimes she believes what I do—about Wood Ibis. That a curse has been laid on it to blast every life it touches. And she's greatly fond of you."

"Well, if she thinks an insinuation of that kind—that I'm your cousin's hired agent—"

"Sit down, Dave," Cleo broke in. "We've got a lot to talk over. You can sit on that stranded log. I'm going to stand up—I can think better."

"All right, but I wish you'd let me say one thing. It might end some of this awful strain."

"What is it, Dave?"

"I went to Lizzie's place tonight to meet you and ask you to elope to Georgetown on one of the shrimp boats and marry me at once."

"I don't doubt you love me, Dave. If I did—this would be such an abominable world that I'd want to get out of it soon as possible. I want to tell you about a talk I had with Dr. Sams only about two weeks ago. He's highly intelligent but not very subtle. He lugged into the conversation a bit of history I hadn't heard before— something my father had done when he was a boy. The purpose of the talk was, I think, to prepare me a little for a great shock— in case it happened. Of course you know what shock he meant—to find out my father was a cold-blooded, horrible murderer of his own family."

What I thought was a cold mist off the sea drenching my face was my own sweat.

"I don't believe it, Dave. That had better be plain to start with.

I *know* it isn't true—at least as it seems to Dr. Sams or to you. Papa can be hideously cruel in carrying out what he thinks is justice but he's just not the man who could plan and carry through such wicked and terribly dangerous crimes. I can't tell you why I know that—but I do. So you can see what my stand would be toward anyone who came here to hound him to the gallows. I'd fight him to the last ditch."

"I want to say one more thing right now, Cleo. I'm not your cousin's hired agent. I've never laid eyes on her and didn't even know she was alive. I haven't been hired by anyone."

Cleo who had been making little nervous movements stood still and looked out to sea.

"I believe you, Dave," she said at last. "I was sure of that when Lizzie suddenly stopped hinting—and turned white. Another idea had suddenly dawned on her. The reason I rode this far before I stopped to talk to you was to figure out what that idea was—that was easy—and all it meant. My head worked pretty well. Obo told me something today that helped me think it through. In five minutes I've discovered a good deal."

She had turned to me again and I nodded to her in the moonlight and gave her a faint smile.

"Obo went crabbing along Whale Branch and found some sign he couldn't at first understand," Cleo went on. "He was so puzzled that he investigated it very carefully—and no one understands the swamps as he does or can read sign as well. He found where a trap-chain had been fastened to a root cut off from a cypress tree, and in the mud beside a run he saw where the trap had been dropped and picked up again. It was Cliff Todd's big bear-trap that you took home. It had been set in the run, and tracks and other evidence showed that a man, not an animal, had been caught in it. I told him you couldn't have made Cliff fall in his own trap. He said of course not—but you could knock him out and put him in it and let the spring tide rise around him until he told you what you wanted to know. He said that was what you had done—and you wouldn't have gone to any such measures just to scare him from buying any more stolen goods from the Negroes. You scared him so bad that he left the country. Of course you know I've overheard some of Granny's talk with her ghosts—others have too, I suppose. It's no wonder that anybody investigating the deaths of Papa's first wife and his brother would have business with Cliff Todd."

"Your head worked very well, Cleo."

"Please don't tell me what Cliff told you—I don't want to know. The question I asked myself was, if Cousin Terese hadn't sent you here, who did? Well, it wasn't a very hard question. The piece of history that Dr. Sams told me was that Papa had broken Uncle Noel's back in cruel play when both were boys. Uncle Noel loved Bruce terribly and hated Papa terribly. But why did he wait all this while to try to avenge what he thought was Uncle Bruce's murder? If it was a question of hiring someone, he could have done that years ago. Dr. Sams told me that same day that Uncle Noel had believed in poetic retribution. Everyone knows his mind was affected by Bruce's death—perhaps by his own injury before that. Well, since he didn't have a son to inherit and pay his debt of hate, he could adopt one."

When she paused, I spoke above the sibilant sound of water running through sand.

"And of course you remembered my telling you that I had been adopted."

She was silent a long time, before she had breath to go on. She walked a short distance up the beach and returned. I rose and we looked at each other, pale and trembling, in the moonlight.

"I might have stopped there—but I didn't," she told me. "I followed on to the end. The lame musician in Philadelphia whom Papa thought might be Uncle Noel *was* Uncle Noel. He'd got a man with a humpback to answer the door, and later he went to Baltimore with his adopted son. I played with his son that day—and we went into the woodshed—and made promises to each other."

I craved to speak, but must wait until she had spoken.

"So you *are* Dan Reed, after all," she told me in sorrow deeper than the sea. "I've found you at last. But you can't keep your promise to me—you've got to stay here to put a rope around my father's neck."

My arms hung useless. The ache that spread from my heart to my finger ends—with every aspect of real pain—had no outlet. The first words that either of us spoke were only three, breaking from my twisted throat. "I love you."

"I know, Dan," she replied as though from far away. "I love you. That's what makes it so awfully sad."

We stood side by side, gazing out over the moonlit ocean. The darkness hid all but its shore waters as another darkness concealed from ourselves and each other the unplumbable deeps of our souls. At last my tension passed and I spoke with ease.

"We were bound to love each other, Cleo—as though we'd drunk a love potion. The curse laid on Wood Ibis struck us both. You didn't know that, in the woodshed, but I did."

"Yet we're both innocent. Why should the Furies—?"

"I don't know. But I think you understand now—at least you will as soon as you have a little more time—I didn't break my promise. I only postponed its keeping. Since that day in the woodshed my life has had two great meanings instead of one. Loving Pa—and loving you."

"They didn't conflict?"

"Not then. After I'd done what my love for him demanded, I was going to take you away—and live with you—in the woods."

"Now what are you going to do? I needn't ask, of course. You're going on with what loving him demands of you. After that—but there can't be any 'after that' between us."

"I'm going on to bring retribution to Bruce's murderer—not to any innocent man. I'm going to kill Saul—either by bringing him to the gallows or in defense of you or myself. I don't know what will happen after that between us two—except we'll love each other always."

"Now you've got the right to ask what I'm going to do."

"Yes."

"Tell Papa—of course—that Uncle Noel's alive, living in Baltimore, and has sent you here to convict him of murder. I'll tell him what you did to Cliff Todd. I'll warn him that you're a very dangerous man, and he must do what he can to protect himself from you."

"That would apply both if he's innocent—or guilty."

"Yes. But he's not guilty, no matter how black it looks. I told you how I felt about that."

"You love him and that might shut your mind against the truth. Assume for one minute that he is guilty. The murderer of his wife and his brother—with a hand in the murder of Bert and Slewfoot—wouldn't hesitate to murder another brother or an adopted nephew if thereby he could save himself from the hangman. I ask you to wait two weeks before you tell him. In that fortnight I promise I won't lift my hand against your father—do nothing but work on the plantation. He won't be in a bit more danger at the end of that time than he is this moment. Meanwhile I'll write Pa that your father is going to find out he's alive and what we're trying to do—and tell Pa to hide out until he hears from me. Is that fair?"

"Perfectly fair. I'm not the least afraid of Papa doing anything like that—but I'm terribly afraid of Saul. He'd kill anyone he thinks might stand in the way of his inheriting Wood Ibis—including Papa himself. I believe that—and I'll say it. I believe he'd kill Uncle Noel just to get Little Ibis, if he could do it without risk. Of course he'd kill you if you're enough in his way. Another sudden death out here would look mighty bad—" Her eyes had got big.

"He wouldn't take that chance, Cleo, unless his and your father's position is desperate."

"Well, then—I won't worry—so much—about you. I mean—it could hardly be that desperate unless Papa's guilty—which I know isn't true. . . . But look out, will you, Dan? Saul might think the evidence is so black—"

"I'll be on guard against him."

"I take it back—about not worrying. I'm terribly afraid for you. In these two weeks take every precaution you can. I wish you'd go away—but there's no use asking you to."

"No. It's got to be this way."

"Then there's only one more thing to say. I'm breaking our engagement."

"Is that necessary, Cleo?"

"Dan, I can't be engaged to the man who's trying to destroy my father."

"But later—if it turns out—"

"I don't want to look into the future, or think about it at all. It's too black and terrible. I love you, but we're no longer engaged."

When I could not reply she spoke as in a dream. "Mama ought to be right pleased. I won't tell her the real reason and she'll think I did it for her. So I'm not a traitor after all."

She turned to me with a dreamy expression on her face. "Maybe it was meant to be this way," she said, "so I needn't be a traitor to Mama. She's still a queen with jeweled eyes and a golden crown."

Her slow movements gave the effect of wakening from sleep. "I'm going home now, Dan."

"Can we kiss each other goodbye—until we meet again?"

"Yes—if we ever do. Goodbye, Dan."

There was this world—of new moon and sand and sea—and another world. That was compact of a vacant space behind stacked wood, the piney smell of sawdust, a narrow shaft of sunlight in which dust motes floated, and Cleo and I crouched with our arms about each other's naked bodies in the sharp shame of innocence, pressing tear-wet lips. Those two worlds became miraculously one. During that brief junction, Cleo and I were one.

Obo brought our horses. He looked at Cleo in the moonlight and, bending a little in great pride, he had her place her foot in his mighty hand and soared her to the saddle. He did not give her the reins but led the horse away, as though she were a child just learning to ride. I stood holding my horse where the foam of the highest waves stranded and died, until my visions, rushing dimly upon my soul, stranded and died on a beach of time and place. There was the sand and the new moon and the sea, and a light in Lizzie's window.

Sam Childer looked at me wide-eyed as I entered the store. Leaving some fishermen to serve themselves from the jug on the counter, Lizzie led both of us to a small kitchen and closed the door. It was the second time I had seen her without her mask—the first time was hardly two hours ago when she had suddenly stopped talking about Terese D'Arcy. A voice can wear a mask as well as a face, and the one hers had worn had fallen off. Oddly enough she appeared younger and more handsome as well as stronger and more womanly. Her voice was richer and warmer than I had ever heard it, except those times she had burst with ribald laughter.

"Dave, did I cook your goose?" she asked.

"Do you mean, as far as my job here is concerned, or with Cleo?"

"Both, I guess."

"In both ventures I've suffered severe defeat."

"For the Lord's sake, let me tell you why I did it, and then forgive me if you can. It's going to be mighty hard to forgive me for trying to break up you and Cleo—if I succeeded, maybe you never will. I couldn't stand the thought of you marrying Ralph Dunbarton's daughter—half-sister to Saul. If I could just delay you awhile, I thought, you'd find some other girl you could be happy with. I still think so—young love isn't as all-important as it seems to young lovers—at least, it wasn't so with me or thousands of other cases. Honestly, Dave, for you to marry into the Dunbarton family would be in my opinion the most ill-starred, hopeless marriage you could let yourself in for. I'm mighty fond of you, and I was doing what I thought best for you both."

"So did Madeline think so—when she refused her consent."

"I know how bitter you feel toward me. But you know too much about the Dunbartons—and before long they'll know too much about you. Just keeping on with the love affair puts you in awful danger from both Ralph and Saul. I still think Cleo's only hope for a happy marriage is to go a thousand miles from Wood Ibis and marry someone who never heard of this hell spot and knows nothing of her history. That's all I can say about that. If you believe I'm mistaken, still believe I'm sincere."

As far as she had gone, I did believe it. I thought there was much farther that she could go, if she would.

"Now about letting the cat out of the bag to Cleo. Ever since I began to suspect you were gunning for Ralph, I jumped to the conclusion you were in Terese D'Arcy's employ. Both Sam and

I have long been expecting her to send an investigator here. She's tried to do some investigating herself—written letters to Low Country officers and fellow aristocrats—once sent for and questioned a man from Bull Island who was visiting in Wilmington. Madeline is getting close to forty-five. Terese could see herself coming into a fourth of Wood Ibis—provided Ralph lost his ownership when a jury brought in a verdict of guilty. Well, assuming she'd finally done what she's threatened to do so long—hired a private investigator—I didn't in the least mind throwing a monkey wrench in the machinery if it would break up you and Cleo. I saw Terese before Madeline's first marriage—a beautiful but silly girl. I hadn't the slightest belief you could uncover anything important after all these years—you were wasting your time—she probably wouldn't even pay you what she promised—you'd already tipped your hand to Cliff Todd and he had skipped the country—you were in for serious trouble with Saul—had a lot to lose and nothing to gain. Cleo would, of course, tell Ralph that you were in Terese's employ, but that would reduce instead of increase your danger. Even Saul wouldn't dare play too rough with Terese's agent—if anything happened to you her shrieks would be heard from here to the White House. In fact, unless I could make you quit the undertaking, I was going to throw out the same hint to Ralph himself, so your life would be safer here."

"But tonight you got another idea? What was it?"

"As I stood there talking to you something came into your face. It wouldn't have come into the face of a young man hired by Terese—it went too deep for that. I should have kept on talking along the same line—so Cleo would have no doubt you were Terese's agent—as though I still believed it myself. Instead I stammered and backed-water and almost fainted. Tell me, for God's sake—does Cleo still think you're working for Terese? If she does, I can rest fairly easy in my bed tonight. But if my strange behavior has made her look for some other explanation for your coming here—"

"Let that go for now, Lizzie, please. What other explanation occurred to you?"

"Occurred to me! It hit me in the face. Hell, I knew the truth in one flash—I was blind not to guess it before. You came here not for money but for love—and for a lame man's hate. A ship's officer I knew saw such a man on a ship from Philadelphia bound for Baltimore—he thought it was Noel Dunbarton—and there was a boy thirteen or fourteen traveling with him. Sam and I wondered at the time if Noel had adopted a son. But so many years have passed—the officer wasn't sure of the identification—and when you showed up I took the wrong tack."

"Well, the cat's out of the bag," I told her, when capable, thoughtful Sam had served us both a tot of rum. "Cleo has promised to wait two weeks before she tells her father—provided I don't move against him in the meantime."

"Damn my loose tongue! But there's just one consolation, Dave—the secret was bound to get out very shortly. If Ralph and Saul were to discover it for themselves, you wouldn't know they knew—they could work in the dark. As it is, you're forewarned."

"What's the first thing you're going to do?" Sam Childer asked.

"Write a letter—right now—and get one of the shrimpers to mail it. It's to tell Pa—Noel Dunbarton—to leave home and go into hiding."

"That's just what Liz and I figured you'd do. If you didn't—you've got a lot to learn yet about the Dunbartons."

"I knew that much—but I've got a lot more to learn," I said. "Are you two going to help me?"

"You're damned right we will," Lizzie cried, while Sam answered with a quiet, "Yes, sir." Yet I believed Sam meant exactly what he said, while Lizzie intended very much less—or perhaps very much more.

When I remarked that I could accept no help in the next two weeks, Sam nodded "of course" but Lizzie looked for a hole in the contract. "There's nothing to prevent Sam and me talking over the case between ourselves," she said. "If you happen to overhear us, it's nobody's fault."

"Dave, that's what makes women so interesting," Sam observed, as he handed me paper and pen to write to Pa.

When Sam had dispatched the letter to the Charleston post office in care of a fisherman, I bade my friends good night and reported the new developments to Dr. Sams. He was deeply discouraged, and only by the most careful maneuvering could I persuade him to go to bed, instead of starting a solitary drinking bout that might last for days. Days waxed and waned thereafter but with the effect on me of the waxing and waning of the tides, which left the sea precisely as before. I drove the work-crews and myself all day in the sun, and before dawn and after dark took long, hard walks alone, so I might sleep at night too deep for dreams. Even so, I could never follow a train of thought for more than a minute or two without it arriving at Cleo.

On the third day after my parting with her, the news came that Saul had returned to the island. On the tenth day, Dr. Sams showed me a letter, posted in Washington, that contained a single scratchy line: "Neither you nor Dan must attempt to communicate with me until further notice," and signed "Noel." It was hard for me to believe that this was the reply to my letter. Indeed the post was rarely fast enough between Charleston and Baltimore to permit such a rapid exchange. Perhaps Saul had traveled farther than we knew and again Pa had been forewarned in time to run. But how did I know that he had not written the letter by Saul's ungentle persuasion, and while the sea birds on the Bay might have news of him, I never would again?

When that night I proposed to go to Baltimore in search of him, Dr. Sams told me it would endanger both of us. "Trust to Noel's cunning," my friend said. "He has great ability to survive. I think we're approaching a crisis, and your love for him as well as for Cleo demands you here."

On the following day the demons of Wood Ibis struck again. They had employed cunning ministers. For the past several days I had been draining a low-lying piece of land on Little Run, and the short cut I took in going back and forth was across a hummock where heavy-footed Paddy was inclined to bog. Therefore I had made a practice of picketing him in the meadow and crossing on foot, along a narrow trail worn by deer and wild pigs through the heavy growth. As usual on this morning, the sun had barely topped the sea-rim when I approached the fen, and the instant I pushed through the vines, it seemed to sink again.

Here I paused, as before—well concealed behind thickets—until my eyes became accustomed to the dim, greenish light, then my winter on the duck marshes would stand me in good stead. There were only a few vantage spots from which a rifleman could safely

227

pot-shoot a traveler on the trail, and these I scanned with such care before venturing in sighting range. Also I was no rabbit, to be shot and to kick and docilely to die. Of late I rode abroad with my rifle in a saddle scabbard and carried it in my hand whenever I entered thick country—a common practice of white foremen hereabouts, who liked venison for the pot and wanted to be ready for any slave who might run amuck. The brightest hope I had harbored these past days was that I might locate Saul's big body in ambush by the path. Taking careful aim from behind a screen of vines, I would be done with him.

This morning the swamp-folk and I had the fen to ourselves. Every sense I could knowingly employ and something like an extra one that scouted for the others assured me no other human being was in rifle range. Actually a killer would be hard put to it to pursue his trade here at this time of day—he could hardly creep away without being seen—and there would be far more danger of his attacking at sundown, when I started home. Completely assured, I devoted my attention to a delightful subject—a doe and her fawn that had traversed the trail ahead of me not more than an hour or two before. Their tracks were plain in the soft ground— the fawn's not much bigger than a dime—and were barely wet with dew.

Midway the fen they told me a little story. The doe, leading the cautious way, had suddenly sensed danger. She had stopped dead still on all four feet, ready to bound; the fawn had crouched down as instructed by its mother or by a greater Mother. I was not surprised that the two had then left the trail, but wondered a little at their leisurely pace—their strides were no longer—and marveled greatly at the direction they had taken. Following the tracks into the thickets, I found them making a short turn back to the trail and continuing on. The animals had merely made a narrow detour around a twenty-foot length of the trail.

Perhaps a big water moccasin had been lying there. But grown deer are not afraid of such creatures. To make the woods safer for her fawn the doe would have more likely chopped the snake to pieces with her front hoofs. I returned to the point where she had left the path, and advanced very slowly and carefully. Thinking of Cliff Todd's bear-trap, I examined every foot of the ground. My thoughts and my heart were hot, my eyes cold.

What had frightened the deer was the faint taint of man. I soon found where the man had been and what he had worked at. Supporting an inch-deep layer of leaf-strewn dirt was a web of vines over a yawning hole. It was neither wide nor long nor very deep—it did not need to be. Imbedded in its walls were two pointed stakes.

In the fall prepared for me, my foot might have deflected the aim of one of the stakes, but assuredly not both. Impaled through the groin or lower belly I would have died not decently and silently, but turning the solemn morning hush into a screaming horror.

There is a degree of rage and hate in which a man no longer burns and trembles but turns icy cold. The lust to kill charged every particle of my blood but did not derange my mind. I would not attack rashly, in the open, or too soon. I was not in the least stunned by the enormity of evil hatching the hideous device—Dr. Sams and Cleo had warned me, and I had smelled it everywhere. The murder was to have been a fit successor to that of Sadie, Bert, and Slewfoot. Only Bruce's, although a fratricide, was of another and more human ilk.

With Bruce had died his Negro boatman. I did not know why I remembered him in this moment's count of the slain, but the memory posed a question. Why had Dr. Sams made so little mention of him? Indeed, he had spoken of him only once and did not even tell me his name. Truly that name had its place on the scroll—a Jim or a Tom or a Ben designating a real and powerful man, a lover of women and wide waters, knowledgeable of winds and tides, full of life as a young mule till the boat blew up. Ralph had had no grudge against him but could not kill Bruce handily without killing him too. . . . It was only an unfortunate accident . . .

Unwilling to leave the deadfall a moment until it was disarmed, I shouted for Joshua. He listened to my low-voiced instructions and made off; three swift hours later Cleo came riding up Little Run, Obo pacing behind her. I called to them that if they would tie the horse, I would show them a pretty sight.

As they gazed down into the pit, I stood where I could watch both their faces. I had never seen drama as terrible, or as moving in its brevity, in the smallness of its field, and in its silence. It was all enacted in two human countenances, one black and one white. The white face turned gray and all its expression, even its individuality, it seemed, was wiped away as by the sponge of death. Truly Cleo died for a moment. She was simply not here; there was no life in her lovely body; it returned slowly and with regret. She tried to turn her eyes to mine but they would not obey her will. Her gaze kept falling in the pit. She was gazing far below the stakes set in its walls and beholding what was not well for any earth-child to see. I would have spared her the revelation, if I could. Perhaps she would not care to live, after this.

Obo did not turn gray: instead a distinctly red flow diffused his black skin. For a few seconds the sweetness and the gentleness that his love and care of Cleo had bred in him passed away like a flame in the wind. His eyes blazed in a terrifying way. His lips drew back from his glistening teeth. He was again a Congo king, driven mad by the drums of hate and going forth to slay and burn. He cried out something in his native tongue that he too, no doubt, thought he had forgotten. Then he turned to Cleo and spoke slowly in English, and his tone was like the snarl of a lion.

"Miss Cleo, if you say I kin, I'll bus' Mas' Saul to bits wif my two hands."

She shook her head. It was a strange thing to see the glare pale and die in his eyes and his face slowly resume its normal aspect. Then his nobly carved lips curled a little in a sorrowful smile.

"Mas' Dan, we was goin' to be in de same boat, wasn't we?"

"Yes."

"No, mine would be heap wuss. You was to die wif de stake t'rough yo gut, and I was to die wif one t'rough my heart. I wouldn't care for de rope 'round my neck, 'cept for leavin' my little girl. But to have de people believe I'd killed you for loving her—and dat was fo' why I love her all dis while—and dat was de way I pay her for savin' and lovin' me—Ol' Debil in Hell couldn't do me bad as dat."

"Oh, Obo!" Cleo burst out weeping, clutching his big hand. "No one would have believed it!"

"Dey plenty who would believe it of a black man, Miss Cleo."

"You said he isn't a human being, and I know now it's true," I told Cleo, when she had stopped crying. "Obo, I'll tell you what we've got to do. I don't want Saul to know we've found this thing, and still we can't leave it as it was, to kill the first person or animal that comes along this path. Saul won't come near here for some days—he'll be afraid of being seen. I don't think he'll risk coming at night even, for fear we're laying for him. We've got to do something like we did about Cliff's bear-trap."

"I could git some chicken blood and smear one of 'em stakes and mash 'm bof down. I could make it look like a bear fall in de hole and got out wounded and run away." He paused, and a dim grin burst through the sadness on his face. "Bless God!" he went on. "Jus' dis morning I found where a big hog bog down and smodder in de mire—not a mile from dis place. I'll fetch him and t'row him in de pit and Mas' Saul t'ink dat what he caught."

"Take my horse then, Obo, and try not to let anyone see you."

"I'll come up Little Run where nobody see me. But while I gone, you and Miss Cleo sit in de open in plain sight of de men workin' on de ditches. No deer will fall in de pit wif de screen off."

He left, and Cleo and I were glad enough to go out of this dim lair, into the sunlight.

"If you can stand it, it's time to talk plain," I told her, when we were seated in the grass.

"I know it and would be ashamed not to stand it."

"Why did Saul do it, Cleo?"

"I'd like to think he's a homicidal maniac—who kills for the sport of it."

"He's no kind of a maniac. He's most terribly sane in a subhuman way—and remarkably intelligent. It was an African deadfall—Obo once dug one for your father as a warning not to whip you any more—Saul counted on killing two birds with one stone. Maybe he didn't intend Obo to stand trial—more likely he was to be hunted down and shot when 'trying to escape' by your outraged father and brother. But lots of people would know it wasn't Obo's work. No one on the island would be in the least deceived. Saul didn't care about that—he'd get a lot of amusement out of it—provided his plans didn't slip up and he himself went to the gallows for a hideous murder. He was willing to take that chance."

"He took another chance too, whether he knew it or not. If you'd fallen in that pit, I would have tried to kill him."

"What was his reason for running a real risk? Saul doesn't kill for hate—only for calculated gain. You can be sure he didn't make Lizzie's mistake—he knows I'm no hired agent of an old maid in Wilmington. Obviously he's figured out I'm Noel's foster son.

But that isn't a good enough reason either—unless he's also figured I'm a mighty dangerous enemy."

"I know what you're leading up to," Cleo told me quietly and calmly. "But for you to be killed would make people remember all the other deaths—maybe lead to a complete investigation—"

"That's the weakness in my argument. I don't see how he arrived at the opinion I was dangerous enough to justify the hue and cry. I am, but for reasons that don't show. There would be a hue and cry. This is the middle of the nineteenth century—Wood Ibis is no longer a secure island kingdom where the king can do no wrong. Maybe he thinks I know more than I do—or Pa has told me something that doesn't seem important to me, but that some day, if I live, will hang fruit on the gallows tree. I tell you again, Cleo, he didn't do this for hate, or because he's insane. There's only one other answer—that he's in mortal fear of me for reasons we don't know."

Cleo had turned very white but her gaze did not flinch from mine. "That's true, of course," she said.

"The fear may rise out of the deaths of Bert and Slewfoot."

"Tell me everything you're thinking, Dan."

"It may not concern the deaths of Sadie and your Uncle Bruce. But if those deaths were fastened on—Ralph—Dunbarton—Saul would not inherit Wood Ibis."

"You don't have to say any more, unless you want to. I don't know if Papa could have saved Bert and Slewfoot—I do know he didn't. I do know that murder has run riot around here for a long time. I want it stopped, no matter who has to die on a rope. I want —the murderers—dead."

I heard her voice above the chanting of the work-crew in the field. The sun was high and blazing, the sky serene, the shadows sharp and small. It was a scene for a commonplace conversation— at most for making love—not a pronouncement of this magnitude. She was a slim, young girl: it was hard to believe that such words could fall from her delicate, lovely lips. I did believe it, because I knew her bravery long ago.

"There's only one more thing," I told her. "We can't know—we can't imagine—what will happen next. I want to make you safe as I can. Will you marry me at once?"

"Are you sure you want me to marry you now—Saul's half-sister —Papa's daughter?" Her eyes were dry and steadfast on mine.

"I never wanted to as much before."

"Then I wish it could be this minute."

"I'll need until tomorrow night to get everything ready. I'm going to take every precaution possible, so no one—nothing—can separate us again."

Her throat worked, then she spoke. "Maybe the demons didn't hear you, that time. Maybe they stay out of the sun."

25

The night was clear, warm, and almost still. The moon had shown her full face to us yesterday; now it looked shortened with puffed cheeks, the first symptom of a fatal sickness with which she would waste away.

She had risen only an hour later than last night, when she had set sail in the fullness of her pride and beauty. Grandly she set forth again as though nothing was wrong with her that a sky voyage could not cure. She was like a queen riding with pomp and splendor up a boulevard of her capital, so none would know she bore a taint of leprosy. . . . But the envious great stars, their glory dimmed of late by her resplendence, knew well that Death had touched her with his cold hand. "We will shine again, and soon," they signaled dimly to one another. Out of the seeming empty deeps of the sky rose a triumphant prophecy. "Even we little stars will soon shine again."

I thought that the moonlight was slightly more gray than last night, with a little more alloy in its lustrous silver, but that might be a trick of my eyes. It was a trick of my mind, perhaps, to invent ill omens, at least to notice every little sign that might be bad, so not to anger the gods of evil fortune. I would confess their powers to blast my hopes this night of nights; I would tremble in their sight. Thus, perhaps, they would not move against me to teach me a lesson. They would not punish me for being uppity. So high were my hopes this night of nights, so deep my fears.

For my own part I had raked and reraked by brain to provide the maximum of safety, the minimum of risk. No trawler had stopped today at Turtle Inlet whereby we might sail to George-town, and we must go by land and ferry to McClellanville, but at sundown a boatman and I made a false start for Bull Island in Dr. Sams's little sail-boat, while Cleo, tired from a jaunt with Obo, went early to her room. Every lamp was out and candle expired when she stole through a side door—it was eleven o'clock and the marsh hens would not holler until after one. I was waiting with

235

two horses beyond the live-oak aisle, and would have had three save that Obo could travel faster through the night, see, hear, and smell more, and protect us better, on foot.

Cleo and I exchanged hardly a word as we mounted and set out for the wide tidal river that separated Ibis Island from the coastal isles. We kept on soft ground until we were out of hearing of the houses, then rode wildly to our rendezvous with Obo, who for safety's sake had left the Quarter only a few minutes ahead of us. We had almost reached the border of Wood Ibis without sight or sound of danger.

"Is it all right, Obo?" Cleo murmured.

"I aint seen nothin' yit, but I aint had time to look."

He bade us again take to soft ground as we approached the river, and had us wait in the tree shadows while he scouted alone. He was gone a long time. Cleo drew her horse close and slipped her cold, trembling hand into mine. Still Obo did not come. The little drum beating so wildly for so long was my own heart. A slow-moving 'possum had time to appear in the moonlight, approach us within a few feet, and disappear. We heard a mockingbird in her bowers, but not Obo's happy whisper that all was well.

He returned a different way than he had gone. He stood beside us and I heard him draw a long, deep breath before he spoke.

"De news mighty bad, Miss Cleo."

Her hand jerked a little in mine, then she replied,

"Well?"

"Dey got de boat on de odder side. On dis side dey got a heap o' mens—scatter all along de bank. Mos' of 'em Old Massa's slaves but two or t'ree white in de lot. And dey all got guns."

"Can we swim the river?"

"You know we can't do dat. De horses would mire down befo' you git to de water and de tide runnin' so fast he sweep us out to sea. But dey didn't need all dem men to stop us. Mas' Saul know dat; he need only enough to keep us from gittin' de boat. What you reckon he want of all 'em men wif guns?"

"What do you think, Obo?"

"I t'ink Mas' Saul gwine kill Mas' Dan, like he kill Slewfoot. Dey pretend to chase us, to git you back, but de guns will fire for signal, and one of de bullet fly straight to Mas' Dan. Dey want

236

Mas' Dan dead right away. Dey want him dead befo' he marry you. Dey mighty 'fraid for Mas' Dan to live no time mo'. And we mighty lucky if he las' out dis night."

"We've got to get back to Dr. Sams," I said. "We've got to keep him with us every moment—they won't dare murder me with him looking on."

"Yes, but we can't go back de quick way, down de road. Dey's men posted there—I thought I smell 'em as I came by. Dey let us pass cause Mas' Saul told 'em to—he want plenty men after us when Mas' Dan get kill—but dey'll head us off at de first causeway. We got to go into de woods and maybe into de swamp. Dat depend—"

Obo paused, and lifted his head to listen. I too thought I heard a sound like one board being drawn across another a long distance off.

"What is it, Obo? You say we won't have to go into the swamp unless—"

"Dat's it. But it stand to reason Mas' Saul bring his pack o' hound."

For perhaps ten seconds he stood in thought. They grew long, but neither Cleo nor I broke into his reverie.

"If he got 'em hounds he'll put 'em on my track," he said. "But 'taint no good for me to go into de swamp while you light out wif Miss Cleo for Dr. Sam'. Mas' Saul trap and kill you sho. You all 'pend on me. It de best hope of livin' t'rough de night. You do what I tell you, and go where I take you."

"We will, Obo," I said.

"Follow me, please, Miss Cleo and Mas' Dan."

He set out in an easy run, much faster than it looked: to keep pace I held Lizzie in a quiet canter. At first he weaved through the shadows, careful not to cast his own in the patches of moonlight; a furlong farther on he tacked only when necessary to maintain speed. To my surprise he cut no corners through the thickets to shorten the distance to Little Ibis, and his course brought us ever nearer the Swamp. Plainly he preferred to run a longer way than walk a shorter one, even though no time would thus be saved.

But I had time to think now, and soon had little doubt of what he was thinking. A glance backward through a break in the timber

237

revealed a converge of lanterns and pine torches half a mile behind us. A glance inward by the light of imagination disclosed the scene enacted there—a search being made for what human senses could not perceive. That search would not take long. . . .

Only a moment later we heard a hound give tongue. It was a hoarse, savage, triumphant outcry in the silent night—the beast that had already sniffed at an old garment or scrap of bedding taken from Obo's cabin had found the same scent on the riverbank. His questing pack-fellows bounded to the spot; each sniffed and lifted his head to bay; the chorus swelled until it filled all the distant hollow of silence with fierce song. I was expecting it, but my heart leaped in terror. It steadied a little only when I looked at Obo, leading us on. He did not glance back. As he veered swampward across moonlit ground he did not increase his pace.

A mile or so ahead of us other hounds bayed. The grim picture was filling in well: Saul had kept back part of his pack at the last causeway we had crossed, and one of his men had now set the crazed beasts on Obo's tracks. His obvious purpose was to drive us into the swamp, where premeditated murder could be more easily disguised as accidental to a man hunt. Yet I never doubted that Obo's plan of entering the swamp—apparently in the panic of terror—and then circling back to Wood Ibis was my sole chance for life. I would not be permitted to surrender to my pursuers. Guns would blaze at first sight of me—unless broad daylight and the presence of a feared but fearless witness held their fire.

Saul had not overlooked another method of inspiring terror. The baying of the hounds ahead of us was evidently a signal to a henchman left at the Quarter. Weirdly over and under and through their blood-lust song, clamored the great bell of Wood Ibis. It was summoning man and beast and even the evil spirits of the earth and air to join in the chase. It bade the waters drown me and the quicksand suck me down. Sometimes the hounds fell silent as they quested for the scent but the bell never ceased or slackened, like despair unriven by hope, so that my heart would beat fast and faster until it kept time with the frantic clanging—but a human heart was only fragile flesh, and the bell adamant brass.

Obo did not appear to hear. He was following a little brook that flowed toward the swamp—running when he could, calmly walking

238

when he must, crossing frequently from bank to bank, and wading every long, level flow. Now Cleo and I were crossing stretches of boggy ground where the horses plunged. Thickets began to bar our way.

"Leave 'em horses here," rose Obo's soft tenor voice. "But bring yo gun, Mas' Dan. You got killin' to do befo' dis night go by."

Obo had brought the coil of rope he always carried on his jaunts with Cleo, and his stout oaken pole. I wished he had brought his harness whereby he could ferry her across deep waters; for the hour might strike when they should go on alone across tidal rivers to distant settlements, while I remained in the swamp. Such a notion had crossed the minds of neither of them. We were a team of three who seemed to share one heart. Obo, our captain, led us ever deeper into the labyrinth, his head constantly turning, the treacheries of the moonlight impotent to harm him, the weird shape of things never beguiling him, and even the heavy darkness of the thickets unable to blind completely his swamp-fox eyes.

Mosquitoes assailed us in humming swarms. Obo paused, and plucked the leafy stalks of a spicy-smelling plant. "Mash 'em leaves and rub 'em on your faces and hands," he told us. " 'Twill keep off the worse of de skeeters. I'll find some more befo' dey git bad agin."

He kept to the wettest ground that would give us passage. We waded the brook except when mire or snag dams barred the way. We plunged through bogs and over fallen timber, but never at a pace that would soon exhaust Cleo or me. Once in a patch of moonlight Obo stopped and gave us a smile.

"De goin's *too* easy to suit me," he said. "I wish dis was Deep Swamp, whey dey bigger runs and a heap mo' water. Some of 'em dog of Mas' Saul—dey old and mighty wise, losin' de trail but knowin' how to pick it up agin. We got plenty trick to play, if we gwine shake 'em off."

The hounds that had first given tongue had gained on us at times, chilling our hearts. When they had lost the scent we had gained distance, and now their clamor was no louder than at first. The dogs held back at the causeway had fallen silent after a few minutes of fierce baying: undoubtedly they were on leash and their handler had taken them off the course and was bringing them across country to join the others on the warm trail. The savage chorus suddenly swelled as he slipped their leashes and the two packs became one. No doubt Saul exulted at the doubled uproar, thinking it would panic us into climbing trees. Even Obo was not sure I understood the situation and spoke gently over his shoulder.

"Dey aint any nearer, Mas' Dan. Dey jus' more dogs."

Soon thereafter he led us away from the brook and shortly I perceived that he was following a well-worn deer trail through thickets and across a white-oak hummock. Here the pack could follow us full tilt, still I did not need to borrow some of Cleo's trust in him to conquer terror. As Obo kept to the same rapid walk, his voice flowed softly back to us again.

"We gwine have a mighty close shave right soon now," he warned me. "But it de onliest chance we got to lose dem dogs and circle back to Little Ibis."

"All right, Obo."

"Dey plenty deer and bear come along dis path dis evenin' and 'em dogs gwine get de smells mixed. Dey aint people, dey only mighty mean dogs, and dey more used to runnin' deer and bear dan dey is folks. Pretty soon we gwine take a long swing off de trail. By den most of 'em will be so hot on de scent dat maybe dey keep right on after de critters and not stop and look for us. Maybe de whole passel will chase dem critters far 'way into de swamp, still raisin' sand, and Mas' Saul and de men will foller 'em in. Dey won't look for one footprint while dey cuttin' corners to catch up wif de dogs. If some of de hound foller after us, we got to lose 'em some odder way."

"Well, they're gaining pretty fast."

"Dat all right. Dey goin' to be a heap closer befo' we be in de clear, and maybe some of 'em catch up wif us. But de men are mos' a mile behind de dogs. I seen de lights jus' now."

We came to where the trail followed the bank of a run some five yards wide. Obo was looking for a place to wade it, I thought, but instead of leaving the trail, he presently stopped by a tree whose foliage overhung it. He turned with a faint smile, lowered his palm to receive Cleo's foot, and swung her up until she could grasp a limb. Then he gave me a boost, and from a secure perch,

I lowered my hand to grasp his. When we were all aloft we crawled one by one along a lateral bough and dropped off on the opposite bank.

Obo led us a bare ten paces from the run and stopped by another tree. "Dis is de babah-shop where we gwine take dat shave," he told us. "It gwine be mighty skeery, but you gotta keep cool, Mas' Dan, so if you gotta shoot dat gun, you can shoot straight."

Again we climbed to the branches, and now Obo took pains to find me a firm seat that commanded the moonlit game path and the ground below the tree. The long, deep baying grew louder. It changed to a chorus of sharp, savage barks as the pack emerged on the game trail and need no longer seek the scent but could follow it on the run. Our hearts stopped as they came in sight, the whole wolfish band compact and lusting to worry and kill. As they neared our bridge across the water, I heard Cleo's breathless whisper behind me.

"Don't stop, don't stop!"

The pack appeared to change step at the foot of the tree, and their barking stopped short. Then by far the greater number joined in a resounding exultant bay as they bounded on, hot on the false scent. Only three of the band, big dogs and cunning, old hunters of sly foxes and wily lynx, remained to search out our trail.

"Shoot fast, but don't miss once," Obo whispered.

He had placed me where the moonlight shone on my silver sights. Even so, I had to call on some sharpness of vision beyond my normal powers to see the bead against the dark target. The instrument was my will, exerted at full force, and controlling every nerve. When I touched trigger the hound dropped quivering.

I had never reloaded so fast, ramming down the powder, ball, and wadding, and affixing the cap in the lock. My second shot was again a clean kill. But my hands were shaking at the third and the wounded animal ran off howling.

Instantly Obo dropped to the ground, waded across the creek, and carried the two carcasses by the scruffs of their necks a good way into the black growth beyond. When he returned I saw him carefully efface some dark blotches on the game trail. Plainly he did not want Saul stopping here, to examine the ground. Perhaps

Saul would think I had fired in panic, missing every shot, but had somehow delayed my pursuers long enough to continue the race.

Obo joined us and we struck off at right angles to the trail. We had gained less than half a mile when we saw what resembled a little swarm of fireflies glowing and expiring in the thickets behind us. The lights vanished behind thick timber as we cut back toward the rim of the swamp.

"Mas' Saul may not follow 'em dogs very far," Obo told us. "He may git to wondering why we aint treed by now. But he can't track us no mo' tonight."

"Oh, thank God!" Cleo cried. "But Obo, if we'd tied our horses instead of turning them loose we could go back—"

"Saul would have found 'em and knowed we was goin' back for 'em. Don't you worry no mo', Miss Cleo. If we can't git to Little Ibis we can take agin to the swamp. Wifout dem hounds he ain't got a chance to track us—we could live dere till nex' summer if need be."

His voice rose a little and grew resonant. "Don't you and Mas' Dan feel bad no mo' tonight. We done got away."

CHAPTER 26

Skirting the swamp still two miles from Ibis Hall, over seven from Little Ibis, we saw a bobbing lantern on the carriage road. If some of our enemies were passing there, we could ill afford to remain unaware of their enterprise; if our only certain friend was out looking for us, we must not lose him in the dark. Bidding us wait at the edge of the thickets, Obo took a short cut that would fetch him to the roadside well in advance of the traveler. There was not the slightest danger of him betraying his presence to a foe.

Cleo and I saw the lantern stop and lift. It stood still for a long moment, then began to move toward us. Obo was beside us long before its yellow light revealed black Joshua on Paddy's back, and behind him, both mounted, Ben and Dr. Sams. The two Negroes at once dismounted.

"Great God!" Dr. Sams cried. "Cleo, you and Dan get up and ride like hell for Little Ibis. You three men follow on foot as fast as you can."

"I won't be long a-comin'," Obo promised.

"Ben and me won't be able to keep up wif Obo, but we'll git there fast as we kin," Joshua told him.

"Joshua, would you be afraid to wait by the Quarter, and if the hunters start for Little Ibis, ring the bell?" I asked.

"No, suh. I kin give the rope a few yanks, befo' they take after me."

"If they catch you, they'll kill you."

"Dey aint goin' to catch me, Mas' Dan, in de dark. Dem hounds is way deep in de swamp and won't be home tonight. I heared 'em faint jus' a minute ago."

"I'll see you're well rewarded—both you and Ben," Dr. Sams said, his voice trembling.

Not until we were fetching a wide loop around the Quarter at Wood Ibis did our slower pace permit a low-voiced conversation between Dr. Sams and me. "I guess you know I've been hitting the bottle hard, ever since you told me about the pit," he said.

"No, I didn't notice it."

"No wonder, with all that on your mind. Well, the booze kept me from worrying too much about your and Cleo's elopement. I see only the bright side when I've got enough down me. I reckon that's why I drink it. If I'd been sober I might have found out what the Dunbartons were doing, and warned you. I have entrée to Ibis Hall, and you don't. I could have been paying them a visit tonight and at least—"

"Please don't think about that," I told him, roweled by the torment in his voice and moonlit face.

"Once before my drunkenness cleared the way for murder. It didn't happen tonight, but no thanks to me. I'd assured myself there'd be no trouble—you and Cleo had got clean away. Then I heard the bell—and it sobered me up."

"Well, you did us a mighty good turn, when you started out to help us."

"So late! But Dan, the whole shooting match has gone crazy. Obo told me they were out to kill—I know it's true—but what's happened to turn them into mad dogs? Digging that pit was risky enough. It showed they're in terror of their lives, even though they planned to blame it on Obo. But to chase you into the swamp and kill you—even though nobody was to know who fired the shot—why, that would have aroused the whole Low Country and brought the provost here like bees. Ralph thinks he's a king and Saul is subhuman as well as a desperate gambler—but neither would go that far unless driven to it by something we don't know."

"That's all true," I answered, shivering. "But what now?"

"I'm getting soberer every minute. A while ago I thought you'd be safe in my house—they wouldn't break in the door and shoot you down—but I'm not even sure of that. They'd find some excuse to try to save their necks. It seems to me—but we're almost back on the road. Take all Paddy's got to the house."

I could not talk with Cleo or Dr. Sams above the drumming hoofs, but the time was not wasted. When we sprang down by our paddock, I had something to say to them both.

"Dr. Sams, I want to marry Cleo at once."

He stared at me but I did not wait for his protest that such a thing was impossible tonight.

"I know she'll be safer. I think I will too, instead of in greater danger if that's possible—I haven't thought out the reason but can feel in my bones. We've tried to get to an ordained minister to sign the certificate and perform the ceremony. We were restrained by force. But old Absalom is a Negro preacher—he's married some of your slaves and performed burial service." I whirled to my betrothed. "Cleo, are you willing that Absalom perform the ceremony now and the marriage be consummated tonight?"

Her face became luminous in the lantern light. "Yes, Dan."

"Dr. Sams, will you send your houseboy for Absalom at once?"

"You're damned right I will."

When the boy took horse for Absalom's cabin, I got some clean clothes from my closet and Dr. Sams took from his store a dress of the kind he provided for the housemaids and a fair fit for Cleo. Absalom was not due for another quarter of an hour; anyway the bell at Wood Ibis was still mute, and if Joshua had not quit his post, we were sure of at least twenty minutes leeway before the Dunbartons could strike again. Cleo and I went down to the dock, and only half its length apart, took off our muddy clothes, slipped into the warm water, and bathed. The glimmer of her white body in the moonlight brought a memory-scent of sawdust fragrant with balsam and an intimacy with wonder long ago.

Venerable Absalom, white-haired, noble of countenance, wearing a little beard that looked like cotton, arrived with his Bible that he could not read almost the same moment that Obo paced out of the dark. Neither Negro had ever before entered a white man's parlor, but Obo had been a king's son in his native land and Cleo was his deeply beloved, and Absalom had been called to the ministry of God by higher authority than the governors of a diocese. Dr. Sams had closed the blinds and drawn the curtains against attack from the dark, when Cleo and I took our places before the priest.

"Brovers and sisters, we is gaddered togedder tonight to solemnize de marriage of dis man and dis woman. . . ."

Only once during the brief simple ceremony did my heart fall,

245

then only briefly and for unknown cause. It was when the minister declared that if any person had reason why Cleo and I could not be united in marriage, let him speak now, or forever hold his peace. I thought I feared a bullet through the window. But there was no sound from anyone, and a few minutes later she and I were declared man and wife.

Until that moment it had never occurred to me that the giant Obo could weep like common men.

Our host had already provided a bottle of wine and a small fruitcake—back of all else he was a Sams of Beaufort—and now he offered us a greater safety than we had counted on.

"Dan, if Saul comes tonight"—and the considerate man did not mention Ralph—"of course this house is the first place he'll look for you."

My first thought was—"Let him come!" I needed only a brief warning and his merest threat, to treat and break this burning fever. But I thought upon my bridal night, and it was slaked for a little while.

"You know Rhoda's cabin, a little back from the row?" he went on.

"Yes, sir."

"She moved yesterday with its furnishings to live with her daughter. She left it spick and span, as she always kept it. I was going to have Nathan and his new wife move in there, and provided brand-new furnishings"—Dr. Sams' color deepened slightly—"from the store. Why don't you and Cleo spend the night there? It's the last place anyone would look for you. Obo will stand watch at the road, and I'll do penance for my sins by sitting on the dock where the breeze will keep off the skeeters. Dawn will crack in about three hours."

"That would suit us very well, Dr. Sams," Cleo said quietly.

"Well—just in case—I'd better remind you both—of what Dan said—" He stopped.

"Don't worry about that, old friend." Cleo kissed his florid cheek.

We were both well suited by our bridal chamber, hidden away by its very humbleness. We could imagine it, if we tried, a hut in the woods that we had built after keeping our ancient promise to one another; its smallness and roughness could, if we liked, remind

246

us of the place we had made that promise. Both of us had had hard schooling in self-preservation in the broadest sense of that term, which includes self-mastery and making the most of every chance. So we dropped out of our minds all that had happened between the alarm at the river, and our meeting with Dr. Sams on the road, as though it were a bad dream in the night; and this little cabin became our destination from the first, the scene of our honeymoon. We shut out of our minds all vistas of the future when we must treat with time again. Neither of us would take any thought of danger striking now. We would not make unseemly haste; we would not interrupt love's language to listen to the dark; we would not look out the window save to see the charmed light of the moon. If, despite these resolves, shadows out of the past or cast by coming events crept across our floor, we would only drink more deeply of this brimming cup of now.

We needed no lamp but the moon shining through the windows. Our cabin appeared as dark as any in the row, and seemed as silent. We felt the wonder of that, since we were so wide awake, speaking to each other with such fervor in so many tongues, while her beauty shone. Joy was so bright; there was such music in every word and act. I had her lie across my breast awhile, as on the bank of the cypress pond where the otters played, and now I was gloried to think we need not watch the tide, for soon we must start back. Each glimmering moment would bring us nearer to our fulfillment instead of to thwarted yearning. Unlike in our hiding place at the beach we need not compromise with thirst and hunger, lest we be parted soon.

On our last night on shipboard a jeweled pin at the collar of her dress had become unclasped. When the beauty of her face waxed to the full—no, that was yet to come; yet I had never seen it so moving—my trembling hand went to her throat again, and with no stealth now. But I had hardly bared her bosom to my lips when a little tremor passed over her body and she laid her hand on mine.

"Are you sure, Dan?" she whispered. "Both of us must know."

"You're my wife, Cleo."

"Not yet. I want to be—right away—I can hardly stand to wait any longer—but there's still time to draw back. I had given up hope of being any man's wife, let alone yours. Will you stop and think one minute more before you decide?"

"You should trust my love by now."

"I do trust it. I know how great it is. That's why I had to give you this last chance to let me go. The ceremony took place so suddenly—it was over so quick—I looked at you when Absalom said that part about 'let him speak now,' and something came into your face. My heart was singing for joy—but it stopped—and turned to stone."

"Cleo, it was only fear we might be parted—"

"What caused that fear? Was it thinking how I was Papa's daughter—Saul's half-sister? Now I've got to say something we want to forget tonight—but remember we can't forget it—it will stay with us always. I've got to say it in plain words. Saul tried to kill you—twice. He did kill Bert and Slewfoot. And Papa—"

"Oh, I ask you not to—"

"I've got to, Dan. As much as I've fought against it, I believe he alone has to answer on earth or in heaven for the deaths of four people."

I heard her say "four"—or thought I did—but I did not think she had heard herself say it. It was only a very strange slip of her tongue, or my ears had played a very strange trick. Yet I did not correct the mistake directly—and I did not know why! I found that my heart had no room, just now, for pity on her torment or for wonder at her bravery: it was too full of foreboding. It was leaping a moment ago. Now it was fluttering, with an ever faster beat.

"I've considered all that, Cleo," I told her out of a clamped throat. "His own wife Sadie—his brother Bruce—a Negro boatman—" There I paused.

"And a helpless baby! That's haunted me the worst of all. Mama's first-born by the man she loved. He was sick that night. I guess you know about it. Uncle Bruce started for Bull Island to take him to a doctor. Instead both of them were going to meet death."

I was silent and still a long time. She was waiting for me to tell her that all the demons in hell could not make me let her go—

waiting for me to make some move to show her that no evil could ever taint this good—but my tongue was frozen and there came an unliftable weight on my hands. The warm, close room was turning sinister. The moonlight shining on the bed was cold and gray as death.

Her eyes darted to mine, then leaped away. "I had to speak of this, Dan. Don't blame me—"

"Why, how could I? You're just being true to yourself. What was the baby's name, Cleo? I don't believe Pa ever told me—"

"Donovan."

"Your little half-brother you never saw. Is he buried in your private cemetery? I passed by there not long ago—and looked in —but I don't recall seeing his grave."

"I suppose it's there. It's queer—I don't remember seeing it either —but I haven't been there since I was a little girl. The moss on the trees is so mournful—and I—even then—was afraid of ghosts."

"Yet his body was found on the boat—"

"Why—I—suppose so. It seems I heard someone say so—but I can't really remember—"

Only with a violent surge of my will could I break this smothering silence.

"Poor little fellow. Perhaps blown to pieces by the explosion. Thanks for being so fair, Cleo—it wasn't necessary though. How could anything in the past change what's between you and me?"

She lay very still. I could not hear her breathe. Finally she spoke in a guarded tone.

"Your voice sounds so strange."

I bent and kissed her lips. "I love you, Cleo."

Again she lay still. When she spoke again, the guard of her tone was no longer strong.

"Your lips—felt—cold."

"I guess I was still thinking about what you told me."

She gasped and said, "I wish now I hadn't."

"What do you mean, Cleo?"

"It *has* made a difference. You're thinking about me being Papa's daughter—and Saul's sister. I knew it would."

I could only say, "Oh, you don't know what you're saying."

249

"Maybe not. Maybe this would have happened anyway."

"Nothing's happened, except what we've both been through to-night—enough to drive any two people out of their minds."

"It was a bad night to get married, wasn't it? We've been through too much. We're not fit to go on with it—are we?"

"Well—we haven't much time until daylight. If you think—"

She sat up and leaned against the wall. "I knew it was all a dream."

"Oh, Cleo!"

"A door that had been shut all my life opened once—and closed —then opened again—and now it's closed again. But it isn't be-cause of Papa—or Saul. I guess it's because of Mama, who's so beautiful. When you think of her—and then look at me—"

"Don't say that. You're the most beautiful—"

"I shouldn't have betrayed her. She's all I had. She didn't love me—she couldn't after she had seen herself in the mirror—remem-bering the way she looked when she was young—but she let me adore her. Because you thought I was beautiful—because I thought you loved me—I've lost that too."

"Great God, I do think so! You're wonderfully beautiful to me. I do love you—"

"We both thought you did. And I became beautiful a little while because of it—it was like light falling on my face in a different way. But I ought to have known the truth. I had offered you my body, and you refused it. You could have done with it what you liked—played delicious games with it, or got warm by it, or used it for making sons and daughters. If you love me, why don't you kiss me? Why don't you go ahead and undress me, as you started to? You would, if you love me, no matter whose daughter I am. Even if you couldn't bear to keep me, you would have had me tonight. Wouldn't it be more pleasure than to go with a tavern girl?"

"Cleo, it isn't that. If you only knew how I love you and want you! But I've got to find out something—"

"Tomorrow? This is tonight. I've a pretty little body, Dan. You saw it when I was a child—didn't you think it was pretty then? I look at it in the glass and it seems pretty enough for a young man to want at least for one night—the first ever to have it. Shall

250

I show it all to you? Will that make your lips turn warm again? You don't need to answer. You know there isn't any answer that's any good. I release you from your promise. I'm going to get up and go into the woods with Obo and watch the otters one more time and then I'm going to die. That's all I want now. Not another thing. Death will take me in welcome, and not offer any excuses. Obo will come too, when I go."

I had taken her by the shoulders, holding her firmly, but it was a long time before the immense pupils of her haunted eyes contracted a little, and I thought she could hear what I said.

"Cleo, will you listen to me now?"

"Yes, Dan."

"Wait here a few minutes. I've got to ask Dr. Sams a question. If the answer is what I hope and believe, I'll run back here, and then you'll find out how much I love you and want you. No doubt will ever cross your mind again, I tell you! Don't ask me what the question is just trust me. Will you?"

Her eyes met mine in one great wondering glance and she nodded. I sped out the door, and ran wildly to the dock where Dr. Sams kept watch of the road. He saw me coming and sprang to his feet.

"Oh, my soul, what's the matter?" he gasped.

I had to catch my breath before I could speak. "You never told me about Donovan—Bruce's and Madeline's baby—"

He reeled a little as though from a blow. "On reflection—I dare say—I didn't."

"Why? Was it for some reason you didn't know—something in your mind that wouldn't come out—"

"I know at least one reason. The most awful shame. But maybe there was another—"

"Don't take time to tell me now. Just answer one question. Was the baby's body found?"

"Why, yes."

"Thank God!"

"It was several days afterward. Ralph brought it here—and I signed the death certificate—"

"Oh, thank you, thank you! That's all. I'll see you later—"

I turned and started to run but he spoke again.

"Wait just a minute."

I stopped but it seemed a long time before I could turn back. There was no blood in my heart or bravery in my eyes. I kept looking at the trees, wondering at their pleasant shapes against the moonlit sky. When at last I faced him, he had his hands pressed to his temples and the travail in his brain had drawn his countenance almost beyond recognition.

"Dan, Dan!" he burst out. "I'm trying to remember. I was drunk —I had been for days. They came at night—the little thing was wrapped in a canvas—and tied up with a rope. It had been in the water nearly a week. One of the slaves had found it washed into the reeds. That was what Ralph said."

"Did you look at it? You've got to remember."

"I can remember dreading to. I remember Ralph saying, 'I'll spare you seeing him, if it's all right with you. He's in bad shape, Doc.'"

"Did you look at the body? You were a doctor. You wouldn't have signed the certificate—"

"I touched it. It was limp—and soft. No! I didn't! I didn't look at it! I flinched from it as I've always flinched from everything I didn't want to face. I signed the paper that swam before my drunken eyes. God help me."

When the rocking sky grew still again, I heard my quiet, sane reply.

"Thanks for telling me. You know why I asked. We'll talk it over tomorrow."

I walked back to the cabin and found Cleo waiting for me by the door. She too had recovered herself. Her eyes in the moonlight pouring through the doorway were wide and dark with dread, but, alive and beautiful and brave, she was looking at me, not yearningly into void. I thought that in my absence she had surmised my errand.

"What is it, Dan?"

"I love you forever and ever, but we can't have each other tonight. Perhaps we never can. Do you know why?"

"Yes, Dan, I know. But I love you forever and ever."

"Forever," I had said. And she had replied, "Forever."

Our fingers intertwined—as on that day we waited in Philadelphia for a carriage to come for her—Cleo and I stood in the moonlit doorway. The tide was very low. I thought it was still going out, but took comfort soon in seeing that it had turned back. A thing more than comfort was in the warm clasp of our hands. Thereby our hearts had reassurance that this plighting of our troth was real—never to be mistaken for something else, perhaps a valiant sparing of ourselves and each other from shame and guilt. What we had done in innocence would not turn on us and haunt us.

Cleo uttered a little gasp. "I don't believe it, Dan."

"I don't either. Even if by some miracle a baby survived the explosion, how could he stay up—"

"That's right—but I was thinking of all that's happened between us. It couldn't have happened—could it?—if—if—what we fear is true. We wouldn't have become sweethearts. Instinct would have—"

"I'm afraid we can't trust to that. It wasn't as though we'd grown up with any such possibility in our minds. There've been other cases where people married without finding out such a thing. But it won't be hard to find out—and it hadn't ought to take long."

"Well, let's not hide here any more. I haven't a drop of fear left —except about this. I *do* believe that instinct would have warned us. It isn't even warning us now—when we know the possibility. Every prayer in my heart is—it isn't true. That means I still—"

"I do too, Cleo. Well, let's go to the house. We'll talk a minute to Dr. Sams—then wait for daylight."

Dr. Sams met us at the door, looking gray and drawn under the lamp. He put his arms around Cleo and kissed her; to me he gave a wan, weary smile.

"Ralph and Saul may be here soon," he said. "I don't think we'll have the least trouble with them tonight—I've thought that much out. But what are we going to tell them?"

"You decide, Dr. Sams," I said. "My head won't work."

"Well, I believe it best to tell them you two are married and let them think the marriage has been consummated. I'll maintain the legality of it till hell freezes over, if it's otherwise possible. Dan, I'll explain to you shortly why I think it's the best move now. Cleo, I want you to go to bed."

She nodded, kissed me lovingly, and climbed the stairs. Dr. Sams and I took seats in the unlighted dining room where he could watch the road through the window.

"Dan, I would have told you about little Donovan," he went on, "if I hadn't assumed that Noel told you. True, I flinched from it in that first talk with you—before I knew Noel had sent you here —and continued to flinch from discussing it, since you didn't mention it. Naturally I thought that was out of consideration for me. If you look back, you'll notice I said very little about Webb, the Negro boatman who was killed in the explosion. The reason was, of course, any mention of him came too close to the baby."

"I did notice it, Dr. Sams."

"You see, Dan, I felt myself responsible for the baby's death. If he was blown up or drowned, which I still believe, I'm still responsible. At least he wouldn't have been killed that night, except for my criminal negligence. I knew he'd been ailing but got drunk just the same." Dr. Sams was speaking in dull, dry monotones, painful to the ear. "That's what Saul meant when he said I got drunk once too often and now I'm in a more respectable business than doctoring sick people. Because I was unfit to treat the baby, Bruce started that night for Bull Island in search of another doctor."

"You told me on the dock tonight there was another reason you never mentioned him to me."

"Did I?"

"Don't you remember?"

"No. I can't think of any other reason. I'm sure there is none." He spoke on quickly. "I want you to know not the slightest suggestion of a possibility ever crossed my mind that the baby might have—survived."

"Of course not, or you would have warned Cleo and me."

"Why didn't Noel tell you about him, Dan?"

"I don't know—but it scares me. Actually he told me very little of the detail—he wanted me to find out everything for myself—but he never counted the baby as one to be avenged, in spite of him being Bruce's son by Madeline."

"It's very strange, I grant you. Not only Bruce's son—but the heir to Wood Ibis."

Thinking of that, Dr. Sams gazed out the window and up the moonlit road. My skin prickled all over. If I were Donovan Dunbarton, my legacy might be Wood Ibis and it might be death. Each had been willed me by my kindred. I wanted neither, only to live with Cleo.

"I thought you said Madeline inherited by Bruce's will."

"She did—provided Donovan died without issue. She came again into the estate when I signed his death certificate."

"Well, before we know anything for certain we've got to deal again with Ralph and Saul. They may come any minute. We've agreed to tell them that the marriage has been consummated."

Dr. Sams wanted to ask a question. It was like fever in his face. He could not bring himself to do so, so I spoke.

"Cleo is still a virgin, Dr. Sams."

"Thank God! That sounds like I believed—I don't, I tell you—still we can't shut our eyes—"

"What else are we going to tell Ralph and Saul?"

"Dan, if that was not Donovan's body they brought to me that night—in twenty-four hours we may discover that it was, but we may not—it might account for what happened tonight. Undoubtedly they know by now you came from Noel. Saul knew about Dan Reed—Ralph had been to see a Professor Reed in Philadelphia whom he thought might be Noel, and who had a son—as soon as Cliff Todd took flight they'd begin to put two and two together as Cleo did. But if Ralph had faked the finding of the body, he'd go farther than Cleo did—his mind would leap where yours leaped tonight. That was some weeks ago, I believe. I think Saul left here to look for a lame musician in Baltimore; if he proved to be Noel —and Noel had an adopted son answering your description—why not another murder added to the grisly list? Saul would weigh the risk against the safety gained. Noel owned Little Ibis and was an implacable avenger. But if in addition to that he had planted a baby in an orphanage to adopt him later, and his testimony alone could prove—"

Some words I could not disown forced themselves out of my corded throat. "Maybe that murder is already behind him. That letter Pa wrote—"

"Put that out of your head. Noel's a long-headed, cunning man and would have kept close guard all the while you're here. He'd have counted on them becoming frightened and striking right and left."

"They're frightened right now. We'd better hurry this up."

"If an armed party starts this way before daylight, Joshua will ring the bell. Don't fear he won't! Anyway, that's not the way they'll work."

"All right. Go on."

"Sitting on the dock—after you asked that question—I tried to put myself in Ralph's mind. Assume he faked the finding of little Donovan's body. Still it never occurred to him until a few weeks ago that the baby might have lived. He wanted a death certificate to avoid legal difficulties—so Madeline could come immediately into the estate, which he would get when he married her. When the idea did occur to him—a terrifying possibility—he came across a very strange fact. The fact was—mark it well, Dan, because it's awfully important—you yourself didn't suspect you might be Donovan. In other words—Noel had never suggested such a thing to you."

"I see that. If I suspected it, I wouldn't be trying to marry Cleo."

"Exactly. Well, how would he explain Noel never telling you? A mad vagary? That would be hard to swallow. I know Noel far better than Ralph does and it wasn't a mad vagary. If you are Donovan, Noel had a deep but as yet incomprehensible motive for concealing it from you. But wouldn't it be a strong argument to Ralph that you weren't Donovan, merely a waif Noel had adopted?"

"It might be so. But notice he went ahead anyway. Perhaps an attempt to kill Pa—certainly two attempts to kill me."

"That's the point I'm making. He and Saul might have risked the pit murder with less motive. Obo was to be blamed for it—the state could hardly hope for a conviction. But they wouldn't have risked the hue and cry to follow your death in the swamp unless —I put it straight to you—they have reasons we don't know, over-weighing Noel's strange silence to you, strong reasons to convince them perhaps beyond all doubt that you *are* Donovan Dunbarton."

"I agree with you, I regret to say."

"What did Saul find out while he was away? And mark you, Dan, they wanted you dead before you married Cleo. Do you know why?"

I drove my dizzy brain. "So if it turned out later I was the lost heir, she'd not be owner of Wood Ibis by marriage to me? No, that won't hold. We couldn't have been married. No legal marriage can exist between half-brother and -sister."

"No, but the ceremony—performed innocently—would show your intent. Any judge with a sense of equity would award Wood Ibis to her."

"Then that's why you want to make Ralph believe the wedding was consummated."

"They may suspect the worst—but what do we care if it adds to yours and Cleo's safety. At least it will give us an excuse for keeping Cleo here. They can't charge it is an impossible marriage without letting you know their suspicions, which they assume you don't know. If you'd been killed last night, they might have come out with them as an excuse for the man hunt. Saul would think of that, no doubt—that you *knew* you might be Donovan but had eloped with her just the same—"

"Yes, it would be quite in character. Well, there's one thing I can do. I'm going to write a will right now, leaving Cleo every-thing I own. I'll wake up Cleo and get her to write one, leaving to —charity, I reckon—all she owns. How are we going to put that over to them without showing we suspect—"

But that question was a relatively simple one.

There were others at which we could only guess; so we had no assurance that the program we had adopted temporarily was the best or safest. The night wore out without a warning bell or any sign of the foe; half an hour after sunrise Joshua brought word that Ralph and Saul had returned bedraggled to Ibis Hall two hours before, leaving their kennel boys to retrieve the dogs from their rampage in the swamp. The armed Negroes had turned in their weapons and were going to work, while the low whites Saul had recruited departed to their homes on the coast isles. Dr. Sams and I drank black coffee and awaited the enemy's next move. However ill we had prepared for it, only then could we decide on our own.

It came in midmorning in the shape of Ralph riding sedately down the road, accompanied by a groom. He dismounted and gave the man his reins, but Dr. Sams did not wait for him to approach the door. While I stood in easy hearing, he stepped out on to the veranda.

"What is your business here, Ralph?" he asked in a quiet, impersonal tone.

Its effect on the master of Wood Ibis was stronger than he wanted us to know. His expression changed subtly; his manner became less imperious; his gaze less bold. Its effect on me was thrilling. I had not been certain until now Dr. Sams was this much of a man.

"Why, to pay you a neighborly call—and talk a bit with you and the two young people. Shall I come in, or shall we sit on the porch?"

"My door is closed to you, from now on. You can say what you have to say, where you are."

Ralph could hardly believe his ears. When he thought upon his riches and power, his twenty years reign of an island kingdom, still the words echoed and re-echoed, too clear to mistake. He had climbed so high—did the ladder crackle faintly, sway dizzily? Did the shadow of a buzzard in flight flick over the ground where he stood?

"That's a fine way to talk! Well, I'll keep my temper for old time's sake. You're making a mighty big mistake, Doc, taking a stand like this. You may be within your rights as far as closing your door to me—it depends on whether my brother Noel is still alive—but you heard me say I want to talk to my daughter. I mean face to face. To be plain with you, I came to take her home and I'm going to do it."

"Her husband will have something to say about that."

"Her husband! What in hell do you mean?"

"Cleo and Dave were married last night. I witnessed the ceremony. It took place in my house. It was performed by a preacher who has performed other weddings, of free Negroes. If you think it isn't legal, go to the judge. He'll tell you a marriage is nothing but a contract sworn to before witnesses. The couple were restrained by force from getting a marriage certificate, but they will have one as soon as I can go before a magistrate. After what you did last night, you or Saul had better not make any move to take her away from here by force."

Ralph resisted any temptation to reply at once. He stood slapping his boot with his riding whip, a glower on his face, while he taxed his brain for cunning. For the present he decided to tack.

"Well, I'm not enough of a lawyer to know whether a marriage like that—performed by a nigger, I reckon—is legal or not. All I know is, I'm not going to have my daughter livin' with a man she's not married to legally—if I have to set this house on fire to get her out."

"I wouldn't even talk about that, if I were you." Dr. Sams had turned fiery red. He had been under pressure too long.

"You're talking mighty high and mighty. 'After what I did last night,' you say. What did I do but try to keep my daughter from running away with a man I don't know anything about—who he is or where he came from or maybe his real name. What's wrong with that?"

"You risked both of their lives by arming your Negroes and white men and by setting the dogs on them. I think you can be sent to prison for that alone."

"How did I know he was even going to marry her? Well, I aint goin' to argue that with you. I'll ask one question—and you'll hear from me later."

"What is the question?" Dr. Sams had begun to tremble.

"What do you know about that fellow? Are you even sure he got married under his right name?" Sensing his advantage, Ralph moved ominously nearer.

I stepped out on to the porch. "I'll answer that, Mr. Dunbarton. I married Cleo under the name of Dan Reed, the name I was given when I was legally adopted by your brother, Noel Dunbarton. I also signed 'Dan Dunbarton,' on Doctor's testament."

Ralph feigned amazement. "So you're my brother's foster son!

If you'd told me that, instead of sneaking around under a false name—well, at least be man enough to tell me if my brother's alive."

"Yes, sir, he is."

"And that's why Doc would talk so big about shutting his door to me. All I can say is, you'll hear from me later."

"I've got one more thing to tell you. After last night, I don't know what lengths you may go to. If anything should happen to Pa or to Cleo and me you won't get Little Ibis back. I'll inherit it by Pa's will, and I've written a will leaving it and all my other possessions to Cleo. Cleo has written one leaving all her possessions to charity. Dr. Sams witnessed them both. Both have been sent to a safe deposit."

The latter statement was not true but it would be true before Ralph could move again. Actually the shot appeared remarkably effective in the way of counterattack. He appeared stunned, unable to reply, plainly without present resources to combat it. But I had no sense of triumph, only of unutterable dismay. What would Ralph care about such a will as I might make, unless he believed that I were heir to Wood Ibis?

Gray of face, Ralph rode away. Dr. Sams braced himself with a drink. "Great God," he burst out. "How I've longed for the day I could see retribution moving on Ralph Dunbarton."

"It hasn't got to him yet."

"No, you have a long way to go." Dr. Sams spoke with sudden, deep weariness. "I dread the last half of the journey more than I did the first. The closer Ralph and Saul are pressed, the more frantically and savagely they'll fight. At least that's true of Saul. As long as I've known Ralph, I still can't diagnose him. And you can't chart Saul's moves, because he's not a human being. He doesn't think and feel like a human being. Ralph thinks he's king of Wood Ibis, and his wish and word are law. Saul doesn't know what the word law means."

"Haven't we checkmated them with those wills? Provided they think I'm Donovan, which God forbid?"

"Hell's fire, you may meet with an 'accidental death' so perfectly contrived no charge of murder can be made. They'd take their chance on Cleo being owner. As long as they can deceive Madeline, they've got a mighty big hold on Cleo."

"The first thing is to prove I am Donovan—or I'm not. There can be no middle ground." I was fighting a small, growing fire of frenzy in my brain.

Lost in somber broodings, Dr. Sams hardly heard me. "And when you reach the end, what then? The door of Bluebeard's room thrown open, and you stand there holding a light? What's hanging in those closets? What demon rises up out of what pit? Will life be worth living for any of us after that—provided—any of us— are still alive?"

I had been pacing the floor, but I stopped to gaze at Dr. Sams at once in profound wonderment and pity. He looked up and saw my face, and by the same token was wakened from his evil dreams and came back to me.

"Forgive me, Dan," he cried quickly. "I keep forgetting what this means to you and Cleo. I suppose in my inmost heart I want you to be Donovan—so I won't have his death on my conscience. That's natural enough, isn't it? Besides—I'm out of my head from strain."

"It's natural enough, Dr. Sams. Tell me straight. Do you believe I am?"

"It doesn't seem possible a baby could survive. But yet—"

"Where is he supposed to be buried?"

"That's another thing. Instead of taking the body—what seemed to be the body—to the D'Arcy private cemetery, they buried it as soon as they left here in a little graveyard back from Turtle Inlet. Bruce and Ralph's father were buried there—so was old Gustaf Neilson—and some fishermen drowned at sea. Ralph told someone that the body was in such bad shape he couldn't bear to take it any farther. Still that wouldn't indicate—"

"Can we look at it tonight?"

"Yes. We can still tell something."

"We can drop in at Turtle Inlet to mail those wills to your lawyer in Charleston. The mail boat's due to touch there tonight. After they're off—"

"All right, but get in bed, whether you sleep or not. Pretend I'm a doctor again. No one can steal a march on us—I'll see that the house is well guarded."

I lay down on a couch in the same room where Cleo lay in deathlike sleep. What was she dreaming now? Hours passed, and she, Dr. Sams, Obo, and I stood in a little graveyard where palm trees grew crooked from the wind's rough games, and the moonlight lay cold and gray. The doctor had already posted the documents. He had talked briefly to Lizzie and Sam, telling them no secrets but promising to revisit them soon to give them a full account of Cleo's and my elopement. Obo had scouted the territory, reporting there was no sign of the enemy, and there was no danger of him approaching within rifle range in this almost barren region. Cleo stood well back from a small grave with its white stone as I bent my back to the shovel.

An hour later the blade struck wood. I lifted out a plain wooden box that might once have held ship-stores. . . . Surely Ralph could have had a slave carry it a few miles farther for interment among the D'Arcy dead—Madeline's son by his brother Bruce. . . . My hands were shaking as with claw hammer I drew the nails and raised the lid.

"Dr. Sams, will you please come here a moment?"

He did not want to come but he knew he must. Kneeling on the opposite side of the box, he looked in, gasped, and then lifted his eyes to mine.

"Nothing but rags—and sawdust—and the head of a China doll."

After a long time, I asked,

"Shall we carefully replace the dirt, or does it matter?"

"I reckon we might as well."

"What does this amount to as evidence? Anything?"

"Ralph can say the body was stolen for Negro conjure. Or he can say he never looked at the bundle the Negro brought—he didn't have the heart. The Negro knew he wouldn't—grieved and shocked as he was—and cheated him out of the reward."

We both stood up. "Who was the Negro? Can you remember?"

"Yes. It came to my mind only about an hour ago. I tried hard —and remembered. I wish I didn't."

"Well?"

"His name was Slewfoot."

CHAPTER

28

A seaward breeze sprang up before we left the scene, rattling the dead palm leaves and making dry, creaky rustlings in the green tops. We rode home in the face of it and perhaps the fresh rush of air, stimulating our bodies, also quickened our minds. In Cleo's case, it had an additional effect that might tend to counteract straight, clear thinking. It whetted, one might say, her instincts, which were a medley of subconscious perceptions and inarticulate emotion. She was very intimate with the moon, the open ground, and the winds. They had been her salvation all her life. Tonight she listened to their voices, so she thought, but perhaps she was only hearing the drum-telegraph of her own heart.

"I still don't believe it," she told Dr. Sams and me, when we were taking a kind of ease in his little office. "If the baby survived, which would be almost a miracle, Dan isn't he."

I could have reminded her, if I could be so stern, that she had refused to believe in her father's guilt, and even now harbored unreasonable doubts of its total blackness. As it happened, she was reminded of that herself. She was not flinching from anything tonight.

"If I could be so wrong about Papa, why can't I be wrong about this?" she went on. "Well, I still don't believe I was completely wrong about him. If there is such a thing as conjure—and I reckon I believe it in my heart—I would swear that if he killed his wife and then rigged the boat to blow up Uncle Bruce and the boatman and the baby, he'd been conjured. I can believe he thought he was fated to be king of Wood Ibis. I know he's horribly cruel in carrying out his beliefs. I can believe that after he became king, with Saul grown up into some kind of monster who loved to kill, he would consent to or even take part in one murder after another, to keep his kingdom and his life. Bert—Slewfoot—now you, Dan, and Uncle Noel, if he thought you were dangerous enough to him —a horrible tidal wave of blood befouling Wood Ibis forever." She stopped, her face drawn in revulsion, then spoke on bravely. "To be absolutely honest—I can imagine his fixing for a helpless baby to be blown up or drowned—the heir of Wood Ibis—easier than the rest. I never thought of that before—it's an awful thing to think —as you both know, until I saw that pit I wouldn't let myself think of any of this. Not that I loved him—I know now I didn't—but I wanted him to love me. Do you understand that, Dr. Sams? And if I let the idea enter my head he was a murderer, I couldn't take his love."

She had turned her lovely hazel eyes, with a little quiet luster in them yet, to her old friend. I looked at him too, deeply troubled. Sweat-beads stood all over his face and the skin had tightened over the bones and he was fighting private demons that her words invoked.

"I reckon you craved somebody's love, Cleo, to try to even up for your worship of Madeline," he answered.

"The boatman, Bert, and Slewfoot were Negroes," Cleo went on with deep self-search. "He's taught himself to believe that Negroes aren't human beings—only chattels whose lives don't matter. But it was the deaths—I'll say the killings, because I have no more doubt they were murdered—of Sadie and Uncle Bruce that still— if I were on a jury—I couldn't hang him for. It's true that traps were fixed for them both. He didn't kill them with them looking at him. That makes it more credible to me—but still it isn't enough."

"You've wandered away from the main subject, Cleo," I told her, forcing a quiet, calm tone. It did not betray the wild throbbing of my pulse from seeing her so near me, her slim body curled in a chair instead of in my arms. I wanted its warm length against mine. That craving again kindled a frantic fire to burn my house down now, rather than be locked outside while I waited for it to be blown down by the winds of fate. I could not know that fate until I could question Pa, if ever I saw him again; but I was compelled to surmise it now—to find out how black was the evidence that I was Bruce's son.

"That's right, Cleo," Dr. Sams said quickly—it seemed to me as though in profound relief at the changed subject. "You were saying you didn't believe the baby could have lived."

"I said if he did live, Dan isn't he."

264

"Cleo, do you feel equal to lining up and facing all the facts we have to see where they point?" I asked.

"Of course. I slept all day."

"Then let's begin at the beginning. Dr. Sams, you were on the boat that went out to the wreck. Was there any indication that either Bruce or the Negro Webb had not been killed instantly? Could either of them have lived long enough to do anything for the baby?"

"I can answer that question fairly reliably. I was drunk, as you know, but pure medical instinct made me look closely at the bodies. Bruce was obviously killed instantly. Webb's legs and pelvis were smashed, but he had crawled from the stern to the cabin—he left a trail of blood on the shattered deck—and then—to the rail." Dr. Sams's tone became hollow with wonder too great for utterance, and his eyes round.

"Was there a lifebelt missing?"

"My God, one was usually fastened to the rail at that very point. I'd seen it often. I can't remember whether it was gone. If I'd noticed it was gone, I would have thought the explosion—"

"Webb was a good boatman. He might know how to tie the baby in the belt so his mouth would be out of water and he could stay alive a good while. But would he set him adrift?"

"He might, if he thought the wreckage was going to fall apart any instant. It would have, if it had floated into the tide rip through the reefs. Actually the bow anchor line had fouled under the boat —where Webb couldn't have seen it—and by a hundredth chance the hook caught and held in a shoal. Even so we marveled that it stayed up as long as it did."

"Pa went out to the wreck with you. He was frantic with grief and terror, you said, but he's a strong man inside and amazingly cunning. He saw Bruce dead—next he would look for Bruce's and Madeline's baby. You can be sure he saw that blood trail and if the life preserver was missing, he'd see that too. He never had the slightest doubt that the explosion was rigged and if by any chance the baby was alive—floating on the sea or washed into shore—he would try to hide the possibility from Ralph. Little Donovan was the heir to Wood Ibis. His life wouldn't be worth a straw if Ralph got hold of him. You saw Pa drop something into the sea. Could it have been, say, a piece of rope that had fastened the life preserver to the rail—or maybe just one of its strings Webb had jerked off to tie the baby better but hadn't used?"

"That's possible," Dr. Sams answered, after a long silence.

"Did Pa show any eagerness to get to shore?"

"My soul, he was frantic to get there! He kept yelling that the wreck would fall apart—the bodies would sink and we couldn't find them—a messenger had to be sent to Madeline—"

"You said he disappeared after the boat touched shore and wasn't found until the next day, exhausted, incoherent, and covered with mud. Was he found upwind or down from the wreck?"

"Dan, he was found where the tide and the wind might carry a baby floating alive or dead into shore."

"He couldn't make much of a search alone. He'd have to have help from some Negro whom he trusted—one who loved him and would keep faith with him. A few years ago such a Negro was whipped again and again because Saul thought he knew something he wouldn't tell. Finally he swam out to sea and drowned, carrying down his secret with him. His name was Bert."

"God, I can't stand this." Dr. Sams rose and went to his liquor cabinet.

"Dan, you're certainly building up a fine case to prove you're the owner of Wood Ibis," Cleo said in a flash of anger.

"I can't help it."

She smiled at me forgivingly. Dr. Sams, steadied by the drink, resumed his seat.

"Granted that Bert found the little castaway alive, Pa hid him until he could take him out of Ralph's reach. He was a marked man—people would remember seeing him with a baby—soon he left him at the door of an orphanage dressed in rags and with an ill-spelled note asking the people to be kind to him. He wrote that the child's name was Dan—not far from Don. It was the best and perhaps only way to get shed of him until he could become Professor Reed, a music teacher, and adopt him without arousing suspicion. You spoke once, Dr. Sams, of how Pa believed in poetic retribution. Also he was not always in his right mind. Even then he was planning the most poetic retribution he could conceive—not a hireling to destroy his brother's murderer—not a waif from

266

an orphanage—but the murdered man's own son. No wonder he was willing to wait twenty years for such a fulfillment as that."

I stopped and the room was deathly still save for the ghost of Pa's voice returned from my childhood.

One whose name is lost. . . . One who has naught to gain for himself save that one he loves may die in peace. . . .

Then I heard my man's voice in this room, uttering against my will words that smote my heart and cast adrift my hopes.

"I know now—if this is true—why Pa never told me."

They did not ask what the reason was, and waited for me to go on.

"It was pretty hard on a baby boy, to leave him to the mercies of an orphanage, but Pa figured five years there would put iron in my soul, for the job ahead. When he adopted me and loved me, I'd do anything he wanted. As you said, Dr. Sams—he's a cunning and ruthless man. He kept watch to see no one else adopted me. He was ready for that contingency. And there was no danger of his ever mistaking me for some other orphan." I held up my hand, to reveal the useless little finger against my palm. "I got that, I guess, when the boat blew up."

Cleo spoke softly. "So I did see it that day in the woodshed—didn't I?"

"Yes. Well, we can skip till last winter, when you, Cleo, came to see Pa. When you'd gone—and I told him I was taking the same boat—he warned me in most solemn way not to make love to you. He gave the excuse you were Ralph's daughter as well as Madeline's—but a better reason would be, I was Madeline's son by Bruce. When Granny came in to talk to me she mistook me for a ghost. Well—if this is true—I'm a living ghost."

"I wish you'd stop," Cleo said quietly, "but you won't."

"There isn't any use stopping. I remember now when I got back to Baltimore Pa questioned me closely with a desperate look, as to my relations with you. I told him I had not had you. He was prodigiously relieved, but had a deep sense of guilt over something —I felt it when he played to Madeline's picture. It might have been the awful chance he had taken for sake of his vengeance—of our committing incest unaware."

"But Ralph is willing to take that chance," Dr. Sams said. "Not just Saul, Cleo—but your father. Of course he hasn't heard the evidence Dan has presented tonight. Do you suppose he figures that when the truth comes out—if it is the truth that he at least suspects —you'd be so horrified that you'd hate Dan—couldn't bear to see his face again—maybe go mad—and when Dan was neatly disposed of, he'd get control of Wood Ibis again?"

"Hate Dan?" Cleo echoed in childish wonder.

"Is that all?" Dr. Sams asked, looking at me.

"All that I know."

"I'm going to bed," Cleo said. "Dan, will you come with me to the head of the stairs?"

"Lock all your windows, Cleo," our friend ordered. "You'll get the sea breeze through the door. Obo's going to sleep in the store."

At the door of her room Cleo put her arms around my neck and kissed me passionately.

"That means I still don't believe it," she said.

"I wish I didn't. Well, I'll tell you one other thing I thought of —it was a little too private to tell Dr. Sams. In my first dreams the girl who loved me and cared for me had golden hair—like Madeline's. That's not as important as the signal I told you about—in the dream I had so often—and how then I'd find myself in the orphanage. It was like a gun going off."

"If you're Donovan you were not yet two years old when that boat blew up—"

"I've heard that people sometimes dream about things that happened long before they can remember anything."

"I remember loving you almost from the moment I saw you. You told me what you dreamed about me when we were parted— and I told you. We weren't half-brother and -sister—we were sweethearts—and then real lovers. Mama could say you're Donovan —or Uncle Noel—and I still—"

"Don't say that, Cleo. You'd have to go back on it."

"If I had my way I'd never ask them."

"Good God, Cleo!"

"I believe my heart—not a lot of evidence. Don't you believe yours?"

"Mine doesn't speak so plain. Mine isn't as brave as yours—it won't stand against the terrible doubts in my mind."

As she stood in the lamplit doorway, I was minded of another night, when she had opened a door to Saul and me. She was as erect as then, and as proud, and as wonderfully beautiful. But there was no infamy, as on that night. Not even a shadow of it when she spoke again.

"If your heart tells you what mine is telling me, you'd sleep with me tonight."

I did not dare take her in my arms. She gave me a proud smile and turned away. Dizzily descending the stairs, drunk with hope with which my brain would not treat, I dared only know that I loved her with great passion and nothing could keep me from it as long as I lived.

CHAPTER

29

It was late the following night. In terms of what men call fact I had been asleep in a narrow bed about three hours. By another truth I had wandered without restriction of time and space, revisiting distant scenes in the twinkling of an eye, reliving long sequences of event in the course of a hundred heartbeats, perhaps perceiving their meaning more clearly than when my eyes had been open, maybe beholding vistas of the present and future curtained from my waking mind. Then Dr. Sams came into my room and called my name.

"Obo sent Joshua to warn me there's some people coming down the road from Wood Ibis," he told me in a low, calm voice. "He's heard only two horses and they're traveling slow. He's gone to see who they are."

Obo himself was at the door by the time the doctor and I could get downstairs.

"It aint nobody but Mas' Martin and he wife," the giant Negro reported. "Mas' Martin got him a gun but it aint agin us. He comin' on private business."

In the dim light of the wasted moon I saw the riders move off the road onto soft ground as they passed our Quarter. Obo took their horses and tied them in dense shadow. Dr. Sams did not keep them waiting on the porch, but led them straightway into his office, where often wakeful slaves saw a lamp burning from dusk to dawn. Although clad in an old dressing gown over his nightshirt, slippers on his unsocked feet, he did not excuse himself to dress. The indignity of receiving visitors in such attire went hard with a Sams of Beaufort, but by the same token he paid his obligation to their stealthy haste.

I had had time to slip into trousers and shirt. On the contrary the two Martins were as well dressed as their position and exigencies of the saddle afforded—attire such as they wore in church or at election day in town. Jud Martin was a figure of indubitable dignity in his dark suit and hat. His plain, honest, weathered countenance was imposing tonight, and suddenly significant of humanity. Heretofore I had not much more than glanced at Belle Martin, on the very few occasions I had encountered her around the Quarter. She had seemed so typical of overseers' wives, and untouched by and unimportant to the tragedies of Wood Ibis. I had forgotten a quotation from ancient Greek that Pa was wont to give: "Common men marvel at strange things; wise men marvel at common things."

Belle Martin was a po' white—a vastly different thing from a low white. She would be called a cracker in up-country Georgia where she was born; she had come up in the world to marry Mr. Martin, an overseer of an immense plantation, and to live in such comfort. I saw now, though, why he had chosen her and was proud of her. She had a pleasant face with a sweet expression; she kept herself clean; her manners were modest and womanly. She thanked Dr. Sams for the chair he offered her with grave courtesy, then waited for her husband to speak. He sat holding his hat between his big, bony knees.

"Belle and I came on what we figured was important business," he began at Dr. Sams's invitation. "But first, I want to tell you both—and I'd like Miss Cleo to know it too—I didn't have nothin' to do with hunting you, Mr. MacDaniel, and her, in the swamp with them dogs. I told Mr. Saul I wouldn't have nothin' to do with it, and I didn't. I would have helped you if I could."

"I thank you, sir," I said. "I'll certainly tell my wife."

"In a way it led up to us comin' here tonight. Belle and I have hardly closed our eyes since then, trying to see what was beholden on us. We made up our minds at suppertime tonight, and got here soon as we could without too much danger of being seen."

"We'll keep your visit here in the strictest confidence," Dr. Sams said.

"I know you will—as long as it's fitten. Well, here's what it is. When Mr. Dunbarton offered me this job, five years ago—he knew an uncle o' mine when they was both young men—I'd heard bad report of Wood Ibis. There was whisperings about the death of his wife and Mr. Bruce. The reason the overseer before me quit—you remember Tom Harkin, Dr. Sams—was on account of what happened to Bert, that bright-colored nigra who run away and was drowned. Tom said right out that if ever a nigra was murdered, it was Bert. Tom gave up a mighty good job but he wasn't goin' to stand for anything like that, while he was in charge of the slaves."

Dr. Sams's eyes looked haunted. He remembered that he had stood for it, when he was in charge—or at least had been charged from On High, as all men are, with the keeping of all mankind. He had stood for much more than that, since first he dissected the head of a water moccasin twenty years ago.

"But it was a better job than I'd ever had, in the way of pay and livin'," Jud Martin went on, "and besides times was hard on account of the war with Mexico. Though Belle asked me not to, I went ahead and took it. If I'd known what it was goin' to be like, I wouldn't of. Few folks have paid a higher price for butter and meat and white bread on their table every day than Belle and me. But when twice I said it looked like I might have to quit, Mr. Saul just stood there and smiled. To be plain with you— shamed as I am to say it—I was half 'fraid to quit."

"You needn't be ashamed to say that, Mr. Martin," Dr. Sams told him. And for the first time I perceived the courage that this furtive visit had demanded of them both.

"Belle kept tellin' me to go ahead and quit anyhow. We didn't have no chillen we had to look to. But Mr. Dunbarton and Mr. Saul together—why, it didn't seem there was anything they couldn't do. They was like kings in the old countries. They clean took my manhood out o' me, the way they always come out on top. I kept puttin' off and puttin' off takin' any stand agin 'em. Now Belle's got somethin' to tell. She never told a livin' soul but me—and that's my fault too. She wanted to tell the sheriff; but I told her to stay out of trouble, and she obeyed me. I'm ashamed of it but now I'm tryin' to make amends. I want her to tell you, 'stead of me, so you know it's true. Go ahead, Belle."

There would be no question of its truth. No jury on earth would doubt it, when Belle Martin looked the men in the face and spoke in her low, clear voice.

"An old hen was hatchin' some biddies in our henhouse," she began. "I was standing there quiet, watching her, afraid she'd get off the nest with some of the eggs unhatched. Mr. Dunbarton and Saul had walked by the horse lot and stopped just outside. I could hear 'em as plain as I hear you all. After their first words I didn't dare make a sound and was scared half to death they'd find out I was listening to 'em.

"Mr. Saul said, 'You're going to get in up to your neck. That's where the hangman will put the necklace, if these chickens ever come home to roost. I'm not going to be dancing and kicking for the happy throng, while you stand down and look pious.' Them was his real words, as close as I can get 'em. I went over 'em in my mind a thousand times and they're mighty close. Anyhow that's what he said amounted to."

I did not doubt they were Saul's word-for-word utterance. I went into the henhouse with Belle, glanced at the restless hen, heard her excited cluckings, saw the hard, gray ground, the roosting bars, the gray dung everywhere, and standing with her, listened to Saul's vital voice. Then I left her and went outside and looked at Ralph's face. It made me think of chicken dung, it had turned so gray. . . . But Belle, who had paused, was speaking on. . . .

"Then Mr. Dunbarton said, 'What do you want me to do?' Then Mr. Saul said, 'Call him over here and give him his orders.' Then Mr. Dunbarton said something you won't hardly believe, but I heard him just as plain. He said, 'You better do it, Saul. You know my weakness—how my voice croaks.' Mr. Saul laughed his loud laugh and there was a sound like he'd slapped his leg or Mr. Dunbarton on the back. 'Then croak like a bullfrog, old man,' he said, as he was walking off.

"There wasn't a sound for a minute or two, and then Mr. Dunbarton called, 'Come here a minute.' His voice *did* sound queer. I didn't know who he was talkin' to until I heard a nigra answer close by, 'Yas, massa,' and I knew right away it was Slewfoot—before Mr. Dunbarton called his name. Slewfoot was a big, thick-headed, laughin' nigra who went around with Saul. Mr. Dunbarton said something about he'd picked him out for a very special errand, and he wasn't to say nothing about it to anybody. 'I sho won't,' Slewfoot said. Then Mr. Dunbarton said—as close as I can come to his exact words—'Slewfoot, I want you to go into Fern Creek swamp where Cliff Todd has his old still. He's got a five-gallon keg of whiskey hidden in the nearest clump o' brush. He owes me that whiskey and he's took too long to pay me. I'll give you a drink when you get back, but don't tell anybody where you're goin'. Just light out.'

"Slewfoot said, 'Yes, massa, I sho won't tell a soul,' and I didn't hear him any more. Mr. Dunbarton walked on and as soon as his back was turned I slipped out and ran to find Jud. I didn't know what else to do—I couldn't think—I knew Slewfoot was going to be killed but I didn't know how to help him. By the time I found Jud, Mr. Saul had rung the bell for a runaway, and then turned loose the dogs. That's all I know, 'cept what happened, what you know too."

Dr. Sams waited for me to speak—and he need not wait long.

"Mrs. Martin, will you let me write that out, and you sign it, with all of us witnessing it? I promise Mr. Dunbarton or Saul won't know about it until they're under arrest."

"Yes, sir."

"She's been wanting to go to the sheriff with it, but I was 'fraid," Jud Martin went on in a dull voice of shame. "I done told you my manhood has been knocked out of me. Maybe none of it would of come back, if you two men hadn't stood agin 'em, about Miss Cleo. And now I'm goin' to quit the job and we're goin' to shake this dirt off our feet."

"Will you wait a little longer before you quit?" I asked.

The two Martins glanced at each other. "We'd like to be a good ways from here, soon as we can. Mr. Saul has a way of findin' out things, and if he found out we was here tonight with that story—"

"Yes, there's danger for everyone who knows anything against him. But this isn't enough in itself to send either one of them to the gallows—it's going to take weeks and weeks and maybe months to get enough. We know we can trust you and Mrs. Martin. You're with us and add a great deal to our safety. If you quit, he'll get some of those men from the coastal islands who took part in the hunt. We need your help."

Belle gazed at her husband. Jud Martin shifted his hat in his hands.

"Well, I know what Belle would say to that, and for once I'll say it fust. We'll stay as long as you need us."

274

I fixed two statements for the Martins to sign, one to be kept in Dr. Sams's safe and the other to be dispatched to his lawyer in Charleston. Our visitors made a dignified departure; when Dr. Sams had paid his due to the bottle-demon he read over the documents without them rustling and trembling in his hands.

"You're right, Dan," he said. "This isn't nearly enough by itself. Taken with Cliff's statement it might hang Ralph—the State would want a lot more, to make sure—but Saul could ride through it with a six-horse coach."

"I wish he'd been there when Ralph gave Slewfoot his orders. Still—"

"Saul could swear that Ralph tricked him. Belle misunderstood him—he had been trying to dissuade Ralph from a crime of some kind—of course one for which Saul, an innocent man, might be blamed—so Saul told him he had to give Slewfoot certain orders meant to save the Negro from the deathtrap set for him. Instead Ralph sent him into the swamp where Cliff would be laying for him by his still. Saul knew his only hope was to catch him and stop him before he got there—that's why he rang the bell and turned loose the dogs. He wasn't in time."

There was nothing I could say except, "How about putting the bottle away and both of us going to bed?"

My friend nodded, and while I held the lamp for him, trudged up the stairs. I carried the lamp through the open door of Cleo's room, and sitting by the bed, watched her dreaming. She lay without a sheet this warm weather, her gown drawn up above her knees, and the lovely round of one breast had escaped the cloth. Cleo, my lips would not now be cold!

I want to lie beside you, Cleo. I want your head in my arm, as I listen to your quiet breathing. I need your sweet warmth, testament to your being alive while I am alive. If I speak to you, Cleo, will you hear me in your sleep? If I address you only in my thoughts, will they color and warm your dreams? Sitting here silent and still, I will make love to you, spurning my body's torment for the sake of possessing you in imagination. You looked at your little body in the glass, you told me—it seemed to you pretty enough that I would want it for at least one night. To me it is the most beautiful house of human being I can conceive. I want

275

it as long as I live. There are no words to tell you of the power of that wanting.

Are you dreaming that I have it? A faint flush steals into your face, your arms cross and press against your breast, and you whisper something. I am dreaming the same. Beside you, I have kissed you until you stirred—you give me childish drowsy kisses in return—suddenly you are wide awake, your eyes lustrous, your face luminous, your arms have other use than clasping a figment of your dreams; I can hear you whispering your secrets. The night is hushed. The dawn will lie abed a long time yet. We need not make haste, my bride. Shall we play the delicious games you promised? Shall we woo each other with manifold addresses ere we both surrender? The night is ours—we are endowed with all the time there is, a kind of eternity. We are wide awake at last, with a wakefulness beyond sense. We are completely, incomprehensibly alive at this shared point of time and space, and death is a dream in the night.

A cloud drifts across the sick, gray moon. . . . Swiftly upon that realization of supreme life, there comes so deep upon me that I can not plumb its meaning, a state of trance. Its mists flow backward against the tide of time: I do not know what is hidden in them of past event. I remember sitting beside Cleo's bed and the catching fire of my imagination, but do not recall rising from my chair. Perhaps I can do so, if I try to throw off the spell; instead it changes gently into dreams, as I fall asleep in my own room. I will not try to rejourney a forgotten reach of my path. All that I know is—a blessing on our love whatever its future fate—my dreams are unshadowed by either shame or guilt.

On Sunday morning—a cheerful time on any great plantation when man and beast rest from their labor in their fields, and the cooks make great stir—there came another visitor from Wood Ibis, this one from the very Hall.

It chanced to be the first sunlight after a heavy shower of rain, and Dr. Sams, Cleo, and I were outdoors to enjoy it. We were standing by the paddock fence, enjoying too the friskiness of the horses and the sheen of their coats. Having downed in one quaff their weekly ration of rum, Obo, Joshua, and Ben had been moved to song. They were doing well with "Oh, Susannah," the black giant childishly pleased with his sweet, high tenor rounding every chord, Ben carrying the refrain, and little weazened Joshua chiming in with a lusty bass.

Of these three, Obo alone had been an African spearman, an initiate into the warrior cults, wetting his blade ere he was fifteen, a listener to the bull-roarer in the House of Magic, so it stood to reason he would be the first to see our approaching guest. He rose leisurely to attract my eye, made a little gesture toward the road, then crouched again. As far as my ear could tell he had not missed a note.

Down the open road rode Saul on his big gray stallion. He swung down with feline grace—so impressive in so big a man—tied his horse, then swept off his hat in an arrogant gesture.

"Good morning, Dr. Sams—in order of social standing. How do you do, Miss or Mrs. Dunbarton, as the case may be. Last below the salt—hello, Dan—but it's you I came to see."

"But you didn't bring your dogs," I replied.

"No, they haven't cared to stir out—moping, one might say—since they lost three of their loving little band. The best three, by the way. The only ones who would stick, hell and high water, to one scent. They met with fatal accident in the swamp."

"My wife and Obo and I almost did the same. Sooner or later

you're going to have to answer for it, among other things. Knowing that, will you state your business?"

"Say it—and get out," Dr. Sams told him, his face deeply flushed.

"What a neighborly welcome! How times change! What I came for, Dan, is to sit on yon rail and tell you my inmost thoughts. Perhaps you won't profit by them, but you certainly have nothing to lose. My conduct will be very restrained in front of five witnesses. To be candid—I always hit from the dark."

It may have been intuition that prompted Cleo to speak—certainly it was not panic. "Dan, I think you'd better hear what he has to say."

"You're quite right, pussycat."

"All right," I said.

Dr. Sams and Cleo drew barely out of hearing. Obo and the two hostlers continued to crouch, their heads and harmony close. Saul and I sat on intersecting rails, the very precariousness of our perch causing an impression that we were both disarmed. Saul began speaking in a meditative, one would almost think a nostalgic tone.

"Dan, do you remember the first time I ever saw you? I asked you how you expected to sell stud horses if you got in trouble with me? I spoke of what fun it would be for me if you fell in love with Cleo. Well, I eat my words."

"That might be very flattering, if you did not seem as formidable —perhaps more so—than ever."

"It wasn't meant to flatter you. I'm not such a fool. It was the first move to get at the truth—and it's perfectly true I'm more dangerous to you than ever, because—however incredible it seemed a few months ago—I'm at bay. I, Saul, have been brought to bay by someone I mistook for a horse-trader. While very exciting, it could also be completely disastrous."

Saul was speaking with his usual animation, in a cheerful, almost blithe voice. I had never appreciated its musical quality until now, as it blended with the mellow voices of the black trio. The rail crackled beneath him but I could not see that he spared it his full weight.

"You don't seem at all worried, Saul," I said.

"I'm incapable of worry. That's one of the advantages—possibly at times a handicap—of my interesting condition. For that matter, I'm incapable of fear, in the usual sense of the word. I react quickly and vigorously to danger—with flight or battle—but I'm not in the least afraid. You may not believe that, but I assure you you'd better."

"I think it could very well be true."

"So we'll both do well to stop this game of hide-and-seek. I'm going to tell you how much I know about you, and how much I merely guess. You'll be better able to consider the offer I'm going to make you. I know, for instance, that you almost stepped into a mighty pretty deadfall only the day before Cleo and you eloped."

It was not the first time since I had come to Wood Ibis that a sense of unreality, evil-dreamy and haunting, made me doubt not my ears but my sanity. I could believe Saul had said this if we had met in the deep swamp or under a leprous moon, to taunt me ere he killed me, but we were sitting on the rail fence of the paddock on Sunday morning; a big Negro and a middle-sized one and a little Negro were crouched a short distance away singing "My Old Kentucky Home"; Dr. Sams and Cleo were looking on, and the horses were getting sleepy in the sun. Saul's tone was cheerful, almost friendly. I had thought and dreamed many times about the hideous death he had devised for me and today had resolutely barred it from my mind, lest accompanying storms of hate and fury cloud my cunning. Saul's big handsome face appeared as shameless as might a pet mastiff's that had just killed a child. When I could not speak, he glanced at me.

"By God!" he burst out. "That knocked you all in a heap, as the saying goes. I wonder if, in the way of understanding each other better—in view of the offer I'm going to make you—I should attempt to explain an odd thing about myself. That is, it strikes you as odd. I'm so used to it by now that I don't think anything of it. You picture yourself impaled on one of those big stakes. You see—if an African savage had dug that pit for a wild pig—or even for a tribesfellow—he would have used a big stake. He would want to make sure that if his prey wriggled loose and climbed out, he wouldn't run far. The pit dug for you was to be a bang-up job. Its digger took pride and pleasure in its artistry. No more than an African savage—probably a great deal less—he didn't worry about the discomfort of his catch. To be candid—he was no more concerned than a man-eating tiger over the size of his fangs."

"You're not a human being," I said.

"Of course not. The general assumption is that I have no heart—actually that's not the right diagnosis. It's true I haven't the slightest conception of pity. It surprises me in—I was going to say in other people, but that's not right—I'll say in real people. Naturally I can't feel love or hate. Well, just as a good dog has a near-human love for his master, I have a near-human hate for Cleo. I've tried to figure it out, but I can't—I can only find an interesting comparison in the extreme hate wolves have for their tame kinsmen, dogs."

Saul stopped and listened to the music. "The man who hath no music in himself—" he quoted thoughtfully. "You'd think I wouldn't care for it—but I do. I like harmony especially—I'm a very harmonious fellow. That little Joshua—who turned loose my horse—you said you did it, but you lied—sings pretty well."

"You were talking about Cleo."

"Pardon me. I was starting to say that ordinarily I'm no more cruel than a wolf. If pity is left out of a man or an animal, he can't be called cruel—cruelty is a denial of pity. I kill only for meat, or survival, or sometimes the pure pleasure of the chase. But I spent a lot of time and went to a lot of trouble to torture Cleo. It was quite foreign to my nature, I assure you. You crave and are planning to kill me for it, but actually it's the most near-human behavior with which I can credit myself for many years."

Weep no more, my lady,
Weep no more today—

"Are you insane?" I asked.

"That's funny, Dan. Don't you ask the same question about Granny, Madeline, Papa, Uncle Noel, quite possibly Cleo and Dr. Sams? Do you think Wood Ibis is a lunatic asylum? Granny tries to slip out of reality into the fog—makes only half a go of it, because her senile but otherwise sound mind keeps jerking her back—and Uncle Noel is somewhat eccentric, I hear. But when you know the truth about Wood Ibis—which will be, if ever, when you're one of Granny's spooks—you'll see what looks like insanity in all of us is just the logical effect on our various personalities of one underlying cause. One extreme passion, itself sane under the circumstances, has turned Ibis Island to a shambles. There's no harm in telling you that—you'll never grasp the truth as long as you live—which—after all—may not be very long."

"It will be longer than you live, Saul, I think. I've heard of people selling their souls to the Devil—"

Saul laughed boyishly. "That's what the niggers think about me. They say I went through some hocus-pocus with a conjure woman and sold my soul to Agoun, the conjure god of Haiti. Dan, I can give the Devil cards and spades. He's a bit of a gentleman when everything is said and done—really just a bad angel—still fighting God while I plumb flew God's coop. I got away. I escaped into the Swamp—one of the few creatures in human shape who ever did. But let's get back to business. Throwing the dead hog into the pit so I wouldn't know you had discovered it was a good trick, but I saw through it. But meanwhile you'd begun to see through a lot of our tricks."

"I may have missed some of them. Since you're being so honest—"

"It's the best policy, now. For instance, an idiot would have perceived that digging that pit and hunting you with dogs were acts of desperation. Dan, you spoke of Cleo as your wife. I don't think she is, as yet. Pa thinks so—but he's not very clever, you know. If she became so, that night, you've parted since. Suppose it just recently dawned on you that you might be little Donovan. Why so late, I can't imagine—but what would be your next move? First, to ask Dr. Sams if he saw the child's body. He'd tell you—provided he could remember anything from his big drunk—that he didn't. Then you'd dash over to the graveyard back of Turtle Inlet to look into the supposed grave. If I'd thought about it in time, I could have fixed an infernal machine in the box—later filled in the hole—straightened up the gravestone—Donnie where he ought to be, better late than never. I missed that trick. But I saw, plain as a pikestaff, you'd been there. And now where are you?"

"You tell me."

"Desperately and passionately in love with Cleo, but reasonably certain she's your half-sister. You are on the horns of an interesting dilemma. If you prove to be little Donovan, you're the owner of Ibis Island—but you lose Cleo. Will you mind telling me which you'd rather have?"

"Cleo, of course."

"You're the craziest of us all. Willing to swap a ducal manor for a hundred and ten pounds of skinny bone and flesh! Hell, I wouldn't give one good strapping Shanti wench for a couple like her. But naturally enough, I rejoice in your insanity, and have come here to arrange for the swap."

Two field hands had joined the trio in singing one of the "shouting" spirituals. A young Negress clapped her hands and swayed. I was trying to resist an intense, guilty excitement in what Saul might say next.

"As yet you're only reasonably—not completely certain," he went on, "and with great kindness, I'm willing to help you stay that way. I'll help you fabricate evidence that little Donovan was drowned—that will be relatively easy. Indeed there's only one person who can present any evidence to the contrary—your foster father, Uncle Noel. My natural methods of repressing his evidence wouldn't appeal to you. But there are other ways."

"They will be ingenious, I'm sure."

"He was mad as any hatter when he left here twenty years ago. Plenty of people will testify to that. Running all night in the swamp—muttering and seeing visions. One of the visions he saw was little Donovan, saved alive from the flood. Later a man met him in Charleston babbling about the baby he held in his arms—but there wasn't any baby. Still later he had the illusion of having left the baby at an orphanage in Philadelphia, but the one he later identified as his, had been abandoned there by an unmarried mother—a reliable witness had seen her do it. You can go right on being his foster son—you'll love each other just as much. He shall live happily with you and Cleo whatever part of the world you choose for your abode. Moreover, you won't go there penniless. Noel can sell Little Ibis to me—I will deed to you, to be sold, the land below Fern Creek that was once intended for Madeline's cousin, Terese D'Arcy. Thus the affair of Wood Ibis will have a happy ending for all—or almost all—concerned."

I got down off the fence; perhaps it was a token of revulsion from my temptation of a moment ago.

"What's going to happen to your father?" I asked.

Saul shook his head with mock woe. "I'm worried about Pa. He's suffering pangs of conscience from various peccadilloes of his youth. In plain words, Dan—he's losing his grip."

"And your stepmother?"

"The queen will continue to reign of course. Long live the queen!"

"Did you really think I'd accept?"

"You might 've. You're not the psalm-singer some might take you for. By the way—you haven't inquired as to the alternative."

"I'd be interested to hear it."

"Neither Cleo nor Wood Ibis." Saul too got down off the fence, dusted his hands, and smiled. "A much more common reward. The consolation prize Fate pays to fools."

"Death?"

"Of course." Saul laughed loudly.

"I thought I said you were going to get it first."

"You did say so, but you're wrong. I think you may be in a position to wipe out Pa. You may be able to keep me from getting Wood Ibis. But you can't keep me from killing you, once I have determined that's *my* consolation prize—the only one I can win. I told you I occasionally killed for sport—only bears and such like until now—and your hunting-down and death at my hands will be excellent sport. You see—I have an insuperable advantage over you."

"What is it, if you don't mind telling me?"

"It arises out of what I told you before. I'm not a human being and don't have human limitations, fear being one of them."

"How did that happen? Do you know?"

"I know perfectly well but I'm inclined to regard it as a little secret between—well, let's say God—and me. I don't blame Him, you understand, for the mistake—I won't tell on Him." Saul's eyes gleamed with mirth.

"You're not afraid of death? Most animals are."

283

"No, they're not. They don't know what it is. They shy from danger but can't comprehend death. I'm not afraid of it because I do know what it is. You see—I've been through it. I've already died."

He spoke as though it were quite an amusing situation. If Dr. Sams or any other man I knew had said it, I would have known he was mad; Saul's saying it seemed to make more manifest some awful sanity I surmised in all his actions—not human, not diabolical, but of the swamps that lay between.

"You don't look dead to me," I told him, grinning.

"I am, though. That's why I haven't a soul. You know what happens when people die—their souls pass on. Death took mine. He let my body go—I rose and walked—but he kept my soul. I haven't hide nor hair of one."

He began to untie his stallion. "That's why this wild brute and I understand each other so well—that's why dogs like me so much in a kind of guilty way. Interesting, don't you think?"

"Very." My scalp crawled about on my skull, because Saul was not insane.

"But I have a high old time," he went on, as he swung into saddle. "A barrel of fun, Dan—living in the swamp."

He hauled the stallion up on his hind legs, waved his hat, and galloped him down the road.

Dr. Sams examined the symptoms of the developing crisis and made his diagnosis.

"We're in an armed truce," he said. "It might break any moment, but I don't think it will break as long as Ralph and Saul are in doubt as to whether you're Donovan Dunbarton. It may last quite a while after they become certain. The wills you and Cleo made have checkmated them; they don't know how dangerous you are to their necks and their riches, and whether they will have to lose the latter to try to save the former. They can't calculate the risk and the gain of any action."

"I'll tell you one thing," I replied. "Saul will run no risk at all to save Ralph."

"Or vice versa."

"I don't know when I can find out from Pa—if ever. But there's Madeline who might throw some light on the question. She's at least an interested party."

"A mild way to put it." Dr. Sams spoke in a sardonic tone and gave me a wry smile, but these were shields for a sudden, extreme tension.

"I doubt if Ralph or Saul have told her of their suspicions. Wouldn't it be—dangerous—to do so? If she thought her own son might be alive, wouldn't she come out of her cloister? It stands to reason she'd join forces with us."

"Of course she would, if she had the least inkling it might be true."

"Dr. Sams, would her instincts tell anything? I've heard of cases—"

"I wouldn't bet five cents on 'em. But she might have some factual evidence."

"How about Lizzie?"

"I'd like to hear what Lizzie would have to say. She's thought a lot about this that she's never told anyone—perhaps knows something she's never told—and I see no possible harm in taking her the rest of the way into our confidence. There's no question of her essential goodness."

"No, but there's a great deal of question how she feels about Madeline—and Cleo—and would feel about Madeline's son by her lost sweetheart. She's no shallow woman. I think she's a woman of deep passions."

We decided to visit her that afternoon, taking Cleo with us because we dared not leave her at home. Since Lizzie had opposed our marriage, I thought Cleo would want to avoid talking to her and would wait on the beach with Obo: in that I misread her character. She was determined to hear all Lizzie might say in regard to the mystery and to watch her while she said it. In the upshot the four of us sat on Lizzie's little tumbledown dock over the oyster beds, the beryl-green water below us, the turquoise-blue sky above, and—another sort of aspect of nature—a seeming feature of the landscape—jet-black Obo guarding us not far off.

"Did it ever occur to you, Lizzie," Dr. Sams began, "that Madeline's baby might have survived?"

Lizzie was looking into his face as he began the question; before he had quite finished she had wheeled her gaze to a white tern in erratic flight. She continued to watch the little fisherman several seconds more, as it checked at many a false clue, fluttering fast to keep aloft, and finally dived at its prey. Her brow was furrowed as though in deep thought. The tide made lapping and gurgling sounds, as we waited. Finally she spoke buoyantly and cheerfully.

"Doc, I had to stop and think if the idea ever crossed my mind. Maybe I toyed with it a little the first few days on account of Noel's strange behavior, but didn't put the least stock in it. After the report of finding the little body—and you signing the death certificate—of course I never thought of it again."

"Ralph faked the finding of the body so there'd be no trouble about Madeline inheriting—"

"Do you mean that little grave—close by my father's—has been empty all these years?"

"It held a big doll. You can figure out, if you try, how I came to sign the certificate—without looking."

"That's all right, Doc. We've all got some rotten planks in our hulls—no one's altogether seaworthy. But every time I put

286

flowers on my old man's grave I used to lay a few on the baby's."
Fiercely she rubbed her eyes. "God damn Ralph's soul to hell."

She looked up at Cleo, her expression changing, and spoke in a
voice not as becoming as a moment ago. "Excuse me for speaking
so about your papa. I really couldn't hold in."

"Thank you, but Dan says we've got to find out the truth."

"I don't see how I can help," she told us, slowly and thoughtfully. "You'll have to go to headquarters—not Madeline, 'cause
she wouldn't know any more than I do—she gave her baby up
for lost twenty years ago—but Noel. If Noel got his hands on
little Donovan unbeknownst to Ralph, it would explain Dan pretty
well. Noel's just crazy-sane enough to plant him in an orphanage,
adopt him, and raise him to be his father's avenger. On the other
hand, Dan doesn't remind me of Bruce, and God knows he doesn't
take after 'the most beautiful woman in the world.'"

I was expecting her to look at me—it would seem a natural
thing—but she did not.

"Perhaps when I tried to interfere with Dan's and Cleo's marriage," she went on, sweat suddenly bursting from her skin, "I was
in the right barn but the wrong stall."

"You are a woman of remarkable instinct, Lizzie," Dr. Sams
said, "but I doubt if it would go that far."

"I understand now, why Dan and his bride separate at bedtime—
to express it delicately. I'd heard it, of course—the housemaid tells
her sister about such queer goings-on—and it trickled over to me.
Granny's complaint with Wood Ibis—she's made it several times to
various people—doesn't hold in this case. She said there was too
much crawling into wrong beds hereabouts. Quite a sapient ob-
servation on the whole—"

"What in the hell has got into you, Lizzie?" Dr. Sams demanded.

Lizzie turned white. "I'm only trying to make interesting conversation. If it's indelicate, remember I'm not a D'Arcy of Ibis
Hall, only a rough sailor's daughter. You might also consider I
'kept company' with Bruce when I was a very young girl. Tough
as I am, still it's a little jar to think that his son by the beautiful
lady who took him from me might be sitting right now on this
damned, dirty, little dock."

"Lizzie, I never thought you took that to heart—"

"Doc—not a damned dirty one but a nice one—what you don't know about a woman's heart would fill a book."

"I never thought your spite against Madeline was real—"

"It isn't, but let it go at that."

I could not keep silent. "Lizzie, if I'm a painful reminder to you of the man who may or may not have been my father—"

"I said, Dan, it was a little jar, but I hope I'm woman enough after all these years not to throw any sentimental fits. I'm no end fond of you, whoever in the hell you are."

Cleo looked into the water and spoke quietly. "Lizzie, if your spite against Mama isn't real, why do you hate me? I'm not Bruce's daughter."

"I don't hate you. Since you put it to me, I resent you—everything about you—as long as I've known you—for reasons I won't explain to you or to anybody. Since it's gone this far, I'll tell you what I dodged telling Dan and Doc. I do think he's Donovan Dunbarton. I haven't a bit of evidence to offer, but I'll bet my petticoats. That means you'll have to go on parting with him at bedtime, forever amen. Aren't you surprised I don't break down and cry?"

Dr. Sams got quickly to his feet, and Cleo and I followed soon. "We're leaving right now, Lizzie—and forgetting everything that was said. I'm sorry I misjudged how you felt about Bruce—of course you're not yourself. Goodbye for now, old girl."

We made a hurried departure, but I could not leave without a backward glance, stolen when Lizzie thought we were out of sight behind the building. Despite her sarcasm, I had not been at all surprised that she did not break down and cry in front of us. But neither was I surprised, now that we had gone, to see her bright head in her arms, and her staunch shoulders shaking.

"I suppose your next move will be to talk to Mama," Cleo remarked in a dry voice, as we were riding up our little driveway.

"It would seem the logical one," I answered.

"You should have gone to her first. After all, it's Mama's affair, not Lizzie's. If she says you're her son—" Cleo paused.

"Don't go back on what you said, Cleo."

"You're going to believe her, aren't you—or Uncle Noel?"

"I don't know."

"Well, if you don't want me to believe her, don't let me hear her say it. Don't let her be looking at me, with jewels for eyes. I disobeyed her—but she's still queen."

"Dr. Sams and I will talk to her alone. I don't see yet just how we're going to manage meeting her—"

"If she has any suspicion by now, she'll manage it herself."

Cleo's prophecy came true, but not in any way she had reckoned. I was not summoned to the palace as before; instead a black courier came, horsed and in livery, to notify Dr. Sams and the young man, "hitherto known as Mr. Dave MacDaniel," that Mrs. Dunbarton of Ibis Hall would leave cards at Little Ibis at four o'clock Wednesday afternoon. Actually both Cleo and Dr. Sams were more stunned by the lavender-scented message than I; perhaps no wonder, since she meant so much more to them than she ever could to me.

"My God, it's the first time she's gone farther than the garden in ten years," Dr. Sams burst out, his face flushed, his eyes glowing.

Cleo was terrified at first and tried in vain to conceal the fact from me. When I took her on my lap and held her chill, trembling hands, she confessed and thus eased some of her fears, but there were deeper ones that she did bring to light, perhaps because she could not identify them, or would not admit to them either to herself or to me.

"I've got to sit there and listen to her," she said. "She'll expect me to—she'd send for me—I'll have to obey her. I'll believe what she says. If she isn't sure you're not her son, I won't be sure any more. If only we could run away—and live in the woods with Obo—"

I stopped her lips with mine, but there was not much that I could say to reassure her. "We're going to believe the facts and nothing else."

The house was swept and garnished, the servants agog. Pat on the appointed hour we saw the queen's equipage on the road. It was not the two-horse carriage in which Ralph sometimes rode abroad but an ancient coach, once the pride of René D'Arcy, and drawn by four horses. A black footman and a driver perched on the high seat, and on each side were outriders.

It was not this that astonished Dr. Sams. Lesser ladies than

Madeline rode forth with equal state in the Low Country. But as he stood at the window, in order to time well his meeting her at the door, he turned to me in bewilderment.

"There's another woman in the coach with her."

"Isn't it her maid?"

"There are two colored women. This is a white woman. She looks old—I believe—good God, it's Granny! They've got her dressed up—that's Lucy taking care of her. I don't know what it means."

We would find out, I thought grimly, in due time. The footman helped only Madeline to the ground; her maid followed her to the veranda, while Granny and Lucy remained in the coach. She came in with a shy expression and I would have sworn she looked younger and more beautiful than I had ever seen her. I could not stop my heart from racing until I looked at Cleo. Our eyes met, and that steadied us both, I thought.

Was this regal, almost incredibly beautiful woman my mother? I searched her face with all the honesty I could force into my eyes and had not the slightest inkling of recognition.

"You see I've come in some state," she said to Dr. Sams. "It's the least respect I want to pay to my future son-in-law—if that is to be his relationship to me—or to my son."

It was a curiously impressive announcement. I wondered if it were studied—her shy smile and simple manner seemed to testify otherwise. She bent and kissed Cleo and received a chivalrous salute from Dr. Sams.

She had returned my bow when she had come in, but did not glance at me again until we were all seated. Then she looked at me with luminous, eager eyes.

"I want to tell you first, Dan—I'll call you that until this mystery is solved—that if Cleo and you are eligible to marry, I withdraw all objections. I realize the present status, but would want you two to go through another and more formal ceremony, and perhaps invite some of my old acquaintances in the Low Country."

"We were very well satisfied with the ceremony, Mrs. Dunbarton," I replied. "Anyway that can be decided in the future."

"I've been unable to imagine what it would mean to me if Donovan has survived. I've often dreamed that he did. You would be master of Wood Ibis, and of my own blood. The danger is, I would be too quick to believe it. Yet in the last analysis, I must be the one to decide the question. You realize that, I suppose."

"I thought my foster father, Noel Dunbarton—"

"If he testifies you are not Donovan, of course he will be believed. He would have nothing to gain by falsehood. But if he testifies that you are, the court will demand proof, since thereby his foster son would become master of a great plantation. Besides, his great yearning that you might be my son by his beloved brother Bruce might have affected his mind."

"Mama, that's perfectly true," Cleo said, her eyes shining.

"Thank you, dear." Madeline gave her a queenly smile. "On the contrary, Dan, the court will believe me without question. The judge will trust my mother's instincts, since there is no proof of little Donovan's death."

Cleo did not speak again. Her eyes had dimmed a little, and widened a great deal. I knew what she was thinking—the same thoughts were bursting through my brain. If Madeline must choose between Saul and me to own Wood Ibis, there would seem not much doubt of her choice. If she did not deliberately pick a pretender to the crown, her instincts could very easily be misled by her desires. As it happened, such a choice would prevent my having Cleo, in case her mind would trickily play both ends against the middle. It came to me, a stunning inkling, that in the next few minutes she was going to declare me her son.

"Your countenance is reminiscent of my husband's," she went on. "I look for evidences of D'Arcy blood so far without success. My baby had a small mark on his left shoulder—a little above the heart—that might or might not have persisted. It was oval, no larger than a dime, and was slightly whiter than the adjacent skin. Have you such a mark?"

"No, ma'am."

Her head hung for a second or two, I thought, then it rose again.

"Will you come close to me, please, and permit me to look closely into your face?"

I did so, and she gazed searchingly into my eyes.

"I do not recall a blue rim about the iris of my baby's eyes," she said in a forlorn tone, "but on the whole they are of the same color. Certainly my baby would have had dark hair." Her beautiful hand came up, her fingers lay lightly on my cheek, and she turned my head to study my face from every angle. I could scarcely keep it from brightening at the growing sorrow in hers.

"I do not see my son," she said—not to any of us, it seemed— perhaps instead to the ghosts of the D'Arcys assembled in this room. Perhaps they had risen from their majestic tombs for this momentous trial. If so, they knew whether I was a pretender, and were bending to her ear, trying to make their soundless voices heard. She was the last of their line whom they would acknowledge. At Cleo—and me too, if I were Madeline's son—they looked askance.

Madeline spoke again, with great gentleness.

"I invite you to kiss me, Dan."

I did so. Her lips were wonderfully smooth and soft, but there seemed no more life in them than in painted lips of a portrait on the wall. There was no more change of expression on her face.

"There is no longer any doubt in my mind," she announced. "Every instinct and thought tell me you are not Donovan, and so you can be Cleo's husband. But no decision I've ever made—even to marry Bruce Dunbarton—is of greater moment. To make assurance doubly sure, I will ask you, Dan, to undergo one more test."

"I will, gladly," I answered, despite my fears.

"Some people might think it a foolish one. That wouldn't influence me in the least. I have brought with me today my husband's mother-in-law by his first marriage—a very old woman in her second childhood. However, she has a remarkable gift of second sight. She's waiting in the carriage with her attendant, and I ask permission, Dr. Sams, to have her come in for a moment. I want her to say whether Dan is my son Donovan."

The delicate color that had come into Cleo's face was wiped clean away, and her eyes met mine in terror and entreaty. Dr. Sams looked at once alert and fascinated: it was as though he were again a medical student about to witness a momentous experiment. Madeline's voice flowed smoothly as a deep brook into the room again.

"As you know, Granny is not always in her right mind. Doubtless you have heard that she blames my husband for her daughter's death and says wild things. For that reason, I request that none of you question her, or in any way distract her attention from what I am saying to her. I alone know how to get her to answer our question."

At Madeline's request, Dr. Sams sent her maid to speak to Lucy; then he and I resumed our chairs. In a moment Granny came up the little walk, a sturdy figure needing no help from the colored woman holding her arm. Lucy spoke to her in a low voice, then stopped at the threshold to let her charge enter the door alone. It seemed a cruel thing for us to sit so still, no one rising to greet her, no one speaking as her vacant eyes moved from face to face in the breathless circle.

"I'm Sadie's own mother," she said, in a faltering tone. "I've got a right to meet the people." She looked at Madeline.

"Of course you have, Granny. You were invited here today."

"You're the rich lady Ralph crawled in bed with—and I see my little lovely Cleo—and I remember Dr. Sams. But who is this young man?"

Had she forgotten talking to me? It stood to reason, yet I had the eerie feeling that she remembered perfectly well and was employing amazing guile to keep the secret.

"Look at him closely, Granny, and tell me if he is my son," Madeline answered.

She stared at me, then at Madeline. "Your son?" she faltered.

"Yes, my son by my first husband. You were living at the little house then, but the good spirits will tell you if he is my son."

"Oh, I'd forgotten. It has been so long. Don't blame me, rich lady—I am very old and my memory has begun to fail."

"Of course I don't blame you, Granny. You wouldn't be expected to remember. But won't the spirits tell you if he is my son?"

"Yes. . . . They will tell me. . . . Will you take my hand, young man? They speak clearer about people, when I can touch them." This was not guile now, or any shadow of it. Her eyes half-closed, so that the whites showed as glimmering crescents; her face became empty as an idol's. I rose beside her and took her hand.

"Be patient, a moment, while they come in," she murmured. "Yes, they're coming. I can't tell who all of them are—but I see

Sadie. . . . She's crying and holding her side. . . . Sadie, my daughter, stop crying and answer Mama's question. Is this young man the rich lady's son?"

A curtain rustled behind me in the breeze from the sea, and a cold wind blew down my spine.

"No? Are you sure, Sadie? The rich lady wants to know." Granny turned to Madeline, shaking her head. "Sadie says no."

"Will you ask the others?" Madeline murmured.

"There's a Negro here. I think he was account-keeper for Ralph's brother, Bruce Dunbarton. Oh, yes—his name's Bert. There are awful stripes on his back—and I smell seaweed. Will you tell the rich lady, Bert, if this is her son come back to her?"

The silence held long. Granny's hand twisted in mine.

"Won't you speak?" she whimpered. "You rose out of the sea to come here. Was her baby saved from the sea that swallowed you?"

Granny stood leaning forward. A look of bewildered torment came into her face, then slowly faded.

"I could hardly hear him above the noise of the sea," she explained falteringly, turning a little toward Madeline. "The waves rolling and crashing, and the wind blowing. But he said—plain—you're wrong. He was born far away from here—"

"So was my baby, you know," Madeline said in a low, tense voice. "In New Orleans. But that's enough, Granny. You may go now. I know now—"

"His mother couldn't keep him. She went away and left him. . . . Oh, yes, you told me to go. I will—I'll go back to my room—"

"Are there any other spirits you can ask?" I said, holding firmly Granny's rough-skinned, solid-feeling hand, and forgetting my promise to Madeline.

"It's pretty hard on her, Dan," Dr. Sams said quietly.

"If I can stay—a minute more—I'll ask Mr. Dunbarton. Mr. Bruce Dunbarton, master of Wood Ibis before Ralph's turn. It's hard for him to speak of that awful night—his body was broken, and I reckon his heart too. . . . He doesn't say anything but he shakes his head and laughs. . . . It's the first time I've ever seen him laugh since he went away."

"He—he—laughed?" Madeline stammered, rigid in her chair.

"He looked at the young man and laughed. I think he means it's all right for him to marry Cleo."

Madeline raised her hand to Lucy, watching through the open door. "You gotta come now, Miss Granny," Lucy said.

"I've got the right to meet the people—"

"Come in and take her arm, Lucy," Madeline ordered. "Thank you, Granny. You've helped us all a great deal."

"I won't tell a soul about the snake—"

But the mutter died away as Lucy hurried her out of the house and down the steps.

My sanity was returning swiftly as Madeline rose. "I won't keep Granny waiting," she was saying. "Pardon me, Dr. Sams, for not remaining to enjoy your hospitality. Dan, you have my full consent to make Cleo your wife."

"Thank you, ma'am. The moment there's no longer any doubt—"

"How can you doubt both me and Granny? We all know the ghosts are all in her imagination, but she has occult powers. Of course you'll want to talk to Noel—but remember his condition. I'm sorry to have to speak of it, but I did wrong to oppose the marriage, and I want both of you to be happy."

"Oh, thank you, thank you, Mama." I expected Cleo to rush to her mother's arms but she stood still, trembling.

"I never really hoped that my son had lived—and now perhaps there will be more happiness for us all."

So Madeline told us, as she paused by the door, her voice lovely in the room, her beauty radiant. But Dr. Sams did not look at her or seem to hear what she was saying. Gray and drawn of face, he seemed to be staring not at senile Granny's pitiful ghosts, but at a real specter. I knew now there was another reason than his own shame why he had never told me about the lost child. I thought he stood nearer and looked deeper into the evil spring of Wood Ibis than ever before.

CHAPTER

32

A few days later, the question of my identity had to hang, while I pursued my other quest. Lizzie brought me important news that she had heard from her sailor friends. The *Clarabelle* would not touch Savannah on her northern voyage, and so would put into Charleston nearly two weeks ahead of schedule. If I would journey there at once I might, by immense good fortune, find some member of her crew who remembered Ralph's purchase of fuzee, wherewith to rig an explosion, twenty years ago.

There would be no doubt of my going, if I lived that long. Whether or not I was Bruce's and Madeline's son by blood, I was still Noel's son by adoption. The immediate issue was, what care could I take of Cleo? Dr. Sams soon persuaded me that she would be safer at Little Ibis with his and Obo's protection, than journeying to Charleston with me. Lizzie helped me arrange a flying trip by shrimp boat, whereby I could leave their house after midnight, and with good fortune return at sunrise of the following day.

Hardly out of the shadow of Ibis Island, I began to regret that Cleo had stayed behind. I had forgotten how peaceful these seas were, how reassuring the distant clang of bell buoys and the glimmer of shore lights. So long—about a hundred days—had I walked on bloody ground, that I had almost forgotten the cleanliness and kindliness of near-by shores. The windows of the waterfront taverns still glimmered when we gained Charleston harbor. There stood church-spires against the sky.

By commonplace event I gained the deck of the *Clarabelle* in midmorning, and was presently seated in the captain's cabin. He proved to be a blue-eyed Bostonian named Scott, too young to have sailed the seas twenty years ago, but I judged him a man of spirit and imagination who would take a lively interest in my quest.

"I've heard this is a friendship ship," I told him. "Have you any hands aboard who sailed her twenty years ago?"

"Why, yes," he replied. "Once a man signs on the *Clarabelle*, he's apt to stay till we weigh his heels and put him overside. It's our owner's policy to keep on old, tried, loyal hands. There's at least three who were aboard her then, and maybe more."

"I'll tell you why I ask." I related what Cliff Todd had told me and explained the urgency of my errand.

"I'll help you all I can," the bluff fellow said. "I don't hold with murder, when or where it's done. The three men I mentioned are the gunner's mate, Mr. Sadler—a striker in those days with access to the armory—John Hardy, and Pete Willoughby."

"There was a good deal of talk up and down the coast about the explosion. The man who sold the fuzee probably heard it, and put two and two together. Has anyone of those three men shown any fear of getting in trouble with the law—especially when you touch Charleston?"

"No fear, exactly—I reckon that would of about died out—but one of 'em—Mr. Sadler, to speak plain—has signs of something on his conscience. Did you say there was a baby lost in the explosion?"

"Yes."

"Blow me down, but that fits in. When Mr. Sadler's sober, he's cheerful as a cockroach. But let him toss too many pots, and he gets mighty maudlin about babies. He buys candy and geegaws for every baby he sees on the street. He warns the parents to take proper care of 'em, for fear something might happen to 'em."

"I'll bet he's our man."

Captain Scott thought it very likely, but to make Mr. Sadler confess to a theft of ship-stores—occurring no matter how long ago —would be a tricky course to steer. True, there were worse offenses never logged in almost all men's lives. Perhaps if he were shown his duty—to bring a murderer to justice—he would perform it. But the captain's blue eyes were getting brighter—a notion had struck him—a dram of rum would help him chart the course. Would I join him in a glass?

I thanked him, and a Chinese cabin boy whom he called John, boyish-looking despite a little gray at his temples, served the drinks. Then the captain proposed that Mr. Sadler, himself, and I meet on shore tonight, and make the rounds of the grog-shops. When the mate was sufficiently mellow, we would drop in on Professor Rankin, a phrenologist who had his studio next to Tavey's Tavern.

297

We would have already coached the professor—he would say anything we told him to, for a dollar bill—and when he read Mr. Sadler's skull he would discover his bad conscience and divine its cause. Awed by the wonders of phrenology Mr. Sadler could no doubt be persuaded to write the testament I needed.

Captain Scott had required two glasses, each carefully flavored with lemon and sugar by his Chinese cabin boy, to perfect the brilliant plan. But my drinks had not taken hold—I was becoming depressed by what seemed a fool's errand—certainly I must tactfully discourage the visit to the phrenologist. But before I could find the words, Chinaman John, stirring lemon juice and powdered sugar for a third round, spoke in a thin, flat voice.

"Capan, Mistel Saddle no tell about sell fuzee."

"Why not?"

"Cause he no sell fuzee long time 'go, this place. When he plenty dlunk he cly about baby, buy baby in stleet muchee candy, but no 'cause he sell fuzee, blow baby up long time 'go. He talkee me one night why he feel bad about baby. Long time 'go he run off from harbor woman and baby he make. When he come back, baby alleady die."

Captain Scott held out his glass and sighed. "I should have thought of that."

"I sell some fuzee long time ago to big land-lubble," John went on blandly.

"Sink me!"

"When big land-lubble come on board, talkee me he pay one doll' if I steal fuzee for makee rocket. I talkee him can do for five doll'. But I no steal fuzee. I buy Chinee stole for fift' cents. Chinee man got plenty fuzee for makee fileclackle for New Yeal."

"John, did you ever find out the man's name?" I asked, caught up in solemn wonder.

"I heal Capan talkee him by light name. Numble one dlunk, he call him Mistel—Mistel Done—Done—I folget rest. I memble long time buln stick for him on New Yeal, makee good luck, maybe two time makee foul doll' fift' cent. Numble five dlink, Capan call him Lalf."

"You yellow heathen, don't you know he used that fuzee to murder people?" Captain Scott demanded.

"Maybe one, two piecee man make talkee so, but I China man, not Melican, maybe land-lubble use fuzee makee fileclackle, I no make talkee. . . . I stay this side, mixee drink, cookee meat for Capan."

John was perfectly agreeable to testifying to the event, and the leader of his tong, an educated Chinese merchant named Ling, would transcribe his statement into English. This was done in the presence of the sheriff of Charleston County, who was pleasantly excited over the prospect of a sensational arrest. Later he accompanied me to the office of Dr. Sams' lawyer to see the testaments of Cliff Todd and Belle Martin.

"I think it's enough to draw a warrant and get an indictment," Sheriff Willis told me. "Dr. Sams's testimony about the snake, and seeing a piece of fuzee on the wrecked boat, is good supporting evidence. I haven't the least doubt Dunbarton's guilty—but what twelve good men and true will decide to do about it, there's no telling."

He agreed with me that Ralph's arrest at once would very likely result in a stronger case against him. Others who had concealed evidence would be emboldened to bring it forth; without Saul's support and in terror of the rope he could easily lose his head and incriminate himself. The officer told me that I could expect him at Little Ibis on Captain Weaver's boat within a few days.

"You know, I had a notion that Ralph Dunbarton's chickens were about to come home to roost," he said.

"How was that?"

"I was given a hint by someone, as well as some instructions, but I'm not at liberty to speak about it yet."

The fair wind bore me back to our little landing in the deep of night. Obo came smiling to greet me and reported a quiet watch; I called Dr. Sams and told him the successful outcome of the journey. But although I looked through Cleo's open door, longing for her kiss and to hear her voice, I did not waken her. Perhaps her dreams were bright.

In the morning she listened calmly to the news.

"I know Papa did it," she said at last. "I know he's got to answer for it with his life. But there's something about it we don't under-

299

stand. I tell you again, Dan—he was under some kind of a spell. I think it was conjure."

I did not tell her that no such thing existed. How did anyone know the power of the Powers of Darkness?

When Captain Weaver's boat approached our landing three days later I saw his Negro deck hand taking in sail. Plainly she would not merely nose in while passengers stepped off and the mail was tossed onto the wharf. She would dock for a stay of some length. I could already recognize Sheriff Willis standing by the cabin door, and no longer doubted that he had brought a warrant for Ralph's arrest. There was suppressed excitement in Captain Weaver's voice as he called his orders. This was a momentous day in the history of Wood Ibis.

At that moment Dr. Sams came hurrying down the board walk from the cottage. I turned to speak to him.

"Where's Cleo?" I asked.

"She ran to her room when she saw the boat."

"Where had she better stay, while this is going on? I don't want her to see her father in irons. Besides—how do we know hell won't break loose? If Saul should run amuck—"

"I think I'd better have Obo—"

He stopped, because his breath failed. He was staring over my shoulder in the direction of the dock. His eyes bulged and his jaw dropped in stupefying amazement. My heart gave one great leap before my eyes could take in the scene.

Two men, the sheriff and his deputy, had already stepped onto the dock. Slowly out of the cabin came a third, a cane in one hand, a violin case in the other. He need not stoop to pass through the low door; his head would never rise again above the ridge of his back. The wind blew his thin, blond hair.

I ran and lifted him from the deck to the dock. But I could not ask the question. . . .

"You are surprised to see me," he said in his voice like music.

I nodded, my throat still bound.

"I would have sent you word, save that I feared it might reach other ears. Ever since I fled from Baltimore, I have been near you, not only in spirit but in body. Indeed, I left word with Sheriff Willis, that if you presented evidence for Ralph's arrest, he was to notify me so I could be present at the glorious occasion. I have been living at Middleton Plantation, whose mistress was my pupil long ago."

The cords loosened, so I could ask the question shaped on my lips. It could be answered in one word. But the sheriff had bustled up to us and perhaps I was glad of the respite. If today I must come to final grips with Saul I could not afford a dark heart. Anyway today belonged to Pa. It was the day of his triumphant return from long banishment. Tomorrow I might go into exile from Cleo. It would depend on the word Pa spoke—and there would be no way I knew to dodge or doubt it. . . . But I would not ask today.

"Dr. Sams, will you supply my deputy and myself with fast horses?" Sheriff Willis asked.

"Yes, sir." The doctor turned to give orders to Joshua.

"The fastest you have, Doctor," Pa broke in, a vision as of heaven in his eyes. "They want to take my brother by surprise—before he can rehearse answers to the charge—before he can flee from doom. He must be given no chance to procure weapons, wherewith to strike again."

The sheriff glanced at Pa uneasily, then wiped sweat from his face. "Mr. Dan, will you lead us by the shortest cut to Ibis Hall?" he asked, turning to me.

"I'm afraid to leave Pa here—"

"Never fear, my son," Pa told me quickly. "I have made such provision, that my sudden death will not turn victory into defeat. I want you to behold with your own eyes the triumph of our cause. I want you to see Ralph's face, when he sees the face of nemesis. I will not bid you wait for my tortoise gait. I will come swiftly as I can—perhaps my friend will provide a cart or a carriage—but meanwhile your eyes will be mine. Through yours, I shall witness his terror and his despair. But take care he does not turn and strike, like a serpent beneath your heel. All of you take care, for he is an ox in strength, a fox in cunning. In his desperate frenzy he may kill again."

"You can leave that to us—"

But Pa saw Joshua emerging from the stables with two saddled horses, and leaning forward on his cane, spoke on in ringing tones.

"Make sure your weapons are cocked and primed. Give him no chance to sell his life for one of yours. I yearn to see him on the gallows, dancing his last dance, but if he lifts a hand to resist, do not hold your fire. As King David on his deathbed spoke unto his son of his enemy Shimei, 'Bring him down to the grave with blood.'"

As the two officers were mounting the horses Joshua had brought, the terrible melodious thunder of Pa's voice still pealed in the summer silence. "I implore you, Dan, do not risk your life to take him alive. Forego our final triumph at that cost—let the gallows tree be barren of this ripe fruit. If he lies still when I arrive—if he does not rise to greet his long-lost brother—if I ask how fares the master of Wood Ibis, and he does not answer—if I do not see him climb once more to such dizzy height—even so, my cup runneth over. Even so, your vengeance is greater than you dream."

That thunder died away beneath the drum of hoofs, but a flash of lightning had accompanied its final gong; and what I had seen by its glare still lingered before my eyes, a ghost that would not vanish.

We rode more leisurely after the first half-mile. The sheriff's official zeal was dampened a little by the sandy road, the summer heat, and perhaps the lack of an audience. But although it behooved me to ride behind him, and although I knew well there was no real need of haste, and although I had not touched her with whip or spur, Lizzie kept thrusting ahead. Something had passed between my heart and hers, perhaps. Perhaps something about my posture or my hand on the rein made her think I wanted to race.

As we were making our slow way across Fern Creek, Sheriff Willis swore morosely.

"Mr. Dan, would you say your foster father is entirely in his right mind?" he asked.

"Yes, but it isn't a normal mind. It's in accordance with his nature and his lameness."

"I reckon I know what you mean." The sheriff considered shrewdly and, as he dodged the mudholes and picked the soundest timber of the little bridges, he gave by fits and starts as interesting a discourse on Wood Ibis affairs as I had yet heard. Having a big frame and a flare for drama that impressed voters, he also had the good engineer's ability to integrate facts.

"The whole show on this damned island isn't normal either—I feel that in my bones—but it's according to the nature of the place. . . . Not the nature exactly, either. . . . I reckon a kind of second nature that come upon it from queer people living here so long. . . . Lord love me, them D'Arcys were queer to start with. My old man told me about 'em. René D'Arcy couldn't stand for a common man to touch him. I don't mean a nigra—I mean a common white fellow. They say he'd go and change his clothes. . . . But his granddaughter married a man who could hardly read and write. Next time she married a murderer. . . . I wonder how he became one. My old man knew him when both of 'em was boys—he said Ralph was a cruel boy—a bully with the little chaps—

but the schoolmaster didn't have much trouble with him. What made him grow up to kill people like a bad dog kills sheep? 'Pears like that came on him after he went to Wood Ibis. . . . I knew Sadie by sight. I make it my business to know everybody in the county who'll let me. She was a good woman, yet she borned a son who's a regular fiend. . . . Take even Dr. Sams. When he was a young man he never drank too much. Only when he got out here he turned into a sot. . . . All of 'em got a different kind of queerness."

All a different kind of lameness, I was thinking. Only the lame can love. . . .

We came out into the sunlight and, passing the Quarter, we again rode fast. The five great pillars of Ibis Hall loomed grandly, glimmering white, among the green live oaks—emblematic in René D'Arcy's mind of his great and ancient name. Bruce, who could hardly read and write, must have been awed by them; perhaps he had rarely entered the front door. Ralph admired them for their strength—emblematic of his own, he liked to think. Having dismounted and given our reins to a stable hand, now we were passing under them, dwarfed by them. René D'Arcy, whose sleep was troubled anyhow, turned over in his grave. Although he could not stand for a common man to touch him, could not believe his eyes that a "servant reigneth" in the castle he had built, still his dry bones clattered in fury as two minions of Yankee law entered his front door. Even a peasant king was still a king. . . .

"Tell your master that the sheriff of Charleston County has come to see him on important business."

We were given seats in the second-best parlor. My companions looked up at the chandelier and glanced about at the elegant furniture; they were thinking what all this had cost but remained cool and confident. My pulse and my imagination leaped wildly. Both steadied a little as Ralph appeared in the doorway—the instinct of self-preservation demanded self-control. He swayed a little, I thought, at the sight of the company, and his sallow skin had a gray cast, but his back was straight and his head erect. We rose at his entrance. His throat worked once and there was a suggestion of a croak in his voice.

"How do you do, Sheriff Willis," he said. "I know Dan—but the other young man—"

"He's my deputy, Harry Dillon. I asked Mr. Dan to show us the way here from Little Ibis. Besides—he's had a lot to do with our coming here."

"I suspected as much." He said this in a bitter voice and was strengthened by it, but it was not easy for him to speak on. "What business do you have with me?"

"I've a warrant for your arrest."

"For what crime?"

"Murder. I'll read it to you if you want me to."

"That isn't necessary." He said that with a certain dignity, but I could hardly stand his dazed expression, and then the sight of his shaking hand slowly rising to his ashen face and his blunt fingers drawn feebly across his cheek. I wanted him to be fiercely defiant, now that nemesis clutched him: we could expect that much from a Roman king of the wood. I felt not pity, only dismay.

"May I—call—my son—Saul?" he faltered.

"Yes, but anything you say may be used against you."

Ralph pulled the bell cord twice before we heard a soft, distant gong. When he had dispatched a servant to summon Saul, it was a strange thing to see him brace up—a deeply troubling thing to me, although I did not know why. He even recaptured a little of his usual mien of self-importance. When he spoke, it was with a suggestion of pomposity.

"Pray be seated. I'll submit to arrest, of course—the law is above us all—but since the charge is such a serious one—"

"You're right about that, Mr. Dunbarton," the deputy interrupted.

"So utterly unbelievable—made up of whole cloth by jealous or malicious enemies—I want to discuss it—to consult with my son—"

Saul strode bright-eyed into the room—and the very air was different. The dead room became as throbbingly alive as a lair in the Swamp. With vast amusement he swept his gaze over us—it lingered on mine, while he gave me a quick mocking bow—then his big, resonant voice burst forth.

"What a solemn conclave! Don't anyone tell me what's afoot—

let me guess! Pa, you've been elected honorary president of the St. Cecilia Society!" He gave Ralph a resounding slap on the back.

For spontaneous and supreme insolence, Saul had surpassed himself. There was not a man here who could pass the first Negro doorman of that Society.

Sheriff Willis grinned sheepishly, then was ashamed of the grin. "This is no time for joking, Mr. Saul."

"No merry jests? It can't be you've come here in the line of duty. Chicken-stealing? Not hog-stealing, surely. Wife-beating, perchance!"

"I've come here to arrest your father for murder."

"Do tell! Foul and unnatural, I bet you. Well, Pa, there's no reason you shouldn't serve the gentlemen some brandy. It would brace them for their trying task of hauling you to the gibbet. And you had a sore throat only last week! That's adding insult to injury. Dan, how did you come to be invited to the party? Firstly a mere horse-dealer—secondly Cleo's suitor—thirdly an adopted cousin— fourthly a claimant to the throne—now, by God, a copper. How the young men forge to the front on Ibis Island!"

"I think this is all Dan's work, Saul," Ralph said in a quavering voice. "He hates me on account of my brother Noel. In any case, it's a serious matter—I ask you to take it seriously."

Ralph spoke with considerable dignity. I could see that Sheriff Willis was already leaning a little toward him, in his fury against Saul.

"I'd give you the same advice, Mr. Saul," he said sternly.

Saul sat down and folded his hands. "I'm solemnity itself."

"Gentlemen," Ralph went on, "kindly tell me who preferred the charge, and on what grounds."

"We're not at liberty, Mr. Dunbarton, to say what the evidence is, or who dug it up. That will come out in court."

"I assure you, it's fabricated. I have reason to believe that Dan came to this island under a false name for no other purpose than to ruin me. I have many enemies, some of whom he's no doubt persuaded to testify to lies. A poor man who's risen in the world as I have, is bound to make enemies. The very justice I've exercised here for the good of all the people in my charge has aroused their malice and spite. Sheriff Willis, do you believe in Providence?"

306

"Yes, *sir!*"

"Then don't you understand how strange events may occur—strange accidents, some of which may look like cunning crimes—in order that good may come?"

"Precisely, Papa," Saul broke in, unable to repress his huge enjoyment of the scene even if he tried. It stood to reason that he would try, considering the great stakes at hazard, but I knew better. Saul, on a grid in hell, would laugh at the Devil's posturings. Remembering what he had told me the last time we had talked, I doubted if he would land there. I doubted if his present sport, although he would not miss it for any uncertain future gain, would cost him anything. It was at the expense of all the rest of us, not his own. Indeed he might profit by it in ways that he instinctively or cunningly perceived—that was the usual outcome. While utterly real, his terrible mirth was usually adjunct to some wildly exciting game.

In his deadly seriousness, Ralph was momentarily deceived, and looked hopefully to his son. "What were you about to say?"

"There is a Providence that shakes—shapes—our ends. To quote from the illustrious bard—there's a special Providence in the fall of a sparrow. How much more, then, in Uncle Bruce being blown to heaven?"

"Will you shut your God-damned mouth?" Harry Dillon demanded, half rising from his chair.

"Excuse him, sir," Ralph said quickly. "My son Saul is too given to levity, and naturally he's inclined to laugh at such a fantastic charge being made against me. But many a true word is spoken in jest. Let us take the strange accident that he speaks of. My brother Bruce was too easygoing to be a proper master of Wood Ibis. The great plantation supporting more than two hundred men and women went down under his ownership. By a strange accident he was instantly, mercifully killed—with his son and a Negro boatman. Only a few weeks before there was another strange accident, by which my good wife, Sadie, went to heaven. Providence intended that I marry my brother's widow, and so become master here. But Providence did not intend that a crafty foe would persuade my enemies to make false statements showing these accidents were of my own devising."

"Excuse me, Mr. Dillon." It was Saul's voice again, its gravity belied only by the sparkle in his eyes. "Father, could it be that you too have become the victim of a strange accident?"

"I don't follow you."

"Sauce for the goose is sauce for the gander, the sages tell us. Perhaps Providence has decided you've reigned long enough—that I—perhaps Dan—should bear the burden. No doubt he faked the evidence, but it's all for the best."

"It isn't possible, Saul," Ralph answered, so dulled by the crash that he was unconscious of his son's hideous mockery. "I've been a stern but just master. Wood Ibis has flourished under my rule."

I did not know what game Saul was playing—I had only an eerie inkling. Surely he would not profit by it very long—events were moving too swiftly; and I never had a stronger foreboding than of a near and fateful end to my war with Saul—but Cleo might profit greatly. I decided to strengthen his hand.

"Can you buy Providence, Mr. Dunbarton?" I asked.

"What do you mean? I count that blasphemy—"

"You're the one who's committed blasphemy by blaming Providence for your murders. I mean the five dollars you paid a swamp rat. Another five to a Chinese cabin boy. A drink of whiskey for a Negro out of a five-gallon keg supposed to be hidden in the swamp."

Out of the corner of my eye I saw Sheriff Willis straighten in his chair. If, as Cleo believed, her father had been conjured to bloody crime, a little of the spell had lately passed to the hard-headed officer, and I saw him shake it off. But a more grateful sight was Ralph's face. Its very molding seemed to change as though it were soft putty smeared by an insulting hand. At worst, he had thought, Cliff Todd had peached on him.

"Nonsense," he croaked like a senile frog. "Nonsense."

"It aint nonsense that I'm going to serve this warrant, with no more talk," Sheriff Willis said.

Saul's always bright eyes glittered under his heavy black brows. "At least give my father time to say farewell to his beloved wife," he proposed.

Ralph got quickly to his feet. "I'm sure you'll grant that, Mr.

Willis. If I am to go to jail, I may not see her again until after the trial. I must try to calm her fears—"

"You're going to jail, and I doubt if you'll be released on bond. You can tell her goodbye but just remember you're under arrest."

"In plain words, Papa, don't try to hook it," Saul told him. "It's an insult to your dignity you should resent—anyhow he ought to know you're in no condition for a race." He turned to the sheriff. "I'll attend him, if I may. Not to cling to his coattails, but to lend him my good right arm. You see he needs support."

We looked at the flaccid face, stooping shoulders, and sagging paunch—the latter had seemed to protrude impressively only a moment before—of the late lord of Wood Ibis. The sunlight through the windows lit white fires in the chandelier. The mahogany furniture glowed like wine. The deep carpets, the heavy velvet drapes, the noble molding of the walls, and the cold marble hearth all mocked his fall.

"You can have ten minutes," the sheriff said with half-ashamed kindness.

Ralph reeled out of the room, Saul following in lithe strides. "I wish to God it was that Saul we'd come for, instead of his pa," Harry Dillon exploded to his chief, as soon as the two were out of hearing.

"I feel the same, Harry. If Saul had been just a little older when the boat blew up, I'd put my money on him. I myself can hardly believe Mr. Dunbarton could have done all that killing. He just doesn't strike me as equal to it."

I was increasingly glad I had played Saul's game.

Part of that game was his return in less than five minutes. I was watching it now in intense, cold excitement—perhaps the greatest game I had ever seen with my own eyes, the most boldly conceived, the most cunningly played and, if I divined its purpose aright, the most evil. But out of that evil, good would come to one I loved.

One little facet of the brilliant concept was a black butler following Saul, bearing a decanter and four glasses.

"While we're waiting, gentlemen—"

Sheriff Willis sniffed at and then tasted the brandy with the air of an epicure. Spellbound now by the scope of the drama unfolding before my eyes—its all but unbelievable meaning battering my brain—I could hardly endure such low comedy interjected by a Fate as soulless and as profane as Saul himself. I did not want to laugh when it knifed me in the ribs, only to shriek. But no doubt Saul appreciated it; and exchanged delighted glances with his fellow-jester. No doubt he considered it the biggest joke of a hilarious afternoon.

"Excellent, excellent," the officer pronounced. "And a grateful diversion from a disagreeable duty."

"The old man's taking it pretty hard," Saul ventured, apparently sobered at last. I did not know he was capable of such superb dissembling.

"I hope Mrs. Dunbarton is bearing up well," the sheriff replied ceremoniously.

"She just won't believe it. She has the great gift of not believing anything she doesn't want to. Well, I reckon those ten minutes are about up."

The sheriff looked at his watch. "We can give him a little while longer."

"To be frank—I'm a little uneasy about him. He's a very proud man—however he came by it, he's been cock of the walk a long time. I don't know whether he can stand to have the servants see him marched off in handcuffs. I'll ask you to excuse me again."

He moved quickly, and only I—watching with ice-cold, steel-sharp vigilance—saw the ineffable animation on his countenance as he strode out the door. I rose and wandered about the room to a window. It did not command a view of Sweetwater Pond of fadeless memory—the gate to Gator Creek woods, which intersected the labyrinthine swamps of Fern Creek—still my watch was not in vain. A young Negro stable hand rode pellmell under the porte-cochere in the direction of the Quarter, with something that looked like a man's shirt in his hand. It would not be long now, my prickling skin warned me, before three more would be riding fast—the sheriff, the deputy, and me. While my companions waited quietly for the prisoner's return, Fate rode fastest of all.

Suddenly both men sprang to their feet. A regal figure appeared in the door. I had not expected this sub-climax to the denouement, but I might have known Saul would have used her in some telling way—he had been inspired to the greatest playing of his life. Her beauty, always of great power, was all the more compelling because of her terror and woe. Lately I had thought it was not truly as real as Cleo's—that it had a histrionic quality—yet electric chills ran up and down my spine.

"A terrible thing has happened," she told the sheriff in a choked voice.

"What is it, ma'am? Keep cool and tell us."

"My husband—he went into his room to get some things to take with him to the jail. He didn't return to my sitting room and Saul went to look for him. I waited—Saul sent word by a servant that he thought his father had run away—slipped down the back stairs into the swamp. How he could do such a thing when he's innocent—"

"Panic, ma'am." The sheriff spoke in a tone he considered comforting—he was being strong but kind in front of the most beautiful woman he had ever seen—but only Saul would have laughed. I had a sense of the grotesque that verged on horror. "I've known innocent men—"

"I'm greatly alarmed. He may be fleeing from the disgrace—and I don't know what rash thing he'll do. Saul's absence shows he's prey to the same fears—"

"Do you mean—?"

"Yes. No doubt Saul's following him—trying to overtake him before—" Madeline's voice broke.

"Is he armed?"

"No. But there are deep waters—"

"We'll do what we can, ma'am. Come along, Dillon."

"I think he entered at the pond but how Saul can find him in time—"

Apparently Saul would make a determined effort to prevent his father throwing himself into those deep waters. Madeline no doubt thought it would be for selfish reasons, yet it remained her main hope that her husband might live to stand trial and be judged innocent of the charge she could not believe. . . . The curtains fluttered a little outward, and the satin drapes undulated as though something was hiding behind them. The wine-red furniture looked bloody as in a dream, and the shadows had uncanny shapes. . . . I thought of a pit dug for me in dim woods, and my spirit went from me and looked in; but it did not shiver in such cold as was in this room. I too stood near and looked down into the evil spring of Wood Ibis, and saw my own image beside Saul's in the pit-black water. Strange bedfellows—Saul and I. It seemed that in a few seconds more I would be turning the key to Bluebeard's door. . . .

Strident through the open window clanged the bell.

CHAPTER

34

As the two officers and I raced our horses down the driveway, the long aisle between the live-oak trunks seemed like a gigantic telescope focused on a scene some two furlongs beyond.

There were two sets of travelers on the road. The nearest was a two-horse chaise being driven at breakneck speed toward us, the black driver whipping the beasts, and the white passenger leaning out far and very low, apparently in great danger of falling. A little way behind him came two Negroes, each with two hounds in leash. Almost the instant that we discovered them, the passenger in the chaise discovered, evidently for the first time, the party behind him. Patently at his command, the driver tugged at the reins and presently stopped the frantic team. His passenger turned, calling and gesticulating to the Negroes and frantically pointing into the swamp timber at the right of the road.

The Negro kennel boys and their two brace of hounds immediately struck off in that direction. At once the chaise-driver turned off the road and, again whipping the horses, followed them across the narrow field. By now the white passenger had discovered us and beckoned in a frenzy of excitement. At first glance I had hardly dared believe my eyes that Pa had arrived in time to join the hunt —he who had the most right to the great sport—but who else leaning forward in high zeal would lean so low and far? As we veered off the road to intercept the chaise I had the thrilling inkling that for the moment he was our leader. His fine hair waved in the wind.

"Dan! Dan!" he was shouting as we rode alongside the plunging team. "He's in there! I saw him! It is Ralph, and he's running away—"

"He can't escape, Pa, now you've called his trail," I answered.

The sheriff spoke in a voice loud and harsh with alarm. "Driver, slow that team. You'll turn over—"

"But he *will* escape," Pa yelled. "I told you he was crafty as a

313

fox. Whip the horses, Enoch! Make them run. Oh, Dan, did I not warn you? Why did you hold your fire—"

"I tell you, you can't go into the swamp!" the sheriff commanded.

The chaise was at the edge of it even now, rolling and pitching, the crazed driver still whipping the crazed beasts as he weaved between the trees. But when Harry Dillon started to dash ahead and seize one of the bridles, I blocked his way. Neither the sheriff nor his deputy nor I was in charge of this particular hunting-party. Pa was.

"Do you want him to break his neck?" Dillon growled.

Luckily the ground was softening gradually, checking the beasts' rush. Pa's shouts and the driver's whip were alike powerless to speed them on. Presently they were stopped by a dense growth of thickets, and both men appeared to regain their senses at the same instant. The Negro quieted the plunging horses. A kind of shudder passed over Pa's frame, and he relaxed panting in the seat.

"Can you tell us now what you saw?" the sheriff asked.

"Yes. Forgive my distraction. At a great distance I saw a man running from Ibis Hall toward the pond. I surmised it was my brother, but I could not be sure—"

Pa paused, to catch his breath. "It was him, sure enough," the sheriff said.

"I bade my driver drive as fast as the horses could run, meanwhile peering into every break in the trees. Then another man took off in pursuit of the first—or perchance he too was flying from the Furies. My driver cried out that it was Saul."

"Then you caught sight of Ralph—"

"Yes, as he crossed yonder run. We were racing on to warn you when I heard the bell and a moment later saw the kennel boys behind us with the hounds. I stopped and pointed where my brother passed, but they dally on the course. I beg you, speed them on. Give man and beast a taste of your riding whips. Make haste, lest he escape us even now."

"Look out that you don't stop a rifle bullet, Pa," I said.

"Neither my brother nor my nephew had a long gun. I told you, Dan, of the provision I have made. Can you see the hounds? Have they yet gained the watercourse?"

"They're close to it and questing for the scent—"

"Ride on! Press him hard! Ah, there!"

One of the hounds uttered a fierce bay. His companion joined him; a moment later the other pair gave deep-toned tongue. But when I caught sight of them in a break in the timber, they were still on leash. No doubt this was by Saul's orders—it fitted in the picture of his attempt to find quickly and restrain his father from a desperate act, not to heighten his frenzy.

"He'll never get away now, Mr. Noel," the sheriff said. "I can assure you of that."

"Ride on!" Pa shouted. "Ride on!"

I was the first to obey, without remorse, only wishing I could take Pa with me. He was fading from sight as the wood thickened between us. That had been foregone when his back was broken. A deeper wood would thicken more darkly in a parting yet to come, this one its ill-omen, part of the same pattern, it too a foregone end from the moment we had met across a fence—longer ago than that, if my fears spoke truth—perhaps when a Negro named Bert put a half-drowned baby in his arms. At my last glimpse of him he was gesticulating to the driver, who was turning his team toward the road.

Only a few yards farther on, we had to dismount and tie our horses. Making short cuts guided by the deep-throated baying of the hounds we were soon able to overtake them. They were tugging in powerful surges at the leash; their handlers could hardly hold them and were being hauled through the thickets. I did not think the chase would be very long.

Presently a long shadow glided across the trail, and out of the brushwood moved Saul. He was wet to the waist and daubed with mud; but I had never seen him more wildly alive.

"I don't suppose you've caught sight of him," Saul said to the sheriff, falling in beside him.

I was afraid that the officer would recount Pa's glimpse of the fugitive from the road—I wanted no mention of Pa in Saul's hearing—but he only shook his head.

"I thought he'd go down Gator Creek and I tried to cut him off," Saul went on, "but when I heard the hounds I knew he'd cut across country. Do you suppose he intends to fetch a big circle and come out at the Quarter?"

"He might—if he figured on getting a horse and making for the ferry. But it would be a crazy thing to do."

"That wouldn't rule it out. He's gone completely out of his mind. I saw him going while he was talking to Madeline—I should have watched him closer. What I think he'll do—but we'll soon know."

Only once before had I heard Saul talk this long without mockery. Perhaps that very fact amused him—one of many amusing things in his mind just now—for though his face had a solemn set, he could not keep the blitheness out of his walk, and there was a tell-tale sparkle in his vivid eyes. I was wondering, rather calmly, what he would say next. The intense awareness of evil I had felt in Ibis Hall had passed from me, as well as all sense of guilt over helping him play his game. It had only one aspect that I could hardly bear to contemplate—one that might haunt me all my life— but at its merciless worst it was not, in realistic survey, the horror I might imagine.

"After all, the thing I fear might be a good thing," Saul proposed.

"Maybe I see what you mean," the sheriff replied.

"If it's going to happen anyway—and you wouldn't have made this arrest unless it looked mighty black—this would save my stepmother a great deal of anguish. Of course if he were going to be acquitted, that would be a different thing. But if not—well, you can imagine what that would mean to René D'Arcy's granddaughter. If we should find him drowned in one of the ponds, she'd never know whether he was innocent or guilty. She could console herself that he was too proud to stand trial—he'd absorbed a little D'Arcy himself. Her clan would perfectly understand—and applaud."

"Well, I know enough aristocrats to say you've got it figured out right. You've got a good head screwed on your shoulders, Mr. Saul. It's too bad you don't use it oftener. If you've got any good in you at all—"

Saul gave me a delighted wink. "I can't explain some of the things I've said and done, without throwing blame on someone in too much trouble already," he replied.

The sheriff's face remained grave—I thought he even nodded slightly. Saul could hardly conceal his immense joy in the sally—he had never in his life said anything quite so funny. I found myself rather enjoying it too. My heart felt hard as a stone, my eyes small, bright, and cold. Yes, Saul could give the Devil cards and spades, because the Prince of Darkness was yet a prince, a gentleman by birth. He would have nothing to do with Saul of course—never let him in. Nevertheless he must find him an interesting fellow.

The deep, intermittent baying of the hounds changed to savage barks. They began plunging forward, the handlers hardly able to check them. To keep pace we plunged through mud and water, leaping fallen logs and clamoring over snags. The handler of the lead brace of dogs stuck in the mire, and first one and then the other jerked free. They bounded on with prolonged, lion-like roars.

"My God, they'll tear the old man to pieces, if he's still alive," the sheriff cried, setting a perilous pace across the treacherous ground.

"Don't break your neck," I answered quickly. "I don't think we'll find him alive. You'll drop dead yourself at that rate."

Saul gave me a strange, challenging glance.

"Anyway they might drag out and worry his body," the officer added, slowing down.

Suddenly the baying of the runaway dogs became a frenzied uproar of wild barkings and savage snarls. It rose from and remained in one spot perhaps a hundred paces ahead of us. The two hounds still on leash surged on with such fury that their handler could not keep his feet and was being dragged through the thickets.

"By God, they've treed him!" Harry Dillon exclaimed.

I looked at Saul.

"I reckon I was wrong about my old man," he said, glancing at the sheriff, but in reply to my gaze. "He didn't have the nerve."

A few seconds later we came out on a half-acre meadow, its grass green and pleasant to the sight, and inclosed in a broken-down rail fence. I had passed here once before—the scene of one of Honoré D'Arcy's experiments in raising forest herbs, and hardly two furlongs from the road, so circling had been the fugitive's course. At its edge stood an immense live-oak tree, under which the two hounds were baying, barking, snarling, leaping clear of the ground, and, in the parlance of their handlers, "raising sand." But they had not treed their quarry. He had been already treed in a curious way. He was not in the tree but he seemed to be of it, a grotesque excrescence from it. He dangled out of it.

Not only the color of his face explained why the sheriff could stop to gaze. He was familiar with that color, an expert in appraising it. But any layman could interpret the twist and hang of the head upon the neck.

"Well, Ralph Dunbarton did cheat the gallows, after all," he said with some histrionics, but a certain dignity.

"More of an antique Roman than a Dane," Saul said in a low, vibrant voice. That too was for my ears. He would not have wasted it on his other hearers.

We advanced slowly while the kennel boys were confining and quieting the hounds. Harry Dillon, a practical man, considered the best and quickest way to do his duty. Ralph was hanged not as high as Hallam, but the strap that served for hemp—I saw now that it was a belt of a size to encircle a big-bellied man—had been fastened to a stub projecting from a lateral bough about twelve feet above the ground. However, the tree was easy to climb.

"If two of you gentlemen will be ready to ease him down, I'll climb up and cut the strap," Dillon announced.

It was a sane, practical, common-sense suggestion, not in the least gruesome. But on the heels of it, out of the thickets growing dense, between the little meadow and the road, there rose a frantic cry.

"Do not pluck the fruit from the Judas Tree, until I give you leave! I command that you wait."

Five of our party—the sheriff, Dillon, the two round-eyed Negroes, and I—stood leaning and peering in almost the same postures, too spellbound to speak. We saw the brush move violently, and then Pa limping through it, his stick in one hand, clutching the chaise-driver's arm with the other. Not as fast as when he had run to the vision of Madeline smiling in radiant beauty, but horridly fast for one so lame—that very lameness enforcing his hungry haste—he hobbled toward us.

Belatedly I whirled to Saul, fearing I knew not what. He was not even aware of my gaze. An emotion was reflected on his face that was almost impossible to believe. It appeared to be reverent awe.

318

"Is it all right to wait for him, Mr. Saul?" Dillon asked, in a dry voice. "I reckon you have the say."

"No one will be inconvenienced," Saul replied, quickly recovering. "Let us indulge Uncle Noel."

We need not wait long. Pa came through a break in the fence, a strange light on his face. But he stopped some twenty paces from us—I wondered if the others knew why. Closer than that, he could not raise his eyes to the luscious fruit.

"It was my right to bid you delay," he told the sheriff. "It is my brother Ralph whose bloody hand has turned against himself, and I desired to bear witness."

"That's all right, Mr. Dunbarton," the officer answered kindly. "Then if there's no further objection—" He nodded to Dillon.

I was eager to find the answer to one question. I had thought that I would have to ask Saul, some day when we were alone—almost sure that he would tell me the truth—but chance had provided likely evidence here and now. The skin had been scraped from the chin of the late lord of Wood Ibis. It might have happened in throwing himself from the limb, but more likely it was caused by the raking knuckles of a powerfully driven fist. I chose to believe it was a surprise blow, when Ralph had kept a rendezvous at this spot, on the promise of help to escape. Likely he had not had time to realize what help would be given him for what strange kind of escape. If so, it had been not a stroke of mercy, God save the mark—only to facilitate a task that might otherwise cause inconvenient labor and sound. But the comfort to me was the same.

The only answer to that was, I had not hated Ralph in the degree of my duty. . . . But perhaps there would be no comfort—only specters dimly seen, demons beyond the pale of imagination—if I asked why. . . .

"You may carry my brother to the chaise," Pa told the terrified Negroes. "It is only a furlong from here, close to the road. Enoch drove it hence, when we heard the course of the hounds. It will do to carry him for the last time to Ibis Hall."

A rude bier was contrived out of rails from the broken fence. I wanted to carry Pa, but dared not offer to; the most that I could do was to lift him over the obstacles and across the muckier ground. Limping beside me, he did not drop far behind the pallbearers in Saul's charge, and Harry Dillon brought up the rear. Meanwhile I had abandoned all notion of telling the two officers how Ralph had met his death. While the fact might conceivably be fairly well established by footprints and other evidence, I never wanted Pa to know it—half his glory of victory would depart—and such pride and comfort as Cleo might take in her father's seeming settling of his debt would turn to poison.

Could I have Cleo? I could find out, now. If the answer were no, I knew now where to find a dim consolation. That would be *my* pride and comfort, to be sought as soon as possible—the chance perhaps striking today. There was fever in my brain. . . .

The other men were in sight but out of hearing, if Pa and I spoke in low tones. And perhaps this was the time and place—the edge of the swamp, the greenish light dim, life dancing with death in wild abandon.

"What did you mean, Pa, when you said my triumph would be greater than I dreamed?" I asked.

The breeze from across the fields stole in this far and the vines swayed.

"Do you yet not know?"

"I'm not sure."

"You do not know the name of 'one whose name is lost?'"

"I ask you to tell me."

"I will. The time is here. You have won the victory, without thought of gain for yourself. Perchance I should have told you as you gazed at him who had climbed so high—to whom you had come like a thief in the night, bearing fire and sword. Great as your glory was, it would have been magnified a hundred times. But I wanted to be alone with you when I told you—I alone beholding your face."

"We're alone now, Pa. Tell me."

"As Solomon brought down to the grave with blood his father's enemy, even so have you."

"Ralph was your enemy, and you are my foster father. Is that what you mean?"

"Will you still shut your eyes to the truth, because it is so blind-

320

ing bright? Oh, Dan, that is not a tittle of my meaning! As Orestes avenged the murder of his father, Agamemnon, so you have slain the murderer of yours. You are my foster son, but you sprang from the mighty loins of my brother Bruce. Even from them, into the womb of Madeline! Oh, your great heritage, that strums the strings of my heart to reveal at last!"

He stopped, ankle-deep in mud, and dropping his stick, put both hands on my shoulders.

"Can you hear the music? The god to whom we prayed draws the bow in victorious ecstasy, and the strains fill all these woods. Dan! This is his very abode. Close by a tidal creek, steaming hot this time of year, where birds of many feathers light among the palms. Our household god of vengeance and fulfillment! Together he has brought us here, in this sublime moment."

Pa did not see wide-eyed Harry Dillon approach, then stop and stare—or any other reminder of common earth.

"You are Donovan Dunbarton, saved from the sea! You have come into your birthright! You are the lord of Wood Ibis, monarch of all you survey!"

CHAPTER

35

Blessedly, there were men and dogs and horses, and the cooling clay of what was once a man, to disturb the privacy of Pa and me. There were messages to dispatch to Cleo and Dr. Sams, and other bustling business. A little later I was on horseback while he rode in the chaise; so we could not exult together in our victory. But, when at Little Ibis, Cleo looked into my eyes, she instantly read the full measure of my "joy."

"Dan," she murmured, slipping her hand into mine, "don't give up. Never give up. Our hearts are right, and all the rest is wrong."

She did not speak to me of her father's death but she had told Dr. Sams of the mercy granted her in his dying by his own hand. Although the manner of his suicide would haunt her always, her good friend had been able to offer her some consolation even in this regard: according to the sheriff's message Ralph had died instantly of a broken neck. No doubt he had pitched hard from the limb! With his own belt around his neck, he had not babbled to the sheriff of his crimes!

A deep and dangerous weariness set in upon Pa after his great passion, and he slept until late in the following day. When he wakened he told me that if I consented, he would not tell the story of my rescue and the ensuing events until Madeline had recovered enough to hear it.

"You and she share first right to the glorious tidings," he told me. "I want to watch both your faces, as I recount the strange events whereby her son is returned to her, and she and all the rest of your wondrous heritage are returned to you. You need not wait long, Dan. Now that Madeline knows the story of her own tragedy, she will yearn for the testament of its happy ending at long last. Intrinsic to her beauty is great strength."

By token of that strength Madeline sent for Cleo, Pa, Dr. Sams, and me the second day after Ralph's funeral. We were ushered into the best parlor, where we found Sheriff Willis and Mr. Elliott, a small, dapper, almost dainty-looking man who proved to be the present senior member of a Charleston law firm that had handled D'Arcy affairs for nearly a century. Significantly, Saul was not in sight. I had a sickening but irrational fear that Madeline might enter on his arm—the widow and son of the late lord—in which case today's bad dream would turn to nightmare. I sat next to Cleo, our hands in easy reach. She was very white but perfectly composed.

Madeline entered modestly and alone. She was dressed simply in black, unbejeweled save for a diamond brooch at her throat. I heard Cleo catch her breath, but I could not look at her or at Madeline either, so relentlessly were my eyes drawn to Pa. He stood gazing at her from down under his forehead, and the "most desperate, mad, tragic love" Dr. Sams had ever seen, incandescent in his face, was surely the greatest tribute ever made to her beauty. I hoped she knew that. Being a *grande dame* of course she greeted him first, but I thought the way she laid her hand in his was an acknowledgment.

"I honor your bravery, Madeline, for receiving us so soon," Pa told her.

"I was very tardy, Noel, in the happy duty. If I had waited any longer I would have shamed the memory of my grandfather, René D'Arcy. He went to France to say farewell to the old king Louis Désiré, whom he greatly loved. Louis had hardly breathed his last when the princes and princesses and he—and even poor Madame du Cayla—dried their tears and at once knelt before Charles. We may at least emulate our royal rulers in our own affairs—and Wood Ibis is the equal of many a French demesne. If it has a new master, I am in haste to honor him. Besides—in that case—I've found my son."

I wondered if this were Madeline's stately way of hiding grief—or perhaps her lack of it. The sentiment itself was palpably sincere. She gave Dr. Sams and me her hand, and kissed Cleo. When we were all seated she nodded to Mr. Elliott. The little man put on his eyeglasses and unrolled a scroll.

"Late, sad events, which need not be mentioned here, will cause Wood Ibis to revert to the estate of Bruce Dunbarton, deceased," he declared. "We may safely anticipate this decision by the probate judge. By Bruce Dunbarton's will, which I need not read, he left his estate to his son Donovan, to be returned to his wife Madeline in case Donovan died without issue. If Noel Dunbarton's foster son Dan is indeed Donovan, he is master of Wood Ibis. If he is not, Madeline Dunbarton retains possession."

"That's perfectly clear, Mr. Elliott," Madeline said.

"The court must make the final decision as to his identity. All of us hope and pray Bruce's and Madeline's lost son has returned to his own. But in order that we may know where we stand before the matter goes to court—for our personal satisfactions—I will ask Mr. Noel Dunbarton his grounds for believing this to be true."

"It is not a matter of belief, Mr. Elliott," Pa replied, with great self-control. "It is a matter of personal knowledge. I visited the scene of the explosion that had killed my brother Bruce. I saw where the boatman Webb had crawled across the ruined deck to get a life preserver, and then to the rail. As soon as I set foot on shore, the mulatto Bert and I searched tirelessly where a little castaway might most likely float to shore. What little hope flickered in our hearts, and how it leaped to triumphant flame! Webb had done his work well. Providence decreed that the child should drift onto a firm, sloping shore and be cast there by the falling tide. Even so, he could not have survived save for his strength and dauntless spirit inherited from my brother Bruce, and perchance a great love of life learned in his mother's arms. He had crawled some twenty feet up the bank when Bert heard his feeble wail. He was half-dead from exposure, but when Bert had removed his wet garments, warmed him against his naked breast, then wrapped him in his coat while he built a fire, he cried lustily!"

Madeline turned starry eyes on him and then on me. "It is almost too wonderful to believe," she murmured.

"He had many bruises but only one minor wound," Pa went on. "The little finger of his left hand was broken and lay flat against his palm. Bert and I hid him the next day, and on the following night Bert rowed both of us to Bull Island. There I engaged a poor woman, kin to the overseer, to take him secretly to Charleston and from thence to Philadelphia, paying her well for her secrecy and her aid. She is dead now, but I have her signed testament to these facts."

324

"I'm afraid that wouldn't be admissible as evidence, since she has passed on," the lawyer remarked.

"Ah, but I have other testaments, sworn before witnesses, by a man yet living—my friend, Mr. Linsey. He examined the child and made record of his broken finger. He witnessed, and testified thereto, my leaving the baby at the door of the Orphanage—and watched until the keepers found him."

"May I ask why you waited twenty years to tell his mother this good news?"

"The event of a few days ago answers that question, Mr. Elliott."

"I must say then that while personally I have no doubt of the truth, still I must see it completely established in court. Indeed my client, Mrs. Dunbarton, must herself nominally contest your foster son's claim, as a matter of duty. There must be no possibility, sir, that in your grief for your brother you are the victim of an illusion."

"I understand that, Mr. Elliott."

"Noel, it's only the process of law," Madeline told him in her rich voice. "I deplore it as much as you do. Besides my own feelings make it necessary. The others will tell you that my mother's instinct hasn't yet moved me to recognize Dan as my son. I don't know why—it seems to fly in the face of my reason." She turned to me. "Dan, will you forgive me for doubts I can't help? When finally you're proved to be my son—as every sign points—will this diminish your love for me? Remember—it's been twenty years."

"I'll never blame you, ma'am, for doing what you know is right."

"Thank you. To me that's evidence of my father's blood flowing in your veins."

"Then I see nothing more to be done until the trial," the lawyer told us.

Since he must contest them at the trial, he did not ask to see the testaments, yet Pa provided him with copies, the originals being recorded in Philadelphia. We were served wine and cake and, in an unreal atmosphere of casualness, we rose to go. Then Madeline asked Cleo if she and I would linger a moment while the others waited in the hall.

I thought from the forlorn beauty in her face that she wanted to take us both in her arms. Instead she stood by the great hearth, her hands clasped behind her, her head and bosom high.

"Dan, there's another reason I've doubted you're my son," she told me. "It's again based on instinct—not mine, but yours and Cleo's. I can't believe that you two could love each other as you do, if nature had forbidden you to each other. Indeed it's a stronger cause for doubt than my own instinct—which sometimes dims as I look into your face."

"You're right, Mama! I know you are," Cleo told her glowing eyes.

"Yet Noel's story rang so true! Cleo, do you think you should stay here—with me—until after the trial? I know you and Dan will do no wrong, but on account of what people might think."

"I want to be with Dan every minute that I can," Cleo broke in. "If I had my way, we'd be together every minute. I consider myself his wife. I always will. I'll never marry anyone else."

"Neither will I, Cleo," I told her with a ringing heart. "We'll keep each other always."

I could not read the expression, passing swift as a shadow across Madeline's face. All that I knew was, it was the shadow of an emotion unutterably intense—perhaps the greatest that had ever come close to my life. I could not guess its meaning. She stood so straight—but only the lame can love. . . .

Cleo and I returned to Little Ibis. Perhaps Mr. Elliott would prove a true prophet—there was nothing more to be done until the trial. Apparently Cleo believed him—she did not wonder aloud, with haunted eyes, if demons had overheard him. When, on the last day of August's sultry waning amid small summer lightnings, white-powed Absalom sent word by his grandson whether, please, suh, I would 'blige him by havin' a little talk wif him, still there were no signs and wonders in the sky. I thought he might want to borrow a dollar or two, account some trouble fallen on his gray head.

He was waiting in the road. Please, suh, would I walk a piece with him? By now I was getting alarmed. Absalom was a minister of the gospel, old and wise, well persuaded what counted and what did not on earth below, with the power the Negroes called the love of God in his heart; and no little thing could make him tremble as he was trembling now, and no weak presage of evil could fill his velvety old eyes with such ghosts.

"Mas' Dan, we colo'ed people know a heap that's goin' on," he told me, when I had waited his good time.

"I know it, Absalom."

"F'r instance, suh, we know that weddin' I pronounce fo' you and Miss Cleo aint took yet. We know de reason, 'cause you might be Ol' Miss' boy, come out o' de sea alive. Plenty wish you was, fo' den you'd be massa of de whole plantation, but dey feel sad fo' you too, cause dey know you'd radder have Miss Cleo dan all de plantation twixt here and Edgefield County."

He paused and I spoke. "That's right."

"I wish I could tell you you aint de little boy what was lost, but all de people say you is. Dey say dey feel it in dey bones, and it was de secret Bert die befo' he tell. So I got no good news for you, Mas' Dan. Maybe I got de wuss news one man could tell anodder. But it come 'pon me like de Wo'd of de Lo'd Himself dat I 'bliged to tell you."

We were walking slowly, little scenes beside the road coming to meet us, changing a little as our viewpoints changed, and passing on. My heart was only rustling, not beating.

"Tell me, Uncle Absalom," I said.

"Kin I ask one question fust?"

"Yes."

"Do you love Ol' Miss like a son?"

"If you mean Miss Madeline, I don't. I've never been with her enough. But my pa worships her, and so does my wife."

"But I reckon you would git to love her, if it turn out you her son. 'Pear like nobody can be wif her, wifout lovin' her out of de worl'. She like a queen on a golden t'rone. Dat why it come on me I gotta tell you now, 'stead of waiting till de news would break yo heart. 'Cause sometimes, soon or late, I bound to tell you. I kneel befo' de Lawd and I hear de trumpet sound. 'Go down to de road, ol' Absalom,' de trumpet soun' in my heart. 'Go down and speak to Mas' Dan, and tell him what you keep secret all dese years, even if he take you by de t'roat and kill you in his wraf.'"

"I won't hurt you," I heard myself reply. "Speak out."

"Long time ago Ol' Miss had a yaller girl from Haiti, whose

name was Linda, for her servin'-maid. When Linda lay dyin' from de plague—I reckon five year after Mas' Bruce was kill—she call on Agoun, de conja god, to come and ease her pain, and comfo't her soul. Agoun, he didn't come. He always fail dem dat trus' to him. So in her great trouble, she call on de Lawd Jehovah. 'Twas de 'levent hour, but de Lawd Jehovah, He come anyhow, like He do, and stand by her bedside and take her by de hand. Den it mus' be dat He tol' her He couldn't take her soul to heaven till she confess her sin, and try her best to make up fo' it to His chillen, 'cause she yell out de window for someone to run and git me."

The sun was setting amid flaming clouds. I had never seen such glory in the west. A rosy glow enchanted land and sea.

"Speak on, Uncle Absalom," I told him when he paused, aghast at what he thought might be a sign from heaven.

"An old woman heard her and run and tell me. She beg me not to go, 'cause Linda belong to de Devil, and I'd catch de plague and die. To tell truf, I was mighty skeered to go. De reason Mas' Dunbarton let Linda be, wifout worryin' about her talkin' and ravin' in de burnin' fever, was he think no one dast go near her. 'Scusing dat, I reckon he'd post a guard over her, or maybe t'row her some medicine through de window dat would kill her. But I was a minister of de Gospel, and de good Book say to visit de sick whedder or not de sickness catchin', so I went to Linda's cabin in de deep of night, to talk to her."

"Well, what did she say?"

"Fust, she asked me to give her some whiskey she'd hid away. Den she tol' me about Ol' Miss, and when I ask her to write down de gist of it, she had me git her paper and pencil, and de Lawd held her hand steady as de Cross o' Jesus, while she wrote it down in de language she speak in Haiti. I kep' it to dis day, but never show it to a livin' soul. I kep' in my heart what she tol' me, and never whisper it to a livin' soul. What good would it do, I ask de Lawd? All de people dat need to know it was dead—Miss Sadie, and Mas' Bruce, and de baby, and de boatman. Dey was all dead, I thought. I ask de Lawd to 'scuse me, cause 'twas too big a job fo' me, and I thought He say He would. But maybe de baby didn't die—maybe he was save from de sea. If dat is true, de man he grow to be *'bliged* to hear what Linda told me. What he do 'bout it aint my business, but de Lawd say I 'bliged to tell him, even if he take me by de t'roat and kill me. But I know now you won't lay hand on me. I know you fo'give me, when it somethin' I can't help."

"I'll bless you for trying to help me, Absalom." I stopped on the road. "What is it?"

"Linda tell me how she carry message 'tween Ol' Miss and Mas' Ralph, every few days de last year Mas' Bruce was alive. Sometime dey meet, but dey didn't do nothin' but talk. But Mas' Ralph, he go pitty-nee crazy wif wantin' her and wantin' to git the plantation. Linda say Ol' Miss want Mas' Ralph as bad and maybe wuss. She say Ol' Miss know Mas' Ralph gwine kill his wife. Later on she know Mas' Ralph gwine kill Mas' Bruce. But Ol' Miss gwine to be away from Ibis Hall when Mas' Bruce die. So she got Linda to pretend-like she bring a message—handin' it to her in front of odder people—sayin' her uncle is sick at Combahee, and she got to go to him."

There was dull-red mist on the road. There was a pit opening close by, and I was reeling blindly toward its brink. But my heart lurched, and my soul came back to me, and I spoke clearly.

"But Madeline didn't know what means Ralph would use. She had no idea that he'd rig a boat when Bruce was going sailing. At least she never dreamed that her own baby would be aboard. All the lust in hell couldn't make her do that thing. That was Ralph's work—so he could own the plantation."

Absalom reached his black hand and clutched mine.

"I'll tell you de rest, and de last. Linda say dat Ol' Miss want Mas' Ralph so bad, she promise him he can sho be master of Wood Ibis. Ol' Miss' know Dr. Sams on a big drunk, so she tell Linda dat after she go to Combahee, to make out de baby a lot sicker dan he was, so Mas' Bruce take him to Bull Island. . . ."

Absalom spoke a few more words, but I did not hear them. I was listening to Dr. Sams in his little office long ago, when he had tried to warn me against opening Bluebeard's door. He had spoken so wildly that night. . . . If the truth were brought to light, all of us might wish we had never been born. . . .

Some grateful tasks at the stables prevented me from eating supper with Cleo, Pa, and Dr. Sams. Only sullen embers remained of the sunset holocaust, but it seemed to me there were other signs in the heavens of mustering doom. I had never heard the water birds so troubled. They should have settled for the night by now, sleepily murmuring in the reeds, or on their roosts; instead the gulls still clamored as they passed unseen, cranes whooped and whistled far aloft, and the wings of the wood ducks rustled without rest. Dr. Sams was reading under the lamp in his office when I came in and laid the papers Absalom had given me on his open book.

I went out at once. It was not meet that any man should behold his face in the next few minutes. It was hard to believe he would ever want me to see it again or perhaps to look at it himself; perhaps I had dealt him a mortal wound. He might not be able to stand its pain or its loathsome festering; he might seek many little deaths until the big and final one ended the search. . . . No, Madeline had inflicted it, not I, in spite of his love for her. She had struck at his soul; and she thought that if she could not see it bleed, she need not make atonement. How did she dare presume to knowledge of any soul's limits and laws? It was insolence unspeakable, blasphemy without end. . . . I had only lanced the horrid ulcer for good or ill.

My hopes for him hung in a great measure on the event of the next few minutes. If he went to his room alone, leaving me here alone in the pale dark of the veranda, they would fall. . . . Instead the front door opened and he walked firmly through. A sultry haze hid the young moon and the stars, and it would obscure our faces from each other. Sitting close together on the steps, we could talk plain.

"I'm quite sober, Dan," he told me. "I took only one big drink. You see—after all—this came as almost a relief. I don't have to beat it back any more. The Devil has drawn back from me for a little while."

"So there was a reason besides your own shame that you never mentioned little Donovan to me."

"Yes. I realize it now. I couldn't stand to think of him. Her husband and a Negro boatman—if they had been the only victims I might have been able to face it—and fight it. But her own baby. . . ."

"I remember when once I suggested that Ralph and Madeline were strange bedfellows, you told me if I as much as hinted that she suspected him of murder, I would have to leave. I understand that now."

"I do too. I didn't let myself understand it, at the time."

"I remember the torment in your face when I told you I could hardly believe that a man like Ralph was capable of planning and carrying through those murders. You perceived the alternative. But Cleo came closer to the truth than any of us, the morning after my return from Charleston. She said her father had been under some kind of a spell. That he'd been conjured."

"The complete truth," Dr. Sams said quietly.

"A weak man—his very cruelty a symptom of that weakness— all his posturings the same—greedily ambitious to make up for it and conceal it, but with no gifts to get him farther than overseer of a plantation. But his brother Bruce was lord of that plantation. He had for his wife a beautiful, highborn woman coveted by the best in the land. We can imagine his jealousy—but it was only an impotent gnawing passion until—one unbelievable night—he was offered a chance to supplant him. Madeline's beautiful body and the mastery of Wood Ibis—his for the taking. Why, he was a better man than Bruce! Why else did Madeline want him in her bed? Merlin himself never laid a spell stronger than the one that vision put on him. No voodoo-doctor with his claptrap knew what conjuring meant, compared to Madeline with her beauty and place and riches."

I paused, to grant a little mercy to Dr. Sams, but he did not want it. "Ram on," he told me. "That's the stuff! We've got to see it through."

"Get rid of Sadie, get rid of Bruce. That was all he had to do, to get Madeline. Did she tell him so? She didn't need to. She need only whisper, "If we were both free—" But why was it necessary to be free? They were able to meet every few days, Linda told Absalom. They only talked, she said—why didn't they gratify their lust without committing murder? If it was only lust—"

"*Only* lust. Good God, don't you know that lust of the body can be one of the most cruel, relentless, wicked passions this side of hell? They didn't want snatches of it, behind Bruce's back. They wanted long nights—orgies—satiety—"

"At least she did. That's past denying. Ralph was hardly sensuous enough—too dull and coarse—to match Madeline in lasciviousness. You can be sure she was the aggressor, as she'd been with Bruce before him."

"I believed that she loved Bruce terribly. I thought of her as bearing out my maxim—she, too, was lame in some way, I felt—maybe because she'd absorbed too many of René's medieval ideas. But I was wrong. That too was devouring lust."

"I don't think she can love anyone. And since a queen can do no wrong, it was all right to conjure him to wipe out Sadie. For God's sake, let's assume she didn't know the means he was going to use. But I think he balked a little, when it was Bruce's turn. Ralph hadn't been afraid of Sadie but he did fear Bruce. I think it was then he demanded a higher price than Madeline's body and regency of the plantation. He demanded to be king. So Bruce had to take the baby with him—as Cleo let slip, Ralph wasn't the least afraid of a little baby. Madeline might have had a certain natural fondness for the brat and wanted to spare him, but Ralph insisted—"

"Oh, my God, Dan! If there was anything I could say—or do— to help you through this. . . . Getting drunk's no good. I've found that out. I guess you'd better go ahead and talk."

"Look. Am I still hiding from the truth? Trying to go easy on her because she's so beautiful—because I can't get out of being her son? Maybe she thought of the snake herself. Maybe she offered up the baby the first time he put his hand under her dress. Well, what of it? For having her for a mother, I've got to lose Cleo for my wife. I wish to God Pa had minded his own business the night of the wreck. What business had a lame man and a yeller nigger interfering with the queen's affairs of the bedchamber? I would have whimpered and shivered a little while and then gone to sleep, and left here feeling this was a fairly decent world."

"It is, Dan."

"Now when I leave here, I'll go to hell. I know too much for God to let me through those blessed pearly gates. Well, I'd rather go down there. At least it doesn't pretend to be anything it's not— it says on the door 'abandon hope.' People aren't dressed up to look like angels—"

"Be still, Dan." Dr. Sams put his arm around my shoulders. "Stop that awful sacrilege. I tell you, it is a decent world on the whole. There are sinks of evil, God knows why, and you've fallen in the worst I ever dreamed, but remember Cleo—and Obo—Belle Martin —Absalom."

I rose and walked a little way into the dark and came back to Dr. Sams.

"As sinks go, it's first class. I saw you looking into it after Madeline had Granny put on her show. Madeline didn't want her son, whom she'd conspired to murder, sitting at the head of her table. That's all right. It even indicated a certain fastidiousness. But to get me out of her way she was perfectly willing for me to marry her other child. You looked a little sick."

"You're wrong. Although she'd no doubt forbidden Granny to say anything hinting murder, I think the test she put her to was completely honest. Indeed, she wouldn't have trusted a senile old woman to put on a convincing show. She believes sincerely in her second sight—at the end she was completely convinced you were not Donovan, and it was all right for you and Cleo to marry. There's no other reasonable explanation for her bringing Granny here."

"On second thought—none that I can see."

"I knew she was praying you weren't Donovan. I looked sick, because in my heart I knew why—she wanted that ghost laid. But it was a very strange affair. Granny wasn't coached—and yet— unless Noel and all of us are insane—her second sight failed."

"Of course you know Saul's real motive in killing Ralph."

"I didn't know he'd killed Ralph. I suspected it—and knew that you did—but I thought I'd shut that up too, in one of the drawers. His obvious motive would be to hush him up quick—so he wouldn't have to stand in the dock with him for Slewfoot's and Bert's murder."

"That was one motive but Saul had another. He didn't want Ralph to tell on Madeline, a sure thing when the rope began to dangle before his eyes. Saul still thought—quite reasonably—that he could save his own neck. He still had hopes he could keep me from getting Wood Ibis. Even if I did, he wanted Madeline to stay on as queen. She was to be his bread and butter ever after."

The haze hiding the stars had changed to dark-gray cloud and a few big drops of rain thumped the roof.

"It looks like we're in for some rough weather," Dr. Sams said absently.

I laughed a little. "Madeline is—and so is Saul," I told him.

"Dan, you couldn't convict either one of them."

"I wouldn't try, in Madeline's case. But she's not going to live at Wood Ibis, and she's not going to have Cleo back. I don't know what will happen to Saul—Madeline was the last card in his hand. As soon as he finds out it's no good, he'll do something—but I don't know what. It will be very interesting."

"Are you going to tell Cleo—and Noel—about Madeline?"

I had been dreading his asking that question, because I had been asking it of myself this last hour. I could only listen to the first stirring of a seaward breeze that rustled the leaves and changed the rhythm and timbre of the slow rain's sound.

"I don't know."

He nodded as though this were the right answer.

I did know something arising from this night, and that was how much I loved Cleo. I was going to go and tell her, in lieu of all I must conceal, and it was the right answer to my blasphemies, not long since, for which Dr. Sams had rebuked me. This was the truth that laid bare the lies. In this low tide on the darkest night in the lives of four people, I thanked heaven for my soul that could know joy and pain. Out on this evil sea, shore lights still cast their sturdy, steady beams.

It is the nature of truth to lay bare lies. In laying them bare, sometimes it exorcises evil. Still I did not find my way to tell

Madeline's other child, her adorer, and Madeline's other lover, her serenader, the truth of the evil done to their mocked hearts. I could not find the strength—if that was the name of the thing that seemed so opposed to mercy.

I was grateful, somehow, for tonight's strange weather. It was eerie and ominous enough to divert my attention, sometimes, from the Furies; it did not mock my mood and its effect was harmonious with the movement of event. There were showers of rain with intervals of intense silence. As the tide rose, a dim distant murmur at the frontier of sound came and went until finally I seized and held it long enough to identify it as the surf, never before audible against a seaward breeze. I went in and waked Dr. Sams and together we went outdoors to look at the tide. It was unaccountably high for this stage of the moon, backing in as from a strong southeasterly wind. His barometer had fallen sharply since we went to bed.

In the morning a mounted provost, riding all night from Charleston, brought us the solution of these mysteries. A boat half-naked of sails had reeled into Saint Augustine the afternoon before after being brushed by the skirts of a West Indian hurricane, and the harbor masters and lifesaving stations up the coast had been warned by telegraph. There had been signs of a heavy gale off southern Florida four days before; presumably it was moving very slowly in a northwesterly course. There was no telling whether it would strike inland far to the south of us, or swing easterly to rake our shores. If the signs worsened, people living on low-lying islands should make for the mainland.

Coming events cast their shadows before. The great storm three hundred miles distant was already affecting our weather and tides, to the perturbation of the wild creatures. However, many such alarms had sounded in previous years, there was all-outdoors for the hurricane to cross, and Dr. Sams's glass had risen a little. If it fell rapidly again he would evacuate the slaves and his prized stallions; as for ourselves, he was agreeable to our remaining in the cottage, which was strongly built and had weathered many a severe gale.

The surf that day was strong, with a deep-toned roar; it seemed to me the waves ran in faster than their wont but did not appear high. The tide did not reach yesterday's mark and no breeze stirred, although thin gray clouds seemed in troubled motion on top of the sky. The glass did not move a point from dawn till dark. At sunrise it was still stationary; the birds went about their business with decorum, and apparently the danger had passed. Dr. Sams believed that the gale had changed its raving course to the open sea.

But another storm, long-gathering, unexpendable on any ocean, implacably aimed at this island, and predestined from the moment Bert found a whimpering baby in the reeds, broke that day.

I was given a brief, sharp warning. About ten o'clock in the morning Joshua told me furtively that a quadroon girl named Cassie was waiting in a patch of woods behind the barns to give me a secret message. She was alone there, Joshua said; he had made sure of that before he came to me. The reason for his care-taking he need not explain: Cassie belonged to Saul, he having bought her at Port Royal this spring, and was his favorite concubine.

Tall, lean, yellow-brown, with an extraordinarily primitive countenance, she did not strike me as approaching in attractiveness many of the young wenches of Wood Ibis—but that was Saul's business only. My business was the round of her eyes and breathless, frightened tone in which she spoke.

"Mas' Dan, I aint nothin' to do with this, but what Mas' Saul told me to come and tell you."

"I understand that, Cassie."

"He say for you to come where you met Cliff Todd—by de join-up of Little Run and Whale Branch—right away. He waitin' for you there. And he say—bring yo' rifle."

"Is that all?"

She hesitated; it is very hard for Negroes to be the bearers of evil tidings.

"He say—I mighty sorry, but I couldn't git out of telling you—if you don't come, he'll come here—and you won't know when to speck him. He say you'll git what he call consolatin' prize what fools git, wif no chance of givin' it to him, if you don't come. He say he givin' you this chance 'cause he feel like it—he enjoy hisself mo' than if he come here at night. He say Obo can't watch bof you and Miss Cleo all de time, and he could of kill you when you was looking at Dr. Sams's wedder-glass las' night. He say if you don't come, you won't never see him again."

"What?"

"Dat what he say. 'If you don't come meet me, you'll never see me agin.'"

"Is he fixin' to stay awhile in the swamp?"

"He stay there last night—in one of 'em little houses Cliff Todd make—and he say he goin' to stay there till he finish his business wif you. Then he goin' some place, takin' me wif him, but when I ask him where us goin' he jus' laugh."

"Has he his rifle with him?"

"Yassuh."

"Any dogs?"

"He kill every one of 'em dogs, befo' he go off into de swamp. He say dey aint worf a goddam."

"Has he got any money?" He might need some, if what I suspected was true.

"Yassuh. Miss Madeline give him a heap o' money—gol' money I reckon, ten hunnerd dollar worf. But don't tell him I told you. He didn't say for me to, or not to."

"Do you love him, Cassie?" I did not see how this was any of my business; I only obeyed an impulse.

"No, suh. Not like I love Ol' Massa, who sell me to him."

"Do you hate him?"

"Sometime I do. He mighty cruel to me sometime. But no man like him ever stayed wif me befo'. I feel shamed when I think about it, and he pitty-nee kill me besides, but I reckon I'd go to hell to git him to stay wif me."

I wondered if I were wasting breath in order to pass time. I had come on a river from which I could not turn back, and yet dared not cross. All that I knew was, Death was in great haste today, perchance he had important affairs demanding his attention—and if I went to meet him he would strike, hit or miss, and go his way. If I remained here, to await his leisure, Death would stand in the dark, steady his aim, and make sure.

I considered discussing the matter, as though it were a problem of logic, with Dr. Sams. At least I should talk with Pa and Cleo before I walked into the woods, with an even chance of never walking out. I thought of sending Obo to scout for me, lest I be ambushed—but Saul would perceive that possibility, and once before he had tried for two birds with one stone. He had already warned me of his advantage over me—his fearlessness of death. I had laid it aside—there had been nothing else to do, with a fact I could neither gainsay nor yet confess—but now I picked it up and looked at it again. That very fearlessness had afforded me a fighting chance to live. For his pleasure he had tossed it to me, instead of standing in the dark, steadying his aim, and making sure.

It was not easy to think clearly when I was so terribly frightened. Once more I turned to his courier.

"Cassie, do you think he's laid a trap for me?"

"Do you mean, suh, like layin' in de bushes and shootin' you when you come by?"

"Yes."

"I know he aint." A faint childish smile started to curl her lips but she remembered what grim business this was, and became properly grave.

"If you lie to me, the Devil will take your soul."

"I aint lyin', Mas' Dan. He stay awake and figger mos' of de night, how you and him could have it de mos' even. He can't hardly wait, he so happy 'bout it, snappin' he finger. When I started cryin' he laugh and t'row me in de river and den he do somethin' to me dat he say cheer me up. He say if you want to, you can holler to him, and he'll holler back all de time you comin' near him. I pray to God he don't kill you, Mas' Dan. I rather you kill him Jesus truf. Bless Jesus make me feel dat way, I reckon, even while de Devil almos' burn me up to git him to stay wif me. But I *know* he goin' kill you if you don't come. If you do come, one of you goin' kill de odder, but he don't know which."

Well, was not this what I had been waiting for, ever since the night I had met Cleo beside the tarn? Was it not my passion too, for the moment chilled by fear? Could I lay for Saul and kill him in the dark? Not when he walked on two legs instead of four.

I called to Joshua, loitering by the paddock.

"Yes, massa."

"Wait an hour, then tell Miss Cleo I have important business

338

with Saul. Tell her I couldn't get out of it if I tried. She can decide what to tell the others, but say I ask that no one interfere."

"Yassuh!" Joshua stood at his full height and spoke like a soldier.

"Tell her I'm meeting Saul at the mouth of Little Run, where I met Cliff Todd, and that I have every expectation of being back by sundown."

"Praise de Lawd, Mas' Dan!"

"Tell her not to be afraid. She's taught me to believe my heart—and it tells me I'm going to win."

I had weaved safely through the open woods, and amid the thickets close to the rendezvous Saul had replied to my shouts. Now we were sitting on logs deposited here by floods, about twenty feet apart, our rifles leaning handy. Saul's shirt collar was open, revealing his great tomcat neck, and his trousers were slashed off at the knee. There was a sheen on his eyes I did not remember ever seeing before.

"Do I look like a swamp rat?" he asked.

"Quite a lot."

"It's my natural calling, I reckon. Well, I'm glad you came. I knew you would. You don't know, though, and must wonder, why I decided to send for you at this time—what I've got to gain by it, except the satisfaction of settling my account with you. The answer to that is, I've nothing more to gain by waiting. And I'd like to be well on my way, in a safe, dry spot, when the hurricane strikes."

"Pardon me, but Dr. Sams says it's gone to sea."

"I think he's wrong. It's moving awful slow, to judge from the weather and other signs, but I think it's still hanging off the coast. Well, anyway, I've seen the writing on the wall as far as Wood Ibis is concerned. You're obviously Donovan. Madeline knows it as well as I do. With you disposed of, there'd still be Cleo—and only a rope for me. My hopes lay for a while in Madeline, but they're blasted too. What did old Absalom tell you when you and he took your walk?"

"What do you suppose?"

"The nigger I had watching you said it knocked you in a heap. Well, I think he told you about a conjure-woman named Linda who died of plague fifteen years ago. On her last night Pa insisted there was no danger of anybody coming near her, in case she ratted on old Agoun. In fact he thought she had died, so he told Slewfoot he needn't stand guard any longer. But she revived, and was still breathing when Madeline went there the next morning."

"Madeline went there! Linda had the plague—"

"Don't be a low-lived, Dunbarton son-of-a-bitch. Whatever Madeline is or isn't, she's the last real D'Arcy, and don't you forget it."

"I beg your pardon, for doubting the *noblesse oblige* of your stepmother."

"Nicely put. But I think Linda sold her out as well as her voodoo god the night before. Pa was always inclined to take chances—and I was only fifteen at the time."

"It was careless of him to have let her live a day after the explosion," I remarked when he paused. "If you'd got your growth—"

Saul shook his head. "Again you underestimate Madeline. She wouldn't stand for any hanky-panky with Linda. In spite of me—God knows in spite of Papa—Madeline was queen of Ibis Island. But to answer your question about Absalom—a rumor reached me that he'd left his cabin that night, and I had a suspicion he'd visited Linda. I told a wench I was bedding with to ask him—my maiden voyage, as it were—but the wily old psalm-singer convinced her that he wouldn't dirty his Bible, going near a conjure-woman. If he didn't tell you, you were going to find out about Madeline anyway. Dr. Sams has suspected her fine French hand in those murders—but wouldn't admit it to himself—for years. It was plain as the nose on your face."

"So you were bluffing, when you said I'd never know the secret of Wood Ibis."

Saul smiled winningly. "Are you sure you know it now?"

"That's another bluff."

"All right. Anyway, Madeline was my last card—and a deuce. Very sensibly I decided to shake the dust of Wood Ibis from my feet. Since one of us isn't going to survive this delightful day, I don't mind saying I'm heading for the Okefenokee, to join Cliff Todd. Don't feel sorry for me, friend. With Cassie—and a swamp bigger than Delaware—the best hunting and fishing on the continent—a little whiskey still—I'll have a pretty good life. There's a possibility that I'll be happier—really happier—than if I were king of Wood Ibis. I'm not human, you know—the swamp is my natural

341

habitat. But of course I couldn't go without completing my contract with you."

The sun was high overhead; our shadows were small and sharp. I wondered if I would see it set.

"That stands to reason," I remarked.

"I searched my heart—I'm supposed not to have one, but that's a mistake—whether to lay for you and make sure of your disposal, or to have an enjoyable afternoon with you at some risk. Mark you, either was in my power. I could have killed you half a dozen times in the last two days. The trouble was, I didn't hate you. I'm as incapable of hate—except the curious near-human kind I had for Cleo—as I am of love. Also, I haven't the slightest fear of death. I have a rational wish to live, but that's too cold a concept to interfere with my pleasures. And to save me—and this is a great compliment—I couldn't think of anything more enjoyable than a real jig with you."

I listened to my heart, speaking clearly through my clamoring terrors, and told him what it said.

"I feel the same about you."

"Animals fight for pleasure at times. I've thought I've seen them hunt for pleasure—when they weren't hungry—pass up advantages to prolong the sport. I suggest we have a riproaring game of Indian-and-Paleface—for keeps. You start walking up Little Run, I'll head down Whale Branch. Who counts off a hundred steps first, hollers. The other one answers, and the hunt's on." Saul looked at me with great sociability.

"That's entirely satisfactory. There's just one other thing, which you may or may not want to do. As you say, one of us won't be here long. I wish you'd gratify my curiosity about what you told me on the fence."

"I don't know that that's an unreasonable request."

"We're really great enemies. That relationship is as powerful as though we were great friends. You told me you had died—and risen and walked—and your soul had passed. What did you mean?"

Saul's face became wet with sweat, and I knew it was icy cold.

"I find it's not easy to tell you," he said in a low, harsh voice. "Perhaps Lazarus had trouble describing his experience when, stinking, he rose from the dead. I *will* tell you, out of respect for my great enemy. I was only ten years old when it happened."

He paused, the Swamp seemed holding its breath to listen—then spoke on.

"I was a fairly normal boy, I guess—taking more after Mama than my father. He sent me out of the house on a trumped-up errand, and I looked through the window and saw him putting something from a sack in his and Mama's bed. Once he'd hid a present for her there—some new shoes—and I thought this was another present. I ran and did the errand and got back in the house just a few seconds before she was struck. I was in the room, standing by the bed—waiting for her to discover the 'surprise.'"

I wiped icy sweat from my face. There was nothing I could say.

"I died on my feet," Saul went on. "When I came back, nothing in the world mattered any more. There wasn't any law, there wasn't any God, I was cut off from love and hate. The big man there wasn't my father any more—he was just someone to do what I told him. From then on I was a denizen of the swamp. I never really came out of it, even when I was eating and sleeping in Ibis Hall. I brought it with me."

Then he yawned like a dog, and the sheen came back on his dead eyes.

"Naturally I'd pick the swamp for this last jig with you," he told me, immense vitality and abysmal mockery returning to his voice. "Artistic, by—God!"

"For a minute," I said, "I didn't want to kill you. I want to now—worse than ever—but in a different way. I've got to get you off the earth. The sun mustn't look down and see you any more."

"I reckon I shouldn't have told you. I have a feeling you're more dangerous. But I see what you mean."

"I'm grateful to you for making it self-defense."

"I would be grateful—if carrion were capable of gratitude—if you'd succeed. One of my few human impulses. Now I want to say one more thing, which you'll find very interesting—if you survive you'll think about it a lot. This whole pattern fits. Pa was a weak, and hence a cruel, man. That's why he tortured Uncle Noel when they were boys and broke his back—hence his hate. That's why he was clay in Madeline's hands and took a weak, cruel way

343

to kill my mother—letting a poison snake do the job when he wasn't looking at her. I happened to see him—hence me. Granny suspected it—hence her. Cleo was just trying to get away. But back of all this, what set all the rest in motion, was one extreme passion, lodged in one person."

"You told me about that, before. I know what it is now. Madeline's horrible lust."

Saul laughed loudly. "You're a real card, Dan. You've put me in wonderful spirits for the game. By the way—that little human yearning to be carrion won't dull my play. Shall we begin?"

"I'm ready whenever you are."

He rose, shouldered his rifle, and with a little wave at me started down the branch. I took up Little Run, not quite able to believe that in a moment I would be fighting for my life, but readily believing I might be cheated out of it before then by a stroke of treachery. I could not keep from glancing over my shoulder and dodging behind thickets. Either Saul would not stoop to such maneuvers, or doubt of my honor did not cross his mind. He paced in the open or through the thickets as the path led him, without a backward glance. If I had room in my heart for any civilized emotion, I would have been moved to wonder and pity by his trusting me; as it was, the shadows of those emotions flicked across my soul and were gone. Perhaps he thought I was as zestful for the game as he and hence would not cheat myself of the sport, itself a sign of the gulf between him and humanity. But perhaps this was an unconscious acknowledgment of that gulf, such as sometimes glimmers in the eyes of a dog.

The thickets hid me now; I could think hard and fast. My meeting place with Saul had been in the point of the V between Little Run and Whale Branch; he had waded the mouth of the shallow creek to go down the bank of the river. A fallen tree provided a bridge near the junction, but there was no other for a half a mile into Deep Swamp, and the swift, deep tide could not be swum with dry powder. However, there was a possibility of my crossing higher up, circling back with the flood between us, and taking him by surprise.

I envisioned the maneuver on this terrain in one flash of imagination, and had changed my course a little nearer the river when

I heard Saul shout. Musically and joyfully came his "hy-yo!" from nearly a furlong's distance. I replied, and trying to make the most of these seconds' safety, went swiftly in search of a crossing. But the last high tide had washed out the mud-bar at the bend, and the swift, deep waters balked me.

There was nothing to do but swing wide of the river across Little Run while out of Saul's sight and hearing. Unless I fled, there was no alternative save circling back, then stalking my enemy where and while he was stalking me. This, then, was to be the form of battle. On my good hunting and good luck hung my life.

It *was* good hunting. No paleface pioneer chasing and chased by a redskin scalper ever had keener sport. It *was* sport to some being within me, an inner man completely male, irresponsible, passionately in love with battle, reveling in his male powers, unaware of any moment but his present, thrilling own. The moment *was* thrilling beyond intelligence, fraught with mortal hazard as the price of living it, and with lust for victory the loss of which was death. Terror no longer clutched and cramped my heart. It was transmuted to an extreme excitement that did not addle but electrified my brain. Only a few moments shared deeply with Cleo had ever brought me such a wild perception of my own reality; only then had every sense attained such pitch. Seeing or hearing every clue to life or death—my only study to stand instead of fall—I hardly noticed the stage so wonderfully set for the primal conflict, but my heart opened to the harmony and rejoiced.

It was only the edge of Deep Swamp, its waters shallow save for the river, its thickets penetrable, its ground warm and soft but steady underfoot. But its light was a lovely greenish-gray. The noon sky shone in small blue patches amid deep verdure, and what seemed a golden snow was falling where spears of sunlight struck and splintered against the tree-tops' shields. The female vines entwined their lovers' limbs in graceful venery. White cranes took wing and circled, and perchance would betray my enemy's advance by their spurts of flight, but there was an equal chance of their betraying mine. The late-blooming honeysuckle smelled more sweet because life was brief.

I caught sight of my foe too briefly to find my aim. As I was emerging from a thicket I saw his barrel wink in time to draw back. Sometimes his misplaced footstep warned me of his stealthy approach, or gave me a rapturous hint where to seek him; but sometimes a leafy stalk that I thought would bend in silence swished a hair-raising alarm. When I had completed a perfect stalk on what proved to be a wild turkey, I conceived a stratagem. Finding some sun-baked mud on a snag heap, I stood behind dense growth and tossed fragments of it farther and farther into the thickets. The barely audible sounds imitated well those made by a sneaker, and a little rustle of leaves off at one side persuaded me that Saul was closing in. Shielded by vines I waited for him to enter a tree-aisle to meet my bullet.

Nothing came of the trick. My quarry became suspicious and turned back. The game went on, more desperate every second, for we had closed within fifty paces, and the intense strain was surely telling on him as it was on me. False steps became more frequent. Our nerves were too taut; our eyes were getting tired. Suddenly we might meet in a break of the thickets, both fire the same instant, and each know not his victory or defeat.

Assured that I was hidden, I purposely let the foliage rustle as I moved parallel to the river. Then, very softly, I retraced my steps. Peering through the vines, I distinguished a dark shape in the dense growth close to the bank. I could not have told in what way its color differed from the multiple hues of the swamp, but my eyes had no doubt. I moved a short distance so that I could raise my gun in silence and clear my sights. My heart stood still. . . .

My gun was slipping to my shoulder when some aspect of the target foreign to life darted through my brain. I need not stand and stare—in an instant the effigy lost all human likeness and was revealed as a man's shirt fixed on a snag. That instant had not quite passed before I was pitching down—not yet from a bullet's blow, instead by the thrust of instinct to dodge one—but despite the terror-driven speed of my fall, I might not live to land.

I was flat on the ground when the hovering silence fell apart from the roar of a gun. Saul had fired and missed, I thought, and now he was in my hand. I had only to leap up, locate his ambush by the powder-smoke, and close for a sure shot before he could reload. Instead I lay still. My exultation gave way to other states—one of them a mixture of amazement and alarm. Perhaps this was another trick—Saul might have arranged the firing of an extra gun to decoy me into ambush—but I simply did not believe it. Suddenly I was no longer alarmed, but far more deeply amazed. My mind turned back and listened again to the gun's roar—to its memory echo-real—and now marked that it had come from across the river; and on its heels had rushed another sound that I had heard unheeding. It was much closer than the blast and sounded like a rather heavy crashing of thickets.

Barely moving my head, I looked and listened a moment more. No shadow crept and the ancient silence of the swamp had returned. I began a furtive movement toward the scene of the later sound but my caution was no longer enforced by fear; indeed I felt strangely safe. I had gone half the distance when a very dim sensation in my ears began to suggest heavy, troubled breathing. Peering closely I made out a dark shape in the thickets. I was sure that it was Saul but his position denied that he was lying in ambush.

He did not stir as I pushed through the greenery, my gun ready. In a moment more I was gazing down at him. He was not aware of my presence. I would not be long aware of his. His stay here was very short, as was betokened by the gushing wound in his left side. He had stripped off his shirt for the ruse he had played and I saw his big chest swell and diminish at ever longer intervals and reduced power.

"Saul?" I called.

He opened his eyes, and after while uttered a hoarse whisper.

"Is that you, Dan?"

"Yes."

"Who shot me? You didn't."

"I don't know."

"It wasn't Cassie, was it?"

"She couldn't have crossed the river with dry powder—"

"Who could? Oh yes, I know. Well—good fun—while it lasted."

"Extra-good. Can I do anything for you, before you go?"

"Not before. . . . The other time hurt, but this doesn't. . . . No soul to pass this time. . . . But after I stop breathing—"

347

"Yes?"

"Take hold of—my—legs—"

"Hurry up. Try hard."

"Drag me—under—some brush—thick—dark—and leave me. Don't let anybody—know. I—don't—want—bury." He drew a deep anguished breath and made a final effort. "We swamp people—we crawl under a bush to breathe our last. We don't—want—man—or beast—or God—to find us."

Blood spurted from his side in a garish fountain. Saul quivered and then lay still.

If the hurricane had set a seaward course it now turned back toward land. Perhaps it was coming in honor of Saul, with gongs of thunder, trumpets of wind—such Mass as the banished gods performed over the corse of Pan. It would fling down the forests and heave up the waters to hide his bones, and change the land forever for his monument.

The white-powed Negroes were the first to read the signs. The third day of September dawned calm and clear, but a sultriness developed toward noon, and the tides rose very high. In the afternoon the air stirred out of the northwest. Seas came running in from the uttermost horizons, their intervals long, but galloping fast, and left an almost straight line of spume as far as eye could reach up and down the beach. During the night the breeze freshened, blowing in long, moaning gusts; and the glass fell sharply.

On the following afternoon Dr. Sams decided to send all his slaves and some of his livestock to the mainland. Madeline had made the same decision, evacuating the Negroes including the house-servants in the care of Jud and Belle Martin, and sending Granny in charge of Lucy to her kinfolk on the Cooper River. At the same time she sent a lavender-scented invitation to Cleo, Pa, Dr. Sams, and me to take refuge from the storm at Ibis Hall. There never was, and never would be a hurricane so mighty that it could raze its adamant walls.

Obo, of course, would come and go with Cleo. At the last moment Absalom asked permission to stay "wif de white folks." He would be useful, he said, tending the cooking fires at Ibis Hall. But I thought he was more concerned with everlasting fires tended by ministers of other worship, and hoped in his simple way to snatch brands from their burnings. Yet I was greatly puzzled by his request. I could not imagine him trying to shrive Madeline. However, he was devoted to Dr. Sams; he had pronounced Cleo's and my wedding service; he believed that his own flock had "de love of God in dair hearts" and needed no shepherding just now;

and who among us could wrestle with the Devil as staunchly as himself? Perhaps he feared that Ibis Hall was built not on the rock, but on the sand. The temple of Baal had fallen despite its pillars of stone. Perhaps he 'lowed a strong prayer-sender would come in handy.

Dr. Sams was touched by the petition and granted it gratefully. All of us were concerned for Lizzie and Sam Childer until they appeared in a mule cart heaped with baggage. "Her majesty has invited us squatters along with her loyal subjects," Lizzie told us with her deep-throated laugh. "It was so queenly a gesture that Sam couldn't refuse. A love for the high-falutin has my Sam, and I reckon he worships the queen from a distance. It's the habit around here—"

"I don't love high tides," Sam broke in in his easy way. "She's high already and rising fast in Turtle Inlet. I wasn't sure the ferry would be working by the time we got there. Lizzie can stand a little lording-over, to save us a drowning."

"Madeline won't lord it over me, never fear," Lizzie said with a slight, knowing smile.

"How did the sea look when you left?" Dr. Sams asked.

"Bad," Sam Childer answered. "Tremendous surges coming in against the wind. It's got a wicked steely color, I guess from air mixed with the water. It's got a sound I never heard before. Every gull's gone from the beach and the cormorants are flying about shrieking and the pelicans have taken off for the North. By the way, the herons and summer ducks have left the woods."

"Any wreckage coming in yet?"

Sam sat still on the seat. "One drowned sailor. A Portuguese or Spaniard by the look of him."

"Let's hurry," Cleo said.

"I doubt if she'll hit till tomorrow. I've seen three hurricanes, and the glass is still too high, and the weather has the wrong feel for one to be close on us, and the flaw hasn't started to veer. But she might take a running jump."

So with Pa, Dr. Sams, and Absalom in the chaise, Cleo and I horsed, and Obo pacing on foot, we were not far behind Lizzie and Sam on the road to Wood Ibis. The trickle of Little Run had swollen to the old size of Fern Creek; the latter had turned into a half-grown river with wide flooded banks; and the corduroy road was a ditch two feet deep. Clouds in troubled motion were gathering and darkening by the time we turned into the live-oak avenue to Ibis Hall.

No window glimmered; every shutter was closed. No black minions cared for our horses; Obo and Absalom, accompanied by Cleo and me, would take them to the stables. When I had helped Pa up the high flight of marble steps, I caught a glimpse of Madeline answering the door. It was an eerie thing, to think of her being alone in the mansion, a forsaken queen, even Granny's ghosts departed with their familiar. Her footsteps must have rung so hollow. The lust that had leaped like the flames of hell was now so cold.

"Let's put the horses in the lot," Cleo said.

"The fence will be the first thing to go. If we want to go riding, we can't."

"The stables would go next. I don't want the roof falling on them. I want them to have a chance. What good would they be to us anyway, out in a hurricane? And what do we care?"

"All right."

"Except for others suffering, I'd want it to come. Maybe it will blow away the lies and leave the truth."

"That would take a big blow." So I spoke, subtly, but I had no reasonable doubt of the truth now.

"Let's sleep in the same room tonight."

"I want to, too."

"My room, whose door Saul was going to break in."

I wondered if Saul had been able to break in a door since I had left him under the bush—hell's door for instance.

"You told me that some day you'd be standing in front of it— do you remember? It made me very passionate to have you say that. I'm passionate now, remembering that passion. Would your lips be cold if I kissed you?"

"No, Cleo."

A moment later she asked, "Does it flow all through you, and catch your breath, and ache—and burn?"

"Yes."

"Is it wrong—or right?"

"It's right."

"Mama doesn't believe you're her son."

"Maybe she believes it—but for some reason—"

"She doesn't believe it. Mama can lie like any queen but she wouldn't lie about that. Do you believe she's your mother?"

"I have every reason to believe I was born to her."

"That isn't what I asked."

"She can never be my mother, if you mean that bond between us—the strongest in human life. It doesn't exist. It can't ever. I know that." But I did not tell Cleo what made me so sure. Perhaps I would not have been so sure if I did not know certain facts.

"We can sleep in the same room. Why can't we lock the door and sleep in the same bed? It may be our last night on earth. That lawyer said it had to be proven in court. How do we know how it's going to turn out, provided we live that long? How could the judge know for sure? Would what he says, sitting on his bench, make us ashamed of what we'd done? It wouldn't me."

"It would me, I'm afraid. You see, Cleo, you really don't believe it. You never will perhaps. But if Madeline said it was true—what then?"

The light went out of her face as though an inward lamp had expired. The lovely passion I saw in her eyes and felt in her arms ran out like a tide that had turned.

"I—don't—know."

"You see where that puts me. My pa *did* say it was true."

"He's not your real father. He could be mistaken. Well, it looks as though we never will know—want each other our whole lives in vain. For a last surprise—when we're too old for it to make any difference—we'll find out it was a false alarm. I thought with Papa dead and Saul gone—never to come back—the curse on Wood Ibis would be lifted. There wouldn't be any more demons. The sun would come out and dry up all the evil. Instead it's going on keeping us apart. It *is* evil doing it—I know it—I feel it in my heart. It's dressed up as something else—the law of God and man— nothing could be so solemn and important—it fools you but it doesn't fool me—it's evil out of hell right on. It's laid off on murder for the present. Anyway the dead don't suffer any more. Slow torture is such an improvement—not just rending and burning our bodies but tearing out our hearts and starving our souls.

Not just two young lovers who can forget and fall in love with others. They wouldn't be worth the demons' time and trouble. But you and I—Dan and Cleo—their chief victims from the first—never having any real parents, either one of us, yours unknown and mine a queen married to a murderer—finding each other when we were children, making a wonderful promise—escaping for a little while—a door opening—clinging to each other so frantically —our love so strong that it could conquer hate! Would the demons miss that chance? The demons and the Furies and the harpies that came up to Wood Ibis twenty years ago."

"Cleo! Look at me." For her pupils had grown so big that they filled all the iris, and she was gazing out of the world.

"Where did they come from?" she went on in a low voice as though she were listening to some other sound. "How did they get out? I can't see them in the daytime but they come to me in dreams in the most awful shapes—"

Her body was rigid in my arms. I was asking her to say no more and she did not hear me. But she heard a long sigh in the live-oak trees that grew into a moan that rose to a weird howl. She fell silent and wonder came slowly into her face and her eyes so black seemed to see a distant, frightened hope.

"It's coming, Dan!" she whispered.

"The hurricane?"

"Yes. It won't turn off again, and this is what I think. When it comes—when it strikes with all its force—then we'll be together always, either in life or death."

She lifted her face to gaze far into the southern skies. A dull-red glimmer of sunset through the swirling clouds tinted their whiteness and was reflected in her eyes.

"Come on, Hurricane!" she cried.

Not knowing the wildness of it, in a great surge of passion I raised my arm in high, long beckonings.

"Come on, Hurricane!" I shouted. "Come on, and blow your damnedest! Show us what you can do. Blow the house down if you want, but blow the devils back to hell where they belong! Come on, you son-of-a-bitch!"

Warm, wind-driven drops of water flung into my face as though in jubilant answer. Then Cleo and I laughed jubilantly, as hand in hand we raced with the roaring rain.

With the help of two good and willing servants, Madeline decided to entertain her guests with a pleasant and memorable supper. It was in the code of the French nobility to make merry when winds howled without the walls—to feast on the eve of battle—to light all the lamps on the darkest, most perilous night. It was one of those romantic, perhaps histrionic gestures that was yet magnificent; it taught that human bravery and beauty must not bow down.

Excited by the storm, Madeline was also inspired by this strange company—all who were left in the island story, all who were still deeply involved in its outcome. If Sam Childer were only a spectator, Lizzie had loved the queen's first husband; Dr. Sams, Noel Dunbarton, Cleo, and I moved mightily in her fate. Perhaps she recognized Obo's great part, as tonight he performed tasks so trivial to gianthood. But she did not know that white-haired Absalom with his cotton-tuft of beard, shuffling back and forth to the pantries on mundane errands, might be the high ambassador of Fate itself.

Although the meal was a simple one, the ancient silver and china and glass were beyond praise, almost beyond price. The cloth was ivory-colored lace, which had glimmered under candles expired these hundred years—which might have reflected the glow of wine drunk to the Valois. Madeline was simply dressed, in respect to our costumes, but her heightened color and the play of light in her jewel-like eyes enhanced her beauty almost beyond belief. It was a marvelous thing tonight, witchery of great power, perhaps abetted by our vaulting imaginations, perhaps authentic phenomenon of inherent gifts made luminous by her mood, by the manifold wondrous gleams of crystal and plate, and by her gay defiance of the swelling storm.

At least two of our company gazed at her in breathless worship—Cleo and Pa. Pa's hands itched for his Jacob Stainer, to tell her of his love. Dr. Sams seemed caught up in a dream, its mists concealing mercifully at times what he did not want to see and what tonight he could almost disbelieve—at times returning him to a day before these days of loathsome revelation, ere ghosts that could not rest rose and gibbered. He toasted her with shining eyes and eloquent tribute; he loved and replied brilliantly to her wit. Occasionally, though, the dream grew thin and he scented the cold, sinister dawn; once, at least, he wakened, and the sick shame and revulsion on his face was a dreadful thing over the glimmering cloth, and the candles seemed to burn low until he slept again.

Of all the guests, Lizzie seemed the most lonely. I thought I saw a profound sadness come and go in her face, sometimes a look of grim resolve, but the spiteful expression she usually wore when she spoke of Madeline did not once appear. Indeed she hardly glanced at the hostess, but her gaze wandered frequently to Cleo, and sometimes she stole guarded glances at me.

I wondered what thoughts moved in the old, wise, lucid brain of Absalom. While cheerfully he plied the platters and the wines, his nobly wrinkled countenance gave no sign.

Ralph had once said that the gales that blew without the walls of Ibis Hall were hardly ever audible within. When we had sat down to dinner we had heard the thresh of rain against the shutters, but rarely the soughs and moanings of the wind. Throughout the meal its sound became ever more insistent; often and more often we had to raise our voices to be heard above its dismal howlings. When we drank our coffee in little translucent cups we heard below our talk a continuous subdued roar. But every candle burned with a steady flame, and the little pools of white light reflected from the water goblets on the cloth lay still and unflickering. Only Obo paid any visible attention to the mounting fury of the storm. Occasionally he would stand near a window, his hand on the glass, listening.

I wished for the cups to empty, the little crystal cordial glasses to tilt for the last time. I had business with Madeline, resolved upon when I had held Cleo in my arms at the stable door; the longer I waited, the deeper my ache to get it done. When at last we rose it was again delayed by events beyond my control. Before I could make an opportunity to talk to her alone, Pa asked me to go with him into a writing room opening off the parlor, for he had something important to tell me.

I lighted his pipe for him as in old time. He sat with his elbows on his knees, his most comfortable posture, since his arms afforded some support for his bowed back.

"There is no doubt in my mind now, Dan, that the hurricane will strike," he began. "There is also little doubt that Ibis Hall will weather it as it has weathered every other gale buffeting its walls, yet the power of the elements is as limitless as the power of God, and no man knows what fury may be loosed upon us. So out of our love for each other, I must exact a promise from you."

"What is it, Pa?"

"I have lived to see my dearest dream come true. My only dream, indeed, that was based on solid hope and not empty figments of my fancy. My star has risen to its zenith; my cup of joy is full. But I am a marked man, and deranged. I am an offense to my own eyes in the glass, and pain is my constant companion, and I am tired from my long labors, and of the breath that wracks me. I would grieve to part with you, my son, and well know how you would grieve. Even so it would be a mercy upon me if this tide now rising would sweep me out to sea."

"I can't bear for you to say that."

"I must say it. More than that, I must ask you to take a solemn vow, lest my heart in its fullness of joy be broken. It may be that before the hurricane sweeps again to sea, you will be confronted by a dreadful duty. It would be to leave me to die in the storm, while you strive on to life and joy. But it is your bounden duty in that pass. I want you to acknowledge it now, and assume its solemn obligation, and perform it, despite all sorrow in the task. If the sorrow is deeper than the sea that swallows me, perform it still. If by staying one second longer at my side, if by lifting your hand once more in my defense, you reduce by one jot or tittle your own chance of survival, you will do me a great wrong. In your good intentions, you will deal me a grievous wound."

When I could not answer, he reached and laid his hand upon my knee.

"If it be true that the dead return, I will return to see you master of Wood Ibis, conqueror of the evil that kept you so long from

356

your heritage and my heart so long from peace, beloved son of Madeline. Could I bear to hover in the shadows and gaze at some usurper wearing the laurels you have won, while you lie low? Shall some stranger sway the power and waste the riches that are yours by inheritance and perilous strife and glorious conquest? I pray that you live, and beget sons to reign after you, and daughters rememorant of Madeline to be chatelaines of the manors hereabouts. Your first man-child shall be named Bruce. But I would that you lie with the beautiful woman you shall marry on the nineteenth, the twentieth, and the twenty-first day of the succeeding March, in the great high bed where you yourself were conceived, and give unto her your plenteous seed. By my calculations, made after long study of natural phenomena, I am persuaded that she may bear you a babe on or very close to Christmas Day; and if it be a boy, or, if you will, a daughter, I would be overjoyed to have the child bear my name."

He rested a moment, smiled at me, and spoke on.

"That, Dan, you may do in my memory. Aye, and I have another whim that, fortune permitting, you may grant. If I perish in the storm, my violin will remain in my hand. It has been my long and loving companion, my solace in my solitude, my consolation for my wound, sometimes the beauty of its singing reminding me of Madeline, sometimes the fury of its trumpets recalling me to my debt of blood. It was fashioned by Jacob Stainer two centuries ago. Its soul is the soul of the Tyrol; it has heard the wind in the pines and the roar of the avalanche. I grieve that it shall sing no more when I am gone, yet God will forgive me for taking with me my beloved, to the world's loss—to lie with me in my grave—since I have never lain with my more greatly beloved in life, or with any shape of living beauty to remind me of her. If I feel Death's hand closing upon my soul, my hand will close tighter on the case—with my last breath will I lock my fingers on its stout grip—so that if my body is found, my treasure will be found with me. In that event I ask that it be buried with me."

He fell silent but it was as though his great accompanist played on. The eerie howlings of the growing gale had seemed choral music harmonizing with his voice, even to rise and fall in accord with its periods. Now they joined in a stupendous dirge, as though

357

all the flocks of Proteus and the wolves of Zeus were lamenting in unison.

"That's a small request," I answered.

"I ask the great one too. Twice we have made bond—the first time over the fence of the Orphanage, the second time before the portraits in our picture-room, now for the last time in your own castle. Put your hand in mine, Dan." And when I'd done so, "Do you promise me, by the love we bear each other, that you will not put your life at hazard in any hope of saving mine? If there is a chance for you to strive on, by token of youth and strength, you will not delay a second in aid to me, or in grief for me, or even to say farewell? I will command it if I must, by right of our first bond; but I would that you swear it willingly, in full assurance of your heart and soul."

"Yes, Pa, I swear it." For this too was a small thing he had asked, compared to what might be demanded of me before the advancing hurricane passed by.

We said a goodbye now, in case we were not given another chance. Listening to the wind, I felt a distinct foreboding of our near and final parting. There were other sounds all but inaudible in the blast, ominous beyond my ken. I could recognize only a few of them—great lateral limbs of the live-oak trees being twisted from their trunks and crashing down, once a reverberating roar that must be one of the giants itself toppling, and sealike waves of rain wind-driven against the walls. Far down the scale from the wind's raving was an unvarying, continuous moan like nothing I had ever heard, and far above rose shrieks and screamings and shrill cries as from a legion of lost souls. When I found Obo still standing vigil over Cleo, I asked him if he thought the storm was approaching its height. Something like pity for me—for he was a giant, while I was only a man—came into his face.

"Mas' Dan, we aint seen even half of it yit, unless it turns off. When I was a boy in Sekondi—befo' I'd wet my spear—a storm like dis came out of de Bight of Benin. It blew like dis, and de witch doctor tol' us it wouldn't blow much mo'. De noise was de same—de sounds you can hear, and dem you can't quite hear. De air feel de same as dis air now. But de witch doctor got de signs mixed. De wind rose and rose till it look like it couldn't rise no mo' wifout blowin' de world away, but it still rose. Dey aint no limit on de wind, once it make up he mind to blow his breaf out. It was noon when de witch doctor make his medicine, and sunset when de wind blow his best. Den all 'twonce it came droppin' down out of de sky like flags haul down at Fort Sumter— flutterin' and fallin' everywhere, and de noise stopped, and you could hear yo' heart abeatin' in yo' breast."

"You were in the hurricane's eye," I said. Then in a wild flight of fancy, "It couldn't see for a little while. You were a grain of dust in the giant's eye."

"De warriors start dancin', and dey was just gittin' hot when de wind start blowin' agin from de odder 'rection. 'At was long ago, but I never forgit. By 'n' by I gwine open de windows under de blinds on de lee side. Dey say dat sometimes de glass bus' out from de wind suckin' at it tru de board."

"All right."

"I tell you what I think, Mas' Dan. I think mo' dan half Wood Ibis already took by de sea."

"What?"

"Dat wind blow ova water mos' of de way here. I can tell by de sound. I think all de land below Fern Creek already flooded by de bitter brine and she won't raise no cotton nex' year, and until de rain fall heavy and wash her clean o' salt, she won't never again. I think de waves roll over Little Ibis like Bull Bay. I bet de house float off, and de barn, and de cabin, and not one board stay. I think you couldn't see de cut of Turtle Inlet or find where de sto' stood. The tide about mid-flow. She'll come up a long way yit. Soon after midnight she turn back to sea, but whedder de waters fall a heap 'pend on de wind. Soon after sunrise she start in again, and dat will be de highest tide of all, if de sign tell true. If you want to take a salt-baf, you can do it by goin' down de fust flo' of de house."

I listened a moment to the wind and then spoke to Obo as though he were an oracle.

"Will the house stand?"

"She built mighty strong, Mas' Dan. I try to think where we could go to be safer, but countin' de time it take to git anywhere, dey aint no place. Dey aint one of 'em oak trees I trust to stand

359

when de water soak tru de ground and de wind trus' agin 'em. If dey was, I'd git into one wif Miss Cleo, and tie her to de trunk. If dey was big cypress, like some far 'way in de swamp, I'd do dat thing. But I study and study ova it, and de best chance is stay here."

I too puzzled a little while, and then agreed with Obo. It seemed to me that the wind had risen very little if at all since I had talked with Pa. And now the time had come to talk to Madeline. I found her playing chess with Dr. Sams, and asked her to leave her king in peril, as the business I had with her was urgent. "My king is all but surrounded already," she answered, as she rose. "Dr. Sams is a doughty fighter."

He did not look the part, just now. He had turned white and a chessman dropped from his trembling hand and rattled on the board.

"Can it be that a queen too is in peril?" Madeline asked, when we were seated in the library on the second floor. She was smiling over this title which even on Saul's lips had been never more than half a jest.

"Do you mean, ma'am, from the storm?"

"No, Dan. My grandfather René D'Arcy built Ibis Hall to mock all storms. You look very grave. I remembered how peril overtook my husband since you came here, and now Saul has gone away and Granny thinks he's dead. Could it be my turn?"

"I want to speak of your first husband—presumably my father. At that time you had a servant named Linda. I have a testament that she wrote on the night she died."

"Excuse me." Madeline took from a golden case a small, brown cheroot; I lighted it for her with a friction match. "I find tobacco very soothing, in times of stress."

"In that testament, her dying statement, she reveals that you plotted with Ralph the death of your husband and baby," I went on, my voice holding steady.

She puffed luxuriously. "You use the word 'reveals.' The word you should use is 'states.' Of course English is not a very precise language. You would never make such a mistake in French."

"I withdraw the word, in favor of the other."

"Thank you. I suppose since you believe yourself to be Bruce's son as well as mine, you feel called upon to tell me this. I don't blame you in the least. Moreover, I can't blame Linda for the delirium that almost always accompanies plague. She was a loyal servant, and I was greatly devoted to her; I regret the figments took such a tragic form. Otherwise the testament is of no concern or importance to me."

"It is of the utmost importance to me."

"That is understandable, as I said. To have the least suspicion that your own mother plotted your murder would make any out-rageous action understandable. Now with your leave, I'll finish my game with Dr. Sams."

"You have nothing more to say?"

"If I were given to making requests, I would make one of you. I would ask that you not show this testament to either my daughter Cleo, or my brother-in-law Noel. Both love you very dearly and find happiness in that love. I think it would be enough to make them hate you."

"You don't ask that I keep it from Dr. Sams."

"It would have no effect on my old friend in the least."

"I brought you here to make a bargain with you—a very base one, in some respects—one that would shame me very deeply, but my love for Cleo and Pa makes me stoop to it. Cleo's every instinct tells her she isn't my half-sister. Granny said the same, and I abhor the thought myself. You appeared sincere when you declared I wasn't your son. Possibly you have evidence—what it can be I can't imagine—to prove I'm not, but which you couldn't reveal without revealing your guilt in the murder of your husband. What the facts might be I can't imagine—unless Cleo is the daughter of one of your unmarried kinswomen, whom you adopted to prevent disgrace to your family name. I don't see how that secret could hinge on a more dangerous one but in any case I'll offer you a high price for it. If you'll furnish proof that Cleo and I are not half-brother and -sister I'll conceal Linda's testimony while you take ship for France and as long as you remain away from America."

Madeline leaned over gracefully, laid her cheroot on a silver tray, and rose.

"Excuse me, but I find this not only grotesque but somewhat tiring. I'm going back to my game."

CHAPTER What little sleeping I did that night, was on but not in a bed with Cleo. We smiled over the difference a little preposition made. We did not lock our door and defy the Furies; I left it open when I was with her, the better to listen to the gale's alarms; I closed it only while I was away on watch with Obo, so she might sleep more soundly. I did not like to have her waken and find herself alone. When I was there, her hand in mine, she slept sweetly and deeply. Truly I spent every possible moment at her side, mainly keeping vigil over her, sweet to my soul as I listened to her quiet breathings and looked at her still face, but sometimes I lay my head on her pillow and dozed a little while.

The wind rose very little more until midnight. Between then and one o'clock it blew with ever greater violence, the gusts longer and more savage, their sound like that of a train roaring over a bridge. From one until nearly three its power did not appear to increase and sometimes we thought it had moderated slightly. When again we marked its slow, steady rise, Pa offered an explanation for its vacillations. In his tireless search for knowledge he had studied Brandes' records of great storms: in his opinion our hurricane was under pressure from the north—fighting against what he called a high-pressure area—and was moving landward very slowly and at times might be virtually stationary. Dr. Sams's glass fell from 28.92 to 28.89 in the next half-hour. The violent rains that had slacked off now came and went in prodigious, brief squalls. But by four o'clock on the morning of September 5 we were deep in the hurricane; and, unless all signs failed, we must bear the brunt of its full blow before very long.

Every candle flame bent toward the lee, apparently from suction through the raised, shuttered windows on that side, since we could detect the merest sprays of wind infiltrating around the edges of the glass of the weather windows. The walls shuddered under the impact of the great gusts but the floors hardly trembled and we had the sense of shelter in an unconquerable fort. The berserk

362

blasts brought flying battering-rams in the shape of debris, some of which seemed of great weight, to deal us resounding blows, and sometimes pictures fell from the walls from the shock, and once all the plates tumbled at once from a rack in the dining room. But the D'Arcys built well, Ralph had said—both their houses and their stock—and massive Ibis Hall still mocked the gale.

Obo and I unlocked one of the shutters of the ground floor on the lee side, and peered out. Ibis Hall was like a great stranded ship in a shallow sea. The east had begun to glimmer, and the waters spread farther than we could see. They were calm below us but wildly harried in every track of wind, low waves sweeping at unbelievable speed across them, and the air dense with spume. Obo climbed out and, wading more than knee-deep disappeared in the gloom. In his absence I envisioned our whole coast besieged by the hurricane, the rivers in tortured flood, the beaches torn apart, the ancient bays and headlands remolded or removed, forests being mown, the wild folk perishing in their sea-engulfed swamps.

"Please, suh, git all de people in Mas' Ralph's office on de lee side fust flo', and blow out all dem lamps," Obo told me when he returned from his survey. "She gwine to be light soon."

He left me, and when I saw him again he was naked save for slashed-off trousers and the harness he had worn the day we crossed Deep Swamp. In his hands was a coil of rope and his oaken pole; but both of these he put in Cleo's charge when we had all assembled. "I think de house may stand," I heard him tell her. "If it do, we'd better git upstairs and ride her out. But de water breaking bad on de wedder side, and she might weaken de foundation. So we better be ready to run for de boat."

He meant Ralph's sailboat, moored in a little cove in Gator Creek close to the dock. She was twenty feet long and built staunchly to ride the open waves. I thought she would have capsized by now, or been ripped to pieces, or been wind-driven out of our reach.

Obo saw the wonder in my face and I could see not the slightest shadow of fear in his. "De boat broke from her moorings," he told me sociably, "and de wind drove her into de reeds. But de reeds was better shelter for her dan a wooden wall. Dey give to de wind and it don't know how to git hold of 'em, and all de while dey breakin' it a little. De mast broke off, but her hull aint hurt none yit."

Obo opened the shutters on the two windows, and a little glimmer of dawn stole through. It was spreading and brightening despite the black, barrier clouds when there came a great crashing noise from the dining room. A flying fence rail had struck one of the shutters end-on, driven through it, smashed the glass of the window pane, and lay leaning against the sill. The gust that had hurled it was dying away—only a narrow draft, powered like a fire hose, drove through the rent. But another gust followed swiftly, and the broken shutter fell off its hinges.

The blast broke open a closed door across the room. Before we could gain the doorway the torrent of air had burst out the pane and carried away the shutters of an opposite window. Obo thrust with all his giant strength against the door and closed it but the latch would not hold against the blast and it flung open again with great violence. Now it hung askew on broken hinges.

An invisible monster of resistless power and demented fury began to destroy the dining room. All its other windows burst out almost simultaneously, the huge chandelier swayed and swung in an ever longer arc, then crashed down on the table. Nothing like a table remained: a wagonload of kindling wood flung against the opposite wall. The chair spun across the floor, and the drapes rose and fluttered against the ceiling. The room could not confine the giant loosed; roaring, he leaped through the arch into the writing room, burst out the windows there, hurled the desks and chairs in ruin, and then charged into the hall and up the stairs. The bursting out of the windows was like rapid cannon-fire. In a matter of seconds the hurricane had ingressed the entire house.

With earsplitting ripping and tearing sounds, the weather boards began to fly off in the wrenchings and pryings of the gale. The roof would go soon—we heard it shrieking—and great rents shot up and down the paneled walls. Obo and I fought our way to the office. Although its chairs had been blown over and broken, it was not yet wrecked, and our companions stood braced against the blast, their faces pale but calm.

Obo at once leaped through the window. Out of my arms to

364

his I passed Cleo, then Lizzie, and then Madeline. When I turned to Pa, he shook his head.

"I will stay here, Dan," he told me. "I would be a burden—"

"Not yet, Pa. I gave you my promise—"

I lifted him down to Obo, who lay him across one broad shoulder, one arm around his knees, and appeared to forget him. Up to me, by some odd suction of the wind, rose Pa's voice.

"I wish you would let me stay. I will be lord of Ibis Hall until it falls. I will make such music—"

"You won't be no bother to us yit, Mas' Noel," Obo told him kindly as he stood picking the best course to the creek bank.

Sam Childer and Dr. Sams scrambled out. I would have helped old Absalom but he grinned at me and nimbly followed the others. When I dropped down into two feet of water, Obo was uncoiling the rope Cleo had ready for him.

"Please you-all hang on to de rope and foller me," he told us in his oboe-like voice that somehow carried clearly through the thunders.

With Pa slung over his shoulder clutching his violin, he strode out from the lee of the shuddering, shrieking building crosswise of the blast. The waves that darted snake-swift over the flood were not high, but thrust violently against our legs and, tugging at the women's skirts, almost jerked them off their feet. Obo stopped.

"Please all de ladies take off dem dresses and petticoats clean down to de shifts," he directed in a high. clear shout.

Cleo, Madeline, and Lizzie obeyed him instantly. Obo strode on, holding a straight course toward the landing. Cleo and Madeline were thrust leeward a distance, but Sam Childer made a strong anchor to windward to straighten our line; and although Dr. Sams, Lizzie, and Absalom swung out behind him, I at the end of the rope prevented a grotesque game of crack the whip. We moved forward in the intervals between the gusts. At their demonic heights we could only stand braced, blinded by the blown spray, at the mercy of the missiles whistling and shrieking over our heads.

A glimpse through the rain squalls showed fully half of the ancient live-oak trees lying in ruin, the rest stripped of boughs.

Sweetwater Pond was indistinguishable from the rest of the sea-scape; not one floating timber remained of the stables. When at last we gained the boat, it was half-full of rain water but floated undamaged save for its sheered-off mast behind its so fragile-seeming barricade of reeds.

Obo stood Pa down and I made a windbreak for him. Sam Childer fished two buckets from under the bow and handed one of them to Lizzie. I thought that the pair of them might be finding a fierce joy in their task of bailing out the boat; both were seafolk, old fighters against the gales; they knew how to bail swiftly and efficiently; even giant Obo could not empty a hull so fast. The latter was breaking out a pair of oars lashed under the gunnels. . . . But Pa and I did not watch the work going forward. Our gaze had followed Madeline's, back to Ibis Hall.

Invisible wreckers busied everywhere at its walls and on its roof. Slates took wing sometimes one by one, sometimes in what seemed coveys of birds taking off, sometimes in large flocks. The chimneys swayed, bent, and crashed. The rotunda appeared to be ripped off in one piece, and then exploded in a thousand fragments. Often sheets of rain and spray cut off our view; when they cleared away, the havoc wrought was ever more. The weather boards ripped off and went sky-sailing, in sharp silhouette against the gray clouds; the lathes flew away in swarms; with an avalanchal sound that rose above the gale, the beams supporting the roof gave way, some of them broken like matchstems in the fall, and its ruin appeared pulverized and disappeared in a streaming cloud of debris. Before the boat had been made ready to launch, all that remained of Ibis Hall was a weird skeleton against the sky—its corner posts still standing, the beams that had supported the floors in place, the five great pillars of the portico above the marble steps erect but their burden thrown down.

Obo picked up Pa again and gently lowered him into the boat. "Please all de ladies git it now and sit on de flo'," he shouted. "De men better help me shove off."

When we were ready, a great heave cleared the boat from the reeds. Obo had already made a sea anchor of a spare sail he had found in the stern-cubby; as we shovers clambered aboard our bow swung into the gale. Sternwise we began to drift, and it was a wonder what an even keel we kept before that stupendous wind. A sheet of canvas dragged on a rope saved us from instantly capsizing. Sam Childer sat at the helm. It might be he could guide the craft enough to avoid some of the hazards of our voyage. Obo crouched in the bow, an oar ready to his hand. Still I wondered if my shipmates' faith felt weak and cold as mine. Only by luck as out-of-bounds as the fury of the hurricane, it seemed, could we clear the shoals and the fallen timber and the reefs of debris between here and any port.

"If we can git to de river we got a fair chance," Obo shouted, as though he had guessed my thought. "She plenty deep and wide and de tide will kay us far up de cypress swamp dat break de wind."

As we were borne along in front of the ruin of Ibis Hall we were given a last glimpse of its death throes. One of the great pillars tottered, and in its sublime fall, collided with another. Both fell inward and although we did not hear them strike the crossbeams of the frame—the pair toppled majestically, with a kind of grace—these and all the corner posts no longer loomed against the writhing sky. They had disappeared like shadows and only the marble steps and the three remaining pillars, rememorant of an Attic ruin, showed where the mansion had stood.

The site was somewhat higher ground than the surrounding fields. The water deepened as we sped riverward, and the islands caused by slight elevations were low and far-scattered. The very violence of the hurricane across these flat alluvial plains had increased our chance for life. No fence stood, young trees and thickets by the brooks had been blown down and washed away, floating debris had been widely scattered. We might reach the river! The prospect brightened with the dim advance of the day. Desperate work with the helm and Obo's oar got us safely past a jam of driftwood on a shoal. Frantic bailing prevented our swamping in the gushing rain.

So swift was our voyage that we approached the river too soon! The tide that would help us upstream had not yet begun to flow; and here it would not be greatly lifted by the hurricane, raging crosswise of the current. We could not cast our anchor and wait. If the cable did not part, the boat would be snatched in two. We did not know where the flood ended and the channel began; and it did not matter in a moment more, because we were being driven into log-jammed shallows beyond.

Sam Childer, our only real sailor, sprang forward and cut the sea-anchor rope. We spun in the wind, all but capsizing, but caring naught for that. Sam held her helm hard over, and some imperceptible pull of the tide bore us down river. We were taking water and going to flounder in a moment more. We would struggle a few seconds and then drown—even Obo's giant strength could not prevail against these destroyers. I wished to God I had Cleo in my arms. Bitter and black remorse that she and I had not lain all night in each other's arms was carrying down my soul when I too saw the dim, wild hope that was turning both Obo and Sam into half-gods of strength and zeal.

We had come into the river only a few furlongs above the ferry crossing. Our captains were trying to make into what seemed a surf-girt island whose crest rose hardly three feet above the breaking waves. A few seconds later I recognized it as the crest of what was called an Indian mound—probably a great earth-covered heap of oyster shells—on the opposite slope of which the ferryman had built a hut.

I knew not by what whim of wind and wave we staggered slowly nearer. I knew not how we stayed afloat this long—a cockleshell in a sea gone crazy amid a hurricane. A man's head and shoulders that appeared above the crest made no more sense than the rest. When we started to sink, the bottom rose out of the sea to smite us; Sam Childer fell on top of me and between his legs I saw the boards parting and green water spurting up in fountains through the cracks. We had stranded on the long slope of the mound, hurling Dr. Sams into the surf, but the waves swept him toward its lee, and he scrambled unhurt to his feet.

The man I had seen came reeling around the side of the mound, slipping and sliding from knee- to waist-deep in a seething cataract. When his own great splashings gave me sight of his face he evolved into Mr. Harper, the ferryman. Obo deftly and accurately tossed his coil of rope: it unwound as if by clockwork and Cleo and some of the others seized it. I flung Pa still clutching his violin on my shoulders and, retracing Mr. Harper's steps, sat him on what seemed a large board shelf behind and extending out from the slope of the mound, hardly two feet out of water. When I rushed back, Obo and Harper were hauling on the rope, dragging in all hands. Some were still erect, some on their knees, Sam Childer flopping like a merman on a trawl, but one after another they clambered around the mound to a seat beside Pa.

A little sunlight of common sense broke through the clouds on my brain, and I saw that the shelf they were sitting on was the slightly-sloping roof of Mr. Harper's ferry-office. Although all but submerged in the tide, it stood in a kind of valley in the little hill, and was thus sheltered on three sides from the main onslaught of the gale. Cleo still clung to Obo's oaken pole. Mr. Harper was shouting something that at first made no sense at all—it sounded like "frying pan." Between the gusts he shouted it again, and now no doubt remained.

"Frying pan into the fire," he was bawling. "This here place will be six foot under water when the tide comes up."

"Well, we're glad to get here just the same," I bawled in reply.

He thought this over briefly, then yielded to a generous and sociable impulse.

"We got once chance but it's mighty slim," he yelled, no strain on his bugle-throat used to far cries. "The steam lifeboat from the station started up here to git me and some folks at Parker's Landing, but I've about give her up."

Obo heard him, meanwhile attending to other business. Standing on the roof he gazed in all directions, with a wonderful expression at once alert and thoughtful. There was not a trace of terror on his face or of forced hope. I felt my will to fight on for my love and life become like steel.

41

Mr. Harper, as though to pass the time interestingly, shouted snatches of his adventures to account for him being marooned on the roof of his ferry-office. He had taken in close to a hundred dollars in the preceding two days; and fool that he was, had concealed the money in a cigar box. Last night he had crossed the river once more to get the hoard, only to lose it and his boat as well. Now he reckoned he was going to lose his life. The greatest tide this coast had ever seen would soon start to flow, and when the wind changed—as it would change when half the hurricane had passed by—the main of the waters of the Santee Swamps would dump into this river.

"Hee come de boat," came an effortless yell from above us.

We sprang up, to see the relief steamboat from the life-saving station laboring around the bend. She had been built to battle storms—her low-sealed cabin wedged in her hold, and driven by a screw propeller—but she could hardly hold her course across the blast and shunted slantwise. Amid waves breaking over her she surged nearer foot by foot; when directly opposite us the captain heaved his anchor and backed in toward us. The full power of the screw in the shallow water could not prevent the payed-out cable from becoming perilously taut. I hoped that my companions did not give way to too great hope. It hardly seemed possible that we could get aboard.

To my amazement Lizzie moved closer to me and put her lips close to my ear.

"Forgive me, for which I did to you and Cleo," she told me. It was impossible for anyone else to hear her.

"If you mean trying to keep us apart—"

"I hate Madeline to hell. To the bottom of hell I hate her. What you thought was spite was my only way to hide it—and I had to hide it from Sam and everyone. She knew. Saul knew too—but he thought I'd keep the secret—and he knew I'd written out the whole story in case I was killed. But I didn't hate Cleo. I only resented so terribly Madeline having a child. To keep you from marrying her—"

A sailor on the lifeboat had thrown a rope. Sam caught the end and pushed between Lizzie and me to find an anchor for it. There was none anywhere in reach and in a moment it would jerk him into the flood.

"Get down off de roof everbody!" Obo shouted.

Sam snatched Lizzie's hand and drew her into knee-deep water. She clutched at the rope and caught it. Dr. Sams and Absalom, both down and floundering in the shallow, grasped it while Sam Childer, in a desperate surge of strength, clung to its end with one hand and the edge of the roof with the other. As it broke Sam's hold on the boards, it swung into Mr. Harper's reach, but Madeline snatched at it in vain. No others could seize it and the crew hauled mightily to drag the five people aboard. One by one we saw them yanked over the rail.

A sailor coiled the rope to throw it again. Lizzie sprang to her feet and clinging to the cabin cleat shouted something I could not hear. But now the anchor cable undulated like a great serpent, and suddenly a length of it shot out of the water and fell writhing. The ship lurched toward the shore. In what seemed a hopeless attempt to save her from stranding, a man in the bow heaved over a sea anchor. Again the life-rope darted toward us—the blue-coat in the stern still minding his duty—but it fell short.

The sea anchor helped the churning screw to arrest the drift of the boat; she stood still, then slower than any crawling tortoise got under way. As she picked up speed the sea-anchor cable grew slack, and the man in the bow cast it loose. She was now too far to throw us a life line and, without an anchor to windward, the captain would not dare lose steerage way again. No doubt he had other castaways aboard and he must not throw away their lives in a vain attempt to save ours. His crew gave us a cheer, for such comfort as we might find in it, as the ship headed down river.

"Will she come back for us, Obo?" Cleo called.

"I don' reckon she can git back, Miss Cleo, befo' de tide rise high. But don't you worry. We aint drowned yit."

I moved closer to him, so I could speak to him unheard by the others.

"Obo, is there any chance you can save Cleo?"

"Yassa. Pitty soon, maybe."

"Is it a good chance?"

"Not too good, but it could be wuss. Mas' Hoppa tell de truf. De wind gwine blow from odder 'rection when de gale half pass by. De tide gwine turn mighty quick now. When it do, I gwine take her up de bank. I gwine make for de cypress wood 'bout half a mile from here. Dey deep water to cross, and big danger to go by, but maybe we git tru."

He paused, and leaning toward me spoke in a deep, thrilling whisper.

"I mighty strong, Mas' Dan. De Lawd give me dat strength to take keer of Miss Cleo. If de wind lull wif de tide maybe I could git two people 'trough to dem cypress wood."

There were five of us here, including Pa and Madeline. We sat on the roof of a hut in no very immediate danger, or, save for the battering into our heads of the wind's raving, in no great discomfort. The rain had stopped an unknown while before. We were in a little backwater of warm air. For the moment all of us except Obo were dazed by the impact of the events just gone—our party cut in two as to numbers, a rescue ship incredibly coming and almost as incredibly going, a rope we had clutched at and missed— and by our own, quiet resignation to being back on the shelf over moiling waters in the lee of a hurricane. . . . Well, I would get over my daze. I was going to quit being a bump on a log. I had great affairs to attend to.

There is only one broom that will sweep lies, and that is truth. It is the only magic that will exorcise evil. Sometimes it is bitter medicine for a malignant growth and sometimes it overwhelms the heart but at long last there is no other.

"Pa?" I called.

He wakened from a dim dream. "Yes, Dan."

"Will you move closer to Madeline, so you can hear what she and I say to each other?"

"Yes, my son."

"Cleo, will you sit close to her on the other side?"

She looked at me wonderingly and nodded her head.

"I did not know we had anything to say to each other, Dan,"

Madeline told me, her voice so rich and full that it carried well. A beautiful forlorn expression came into her face. "I thought we had said everything."

"Well, then, I'll talk to the others, and you may speak as you see fit."

"Very well."

Pa and Cleo took their positions. I crouched directly behind them, leaning forward so that I need not shout loudly to be heard.

"Obo is going to try to take Cleo through the storm to safety. He may be able to take one more. Pa can't go, and I've promised him I won't try to make him. So the choice will be between Madeline and me."

"If you had D'Arcy blood in your veins, there would be no choice," Madeline answered. "The law is older—"

"It will be for Cleo and Pa to decide, not you or me," I broke in. "Both of them love both of us."

The white shadow that dark fear had cast over Madeline's face departed, now that she knew her hopes lay in those hands. But a dreadful anguish came into Pa's face, and wild terror into Cleo's.

"Cleo, you said that your father had been conjured when he killed his wife, his brother, a Negro boatman, and attempted to kill Bruce's son. It was true. He'd been conjured by Madeline's beauty and riches—she'd promised to marry him and make him master of Wood Ibis."

"Lies, lies," Madeline cried.

Cleo fought with terror and won. She turned her eyes to mine. "How can you say such a thing?"

"Because it's true. You already admit the possibility of its truth— I see it in your face. I have a testament from Linda, Madeline's maid, whom Pa will remember. She confessed to Absalom the night before she died. Madeline arranged to be called to Combahee while the people were killed. She had Linda pretend the baby was sicker than he was, so Bruce would start with him for Bull Island in the doomed boat."

Pa raised his head a little. "Dan, it cannot be true," he said in a tortured voice. "Madeline loved Bruce and her baby. There would be no motive for such an unspeakable crime—"

"There was a motive. Maybe it was horrible lust for Ralph. But

373

maybe it was some other not so monstrous. If so, she'll tell you."

"Do you believe this, Dan?" Pa asked.

"Do you think I would say it before you and Cleo, both of you worshiping this woman as you do, if I didn't believe it? I know it. It was Madeline who laid the curse on Wood Ibis. It was she who brought up from hell all this evil. It was her passion that brought about all this bloodshed. She took Lizzie's lover from her and then killed him. Lizzie told me."

"*Lizzie!*" Madeline broke in. And suddenly the mask she wore fell off, revealing a passion of hatred that I would have thought beyond our human pale.

"Then you did do it!" It was Cleo's voice, but there was life in it yet, brave and beautiful and enduring. Her soul had not passed, while she breathed on.

"Lizzie," Madeline repeated, but more quietly now. Why was I able to hear her so plainly? Why did not the roar of the storm drown out her voice? Because it was not now so loud. I had a sense of a brightening sky. The light was slowly growing.

"Lizzie hates me with all the hatred she's capable of," Madeline went on. "She's not capable of understanding me or what I did— only the *noblesse* could understand. But I don't hate her. I don't even blame her. If I tried to hate her, I couldn't. There was room in my heart to hate only two people."

"One of them was Bruce—" I said.

"And the other was you," Madeline turned her eyes on mine and they were two black, bottomless wells of hate.

"Why?" I asked, hardly raising my voice, so swiftly fell and fluttered down the pennants of the wind.

"You won't understand either. You are incapable of it. But Cleo will, I pray—she is my daughter—and perhaps Noel, whose search for learning and his love of me has ennobled his mind. I fell in love with Bruce, my overseer, a man who could hardly read and write, the son of a brewer in Charleston. I rejected my highborn suitors to marry him. But on our very bridal night he rejected my embrace. He told me my lips were cold, and my beautiful body did not stir his passion. In the master's bed of Wood Ibis, in which Valois kings had slept, he told me that. Within a week he was visiting his squatter girl at Turtle Inlet. Her lips were not cold to him—her peasant body stirred him to great passion. To her he gave his seed. By her, he begat his son."

The light cleared. A beam of sunlight flickered goldenly on the distant surge. The waves still rolled in fury, but the only sound was their crashings, and there was not a breath of wind. Obo stood gazing with vigilant eyes in all directions.

"As soon as he found out Lizzie had conceived, Bruce told me he intended to bring the child to Ibis Hall, acknowledge him, and make him heir to Wood Ibis. What could I do to prevent public disgrace to my name and honor? He loved the wench and was a strong and resolute man. Could I listen to the mocking laughter of all the Low Country? I did not know then how easily men died. I proposed to let the world believe the baby was mine. Lizzie agreed, at last, to save it the name of bastard. Each of us vowed to Bruce never to reveal the secret. I went to New Orleans to pretend to be delivered there, Lizzie feigned a visit to kinspeople while she swelled and whelped. Dr. Sams thought she had gone to stay out of temptation with Bruce."

Madeline mused a moment, some splendid guise of beauty on her face, and the rich music of her voice rose again.

"I thought I could endure my shame and balked hate, but I could not. I lay watching my husband asleep, not a dream of what he had done troubling his face; I stood hours looking into the cradle where his and his slut's baby slept or played. It was then I sent Linda to Ralph. He was a weak man who would do my will; I promised he could have Wood Ibis. He and Saul alone knew the secret. You know it now—all of it."

"Did you have any doubt that I'd been killed?" I asked.

"Such a vile trick of fate never occurred to me. Lizzie too believed Ralph's story of finding the body. When you came back to life of course I wouldn't acknowledge you—you'd be owner of Wood Ibis. Lizzie put off acknowledging you because she couldn't bear for you to marry Cleo, whose very existence she resented— when I had flung her own baby in the sea. You will have one question that I can't fully answer. Lizzie knew I had incited Ralph to kill her lover and her baby—why didn't she tell anyone? It was not her own guilt of adultery with the husband of Madeline D'Arcy—she never had any. Her father was still alive—perhaps

375

she didn't want him to know she'd given birth to a bastard. She loved Sam Childer and perhaps she did not want him to know. Perhaps her main reason for keeping silent was that no one would believe her."

"Granny was right," I said, my voice thrilling. "I'm not your son!"

"Did you—hear—her say—that when she asked Bruce—he laughed? My husband laughed. I would have struck again, if I could."

Obo spoke in his soft tenor. "De tide still running mighty fast—faster yit now de wind's down. But she gwine turn pitty soon now, all de waters standing still and den flowin' in de way I want to go. De wind gwine blow agin from todder 'rection. Directly I gwine to start out wif Miss Cleo for de cypress wood, and take wif us one mo' who she say can come, and I want her to pick Mas' Dan."

"Tell him, Cleo, that he must take me," Madeline told her quietly. "Even if you love Dan more than me, still I must be your choice. I have one great duty I must perform before I die. You owe it to your D'Arcy ancestors to enable me to perform it. You know what I did—Dr. Sams knows it—the whole world will suspect the truth when it comes out that Dan is Lizzie's son, not mine. I want to be tried by a court of my peers, and vindicated. I want to cross the seas and tell my story to the kings and nobles of ancient lineage who will understand. Even Victoria, a mere Hanover, will pardon what I did—death to a traitor and his spawn. Louis Napoleon, an upstart, has learned enough kingliness to acquit me. The great kings—the Hapsburg and the Bourbon and the last Báthori—and all the great nobles of the world will applaud! Cleo, the very heavens uphold my cause. They fought for me today."

"What do you mean, Madeline?" Pa asked in his deep, resonant voice.

"The right of kings to punish treason derives from God. Next to them stand the princes and the *haute noblesse*. The whole world believed that but yesterday; today the mob is out of hand but the great plan endures. The heavenly powers could not suffer to see Lizzie Neilson's bastard begotten by my husband become master of Ibis Hall. Otherwise no wind that ever blew could have torn it down. There have been other hurricanes, but in this one they flung the seas down upon all the manor. That is their answer to the pretender. Wood Ibis laid waste."

"It's magnificent, Madeline—but the last mad king in his castle would never believe it."

"What do you know of kings? But you know I was justified in what I did and you love me. Dan is your foster son and he loves you. Tell him that I, not he, must go with Cleo and Obo. If only out of chivalry, he must remain—you understand that, if he doesn't —and it's a trifling reason compared to the great one. Tell him to stay with you, and he'll obey you."

"De tide jus' about slack," Obo said. "We gwine start across de slough in a couple minutes mo'."

"You've forgotten one thing, Madeline," Pa replied gently. "Dan loves me—but also I love him. He is yet master of Wood Ibis that will some day rise from the sea. He will yet dwell in the manor house that he will build. He is my brother's son."

"You can't refuse—"

"I can forgive you for what you have done and I love you still. I can understand such hate—I have borne not its equal but its semblance. But your vindication before your peers is an empty dream—an evil dream if it costs my son's life. In my love for both of you, I refuse."

"Cleo!" Madeline whirled to her daughter and spoke imperiously. "I have asked, and now I will command. I'm your mother, Madeline D'Arcy of Wood Ibis. Tell your slave to take me with you."

The blood in my veins stood still as the waters and the winds while Cleo gazed quietly into Madeline's eyes and made her reply.

"No, we're going to take Dan."

Obo picked up the oaken pole beside Cleo. A rope was coiled in his great, sinewy hand. I bent and kissed Pa's cheek and then took Cleo's hand. As we entered the water behind Obo, each of us holding the rope, Madeline cried out in terror and despair.

"I'm coming too. You needn't help me—only show the way—"

"It won't do no good, Miss Madeline," Obo replied. "We can't wait for you nohow, and you'd bog down in dat fust big slough."

"Do not grieve, Madeline," we heard Pa telling her. "I am still with you and I will love you to my last breath. I will play for you as the waters rise. My music will tell you what my poor tongue cannot—how greatly I love you. Madeline, my own at last! Do you not see how fitting it is that we should die together? We are both so lame."

The flood was deepening swiftly as we heard the first soft strains of the serenade. Obo stopped and fitted the oaken pole into the loops at his belt and shoulder. Standing full in the sunlight ere the black clouds gathered again, he lowered his hand deep in the water. Cleo placed her foot in his palm and lightly he lifted her until she could stand on his shoulders. Grasping the pole her wondrous passage over the waters was instantly assured.

As Obo waded deeper into the perilous gulf she turned her head and gave me, clinging to the rope, a smile at once childlike and mysterious, and I could not withhold my tears.

THE END

378